THE WIFE
BEFORE
ME

ALSO BY LAURA ELLIOT

Guilty

Praise for Laura Elliot

The Wife Before Me

"A definite page turner of a read."

—By the Letter Book Reviews

"A very dark, disturbing and twisted story but one that definitely grabbed me at the first page and kept me reading, (albeit from behind a cushion!), until the very last page."   —Stardust Book Reviews

"Terrifyingly claustrophobic, overwhelmingly emotional and atmospheric, controlling and tense from the very start."

—Jen Med's Book Reviews

Guilty

"Intriguing from start to finish, with meaty characters and unrelenting suspense."   —*Booklist*

"*Guilty* was such a great book. It was filled with so many twists and turns...It was well written and definitely made you wanting more with every page turn."   —Oh My Lit

"*Guilty* is one gripping psychological thriller with a well-constructed plot and realistic and believable characters...Incredibly thought-provoking, it'll make you question everything."

—Novel Deelights

"A mesmerizing psychological thriller...and will leave you completely fulfilled with a flawless ending. *Guilty* is the first novel I have read by Laura Elliot and it will NOT be my last. I found *Guilty* to be impossible to put down, the characters are intoxicating, and the story compulsively addictive."

—Books and Smiles

THE WIFE BEFORE ME

Laura Elliot

GRAND CENTRAL
PUBLISHING

New York   Boston

Copyright © 2018 by Laura Elliot
Cover design by Stephen Mulcahey
Umbrella photograph © Alison Burford/Arcangel
Cover copyright © 2020 by Hachette Book Group, Inc.

Grand Central Publishing
Hachette Book Group
1290 Avenue of the Americas, New York, NY 10104
grandcentralpublishing.com
twitter.com/grandcentralpub

Originally published in 2018 by Bookouture in the UK

First U.S. Trade Paperback Edition: January 2020

Grand Central Publishing is a division of Hachette Book Group, Inc. The Grand Central Publishing name and logo is a trademark of Hachette Book Group, Inc.

The publisher is not responsible for websites (or their content) that are not owned by the publisher.

The Hachette Speakers Bureau provides a wide range of authors for speaking events. To find out more, go to www.hachettespeakersbureau.com or call (866) 376-6591.

Library of Congress Control Number: 2019950515

ISBNs: 978-1-5387-5026-1 (trade paperback)

Printed in the United States of America

LSC-C

10 9 8 7 6 5 4 3 2 1

To my one and only beloved sister, Deirdre Mullally.

Thank you for your love, support and enduring friendship.

THE WIFE
BEFORE
ME

PROLOGUE

Amelia Madison drove slowly down the steep incline leading to Mason's Pier. The road was little more than a fissure carved into the side of the cliff and an earlier rainfall combined with mulching seaweed had added a dangerous slickness to the surface. As she swerved round the bends, she avoided looking down to the rocks below, knowing that her fear, balanced so finely on her resolve, would overwhelm her once again.

At the end of the road she turned left and passed the collapsed barrier of an empty car park. The half-moon cove behind her was deserted, as she had expected it to be. In years gone by the sheltering face of the cliff had made it a popular beach for sunbathing, but erosion and rockfall had turned it into a perilous place to visit. Efforts by the local council to stem the danger with steel mesh had only succeeded in adding to its grimness and underlying its dereliction was the bleak memory of a drowning tragedy that had occurred there years earlier.

In Amelia's nightmares, the cove filled the breadth of her terror. Up close, it looked smaller and more insignificant than she remembered. The slipway was no longer in use and the pier, where local fishermen once cast their lines, had fallen out of favour. Buffered by waves and pitted with potholes, Mason's Pier jutted out over the Atlantic like a grey, forlorn snout.

She did not hesitate as she drove onto the rutted surface. Nor did she look back towards the cove where she had once built an enormous sandcastle with her father. She had helped him to flood the moat by constructing a channel to the ocean, gathered shells and white feathers to adorn the turrets. She had chased a beach ball—no, she would not think about that day. Not now when her mind was set in only one direction.

As she neared the slant down onto the slipway, she slowed her car. At first, when she pulled on the handbrake, she was sure that the wheels would remain stationary; but then she became aware of a slight forward momentum, almost subtle enough to seem imagined. It was a warning, she knew, and soon it would be too late to stop the inevitable slide on the scum of moss and algae.

Kittiwakes screamed as they dive-bombed towards the cliff and a cormorant, standing steady on a nearby rock, watched impassively as Amelia's tyres began to spin. This was it, then. An end to the marriage she had once embraced with such eagerness, such hope. The setting sun lanced the windscreen. She was dazzled by its splendour, yet she must keep looking beyond it towards a new horizon.

The cormorant blinked its dark-green eyes and spread its wings like a cross as her car slid slowly but inexorably towards the end of the slipway.

The ocean heaved.

Part One

CHAPTER ONE

The Present

Elena's red umbrella looks frivolous and flimsy among the sturdy black ones surrounding her. It offers little protection against the rain, and the wind, gusting between the tombstones, threatens to whip it inside out. Thorns from the white rose she holds in her hand dig deeply into her skin as Father Collins lifts his aspergillum to sprinkle holy water over her mother's coffin. Men in baggy jeans, who have been waiting discreetly in the background, step forward with ropes to lower Isabelle Langdon into the earth. Elena is stunned with grief yet, even in the midst of this final ritual, her eyes are drawn towards a man standing opposite her. He is watching her and in that silent exchange his sympathy stretches like a lifeline across the width of the open grave.

Earlier, outside the church, he had introduced himself. "I'm Nicholas Madison," he said as he shook her hand. "I'm here on Peter Harris's behalf. He asked me to extend his deepest sympathies to you and his apologies at being unavoidably delayed in New York."

She had heard his name before. Nicholas Madison... Nicholas Madison... But nothing came to mind as she thanked him and he moved politely aside to allow the woman behind him to offer her condolences to Elena.

She had forgotten him instantly. Smudged him in with the other mourners leaving the churchyard as her mother's coffin was lifted into the hearse.

Not quite smudged him from memory, Elena realises now. His tanned, angular face is a vibrant contrast to the grey complexions of the mourners surrounding him, their lips pinched from the cold. His lips are full but not fleshy, his mouth slightly open, as if he is about to speak words of comfort to her. His eyes, dark-grey and long-lashed—Elena recalls this from their earlier encounter—have such intensity that she finds it impossible to look away. She has seen much sympathy on the faces of those who have supported her since Isabelle died but in Nicholas Madison's expression she recognises an empathy that goes beyond compassion. Instead of sharing this last moment with her mother, she smiles at him. A clown's smile, as grotesque as it is false. Why did she do that? Better than keening, she supposes. The thin wail that acknowledges the missed opportunities, the broken promises, the too-late-to-be-offered apologies.

Stumbling over prayers that were once familiar to her, Elena tears her gaze away. She watches the white rose tumble and settle on the coffin. The gravediggers lay a plank of artificial grass over the open space and place the wreath of white roses on top. No other flowers, she had requested on the death notice. Those who wished to honour Isabelle's memory should make a donation to the Irish Cancer Society where, Elena hopes, a cure will soon be found to prevent the disease that took her mother so mercilessly from her.

The funeral is over. Fr. Collins shakes her hand and departs. Her friends surround her. Tara flew from London as soon as she contacted her. Killian and Susie drove from Galway and the three of them were waiting to greet Elena when her flight from Brisbane landed at Dublin Airport.

They had stayed with her in Brookside, the bungalow Isabelle bought when Elena moved to Australia. No bloodline between them but Elena, an only child, looks upon them as family in the finest sense of the word.

"Are you okay?" Susie smothers her in a damp embrace and strokes her hair.

"I'm fine…fine." Elena has warned them to stay cool, no emotional displays that will trigger another storm of tears.

Tara reads the inscription on the granite gravestone and says, "Oh, my God, Elena! I never realised your father was only thirty-one when he died. He was *so* young."

"Too young," Elena agrees. Her mind blanks, as it always does when she thinks about her father and the silence that filled the house after he died. The rain adds to the dreariness of this bleak cemetery, which she used to visit every Sunday with Isabelle until she was fifteen and deep into a teenage meltdown. "I'm sick of going there," she had shrieked at Isabelle. "Let him *go*." Uneasy memories stir her guilt, but now Nicholas Madison is coming towards her. She is surprised by a jolting awareness of his nearness and the knowledge that she had been hoping he would speak to her again. Her red umbrella gives a last, defiant shudder before the spokes break and it flutters upwards. He takes it from her and snaps it closed before handing it back and shielding her with his own umbrella.

"It was a fitting service for Isabelle," he says as they turn away from the graveside. "Dignified and restrained, exactly as she would have liked." Raindrops glisten like dew on the shoulders of his cashmere coat and his black brogues are sinking in the mud. Elena feels vaguely responsible for destroying their high polish.

"How well did you know my mother?" she asks.

"Only through work," he replies. "Isabelle was a very private person. I liked your homily. It was obvious to everyone in that church how much you loved her."

"She died before we'd a chance to say goodbye." Her voice quivers. Talking about Isabelle in the past tense is not becoming any easier. "Right up to the end I'd no idea...I'd have come home if—" She stops, unable to continue.

"How could you have known how quickly she would die?" He holds her elbow as she stumbles on wet clods of clay. "You mustn't add blame to your sorrow. It's the last thing she would want."

They walk towards the limousine that will take her and her friends to the funeral reception. No words are necessary to fill the silence that falls between them. The knot in her chest eases for the first time since she discovered that her mother was dying.

"Will you join us for lunch at the hotel?" she asks when they reach the car park.

"Unfortunately, I've a business appointment," he replies. "It was a pleasure meeting you, Elena. Once again, my sincerest condolences." She almost expects him to bow and kiss the back of her hand. He has that way about him, an old-fashioned formality, as if his parents had drilled the importance of politeness into him. Always the right word for the right occasion. "Shall I throw that away for you?" He nods at her umbrella and gestures towards a refuse bin.

"Thank you." She hands the tattered remnants to him and enters the limousine, where her friends are waiting.

Tara holds Elena's chilled hands and rubs them between her own. "Who's the guy?" She nods towards Nicholas, who is walking towards a silver Porsche.

"My mother worked with him," Elena replies.

"Is he coming back to the hotel?"

"Afraid not."

"What a shame. He seemed pretty focused on you."

"Don't be ridiculous. He was simply being polite."

"Mmm…" Tara smiles. "There's polite and then there's *polite*."

"Oh, stop it. The only reason he's here is because Mum's boss couldn't be bothered taking an early flight from New York." Elena sounds bitter. She suspects the real reason for Peter Harris's absence has nothing to do with KHM Investments and everything to do with pleasure. After twenty years of working as his personal assistant, there was little about his personal life that Isabelle hadn't known. If she was still cognisant, she would probably throw her eyes upwards and say, "Typical! I wouldn't have expected anything else from him." No more lying to his wife, Elena thought. No more made-up excuses that had caused Isabelle to threaten to leave the company on more than one occasion.

"That's an impressive car he's driving." Tara cranes her neck to get a better view of Nicholas as he zaps the Porsche. "What's his name?"

"Nicholas Madison." The syllables roll easily off Elena's tongue. Once again, she feels a tug of memory and Killian, who had also been admiring the Porsche, turns to her, his eyebrows raised.

"Nicholas Madison?" he asks.

"Yes. Do you know him?"

He glances across at Susie. "What do you think?"

Susie checks the window as Nicholas, his face in profile, settles behind the wheel. "Yes." She nods. "He worked in finance. It has to be him."

Nicholas's car is still stationary as he waits in the line of traffic leaving the cemetery.

"His wife drowned," says Killian. "It was big news at the time."

"Oh, my God!" Tara sounds as shocked as Elena feels. "How did that happen?"

"She was parked on Mason's Pier," says Susie. "It's an old pier close to where we live. No one uses it any longer and there's a warning sign beside it. Her car slid into the sea. It's a really dangerous stretch of water, deep enough even in low tide."

"We were involved in the search for her body," Killian adds. "All the boats in the vicinity took part, but we had to call it off in the end."

"Not that he ever gave up." Susie twists strands of brown hair around her index finger, a childhood habit she still displays when upset. "He was convinced he'd find her if the search would last for another day, then another. She escaped from her car but she couldn't swim. No one discovered she was missing until the following day when a man walking his dog noticed the skid marks on the slipway."

"Oh, my God." Elena gasps, her hand to her mouth. "I remember that time. I thought his name was familiar." No wonder she had found his gaze so compelling. He could hide his emotions in a polite exchange of words but he had been unable to control his eyes. In them, she had recognised the savagery of loss. A yearning she had seen so often in Isabelle's eyes when she heard a song that reminded her of her young husband, or came across old photographs, the two of them arm in arm, wide, happy smiles. "Isabelle phoned me and told me about his wife after it happened. I didn't make the connection. No wonder he looks so sad."

Nicholas, as if he knows he is being discussed, glances across at the limousine and sees them staring at him. Elena sinks back into the seat and turns to Tara, who is still holding her hand. "He knows we're talking about him."

"So what?" Tara replies. "With his looks and his history, he must be used to it."

Nicholas starts his car and indicates left for the city. The limousine driver indicates right and soon reaches the hotel where the post-funeral reception has been organised.

The afternoon passes in a blur. The atmosphere lightens when food and wine are served. The noise level rises. Old friends from Isabelle's single days tell stories about her youthful exploits. Stories so outrageous that Elena wonders if these fifty-somethings, with their trim figures and highlighted hair, are attending the right funeral reception. All-night parties, clubbing on Leeson Street, rock concerts and discos in Ibiza—she finds it impossible to reconcile her mother's contained personality with these vivid descriptions and realises that her perception of Isabelle was formed in the years following her father's death.

Isabelle's friends remember Elena as a baby with a halo of Orphan Annie curls. Her hair is darker now, a deep chestnut, its unruly curls straightened this morning by Tara. They admire everything about Elena and are thrilled, they claim, to discover that she has become such an elegant, lovely young woman. Overpowered by their perfumes and reminiscences, Elena thanks them and wonders what they really think of her.

Can you believe it . . . the grieving daughter? Couldn't be bothered coming home in time to look after her mother. No good pretending that she didn't know the seriousness of cervical cancer. The word alone should have alerted her to pack her bags and do her duty.

If such thoughts exist, she is not made aware of them. Rosemary Williams, a contract solicitor with KHM Investments, embraces her as she's leaving. She was the only friend Isabelle made when she joined KHM and it was Rosemary who broke the news of the seriousness of her mother's condition to Elena. They arrange a date to meet in Rosemary's office for the reading of Isabelle's will. Her departure signals a general move towards the exit. Air-kisses and handshakes are exchanged, promises made to keep in touch.

✦

Exhaustion sets in when Elena's friends depart the following day. That night she goes to bed and huddles under the duvet, convinced she'll sleep around the clock. Hours later, she is still awake, her mind spinning from one grief-stricken memory to another. She cries for Isabelle, for Zac, for the tiny life they had created and which she carried so briefly. A life that will never have a name or a gender, fingers barely formed before sliding so painfully from her. A trilogy of grief. Elena can take her pick, unsure which one she mourns the most.

CHAPTER TWO

Rising every morning, after another fitful night's sleep, is the most important decision Elena is able to make. In Isabelle's bedroom, the wardrobe still bulges with her clothes. Her shoes remain stacked on racks. Neighbours ring the doorbell and are ignored as Elena battles against an overwhelming tiredness. Dishes pile up on the draining board, dust gathers on the furniture. She orders pizzas in the evenings and forces herself to eat, washes them down with beer. Empty packaging and beer bottles litter the floor as guilt-ridden memories she never knew she had suppressed bubble up.

"He was *so* young," Tara had said at the cemetery when she read the date of birth and death of Joseph Langdon. Elena realises she has never thought of her father as a young man. She never mourned him, not properly. At five years of age, what did she know of grief? Or anger at the drunk driver who drove through a set of red lights and killed him instantly?

He was tall and boisterous, she now remembers. A loud laugh and a deep voice lulling her to sleep with bedtime stories; but his youthfulness had never featured in those memories. In time, as she had grown accustomed to the silence he left behind, she had resented the grief that shadowed Isabelle's eyes and lined her face prematurely. On Sunday afternoons while deep in her rebellious phase, Elena would grit her teeth against her mother's silent reproach as she prepared to leave for the cemetery. Why didn't mourning have a cut-off point, a stage that made further suffering impossible, she would wonder, headphones clasped to her ears, *My Chemical Romance* vocalising her angst. Now, they are together again, Isabelle and Joseph Langdon; just a layer of mud and stone separates their coffins—but this thought does nothing to dull her sorrow.

Rosemary Williams rings to remind her that they have an appointment at KHM Investments, and she forces herself to shower and shampoo her hair. Isabelle's last will and testament, handled by Rosemary as a favour to her friend, is a straightforward document and far removed from the intricate contracts she handles on a daily basis. But she shows no sign that this reading is of any less importance when she greets Elena at reception. They travel upwards in the elevator to the eighth floor and enter her glass-walled office.

"Are you eating?" she asks when Elena is seated in front of her.

"Most of the time," Elena assures her. "I'm so busy sorting through Isabelle's clothes and things…" She clears her throat and wills herself not to cry.

"This is a tough time, Elena, and it will get tougher before it gets better," Rosemary warns her. "Have you someone special in Australia—"

"No." Elena shakes her head, vehemently. "But, honestly, I'll be okay."

"You're so like Isabelle. Stoic."

Rosemary opens a folder and draws out documents that she lays on her desk. "It's no harm to cry when you feel like it. I know you're still in shock. I'm so sorry I had to break such sad news to you over the phone."

"Don't apologise, Rosemary. What else could you do?"

A cruel hoax, Elena had believed when she answered her phone in the early hours of that morning and tried to understand what

Rosemary was telling her. But it was no hoax, just the shattering discovery that her mother had been rushed to hospital after suffering a bad reaction to her chemotherapy.

"What chemotherapy?" Elena had demanded. "She never said anything to me about starting chemo."

"Didn't you know she'd been receiving treatment?" Rosemary had been unable to hide her surprise. "She said you knew. I assumed that's why you planned to come home?"

"Her test was clear, that's what she told me." Elena reached across the bed to the empty space where Zac should have been lying. "How seriously ill is she?"

Rosemary hesitated and in that brief pause Elena realised that her mother had been deceiving her for months. Small things that had puzzled her began to make sense. Isabelle's forced heartiness when Elena asked how her smear test had gone. Her decision to take time off work that, she claimed, was due to burnout. Her excuses for not Skyping Elena, some vague problem with her broadband that never seemed to get sorted. Her evasive answers whenever Elena asked when she was coming to see her in Australia, dithering for weeks over which airline to use and the cost of the ticket. Her tears when Elena said she would fly home instead. Tears of relief, obviously, but Elena had been too preoccupied with her own problems to figure it out. And that final phone conversation when it was Elena, not Isabelle, who wept as she poured out her heartache and promised to rebook her flight as soon as it was possible to fly.

"I couldn't understand why you cancelled your flight," said Rosemary. "I wanted to contact you and explain how serious her illness was but Isabelle insisted I keep it a secret. It's important that you come home now. Hurry, Elena. She needs you by her side."

She had booked her flight in the morning and was packing to leave for the airport when Rosemary rang her back. As soon as she spoke, Elena knew she would be too late to say goodbye to her mother.

How could she not have guessed that something was wrong? Not read between the lines of Isabelle's cheerful emails or linked into the mother-and-daughter bond that made words between them unnecessary? Now, when it is too late to make amends, Elena is dazed to discover how much money she has inherited.

Brookside, Isabelle's bungalow, which is mortgage-free, belongs to her, along with all her mother's savings and the investments she made through KHM. Elena, at the age of twenty-five, has become a wealthy woman. She can return to Brisbane and buy a house on the beach. She can give up her boring job as a junior account executive and establish her own company. A bodyboarding and surfing centre, boat tours on the Barrier Reef, a boutique specialising in exclusive beachwear. Her scattered thoughts fill her with exhaustion rather than elation.

She stares down at the Liffey as the river flows between the renovated docklands. Dublin keeps changing. She has been away for only three years, yet she feels like a stranger in the city.

The documents are signed and she is about to leave Rosemary's office when the door opens.

"I'm sorry, Rosemary. I didn't realise you were busy." Elena identifies him instantly by his voice. That glance across the grave… even in the midst of her distress, she has been unable to forget it. When she turns round Nicholas Madison is hesitating in the doorway. "It's not important," he says. "I can come back—" He stops when he recognises her.

"Elena." He enters, his hand outstretched. "How are you?"

"I'm coping, thank you." It's a glib response that he accepts with a smile. He must understand that polite platitudes are the only way to bat aside unanswerable questions.

"I'm glad to hear it." He nods towards Rosemary. "Sorry for the interruption. When would it be a good time to call back?"

"I'll be free to see you after four," Rosemary replies. "Leave the file with me and I'll have a look at it before we meet."

The room seems emptier when he closes the door behind him. It is as if a spark has been extinguished, which is ridiculous; but the high flare of colour on Rosemary's cheeks suggests that even she seems affected by his departure.

"I'll ring you soon to arrange lunch," she says when their meeting ends. "You've a lot to absorb and decisions to make. I'll help you any way I can. I don't make friends easily and Isabelle was a special person in my life. I'll never forget her support when my husband died. I want to give that support back to you. You must ring me any time you feel like talking, do you understand?"

"Thank you." She will weep if she doesn't escape Rosemary's kindness.

The solicitor, recognising her distress, walks briskly with her to the elevator and waits until Elena is inside before turning away.

Nicholas Madison is standing by the reception desk talking to another man when Elena steps out of the elevator. She walks faster. It's too soon after Zac to feel such confused and strong emotions about a man she hardly knows, yet she wills him to turn and notice her. The automatic glass doors open and she is about to step outside when he calls her name.

"I apologise for intruding on your meeting with Rosemary," he says when he reaches her. "If I'd known you had an appointment with her today I'd have organised lunch. I know that Peter Harris is anxious to see you and offer his condolences in person. Unfortunately, he's abroad at the moment but—"

"No need to apologise. Our meeting was just coming to an end." She stands awkwardly before him, aware of his eyes, his intense scrutiny that makes her feel as if all his attention is focused on her only. "Lunch isn't necessary."

"Then coffee, perhaps?" He checks his watch. Impeccable white cuffs, she notices, like everything else about him. His suit fits so perfectly it must be bespoke and his shirt has a pristine crispness that suggests it's been professionally laundered. No mud on his brogues to mar their sheen. She has a sudden image of him on a lofty chair, a shoeshine boy at his feet. Private school, university, a gap year travelling and a junior partnership shortly after he joined the company; these are the details Elena has gleaned from Rosemary, who referred to him as the Golden Boy of KHM Investments. Elena has no difficulty believing her.

"I'm about to take a break," he says. "Would you care to join me? There's an excellent café next door. It'll be quiet at this time of the afternoon."

"Thank you. That sounds good." She has already had coffee with Rosemary but the thought of returning to an empty bungalow holds little appeal. The glass doors close behind them with a quiet swish.

"I'm sure it's been a difficult week for you," he says when the coffee is served.

"I managed to get through it okay." Why burden him with the truth, especially when he must be consumed by his own heartache, which she cannot even begin to comprehend?

Two weeks, the search for his wife lasted, Susie had told her. Boats, big and small, plying the waters, helicopters flying overhead, walkers on the beaches and rocks keeping watch to see if her body had been washed in on the tide.

Her mother had phoned to tell her about the tragedy. Elena had been fruit picking on a farm outside Brisbane at the time and had yet to meet Zac. That would make it about two years ago. KHM Investments had closed down as a mark of respect on the day of his wife's funeral—no…it couldn't have been a funeral. A memorial service, Elena remembers now. How awful it must be to mourn his wife yet hope that somehow, against all the odds, she would return to him.

The sun, breaking free from clouds, shines a harsh light through the café window and emphasises his prominent cheekbones. A nerve quivers in his right temple as if, in that instant, he knows what she is thinking. Should she sympathise with him? What should she say? It's still a recent tragedy, yet not recent enough to offer some bland comment about a woman she had never known. Better not to make any reference to it and embarrass both of them.

"Do you have any plans for the future?" He interrupts her thoughts. "Will you stay here or return to Brisbane?"

"How do you know I live in Brisbane?"

"I spoke to Rosemary about you after your mother's funeral."

"Why?"

"*Why?*" He sounds surprised by her bluntness. "I was curious. Just as you and your friends were curious about me at the cemetery."

"That was Tara." She is embarrassed, remembering their conversation about him. "She liked your car. What did Rosemary tell you about me?"

"That you were still in Australia when you heard Isabelle had died. To receive such terrible news when you were so far away . . . that must have been tough."

The mug of coffee shakes in her hand. Hot liquid sloshes over the edge and scalds her fingers. She struggles for composure as she dabs her eyes with the tissue he hands her. These outbursts come regularly and always at the most unexpected times. She can look at photo albums Isabelle had filled—each photograph dated—and remain dry-eyed. She has managed to discuss the details of the will with Rosemary and stay calm. But small things, like the sight of Isabelle's hair clips on the dressing table or a handwritten recipe she had stuck behind the tea caddy can reduce Elena to wretched, hiccupping sobs.

"How long have you been a partner with KHM?" She changes the subject deliberately.

"Just over five years," he replies. "What about you? How long have you been in Australia?"

"About three and a half years. I backpacked for the first two years, picking fruit and working in vineyards. I worked as a lifeguard for a while."

"Sounds very adventurous."

"It was…in the beginning."

"Oh?" He tilts his head, quizzes her with his eyes.

"I'm with an advertising agency now," she replies. "I was temping at first but I was made permanent shortly before my mother…" She pauses and takes a steadying breath. "Do you ever feel the urge to travel?"

"Travelling is part of my job. I'm in New York next week. A three-month stint this time. You'll probably be back in Brisbane when I return."

"That depends on how quickly I sell her house."

"Is it your childhood home?"

"No. She downsized when I moved. I never lived there, apart from a few holidays. Rosemary doesn't think I'll have any problem selling it."

"You won't," he agrees. "Brooklyn Terrace is an excellent location. I advised Isabelle to buy that property when it came on the market. Could be worth your while holding off selling for a while? House prices are rising again. A year will make a big difference. Why not rent it for the time being?"

"I don't fancy being an absentee landlady."

"What's your email address?" He takes a fountain pen from his breast pocket. "I'll send you the name of a reliable management company who could handle everything for you. The more information you have, the easier it'll be to make the right decision."

"I need the capital now," Elena admits. "I'm hoping to set up my own business when I go back."

He rests his elbows on the table and studies her. "You couldn't do that here? The recession's over. Green shoots and all that."

"I've nothing to keep me in Ireland."

"And you have over there?"

Her fingers burn from the spilled coffee. She doesn't want to talk to him about Zac, to tease out the "what might have been" scenarios. "It's where my life is, now. I'll be guided by Rosemary's advice."

"Of course. I'm sorry." He sits back in his chair and grimaces apologetically. "I appear to be interfering."

"You're not. It's just…" She finishes her coffee and stands. "I'd better go. I've so much to organise."

He accompanies her to the car park. "Be kind to yourself, Elena," he says before they part. "Take time to rest and consider your future. Rushing into a decision when you've been through such a shock is not a good idea." The stretched pull of his lips when he smiles convinces her that the advice he gives must come from personal experience.

When she returns to Brooklyn Terrace, she googles Amelia Madison. It's all there, every heartbreaking detail. How beautiful she looks in the photographs, her short black hair swept to one side, her eyes, so startlingly green and vibrant.

Tragic Family Connection to Incident on Mason's Pier
   Colin Orwell
   A tragic accident took place yesterday evening when a car slid into deep water off Mason's Pier. A dog walker noticed skid marks on the pier and reported his grim discovery to the gardai. Divers soon located the car but the search for the missing woman, Amelia Madison, (30) continues. It is believed that she managed to break the window on the passenger side with her boot and escaped

being drowned inside her car. Serious concerns for her safety are compounded by the fact that she is unable to swim and the water surrounding Mason's Pier is notorious for current and high tides.

Tragically, twenty-five years earlier, her mother, Jennifer Pierce, (31) drowned in the same location. Her death occurred during a family holiday when Amelia, then five years old, fell off the pier. Jennifer Pierce dived to her daughter's rescue but was unable to reach her. An off-duty fireman, Leo Byrne, 44, rescued Amelia but, tragically, was unable to fight the currents that swept Jennifer Pierce out to sea. She was unresponsive when rescued and declared dead on admission to hospital. Her husband, John Pierce, was queuing at an ice cream van at the time and was unaware of the tragedy occurring just a short distance away from him.

Amelia Madison is a well-known interior designer, specialising in commercial and residential premises. She is a regular guest on the television series The Hidden Corner. *Her husband, Nicholas Madison, a junior partner with KHM Investments, is well known for his down-to-earth business reports on radio and television. When he was unable to contact his wife on her mobile overnight, he reported her missing.*

"Amelia and I are in constant touch with each other," he says. "I knew immediately that something was wrong when she didn't answer her phone. But not this. Not with her fear of water. I'm heartbroken but still clinging to the hope that somehow she is alive and will be returned to me."

Amelia Madison had never learned to swim. Elena, who could swim before she could walk, finds this incredible. With such a childhood history, she must have been terrified when the waves lashed over her red Subaru. Elena looks at a photograph of the pier with its slanting slipway and imagines the horror of being unable to stop that slow, relentless slide. Oblivion. She hopes death came swiftly.

CHAPTER THREE

Hi Elena,

I've sent you a link to the rental management company I mentioned when we met at KHM. If you decide to rent, I can guarantee their reliability.

I hope you are well and managing to cope with the difficult task of clearing Isabelle's possessions from Brookside. She loved you very much so use her love to keep you strong. Such memories give us succour and so does friendship. Perhaps it's too soon to look upon me as a friend but if you feel like responding to this email, I'd be delighted to hear from you.

Sincerely,

Nicholas

Hi Nicholas,

Thank you for your email and the link to the rental company. I'm very undecided about my future plans at the moment. Thanks, also, for those kind words about my mother. They come at a good time as I've been battling with feelings of guilt and some anger, too. She should have told me the truth. I would have come home immediately if I'd suspected anything was wrong. She was always the same, keeping her feelings to herself yet blaming me for not appreciating them…that was one of the reasons why I moved to Australia.

I always hoped she would move on and find someone new who would give her the happiness she was denied when my *father died. He died too young but I never grieved for him. I was five years old, for Christ's sake…what did I know about sorrow? Sorrow was my very best friend leaving me for another VBF or jeering me because I was the first girl in the class with nits, my mother being too demented to notice me scratching!! She never moved on, even though there were many in work who fancied the pants off her, and I couldn't cope with her oppressive memories any more. So, I left and met a guy from Sydney called Zac and he certainly wasn't the solution to my problems. In fact, he thoroughly messed up my life and now I'm struggling with depression, which I've probably inherited from my mother, and the only thing that's lifted my mood was your email because, impossible as it seems, I find myself very attracted to you, even though you're not my type, too much of a "suit," if you know what I mean, and I generally fall for the more outdoor type. The dangerous ones like Zac who up and leave as soon as the going gets tough…*

Elena rests her hands on the keyboard and blinks. What is she doing? Pouring out a stream of consciousness to a man she hardly knows? Crazy…downright crazy. She deletes most of the email and begins again.

Hi Nick,

Thank you for your email and the info about the rental company. I'm undecided about my future plans at the moment. How is New York? I've never been there but I believe it's the most exciting city in the world. All well here. I'm tackling the house and clearing it out. Thanks for your kind words about my mother. I appreciate them. Keep in touch.

Best wishes,

Elena

Nicholas emails regularly. Chatty missives about his life in New York. His apartment has a view over Manhattan. At night, standing on the balcony, he feels as if he is part of a vast, starry constellation. How is Elena? He asks this question and she, afraid she will repeat her first frantic email and press "send" before she comes to her senses, writes about jogging sessions, visits to the gym, painting the house to prepare it for sale, photographing the sun as it rises above Broadmeadow Estuary. Reading over what she has written, she marvels at her ability to lie so easily. Her fingers fly over the keyboard and, as the weeks turn into months, Nicholas's emails begin to penetrate the fug of confusion that has trapped her.

A parcel arrives from New York. Inside it, she finds a red umbrella and a card with the words, *I saw this umbrella in Macy's. It reminded me of the first time we met, albeit under such sad circumstances. I'll be home soon. I'd like to meet you again. Is that possible?*

Warmest regards,

Nicholas.

Her heart leaps, then it steadies again. It's too soon. A rebound romance is not the answer to her problems. Nor does she want to be involved with a man who must be carrying his own burdens. As for Zac... she can't go there, not yet, but something is changing within her. An awareness that she wants to emulate this energetic person she has created through her emails. If that means rising at dawn to capture the sun's reflection on the estuary, that's what she'll do. She joins a gym, jogs in the evenings and bins the pizzas. When the house is clean, she takes Isabelle's possessions to the local Oxfam shop and moves into her mother's bedroom. She begins to sleep more soundly and when she awakens in the night it is Nicholas, not Zac, who fills her thoughts.

✦

Sun-bleached sands and challenging rollers, passionate nights and idle days; these are the memories that have tormented Elena. She and Zac were made for each other, she believed when they first met. When their money ran out, they took part-time work until they had saved enough to return to the beach. Freedom— Elena had fought hard for it. She had had no idea what she would do with her life when she headed for Australia but the lure of the waves decided her. This would be her future; but a time came when she needed something more than dreams to pay the rent. She was offered a permanent job with an advertising agency after temping there for two months and decided to take it. The money was too good to turn down and, as she had graduated from college with a degree in communications, the skills she had acquired could finally be used. Zac was working irregular hours in a bar and his evening shifts allowed him the freedom of the beach during the day. Elena tried not to feel envious when she left their apartment in the mornings, trim skirt and jacket, high heels instead of sandals, her heedless days on the surf behind her.

Her pregnancy was unplanned. She was as shocked as Zac when it was confirmed. She sensed his panic, which he tried to hide in the beginning, thinking there must be some mistake. Elena was on the pill. Taking it in the morning was as habitual as cleaning her teeth. They had been away for a long weekend at a rock festival that month and, perhaps, the late nights and the hash, the shots that had her leaning into the bushes to be violently sick…perhaps…perhaps. Zac rocked her in his arms. He told her they were too young and carefree to be burdened with parenting and the responsibilities that came with it. Termination. He made it sound like the end of a bus journey. He accompanied her to the clinic and followed her back to their apartment when she stood up in the middle of the consultation and ran. They faced each other, ships passing in the sunlight, and discovered there was nothing left to say.

Alone in the apartment they had shared, Elena longed for her mother. She organised a flight home, planning to surprise Isabelle with the news that she was to become a grandmother. Two nights before her flight she awoke, her insides in spasm, blood on the sheets. Isabelle understood when Elena broke the news to her. She agreed that Elena had no option but to cancel her flight until she had recovered. Soon they would be together. Two weeks later, the phone call came from Rosemary.

✦

The red dress is an impulse buy and the heels of her designer shoes should come with a health warning, Elena thinks as she slips them on. She loves their precarious height. Her reflection satisfies her, the shadows gone from under her eyes and her skin lightly tanned from working in the garden. She clips her hair upwards into a casual knot and secures it with a comb, then stops, her hands still raised. Her lips are too red, too shimmery, her dress too revealing. Suddenly, filled with an unreasonable fear, she decides to cancel and tell Nicholas that a headache has laid her low. She is about to call him when he rings. He has organised a taxi to bring her to the restaurant. It will be with her in five minutes.

"I didn't expect you to order a taxi for me," she protests.

"It's my pleasure," he replies. "I'm looking forward to meeting you again."

On Dawson Street, people are dining outdoors under colourful awnings. Lights glisten on trees and the city basks in the balmy summer air. He stands to greet her, fixing his eyes on her with that same concentration, and she knows that her red dress was the right choice.

Throughout the meal they talk about music, films, Brisbane, New York. Safe subjects. Anyone seeing them together, relaxed in each other's company, would never suspect the stories they both hid. He asks when she is returning to Brisbane.

"I've changed my mind," she says. The thought of setting up her own company no longer holds any appeal. "I'm going back to university. I've a degree in communications but I've lost interest in working in advertising. I'd like to do media studies or social justice. Last night, I thought it would be wonderful to study zoology…as you can see, I'm all over the place at the moment. All I know is that I need to focus on something. How did you decide to become a fund manager?"

"I've always been a good communicator and I've an analytical mind," he replies. "I make correct decision quickly and am a problem-solver. Throw in a first in maths and my career choice seemed inevitable."

"Is making decisions on how people should invest their money a huge responsibility?"

"Not when you know what you're doing."

"Do you always know that?"

"Always."

"How come you didn't add modesty to your list of accomplishments?" she jokes. "Or self-confidence."

He grins and fills her wine glass again. "Modesty is only an excuse to hide one's weaknesses but self-confidence will always help you to achieve what you want. That's what you need to get back, Elena."

"I never thought I lacked confidence." She is surprised by his comment.

"I'm not saying you do," he replies. "But confidence takes a battering when you receive a sudden shock, as you did. Don't worry. It's a natural reaction."

Is he remembering his own tragic experience? She waits for him to mention Amelia but he asks her to tell him more about her time in Australia.

"I have a sense it was your natural home," he says. "Isabelle was afraid you'd settle there for ever."

The wine has relaxed her and it is easy to talk about the exhilaration of bodyboarding. To describe how she and Zac met when they were carried ashore on the crest of the same turbulent wave. She is nervous talking about the ocean in case it triggers thoughts of Amelia. She searches his face for signs of distress but he shows no indication that his dead wife feared the waves as much as Elena embraced them. She longs to tell him everything about Zac but it is too soon to share such intimate secrets.

"I'm talking too much," she says. "Tell me about yourself."

"Another time, Elena. Our waiter is hovering nearby so I suspect he's hinting he'd like to see his bed before dawn."

She is surprised to discover that the restaurant has emptied out and they are the only diners left. Nicholas insists on taking her home. Will she have to invite him in? And, if she does, what will happen then? She is flustered and flushed from too much wine. "I live in the opposite direction," she protests. "I can easily call a taxi."

"It's no trouble. I'd like to see you safely to your door."

"But we've both been drinking. You should also take a taxi." She tries to sound casual and fails.

He smiles, sensing her nervousness. "I'm under the limit." He gestures towards his wine glass, still half-full. The water jug is empty. Elena doesn't remember drinking from it, which explains the muzziness in her head. She'll have a hangover in the morning, while he'll awaken clear-eyed and remembering everything she said. And everything he didn't have a chance to say because, tonight, she hogged the limelight on anguish?

"It's okay...okay." He leans across the table and holds her hands. "My nights are long and I often drive to pass the time. Tonight, you've given me a reason."

He steadies her when she sways on the steps of the restaurant. The sensation of his fingers on her arm remains with her even though they are now walking sedately apart. He drives at a leisurely pace from the city and brakes outside the bungalow.

"You don't have to ask me in," he says. "I've enjoyed your company and you've shortened the dark hours. I'm grateful for that."

"Thank you for listening to me, Nicholas. I'm sorry if I talked too much."

"You didn't," he assures her. "If I helped a little by listening, I'm glad."

After he has driven away, she sits before the mirror on the dressing table and studies her face. Her lips feel voluptuous, as if he has crushed them with kisses instead of politely shaking her hand at the door.

"I've fallen in love with him." She utters the words to her reflection, then repeats them. Her stomach lurches, as if caught unawares by the giddiness of desire. She believed she was in love with Zac but that emotion now seems like a feeble pulse compared to this sensation of bliss and wonder and terror. She is not ready to be consumed. Not now, when she is so vulnerable, so prone to mood swings that leave her listless or filled with a manic energy. They plan to meet again next week. This feeling that has come upon her like a low fever turned delirium cannot be denied. No more talking about Zac. That conversation is over. She wants to know everything about Nicholas Madison, about Amelia, about their marriage. When he speaks of Amelia she will be as sympathetic as he was with her tonight.

She believed Zac had broken her heart but she had only suffered a mild fracture. Losing her baby and Isabelle had shattered it into tiny pieces—but hearts can mend. Does Nicholas believe that? She hopes desperately that he does. She sways forward, her arms wrapped round her chest, and thinks of Zac, pictures him riding towards her on the belly of a wave... then lets him fall.

CHAPTER FOUR

When they are not seeing each other, Nicholas rings her late at night. An hour later, they are still talking. They tease each other over who will be the first to end the call.

Flowers are delivered to the bungalow when Elena is not expecting them. He books tickets for the theatre and the Concert Hall, takes out membership for both of them at the Irish Film Centre. The films he chooses are interesting, sometimes difficult to understand until later, in a pub, he explains the concepts behind them. He enjoys classical music. This is more than just a preference, he tells her after a Bach recital by a Polish pianist, whose name Elena has already forgotten. Classical music has been proven to help people process grief and other traumatic events from their past. That is why he prefers it to popular music. This is the moment, Elena thinks. The perfect opportunity for him to confide in her. The moment passes.

She has checked everything that is available online about Amelia Madison. In back issues of glossy magazines, she has read about her high-flying career in interior design. She has watched on YouTube her television appearances, where she demonstrates how to achieve harmony and unity within the living and working space.

"Perhaps I should sign up for a course in interior design," Elena says one night when they are dining in a restaurant. "I've always believed I've a knack for optimising space."

He turns his head away. His jaw clenches. Elena wants to bite down on her tongue. She must be more sensitive, more understanding of his emotions, as he is of hers. He has remained a good listener, pressing her hands gently if she becomes agitated, holding her to him when she tells him about the tiny life she and Zac created and lost. He has opened her up in a way that no one else—not even Zac at the height of their relationship—has done.

When she tries to understand the uneasiness she sometimes feels after confiding in him, she can only describe it as being undressed, emotionally. It's as if he can see deep into her soul. Not that Elena believes in the concept of a soul or in a life that continues after the grave. Isabelle's spirit is not haunting the bungalow, nor is Amelia Madison's wraithlike hand on his shoulder when Elena is with him. It's just the power of memory that gives lifeblood to the dead.

She thinks about Zac, his rumbustious passion that petered out as soon as it was challenged. In bed she imagines Nicholas beside her, his probing tongue, his muscular arms and hard, thrusting body. She moans and tosses off the duvet, seeking relief, whispering his name as her body shudders. How long can this continue before her desire spills over and demands more from him than reticence and a chaste kiss on her cheek at the end of each date?

He rings her late one night. "Would you like to come to Kinsale with me for the August holiday weekend?" he asks.

She swallows, her mouth dry. It is three days since he was in touch, his phone going directly to message each time she tried to contact him. She had been distraught, convinced he had decided to end their friendship. That is all she can call this liaison that can sometimes feel more like a therapy session.

"Elena, are you there?" He sounds puzzled by her silence.

"Yes, Nicholas. I'm here." She hopes he can't hear the shake in her voice.

"So, what do you think?"

"Yes. That would be wonderful."

What will they do in Kinsale, she wonders when the call ends. Go for long, bracing walks? Enjoy the gourmet restaurants, then kiss each other chastely as they go to their separate rooms? She breathes deeply and exhales. There is only one way to find out.

✦

They browse the galleries and craft shops of Kinsale, explore the harbour clanging with boats, find small pubs where music is played and singers rattle out old, familiar ballads. A *Do Not Disturb* notice hangs outside their bedroom door. No thoughts of Zac play on Elena's mind as she lies with Nicholas on the wide, rumpled bed.

Quivering from the touch of fingertips, feathery kisses on skin, they are seized by a whirlwind of desire, their nights and mornings tangled up in pleasure, unable to stop laughing, loving, talking. Only one thing mars her happiness. Amelia Madison. Her absence from their conversation has succeeded in making her invisible presence all the stronger.

On their last evening together, they dine in a restaurant with a view of the harbour. Twilight settles over the busy town and the setting sun casts a reddening glow on the water. The light on the ocean intensifies. Yachts, heading towards the marina, stencil the horizon like black Chinese lettering. Amelia must have witnessed a similar sunset, Elena thinks. Had she been so dazzled that she was unaware that the wheels of her car had only the most precarious grip on the mossy surface of Mason's Pier?

✦

Elena had visited the pier, drawn there by a voyeuristic curiosity that shamed her yet nagged her constantly. The sturdy barricade blocking entry to the pier had obviously been erected since
the accident. No more cars would sink into that deep well. She
could see the slipway, its dangerous slant. The shift in Amelia's car
must have been almost imperceptible at first. Perhaps, feeling the
subtle movement, she braked too sharply. The skids on the tracks
still visible on the slipway the following morning suggested she
had lost control, though the handbrake was full on when her car
was lifted ashore. She should have been a confident driver who
knew how to brake gently; her work took her all over the country
and she had written about her love of driving in one of her online
features. Why had she chosen to visit Mason's Pier with its tragic
connotations? Was it possible that her drowning had not been
an accident? Is that why Nicholas was so reluctant to discuss it?

After leaving the pier, Elena had driven to Lemon Grass
Hill, the organic farm that Killian and Susie owned. Killian was
picking plums in the orchard when she arrived and Susie was
grooming their horse, Cassandra. Killian had shown her around
the farm before leaving for a meeting with other organic growers,
and Susie, preparing a lunch of cheese and olives, said, "You've a
bloom about you. Who is he?"

"You met him at my mother's funeral."

"Nicholas Madison?" Susie, who was cutting slices of home-
made brown bread, paused and glanced enquiringly at her.

"Yes. I've been seeing him for a few months now."

"Are you in love with him?"

"I guess I must be."

"Love is not a guessing game, Elena."

"I went to Mason's Pier."

"Why would you do that?" Unable to hide her shock, Susie's
voice rose.

"I don't know . . . she haunts me. And I feel as if she's haunting Nicholas as well. He never talks about her. Doesn't even mention her name. How strange is that?"

"Everyone has their own way of dealing with loss. Let his wife rest in peace. He'll tell you about her when he's ready."

✦

"You're very quiet." Nicholas is attuned to the shift in her mood. "Did I do something to upset you?"

"Of course not." Elena sighs, remembering Susie's words. "Everything's perfect."

"You're thinking of him again." An indent between his eyebrows deepens. Is Nicholas jealous? Has she been too frank in answering his questions about Zac?

"How can you ask me that?" She leans over the table to hold his hand. "You've well and truly exorcised Zac from my life."

"So, what's wrong, then? You're miles away."

"Why do you never talk to me about Amelia?" She presses her lips together and waits for his reply.

His fingers stiffen into a claw-like arch under her hand. He sits back in his chair, his expression daring her to continue.

"You never mention her name or refer to what happened to her. It's as if she never existed. I want to help you—"

"Help me? How do you propose to do that?"

"By talking about Amelia. You've helped me through such a difficult time. Why can't I do the same for you?" Her words sound hollow, childish. They remind her of a woman who phoned after Isabelle's funeral to apologise for missing it. She sounded like an authority on life after death as she informed Elena that her mother was free from pain and at peace. Elena had gritted her teeth, resenting the woman's blithe belief that a few trivial platitudes would ease her loss. Is that what Nicholas believes she is doing?

He cuts into his steak, medium rare, and studies the bloodied centre before bringing it to his mouth. He chews slowly, swallows, dabs carefully at his lips with a napkin. His silence adds to her nervousness.

"So, what exactly are you asking me, Elena? Do you want to compare experiences? Weigh up my pain against yours and see who comes out with the highest score."

"That's so unfair." She sounds defensive, unsure of herself. "You know that's not true. I've been honest with you about my past. What have you told me about yourself? *Nothing*." Why on earth did she start this conversation? "How can you expect me to ignore the fact that your wife died tragically? It must have had a horrendous impact on you. I'm not trying to pry—"

"What would you call it?"

"Concern." When her hands begin to shake, she presses them into her lap. It's too late to back down from the conversation now. "I want you to trust me enough to talk about her. As it is, she's creating a wedge between us—"

"A *wedge*?" His nostrils compress as if the air around him is tainted. "Why not call it an *incident*? That's how it was described in the media. An incident on Mason's Pier."

"Oh, Nicholas, I'm sorry—"

"What do you want, Elena?" He interrupts her apology. "Tears? Do you really believe they'd lessen the *wedge* between us?"

"All I'm asking—"

"You're asking if I'm crazed with grief? Unable to sleep? Unable to focus? Unable to see you without wishing I was looking across this table at her? The answer is *yes* on all counts."

His words, as forceful as bullets, leave her speechless. Two hours ago, she was in his arms. Now, he is pummelling her with his anger, his gaze shuttered. "How dare you assume you'll be able to handle my grief?" he continues. "Just because you feel the need to talk endlessly about yourself and your own problems, you've no right to demand the same from me."

"Stop it! I don't talk…" A feather-like current of air brushes past her cheek and she shivers, goose bumps lifting on her arms. She stands, unsteadily, unable to believe the direction their conversation has taken.

"Where are you going?" he demands.

"Away from you." The weekend is ruined. All that has gone before wiped out by his anger. The man who loves her, or claims to love her, breathing the words into the back of her neck as they spooned together in bed, has become a stranger who wishes she was his dead wife every time they are together. How can they step back from such an admission?

Elena takes two fifty-euro notes from her wallet and flings them on the table. "The meal is on me," she snaps. "Payment for being my grief counsellor."

"Sit down, Elena." He leans over the table and grabs her arm. "You're not going anywhere."

"Watch me." She jerks free from his grip. "I've no intention of competing against your dead wife. Ever!" Her heels click sharply as she walks from the restaurant. She has to find somewhere to stay tonight. She will catch a train back to Dublin in the morning. Why did she ignore Rosemary's advice about putting the bungalow up for sale? So much time lost while she was chasing some half-formed dream. She will contact an estate agent first thing tomorrow and return to Australia as soon as the sale is completed.

She reaches the harbour and leans over the wall. Laughter reaches her from the deck of a nearby yacht. A passing dog pauses and raises its leg. Her eyes brim. What had Nicholas heard when she confided in him? A frivolous recounting of a love that had failed? Two hearts no longer beating, hers broken? And he dared to call that tittle-tattle.

He comes up from behind before she is aware of him and wraps his arms round her.

"I'm sorry . . . so very sorry." His voice is hoarse, his breathing heavy. "You have to forgive me, Elena. I never meant to hurt you. I've no idea why I reacted like that . . . said those hurtful things. I didn't mean them, honestly. You touched a nerve and I reacted. I haven't been able to talk to anyone about Amelia. I can't . . . *can't* . . ." He turns her round and holds her close to him.

Held close against him, she's unable to move. He tells her about nights when he was afraid to sleep because of the nightmares, mornings when he stood with a razor blade in his hand and wondered how long it would take for all the blood to leave his body. But it's different now. Thanks to Elena, he is beginning to imagine a future where he can find happiness again. He curses himself for jeopardising that possibility and begs her for forgiveness. His eyes, no longer shuttered, embrace her, sweep her back into his orbit. His lips are hungry for her and that night, back in their hotel bedroom, he calls her name over and over, as if he is drowning under the weight of desire.

All the love flowing from her, she is frightened by her feelings. Nicholas is inside her, pushing deep, and she locks him to her with a ferocity that seems to overpower love and force her to search for another meaning. Is this obsession, she wonders? This momentum that hurtles her through each day as she waits for him to ring and wills the hours to fly by until she can be with him again.

Their first row is over, already fading into insignificance as he reassures her of his love, whispering into her ear, against her throat, breathless endearments making it possible to forget the other words that he had uttered with such bitterness.

Afterwards, his voice muted, as if he fears that the mention of Amelia's name will disturb the barricades he has erected around his anguish, he says, "She was the love of my life. I never thought I could recover from her loss. Then I met you. Do you remember that glance we exchanged as your mother was laid to rest? That's when my heart began to beat again. You must have known. How could you not feel that shift? Don't ever leave me, Elena. I love you…love you. I believed my life was spent when Amelia died. I don't ever want to feel so lost again."

Finally, he is able to confide in her. She understands why they argued. In order for him to emerge from his crevasse of grief, it had been necessary to punish Elena for forcing him to confront his loss.

She listens, hungrily, when he speaks about his marriage. He refuses to discuss the accident, the memory still too painful, but he tells her about the three blissful years he shared with Amelia before she was snatched so savagely from him. Beautiful, intelligent, charming, kind, gifted: these are the terms he uses to describe her.

"Be careful what you wish for," Isabelle used to say and add, warningly, "Granted wishes can often demand a premium price."

As Elena listens to him, she wonders if the premium on Amelia Madison will be higher than she has anticipated. She tries to find the same tolerance Nicholas had shown when she discussed Zac, revealing more about their difficult relationship than she'd ever intended. In contrast, his marriage sounded like an oasis of tranquillity in their busy lives. This belief is confirmed when she visits his home for the first time.

CHAPTER FIVE

Woodbine is a two-storey period cottage with ivied walls and a long, rambling garden at the back. Wide lawns on either side of the driveway slope towards a high boundary wall. The sense of Amelia is everywhere. She had studied fine art before she switched to interior design and her paintings, a clash of flamboyant colours, hang in all the rooms. Photographs arranged on the antique mantlepiece, on sideboards and occasional tables, prove that Nicholas has not been exaggerating her beauty. Her mouth was slightly on the wide side, a flaw that only amplified her interesting face and gave her a radiance that time can never diminish. Nicholas is in many of the photographs, smiling, hugging, gazing confidently into her eyes. Why did he not remove those photographs before Elena arrived? Have they become part of the furnishings, no longer noticed? If so, how is that possible?

He takes white wine from the fridge and carries the glasses to the terrace. Spicy cooking smells waft from the open kitchen window. Pots of coriander, tarragon, mint and basil grow along the windowsill. He lists the spices he uses in cooking: sumac, saffron, grains of paradise, amchur powder, carom seeds, cardamom; most of the names are unknown to Elena.

"I didn't realise you were a cordon bleu." She tastes the wine, Italian, perfectly chilled. "I'm impressed."

"Amelia was the cordon bleu," he says. "The tagine I'm making is her recipe. Moroccan."

"Sounds delicious."

"As long as I follow her instructions, it'll taste delicious, too."

The late-September sunshine streams through stained-glass butterflies hanging from an apple tree. Honeysuckle twines around a trellis and misshapen but eye-catching animal sculptures, set among the shrubbery, are examples of the attempts Amelia made at sculpting in metal during her student days. What she has left behind, her creativity, her garden, her house with its distinctive décor, have an added poignancy when viewed against the abrupt ending to her life. Elena won't be overwhelmed by her, yet she battles against each revelation Nicholas makes about their blissful years together.

The tagine is as tasty as he predicted. Amelia's hands might as well have cooked this dish. He shows Elena the recipe in a cookbook, one of many, all neatly stacked on a kitchen shelf, spine out. This book is stained from Amelia's floured hands. Old spills of liquid pucker the paper. Recipes that failed or needed an extra pinch of some obscure spice she must have picked up in an Asian market are annotated. Elena hands the book back to him and makes a non-committal comment. She chooses her words carefully, anxious to avoid another Amelia anecdote.

Amelia Madison, she thinks, is the ghost who will never be found out. She will never have to answer for bad decisions, develop irritating habits, have her heart broken or lose the allure of youth while those who remain behind wither into old age. How can Elena ever hope to compete with a woman who died before she reached the age of disillusion?

They take a bath together, soaking in hydro jets that pummel and soothe her. Did he and Amelia bathe together? Did she make love to him with the same wanton passion as bubbles frothed and the water whirled around them? The bathroom intrigues her. It's ostentatious in this house of understated elegance and well-worn antiques. Blue lights on a wall panel that can be dimmed add to the contemporary design and cast his face in shadowy, unfamiliar grooves. She wonders if she looks equally unsettling to him but he shows no signs of restraint as he glides the sponge over her breasts and downwards over her stomach, so taut and flat once again. Later, she sleeps with him in one of the spare bedrooms. She can tell by its exactness, the pristine coordinated décor and empty wardrobes, that this room is seldom used.

✦

He has already left for work when she awakens next morning. She opens the curtains to a view of the Sugar Loaf, its gentle hump rising beyond the trees at the end of the back garden. The glass butterflies shimmer in the morning sunlight and starlings ribbon the sky. She walks along the corridor and opens doors. Only one is locked. The bedroom he shared with Amelia. The handle clunks back into place when she releases it.

Last night, they left the dishes on the table and hurried upstairs, laughing and slightly drunk on wine and desire. He has cleared everything away before leaving for work. The dishwasher hums quietly and the kitchen window is open to clear the air.

"He'll exhaust himself and talk Amelia out of his system," Tara says when Elena phones her. "Just like you did with Zac."

"Not exactly," Elena replies. "Zac is alive and, therefore, fair game for being called a dickhead. Amelia Madison is beyond reproach. I'll never measure up to his memories of her."

"Then don't even think of trying. No one can outdo perfection so just be yourself."

"I don't know what that is any more."

"Yes, you do. You just need time."

"Don't say that."

"It's a cliché, I know, but true, nonetheless," Tara insists. "Susie is afraid you've rushed into this relationship. She's worried that it's too soon after everything that's happened to you."

"I'd be in a deep depression now if Nicholas hadn't been there for me." She wants Tara to understand that he has drawn her back from the jaws of the black dog. Wasn't that what someone once called depression, Churchill or some such warrior, who had heard the long howl? Nicholas's reminiscences of Amelia are difficult to endure but Elena will cope with them for ever rather than return to that darkness.

He has left a note on the kitchen table. His parents are hoping to meet her and he has arranged for the introduction to take place on Saturday. If that is okay with Elena, he will collect her at five.

✦

Nicholas pulls up outside high double gates with the word *Stonyedge* visible on the gatepost and escorts Elena up the driveway.

"No need to be so nervous," he says. "My parents are going to love you."

"Welcome … welcome." Yvonne Madison greets her with a hug. She's small and effusive, a talker, as Nicholas warned Elena on the drive to Stonyedge.

"Nicholas has told me so many wonderful things about you." She draws Elena into the hall. "Come in and meet Henry. And this is Pedro. Don't mind him barking at you. He'll get used to you quickly enough. Oh, my golly, he's licking your hand already. A good judge of character, is our Pedro. Down Pedro, down … *down*."

Nicholas shrugs, throws his eyes upwards as Yvonne flaps the red setter away and flings open the living room door.

"Elena, this is Henry. He's been looking forward so much to meeting you. We both have. Isn't she a sweet girl, Henry? Sit down, Elena. Henry will get you a drink. What would you like? Gin? It's everyone's favourite these days, wonderful with cucumber and juniper berries, I believe, though, personally I prefer vodka—"

"Let the girl get a word in edgeways." Henry rises from his chair and shakes Elena's hand. His cropped hair and craggy face reflect how Nicholas will look in another thirty years.

Yvonne enters the kitchen and continues talking. An open hatch in the wall allows her access to the dining room. She refuses Elena's offer to help, preferring, she shouts cheerfully, to have hysterics in private when her soufflé collapses. No danger of that happening. As Elena suspects, Yvonne is an unflappable cook, who serves starters, mains and desserts with noisy efficiency. Her hands are in constant motion, in contrast to her seamless face. Botox, Elena wonders? Yvonne's hair, blonde and spiked, has that same rigidity. Elena gives up trying to follow her meandering stories about the lives of strangers, suspecting that Yvonne doesn't need a reaction. A nod or a murmur of agreement suffices. When she asks about Australia she interrupts Elena's reply to describe the experience of her friend's daughter, who fell into seriously bad company in Perth.

As soon as the meal is over, she takes a photo album from a drawer in the sideboard.

"Get a grip, Mother." Nicholas groans when he sees it. "Elena doesn't want to look at me running around the beach in the nip."

"I think that could be very interesting." Elena laughs and sits beside Yvonne on the sofa.

The album is heavy and large, each page crammed with photographs. Yvonne has catalogued them with a place and date. She turns page after page, detailing each holiday, each celebration. They are a well-travelled family and the beaches she discusses are in Thailand or on Caribbean islands, the cities Asian and cosmopolitan. The family configuration never changes: a young Nicholas standing in front, each parent with a hand on one of his shoulders. He grows older, his boyish face replaced by a more angular profile and, later again, that roughness smoothing out into the authoritative face of a young adult.

"I never realised you were a biker!" Elena exclaims when she comes across a photograph of him in leather, leaning against a Harley-Davidson.

"Do I look like a biker?" he asks. "Hanging out with the grizzly and obese was never my thing. Biking was a phase of short duration."

"He gave up the leather but he kept the bike," says Yvonne. "It was in the garage for years afterwards. I thought he'd never get rid of it. That was just one of many interests." She shows photographs of Nicholas rock-climbing, another one of him white-water rafting.

Elena is bored by the repetitiveness of these photos. What is it with Yvonne, this compulsion to fill the slightest silence with words and shrill laughter? She reminds Elena of a marionette, those small, busy hands and restless mouth, the tight, floral-patterned dress riding high above her skinny knees. Nicholas has left the room and is outside studying a rose bush with his father. He glances towards the French doors, as if he knows the ordeal Yvonne is putting her through.

"Oh dear." Yvonne slaps her hand over a photograph. "I don't know how that got in here. It belongs to a different album entirely."

"Can I see?" Elena knows it's a photograph of Amelia and Yvonne, seeing her interest, slowly slides her hand away.

A couple on holiday, a mountain in the background. The breeze—Elena imagines its warm friskiness—had flattened Amelia's dress against the curve of her stomach.

"So sad." Yvonne blinks and closes the album. "We were thrilled with the thought of becoming grandparents."

"Oh, God! Was Amelia pregnant when she—"

"No, no." Yvonne glances nervously towards the men in the garden. "Thank goodness her miscarriage happened a year before the accident. She lost the baby at four months. There was a chance, slight as it was, that he—Nicholas was convinced she was expecting a boy—would survive the fall—"

"Amelia fell?"

"From a ladder." Yvonne is angry, her fingers tapping the photograph. "I'll never understand what possessed her to paint a ceiling at that stage of her pregnancy."

"How awful." Elena feels hot, embarrassed, remembering how compulsively she had talked to him about her own early miscarriage.

"Hasn't he told you about it?" Yvonne closes the album without having come to the end of it.

"No." Elena shakes her head. What other secrets has he kept from her? "He's never mentioned it."

"I guess it's too painful to recall." Yvonne's eyes glisten. "He was heartbroken, poor boy. And Amelia too, of course. Don't hurt him, Elena. He's suffered so much already."

"I'd never hurt him, Yvonne."

"I can see that. You've a kind face. Amelia was..." She pauses, as if seeking a precise description. "Headstrong."

"How?" A flaw at last.

"She had a will of her own."

"Surely that's a good thing."

"I agree with you." Yvonne sounds doubtful. "But she was always trying to prove some point or other."

"In what way?"

"What does it matter now?" She returns the album to the drawer. "She's gone from us and far be it from me to speak ill of the dead."

"I appreciate that. I hope you don't think I'm snooping."

"Nonsense. It's natural for you to be curious." She sits down beside Elena again and studies her hands. For once, she seems stuck for words. Elena should be grateful for this short respite but she is greedy for more information.

"Amelia must have been very talented. I saw her sculptures at Woodbine."

"She was multifaceted. Isn't that the modern term?" says Yvonne. "But she was also a diva who loved attention. When she didn't get it, she'd create a drama from nothing. Her behaviour took its toll on Nicholas. Not that he would ever hear a bad word said against her and it's not the place of a mother to interfere. I'm all for women's equality and everything that goes with it but a man doesn't like to be constantly outshone by his wife. That's why Henry and I are so thrilled he's met you—oh, dear..." She flutters her fingers to her lips. "That came out the wrong way. We're thrilled because you're a considerate and caring young woman. Nicholas needs someone who is compatible with him. I can see a change in him already and we've to thank you for that."

Elena knows she will never like this woman, but Yvonne's opinion has at least reduced Amelia to a ghost she can handle.

"It's a lovely evening." Yvonne rises and flings open the French doors. "Would you like to see the roses? They're Henry's pride and joy."

Elena follows her into the back garden, where Nicholas is deep in conversation with his father. One look at her face alerts him that it's time to go. He overrides Yvonne's protests and they leave shortly afterwards.

"You look as if you've had a baptism by fire," he says as he drives away.

Elena shrugs. "Yvonne was just trying to make me welcome."

"I can't believe she produced that album again."

"*Again*? Is this a regular ordeal when your girlfriends visit?"

"Past tense." He squeezes her knee and grins. "My teens were blighted by that album when anyone in earrings called...and that was just the boys."

Elena laughs with him. He's relaxed, glad that the first meeting with his parents is over. She should embrace the moment but the photograph of Amelia, the dreamy expression on her face as she presses her hands against her stomach, soothing a movement, maybe, demands an explanation. To climb a ladder, lean back to paint a ceiling, lose her balance...such recklessness. Elena feels her own stomach lurch in sympathy, and there is anger, too. Why, when she had confided in him and described an empty space that seemed boundless, had he not identified with her loss?

"Do you know that there's a photograph of Amelia in that album?" she asks. "She was pregnant, Nicholas."

"Oh." He clenches the steering wheel, a tiny reflex action, but she notices it and, for reasons she doesn't understand, her heart skids.

"Why didn't you tell me? I wouldn't have gone on so much about what happened to me. It must have been upsetting for you. If I'd known—"

"You needed to talk," he says. "And I wanted to find out everything about you." He checks the rear-view mirror and indicates to pass the car in front. The road is narrow and he doesn't hesitate as he crosses the continuous white line.

"Don't, Nicholas. It's *dangerous*." Elena lifts her shoulders as a woman in an approaching car blasts her horn. "Be careful!" she screams as she glimpses the driver's horrified expression.

Nicholas swerves smoothly back into his own lane. He has narrowly escaped a collision and is now too close to the car he passed. He increases speed, whips around a corner onto a straight stretch of road and eases his foot off the accelerator.

"Stop overreacting, Elena," he says. "We were perfectly safe."

"What's wrong with you, Nicholas? That was a ridiculous and dangerous thing to do." She's trembling, overcome with fury that he would take such a risk with their lives.

"Don't tell me how to drive," he retorts, sharply.

"I could have been killed. That gives me every right to tell you how to drive."

Despite his obvious efforts to remain composed, his knuckles are ridged on the steering wheel. She touches her cheek as it is brushed by a chilled breath of air. The skin on the back of her neck lifts. Someone walking on her grave, that's what Isabelle would have said. Once again, Nicholas increases his speed. His hands are off the wheel before Elena realises what he's doing. He raises them above his head and touches the roof. The car veers towards the pavement before he straightens it again.

"That's what's called ridiculous and dangerous driving." He laughs, his lips drawn back from his teeth, a humourless grimace that fuels her fear.

"What's wrong with you, Nicholas?" she shrieks. "Are you crazy or just plain stupid?"

He drives on, slower now, and indicates to turn into an industrial estate. It's emptying out, shutters coming down, traffic streaming onto the main road. He brakes the car in a cul-de-sac and turns off the engine.

"Are you all right, Elena?" No longer laughing, he sounds subdued, as if her fear has finally sobered him.

"No, I'm *not* all right." She is still shaken by their close encounter with death. He gauged it well. A few seconds more and he would have caused a head-on collision. "What did you think you were doing back there?"

"Behaving like a dick," he admits, ruefully. "I'm sorry for frightening you but you flung Amelia's name at me without warning and I find it hard to cope—"

"What warning do you *need*? You never stop talking about her!"

"You asked me to tell you—"

"I know I did. But then you leave out something as important as the fact that she suffered a miscarriage. Surely you must have known that I, of all people, would understand."

"How much more do you want to find out?" he demands. "I've been as open as I can with you. Some things are more difficult to discuss. I'm sorry I overreacted back there. It won't happen again but you have to respect my boundaries and stop being so obsessed about Amelia."

"*Obsessed*? Is that what you call it?" She is too angry to lower her voice. "We can't go on like this, Nicholas."

"Like what?"

"You're still grieving for her. I thought you were ready to move on but you're not. It's affecting me, my own sense of worth. I'm going back to Australia."

"Has Zac been in touch with you?"

"Zac has *nothing* to do with my decision."

"You haven't answered my question. Have you been talking to him?"

"No. And he's irrelevant to this conversation. Susie's right. I rushed into this relationship too quickly. You need more time and I need to sort out my issues on my own."

"No, Susie is wrong. What does she know about our relationship? My feelings for you? I'd never have told you anything about Amelia if you hadn't insisted. But she belongs to my past. You're here with me and I love you."

"Not like you loved her." This thought, spoken aloud, shames her. How petty she sounds. She presses her finger to her lips to stifle a cry. She wants him to understand the effect his memories are having on her but she will say the wrong thing and he will think she is being obsessive . . . and, maybe, she is. Love can be as demanding as it is selfless, she thinks as she hugs her feelings to herself. In Australia she can start afresh. She imagines hurtling through the surf, carefree and out of love with him. But that can never be.

He nods as if he understands her pettiness, her longing to be at the centre of his life. "Yes, my love for you is not the same," he admits. "Why would you expect it to be? You are different to Amelia. Uniquely different. That's what I love most about you. You make me feel as though I'm the most important person in your life. Amelia could never do that. She played on my feelings. In all our years together, I was never sure of what she would do or say next. It made things difficult—"

"You gave me the impression your marriage was made in heaven."

"I didn't mean to do so." He presses her palm against his chest. The fast thud of his heartbeat alarms her. The front of his shirt is damp and his body exudes a musky odour of perspiration. His adrenalin levels must be off the scale, she thinks.

"I've never been able to speak to anyone about her miscarriage," he admits. "I felt as though the back of my head exploded when you mentioned it."

"I never meant…"

"I know you didn't. And I didn't intend to frighten you. I'm still struggling to come to terms with what happened to her on the evening she disappeared." He sighs, a quiet, shuddering release. "Or what she allowed to happen."

"Do you think she…?" Elena searches for appropriate words and, finding none, leaves the question unfinished.

"I don't know," he admits. "That's what makes it harder to endure. Meeting you has helped me to see the way forward. You can't go back to Australia, Elena. Your future is with me. You must give me another chance."

"Take me home, Nicholas." Her head aches. She needs a darkened room and space to think.

✦

In bed, she replays their conversation over in her mind. What did he mean when he said her future was with him? Does that equate to a proposal? If so, how can that be? Officially, he is still a married man and Amelia a missing person. Elena has checked it out. A death certificate will not be issued until an allotted time span has passed. Seven years. What a sentence to serve before a spouse is allowed to remarry.

The following night he rings her mobile. "Are you at home?" he asks.

"Yes."

"Are you alone?"

"Why?"

"Because I want you to be alone when you look out the window."

A white stretch limousine is parked outside the gate. Nicholas is already striding up the garden path with a Brown Thomas carrier bag in one hand and a bouquet of roses in the other.

"What's going on?" she asks when she opens the front door.

"I'm taking you out on a special date." He hands the carrier bag to her. "Go and get dressed. Everything you need is in the bag. Don't be long. The champagne is on ice in the limo."

The dress he has bought for her is sheer and slim-fitting, an icy-blue shade that enhances her eyes. The weight she has lost since Isabelle's death adds to its elegance. How could he have known her size, and that the style would suit her so perfectly? He has left nothing out: shoes, jewellery, make-up, lingerie. The wrap she drapes over her bare shoulders is made from vintage lace and feels feather-light.

Nicholas whistles between his teeth when he sees her. He has arranged the roses in a vase on the hall table. She is struck by the arrangement; it looks so casual yet, having once temped for a florist in Brisbane, she notices how each pink rose is precisely aligned with white sprigs of gypsophila and fern. The vase he has used is one of many Isabelle collected over the years and kept in a display cabinet in the living room. It seems churlish to resent him looking in that cabinet without permission when all he was doing was finding the perfect vase to display his bouquet.

The driver blinks appreciatively when he steps out to open the door for Elena. The interior of the limousine reminds her of a luxury hotel and, as Nicholas promised, the champagne is on ice. She has never felt as beautiful and as cherished.

He has booked a table in the restaurant where they first dined together. When their meal is almost over, he opens a small box and produces a ring. Blue sapphires in an antique setting. He cannot offer marriage, not yet, but he wants her by his side in Woodbine. She longs to say yes, yes, yes... but a nagging doubt persists. He remains a mystery to her, his tenderness and declarations of love at odds with his sudden unprovoked outbursts. But *are* they unprovoked? It's easy to touch a nerve, as Yvonne did when she spoke yesterday about Amelia's ability to outshine her husband, her bland words implying that such a problem would never arise with Elena. Did Yvonne make that comment deliberately? Whether she did or not, she highlighted Elena's fear that she will always be seen as an inadequate replacement for his dead wife. Is that what Nicholas thinks? And does she want to be a replacement?

"Amelia will never come between us, I promise." His ability to read her thoughts is disconcerting. "I want a new beginning as much as you do. We'll sell Woodbine and buy a new house. Trust me, Elena. We've both been through difficult times but I know I can make you happy."

CHAPTER SIX

The old Portuguese church where they vow to love and cherish each other has been weathered by the prayers of many generations but she and Nicholas are alone under its arches. He will be free to marry her in another five years but, in the meantime, they will mark their commitment to each other before this lavishly adorned altar. They exchange gold rings and read the vows they have written for each other. Elena does not need a priest or registrar to perform this commitment ceremony. No bevy of bridesmaids or pews of appreciative wedding guests are necessary to give their vows the stamp of authenticity. In her mind this symbolic ritual is binding and confirms the love they have declared for each other.

At the end of their ceremony, a musician and a singer enter the church. Nicholas smiles at her surprise and holds her hands while the man plays on his classical guitar and the woman's magnificent voice soars towards the ceiling.

"She's celebrating our love for each other," Nicholas whispers. "Do you feel married to me?"

"Yes." Elena is overwhelmed by the beauty of the woman's voice. "This is as perfect as any wedding day could possibly be."

"Our honeymoon will be just as perfect," he promises.

When the song ends the couple slip away as quietly as they had entered the church and she is alone again with Nicholas.

"There's just one last thing to do before we leave," he says. "And that's to kiss my beautiful bride."

✦

The temperature is high on the Algarve but here in Praia do Beliche, the wind is strong. Waves thunder towards shore and the sand blows fast, stinging eyes and skin. It's three days since they arrived here on their honeymoon—they both refuse to call it a holiday—and Elena is back on the crest of the ocean where she belongs.

The exterior of their villa has walls the colour of pink candyfloss. Inside, it is cool and spacious, as perfect as Nicholas promised her it would be. A labyrinth of paths meander through groves of olive trees and a cooling stream bubbles over stippled stones. They have their own private swimming pool and sun-loungers. Elena has no interest in either. They are only a short distance from the beach, where the height of the rollers reminds her of her tumultuous days on the Gold Coast.

Two bodyboarders standing in the shallows watch as she makes contact with a wave. She's conscious only of the rush of the ocean against her face as she rises on the swell and floats ashore. Nicholas refuses to join her. Earlier, he took a tumble from his bodyboard and now he says he's had enough for today. He's more confident on a surfboard but Elena has been coaxing him to bodyboard, repeating Zac's conviction that surfing is for wusses. She thinks briefly of Zac, agile and eel-like, then he is lost from her thoughts as she wades back out again. She catches the lip of a roller and allows it to carry her upwards. One wrong move and she will fall like a rag doll. The roar of the surf is intoxicating as she executes an air backflip. Giddy with pleasure, she skims past the bodyboarders, who clap and raise their boards in salute. She waves at Nicholas, who leans back on his elbows and watches her from behind his shades. He's turned from golden brown to mahogany. Women notice him, all ages, but he's hers. Elena still can't believe it. To awaken in the morning and see his face on the pillow beside her. To lie down with him at night and feel his long body, aroused and ready to devour her, his hunger matching her own.

Now, he rises from the beach mat and lopes across the sand. At the edge of the ocean he hesitates. The water is shockingly cold on first contact. When Elena is washed ashore she leaves her bodyboard on the sand and returns to the waves, deliberately splashing him as she runs past him.

She dives underwater and grabs his legs. They fall together and surface. Unable to keep his balance, he flounders and topples backwards into the foam. He finds his feet and braces himself against the next wave. The bodyboarders, who have glided back again into the shallows, laugh as Nicholas shakes his head and spits water. Elena laughs with them. There's something comical, almost Charlie Chaplin-like, to his movements as he struggles to stay upright. She pushes towards him and holds out her arms to steady him. His body rigid, his face expressionless, he dives into the water and swims away from her.

She can swim faster and quickly catches up with him. They are out of their depth when he disappears under the waves and grabs her, sliding his hand between her legs, an intimate caress but dangerous here. She surfaces, her mouth opening, gasping for air, her eyes streaming. He swims underwater again and, once more, she is submerged. She tries to free herself but, if anything, his grip is more determined. Her lungs will explode if he doesn't release her. Her heart is pounding hard and fast when he pushes her upwards and she is able to breathe again. She swims towards shore. He passes her but she has no inclination to race him. Her arms feel heavy and the beach with its colourful umbrellas and windbreakers seems far away. She reaches the shallows and staggers to her feet.

Nicholas is already waiting for her, a towel open and ready to enfold her. Water glistens on his skin. A luminous sun god who almost killed her.

They dress in silence. She pulls on a top and harem pants, combs the sand and salt from her hair. Her anger is barely contained as they gather their possessions and leave the beach.

"What the hell did you think you were doing?" Once inside their rented car, she turns furiously to him.

"What?" He pauses, the ignition key in his hand.

"Holding me under the water for far too long."

"Don't exaggerate, Elena. It was a joke. You did exactly the same to me." His teeth, so white against his tanned face, flash. He's enjoying the moment, teasing her as she had teased him.

"You're wrong. We were in shallow water and you were never in any danger. I could have drowned out there."

"What exactly are you suggesting? That I was deliberately trying to harm you?" He's alert to her anger, all traces of laughter gone. "Is that what you *actually* think?"

"No, of course not."

"Then what?"

"You don't know your own strength, Nicholas."

"Perhaps you're right. I'm sorry if I upset you." He sounds impatient rather than sorry as he pulls out of the parking space. "At least no one was laughing at you."

"Oh, for goodness sake! Don't be so childish." She fumbles with the seat belt, her eyes still stinging from the salt water. The entire afternoon has been spoiled by his recklessness. "Surely you, of all people, should be aware of the dangers of drowning."

He brakes so abruptly that she is jerked forward. The wheels skid on loose gravel and a cloud of dust rises. A car following behind narrowly avoids rear-ending them. The driver pulls out and passes them, horn blaring. Nicholas ignores him and steers the car towards the trees.

"Don't you dare. Don't you *fucking* dare remind me of all I've lost," he shouts.

The blow to her cheek is so sudden that, for an instant, Elena is unsure what has happened. The seat belt she had been about to fasten slips through her fingers and she wonders if she has slammed her face into the dashboard. It is the only explanation that makes sense... but she is still sitting upright, and Nicholas is shaking his hand, as if he wants to disown it. She touches her cheek. It's throbbing, hot. Soon it will swell. She draws back when he reaches towards her. He looks shocked, appalled by his behaviour, but his apologies are meaningless to her. She turns from him and stares out the window. She needs ice on her face and a darkened room, alone. Nothing he says or does will change what has occurred between them. Unable to break her silence, he finally drives slowly and carefully from the car park.

✦

She runs into the villa without speaking and locks the door of the bathroom. As she guessed, her cheek is red and swollen. She touches it tentatively, still unable to believe he has struck her. This is the first time she has ever been slapped. Isabelle, no matter how demanding Elena was as a child, never lifted a hand to her. She wasn't bullied in school and her years with Zac, though marked by occasional ferocious arguments, were never touched by violence. Now, in a flash, everything has changed.

Nicholas knocks on the door and asks if she is okay. He sounds concerned but what does that imply? She doesn't know if he is concerned that he has hurt her or that he has revealed a side of his character she never suspected. Has she been fooling herself, refusing to acknowledge that his encounter with tragedy has marked him in ways she will never understand? She slides to the floor and stares dully at the ceramic tiles. Zigzagging lines, a tide of blue waves, the design so often seen on Portuguese walls and pavements. Was she wrong to persuade him to come here? Why not a mountain or a city where there would be nothing to remind him of the ocean's treachery? And that comment she flung at him, heedlessly taunting him. But to retaliate with such violence. How is that forgivable? Her heart pounds when he bangs on the door.

"This is ridiculous, Elena," he shouts. "Open the door this instant and let me in." He is commanding, not contrite.

"I don't want to talk to you," she shouts back, determined to match tone for tone. "Go away and leave me alone."

"I'm not moving from here until you come out." His voice hardens, becomes more determined. "We can't discuss this through a closed door."

"There's nothing to discuss."

"There's *everything* to discuss." The banging intensifies. "Open the door, immediately."

The bathroom is on the ground floor. She drops easily to the grass verge below and runs into the olive trees. Their bark reminds her of the veins on an old man's hands. Beyond the trees she reaches a wall and can go no further.

He is tall and formidable as he comes towards her. She, too, is tall and she has never been conscious of his greater height until now. His skin is blotched. Has he been crying, also? She shrinks back when he hunkers down and brings his fingers to her cheek. But his touch is gentle, his voice muted when he talks about Amelia's drowning.

She had gone to Galway on an overnight business trip and he had grown increasingly anxious as the evening passed without any contact from her. No answer from her phone, not even the answering service. Ringing hospitals, the police, friends—the night seemed endless as he waited for word from her. Then, the following morning, the knock on his door. Two detectives, their mouths moving, but he wasn't hearing them, not really, because what they were saying was so implausible, so utterly unacceptable, that he wanted to silence them with a gun to their heads. Anything to stop them describing the car that had been found at low tide below Mason's Pier.

The weeks that followed, the endless, hopeless searches. Shame fills Elena as he speaks. When he cups her face, she doesn't pull away. She stops his apologies with her lips. She will be more careful in future. Never again will she allow her anger to trigger in him such horrifying recollections.

Grief can come upon him with the rush of a tidal wave, he says. Always unexpected, seemingly unstoppable, yet, no matter how brutally he is pulled down by the undertow, he can cope once Elena is by his side, supporting him.

The moon is waning against an indigo sky when they go indoors. They cling to each other in bed, frantic to recover the carefree happiness they had known before this afternoon. He enters her with a suddenness that takes her by surprise. It is over too quickly, too soon for him to use the condom he had left on the bedside table. His lips are on her, his tongue, his fingers, and when Elena cries out, there is no distinction between pain or pleasure in the sound.

A tidal metaphor, she thinks, when his even breathing tells her he is sleeping. But an undertow does not pull us down. It drags us away from the shore, fights hard against muscle, heart and endurance, and when the fight is done, we sink.

CHAPTER SEVEN

Brookside sells quickly, as Nicholas had predicted. An excellent price, thanks to his negotiating skills. The money is invested in KHM Investments until Woodbine is sold and they can buy the house of their choice. Elena checks the online property sites and tries to endure the bouts of nausea that come upon her with such suddenness. Hyperemesis gravidarum, her gynaecologist—a woman and, therefore, able to invest some sympathy into her diagnosis—tells Elena on her first visit. And likely to last not just three months, she warns, but for her entire pregnancy.

The months that follow blur between brief periods of wellness when she finds the energy to meet with estate agents. She makes arrangements to view houses she likes and is forced to cancel these appointments, either because she is too sick to attend the viewing or because Nicholas has to deal with a crisis at work. Today, they have arranged to meet at noon for an auction. The property for sale, a spacious three-storey renovated Victorian house nestling above Killiney Bay, has an outrageous asking price but it will be affordable when Woodbine is sold and the proceeds combined with Elena's inheritance. The sooner they move the better, as far as she is concerned. Woodbine is dominated by Amelia's spectral presence, the photographs and paintings still in place, the recipe books with her floured fingerprints still slanted on the kitchen shelf. It will take more than a coat of paint and rolls of wallpaper to eradicate her personality and Elena's efforts to persuade Nicholas to have the rooms redecorated have been met with steely resistance. The house is in perfect condition, he argues. Why waste money changing it when it will soon be sold?

He rings as she is about to enter the auction room. He has to fly to the New York office at short notice. Some cock-up due to Peter Harris's ineptness and Nicholas has to sort it out, as usual. There will be other houses, he reassures her. He sounds far away, as if he is already in flight.

That evening, Elena checks the auction site. The house sold for a price they could, at a stretch, have afforded. Unable to sit still, she tackles the living room and moves the armchairs into different positions. She rearranges the photographs so that Amelia's vibrant face is not the first thing she sees each time she enters the room.

On the cluttered sideboard, she discovers a photograph that, until now, has been hidden from view behind larger frames. This is a group photograph that had been taken at a KHM Christmas function. Elena touches her chest instinctively when she recognises Isabelle standing beside Rosemary Williams. Lilian Harris, her mouth pulled downward by discontent or, perhaps, unhappiness, was posed like a ramrod between her husband and Christopher Keogh, KHM's senior partner. The sainted Amelia, sleekly slim in a silver lamé dress, short wings of black hair swinging over her cheeks, was laughing into the camera, while Nicholas was positioned behind her, one hand resting on her shoulder, his downcast eyes gazing tenderly on her. Unable to bear the image of their glowing happiness, Elena hides the photograph behind a sheet of wood in the garden shed.

His face hardens when he returns from New York and surveys the rearranged armchairs. He immediately moves them back into their original positions and demands to know why she made these changes without his agreement. Her skin feels stretched, branded red with frustration. Is he expecting her to walk in his dead wife's shoes? If so, this is unacceptable. Her voice, rising to a shriek, sounds appalling to her own ears.

He stands in front of the sideboard and studies the photographs. "Where is it?" He does not raise his voice but his grip on her arm is tight. "I want that photograph back in its place, immediately."

"Why are you making such a fuss?" she demands. "You hid it behind the others, so you obviously didn't think it was that important."

"Don't you dare presume to know what I consider to be important. This is my house and you had no right to disobey my instructions."

"You tell me you love me yet she's still blinding you to *my* needs? You were hardly aware of that photograph's existence until I removed it."

"I'm aware of everything in this house." He is close enough to kiss her or strike her. The realisation that he could do either fills her with alarm. Has he been so warped by this tragedy that he is unable to see how outrageous his behaviour has become? Is that grief stronger than the love he claims to feel for her? Elena's cheeks tingle, as if brushed by fleeting fingertips, and the sense that another presence, powerful but invisible, is listening to them sends shivers through her.

She pulls away from him and walks out into the garden. Not so long ago, the gentle pressure of his fingers lingered on her skin. Now, her arm is bruised and hurting. The full moon shines on the glass butterflies and the oddly shaped metal sculptures have acquired a pale, ghostly hue. She removes the photograph from its hiding place and hands it to him. Wordlessly, he stares at it. She wants to say something, anything, to break the tension, but there is a warning in his silence that unnerves her.

Suddenly, he slams his fist into the photograph. Glass shatters and falls to the floor. Blood spurts from his hand. He ignores Elena's cry and holds up his other hand, palm forward, to prevent her moving closer. He removes the photograph and tears it in two, flings the pieces and the remains of the frame into the empty fireplace. An ornate brass dragon on the mantlepiece serves as a matchbox holder. He removes a match, strikes it off the dragon's scales and sets fire to the photograph. His blood drips into the fireplace but does not quench the flame. This is ritualistic, almost barbaric. Elena looks away as the paper coils and browns.

She finds bandages in a first aid box in the kitchen and stems the bleeding. The photograph has turned to ash. Her stomach lurches. Bile fills her mouth. She just makes it to the bathroom in time. Afterwards, she brushes her teeth and stares at her reflection. She's losing weight, not putting it on. That's not surprising as this so-called *morning* sickness can afflict her at any time.

Her baby moves that night and Nicholas awakens, as if he, too, has experienced that first fluttery sensation of butterfly wings beating down the months.

✦

Amelia's photographs seem to have multiplied. She knows this is her imagination; she can count, and does, often. How is she to establish her presence in Woodbine when everywhere she looks there is evidence of another woman?

The bedroom Nicholas has allocated to them is spacious and has that wonderful view of the Sugar Loaf. But *allocated* is the word she repeats to herself every time she walks past the locked door. Only Nicholas can enter this room; and that is what he does one evening on returning from work. She hears him walking across the floor, the thud of his shoes when he drops them. She knows, then, that he is lying on the bed, no doubt thinking of those sultry, breathless nights he once shared with Amelia.

Is that why he hits her when he comes downstairs and she demands to know what he was doing up there? The blow is so sudden that Elena staggers backwards before recovering her balance and lunging her fists at him. He takes the blows easily, smiling, as if her fury, simmering on a wave of nausea, amuses him.

"Enough... enough." He holds her as she struggles against him and speaks steadily into her ear. "We've had our fun. Now, let it go. This jealousy is bad for our baby—"

"How dare you call this 'having fun.'" She lowers her voice and goes limp in his arms. "If you dare to lift your hand to me again, I'm leaving you."

He shakes his head, unmoved by her threat. "We made vows, Elena. I love you and I'm trying hard to make our relationship work. We're going to have a child together. You don't walk away from that commitment. You must stop talking about Amelia. All it does is stir up memories. Surely you can see the effect your insensitivity is having on me."

She listens to his arguments, his pleas for understanding, sympathy, acceptance. His sincere apologies that sound so believable. She hugs her hurt to herself and watches his shoulders relax. Woodbine will be sold and as soon as they find a house they both love they can begin afresh.

CHAPTER EIGHT

Yvonne, who has her own key to Woodbine, never phones in advance when she decides to visit Elena. She always arrives with home-made bread and cakes, or Tupperware containers filled with Nicholas's favourite dinners, which, she assures Elena, are no trouble to make. Her key to the front door was cut for her in the days following Amelia's disappearance. Nicholas will never ask her to give it back.

"We seldom have a chance for a girly conversation," she says one evening after she has arrived with a tray of lasagne. "You can heat this up and have it ready for Nicholas when he comes home from work. He loves my lasagne. I used to make it every Tuesday when he was a boy. No prizes for guessing which day of the week was his favourite one."

Elena rises from the sofa, where she had been resting after a bout of vomiting, and tries not to retch as the cheesy smell wafts from the tray. "Yvonne, you'll have to forgive me, I'm not feeling so well today. I was just about to take a nap."

"Poor Elena, you *do* look absolutely washed out." Yvonne pats Elena's arm on her way to the fridge. "Nicholas says you're finding things very difficult at the moment."

"What things?"

"Oh, you know..." She shrugs. "It's those hormones, my dear. They play havoc with our moods, especially at this time. One of my friends was frightened of birds for the *entire* nine months. Said it was like living in that Hitchcock movie."

"Why has Nicholas been discussing our relationship with you?"

"We're very close, Elena. And you needn't worry. I'd never dream of repeating anything he confides in me." Yvonne switches on the kettle and removes two mugs from hooks on the cupboard. "What was I saying? Ah yes, the moods...the *moods*. Remember Molly Blaine, you met her at my house. Big teeth, pudding-bowl haircut? Well, when she was expecting her daughter, she was convinced Susanna had a full set of teeth and was biting her. I mean, *come* on. Was that crazy or what?"

"Yvonne, if you don't mind, I was just about to lie down—"

"You're not having an easy pregnancy but you'll forget all about it as soon as that babe is in your arms." She lifts a ceramic teapot patterned with wildflowers from a shelf and brews the tea. "Nicholas adores you, Elena. When the time is right, the two of you will move from here and into the house of your dreams. In the meantime, we want to enjoy this precious time with you." For an instant, Yvonne's rigid features relax. "Bad feelings create unhealthy toxins and that can't be good for my grandchild. You should practise yoga and do some meditation. Get rid of all that negativity."

Elena bursts into tears as soon as Yvonne's car disappears down the driveway. What is the matter with her? She has never felt so confused. Even when Zac left and the tiny foetus she carried so briefly slipped away from her, she had been able to cope. The shock of Isabelle's death had left her bereft but she had not felt as vulnerable as she does now.

✦

In the fifth month, when she is admitted to hospital suffering from dehydration, Nicholas insists they leave the house viewings until after the birth. His workload keeps increasing but Elena, cooped up in Woodbine, is confined to leaning over the toilet bowl, holding her hair back from her face with trembling hands.

CHAPTER NINE

Spring arrives. Leaves are unfurling, a quivering pale-green lint on the trees and hedgerows, when Grace is born. Her thin cry reminds Elena of a kitten. Her droopy, fledgling neck and puckered mouth, the eyes that have yet to focus and reveal their colour, fill her with a trembling emotion that is part elation, part exhaustion.

"It's obvious her eyes are grey." Yvonne cradles her first grandchild in her arms. "She's the spitting image of Nicholas when he was born."

Henry stands self-consciously beside her, clearly besotted but unable to coo and chirp at his granddaughter as Yvonne is doing. Elena wills them to leave but Yvonne is insisting on relating her own birthing experience. Hours of screaming for relief. Unsympathetic doctors and nurses who left her writhing in agony until they decided it was time for Nicholas to be delivered by Caesarean. She reports all this with relish. It's obvious from the numbed expression on Henry's face that he has heard it all before, and often.

Yvonne looks away when Elena, unable any longer to ignore her baby's hunger, begins to breastfeed Grace. Her daughter is a natural feeder who sleeps peacefully for short stretches before she begins her kittenish demands to be fed again. Elena is amazed that her tiny lungs can emit such a strident noise. That such a tiny mouth has such a vigorous suck.

Grace is a hungry baby, never satisfied for long, and Yvonne's disapproval is obvious when she discovers Elena is continuing to breastfeed. Is Grace getting enough nourishment, she asks each time she visits Woodbine. Is she putting on weight? She frets over the colour of her granddaughter's bowel movements, her frequent demands to be fed, her pale complexion and high-pitched cry, which, she believes, sounds distressed. The weaning process should start now, she states when Grace is two months old. Grace will then be able to spend more time with her grandmother and Elena will have a chance to recover her energy. "Breastfeeding on demand does nothing for romance," Yvonne warns. "You look *so* washed out and you're tired all the time. Grace will sleep all night if you give her a bottle. A man needs—"

"I'm well aware of what a man needs," Elena snaps. She bites hard on her bottom lip. *In Nicholas's case, it's a wife who endures his violence. Oh, yes, your precious son is fond of smacking me around. Why don't you talk to him about that?* She searches for a glimmer of understanding in Yvonne's eyes but, finding none, knows that she can never confide in this self-absorbed woman.

Yvonne's face stiffens. "I've upset you," she says. "That's the last thing I want to do. But you have to understand that it's not easy for Nicholas to cope with a demanding day's work when his sleep is being disturbed by this constant feeding."

Nicholas has that same obdurate expression when he wants his own way and Elena, tired of holding her temper in check, says, "How I feed my baby is my own business, Yvonne. Grace is healthy and strong. I intend to continue breastfeeding until I decide when the time is right to wean her. If you want to continue coming here, you'll have to stop interfering and accept that I know what's best for my baby."

✦

"What on earth did you say to my mother?" Nicholas asks when he comes home from work that evening. "She rang my office in tears when I was in the middle of talking to an important client. She claims you've barred her from seeing her granddaughter."

"I'm sick of listening to her trying to undermine me." Elena braces herself against his anger. "She keeps insisting that I stop breastfeeding Grace and—"

"But she's right." He makes no effort to hide his irritation. "Grace needs to start feeding properly. I'll organise the formula and you can begin weaning her tomorrow. That will reduce your stress levels."

"Grace is not the reason I'm stressed." Elena takes her daughter from the carrycot and presses her against her shoulder. "She's feeding well and I've no intention of taking her off the breast. If I am stressed, it's because your mother is annoying the hell out of me."

"She's only trying to help. Those night feeds are exhausting you." He dips a spoon into the curry Elena has prepared and tastes the sauce. "Not enough cumin," he says. "Amelia made a note of the exact amount you need. Use her book of Indian recipes the next time."

"I know how to cook a Madras curry, Nicholas."

"Don't be offended. This is nice. It just needs something…"

"It needs Amelia's touch, you mean. Why not say it? Nothing I do matches up to how she did it. *Nothing.*" Her mind reels at his audacity. "The *other* reason I'm stressed out is because I live in a house that's like a shrine to your dead wife."

A vein pulses in his forehead. The colour drains from his face. She hurriedly puts Grace back in her carrycot as he walks towards her. This time he will do it, she thinks. She's been waiting for it to happen since their last row but when his fist makes contact with her, it's not her face he strikes but her stomach. She bends double and wheezes, tries to catch her breath. Grace, as if electrified by the dangerous currents, begins to cry. The sound forces Elena to her feet. Still dazed, she has to lean on Nicholas, who holds her upright and leads her to a chair. She collapses into it and struggles to breathe.

"How could you speak about Amelia in that way?" he roars. "I've begged you not to mention her, yet you persist in defying me. Why can't you realise how difficult this is for me? I didn't mean to hit you. It's just…just…" He pauses, seems to be searching for ways to make her understand his desperation. "I want us to be happy more than anything in the world but you seem determined to torture me. If only you'd let her rest in peace, I could build on this life we have together."

His voice comes at her from a great distance. She tries to understand the point he is making. Is he blaming her for his violence? She finds the strength to lift Grace from her carrycot and hold her.

"I can't feed Grace with you in the room," she says, quietly. "We'll talk about this later."

She hears him above her, his footsteps crossing the master bedroom. The bed creaks when he lies down. His love for a dead woman is breaking her heart. She has to leave him. It is the only solution. She must take Grace and run to a safe place. She coaxes her daughter to feed from breasts that will soon be devoid of nourishment—how can they be otherwise when fear is curdling her milk? She cradles Grace and rocks backwards, forwards, backwards, forwards, until he returns, contrite, ashamed, and takes the sleeping child from her arms.

✦

The following morning, she comes downstairs after Nicholas has left for work. Sleepless and still devastated from the previous night as she is, it takes her a moment to realise that Amelia's photographs have been removed. So too have her paintings and wall hangings. He must have risen in the small hours to make these changes. His apology is not in words but in deeds. Her ribs ache where he punched her, the bruise spreading from below her breasts to her stomach. Let him plead for understanding until he is hoarse, kneel until his knees ache. She will never forgive him.

That evening, when he returns from work, he sweeps his arm towards the faded squares where Amelia's paintings had hung.

"Forgive me" he says. "Please, Elena, you have to forgive me." His eyes remind her of pebbles, bleached lustreless by tides. He will never strike her again. He has suspected for some time that he is suffering from post-traumatic stress disorder. Why should that be, Elena rages silently? It was Amelia who drowned, not him. But what does she know about anything? She wasn't combing the shoreline, longing for a solution, good or bad, to the interminable wait.

Post-traumatic stress. It's an obvious explanation. Her love for him rolls over her anger and fear. It quells her awareness that his violence is barely contained and will break out again if she unwittingly provokes him. She has to believe his promises, his declarations of love, his determination to seek help from a therapist. Someone who will lift his memories from him and tame them.

Fishermen had spoken knowledgeably to him about the shoreline where a body could be washed in on the tide. On two occasions, he believed the search was over but the bodies that were recovered from the deep had the wrong dental records. Tooth enamel, it appears, is still death's main identity card.

CHAPTER TEN

Grace adjusts to the bottle, feeding just as lustily as she had at Elena's breast. Elena tries not to feel resentful that this decision has been forced upon her and Yvonne, after declaring that such rude behaviour is understandable when a new mother is highly strung and struggling to cope, decides to forgive Elena's outburst by offering to babysit.

"It's time the two of you went out for a meal to celebrate your daughter's arrival," she says. "Bring the romance back into your relationship again. Men can feel neglected if baby continues to get all the attention."

She and Henry arrive at the house the following evening. The restaurant Nicholas has booked for their meal is renowned for its organic cuisine. Mirrors glimmer on the walls and candlelight adds to the opulent atmosphere. The maître'd, a stately woman in a black trouser suit, welcomes Nicholas like an old friend and leads them to their table. He must have dined here with Amelia on many occasions, if her effusive greeting is any indication. Elena will not let this fact spoil their night together.

They talk about Grace. So much to discuss. Their daughter is an unending source of fascination to them and it is easy to laugh with delight over her antics. Elena won't spoil the atmosphere by mentioning the ugliness of their last row, which, like the others, seems more unreal with every day that passes. When their meal is over, the maître'd offers them after-dinner drinks on the house. The hum of quiet conversation is broken by laughter from a group of women, who are enjoying their night out. It seems so long ago since Elena shared a meal with her friends, who are all scattered now. The yearning that sweeps through her for those careless nights must have travelled by osmosis towards another group of diners, who are being guided to their table by the maître'd.

"Laney Langdon!" Elena swings her head round, startled to hear a name that only one person has ever used.

"Oh, my *God*. Steve!" She stands, overjoyed to see him coming towards her.

She met Steve Darcy on her first day at university. Lost in a bewildering maze of lecture halls and corridors, she asked directions from him. He, too, was just beginning his course, the same one as Elena, but he appeared to have a built-in sonar system that led them unhesitatingly towards the right lecture hall. He made her laugh and forget her shyness, which had caused her so much grief in secondary school. He drew others towards him and Elena; Tara, Susie and Killian, the five of them forming a tight-knit circle that lasted until they graduated.

"Tara told me congratulations are in order," he says as he wraps her in a bear hug. "First of the gang to break the mould."

"Someone had to do it." She laughs as she extricates herself from his arms. "I highly recommend it. Our daughter is adorable. This is Nicholas, Grace's father."

"You're one lucky man." He pumps Nicholas's hand vigorously. "I used all my charms on Laney in university but to no avail."

"Don't mind him, Nicholas." She laughs and nudges Steve with her elbow. "He had so many women surrounding him I wouldn't have been able to claw my way in his direction."

"I *wish*." Steve gives an exaggerated sigh, then cups her face. "I'm sorry I was in Cambodia when Isabelle died and was unable to make it back for her funeral."

"I know that, Steve. I appreciated your calls."

She blinks rapidly, overcome by a sense of loss. Those carefree years they had spent together could belong to someone else. Someone she has trouble recognising. She has broken the mould, all right, and has no idea how she will put the pieces back together. "Are you here on holiday or have you moved back home?" she asks.

"No, I'm still living in Paris. We've been doing a photo shoot at the Powerscourt waterfall. I've opened my own agency. Did Tara tell you?"

"She said you're trying to poach her."

"Some hope. She likes the bright lights of London too much."

How quickly they had scattered when they graduated. Elena had been the first to leave, unable any longer to live in the shadow of a man she could hardly remember. Steve followed, then Tara, the three of them only reuniting for Susie and Killian's wedding. A Druidic ceremony held beside a fairy fort, a high, green mound rising up from the land they had bought. The smallholding had lain idle for years until he and Susie gave up their jobs in advertising, turned their backs on city life and decided to become organic farmers.

"Motherhood suits you, Laney. You look amazing." Steve sits down in an empty chair and holds out his hand, fingers beckoning. "Come on. Show her to me."

Obligingly, she takes out her phone and shows him photographs of Grace. She is conscious of a woman at Steve's table, who keeps glancing across at him, and an increasing pressure from Nicholas's knee.

"She's inherited her mother's beauty gene," Steve says. "Like I said, Nick, you've hit the jackpot."

"I couldn't agree more." Nicholas puts his arm round her. Elena is conscious of its tautness, the stiffness of her shoulders as Steve, oblivious of any tension, talks about mutual acquaintances he meets on his travels. She is eager to know more about his agency and if there is someone special in his life but the questions will only prolong their conversation.

"Why don't you come to Woodbine and meet Grace before you go back," she says.

Nicholas knocks his knee against hers again, two hard taps that express his annoyance more effectively than words.

"Looks like the waiter is ready to take your order." Nicholas stares pointedly across at Steve's table and the woman, sitting beside his empty chair, gestures towards him.

"Duty calls." He stands, his reluctance obvious. "I'd love to see Grace but I'm flying out early tomorrow morning. Next time—that's a definite date."

She should not feel a sense of relief that Steve has refused her invitation but it washes hotly over her and trickles down her spine.

"*Nick*. What's with the fucking abbreviation?" Nicholas asks when Steve has returned to his companions.

"That's Steve's way," she says. "He's always been very informal."

"So I noticed, *Laney*?" He leans towards her. "Would you like to explain that one to me?"

"It's what Steve always calls me."

"Is that why you were so tense with him?"

"Tense?"

"Yes, *tense*. How come you never told me about him?"

"There was never anything to tell."

"That's not what he said."

"Romance wise, we hardly lasted any time. But he was one of my best friends at university."

How long had they lasted as an item? A few weeks, no more than that. They had decided their friendship was more important than the emotional entanglement of a break-up that—knowing how woman were attracted to Steve, and he to them—had been bound to happen.

"Susie, Killian, Tara." He lists the names on his fingers. "It's interesting that I've never heard his name until now?"

"If you're keeping count, then include Steve."

"Don't mock my feelings for you."

"I'm not mocking anything. You need to loosen up, *Nick*." He dislikes having his name shortened, as she discovered when she addressed him as such in one of her earlier emails, but the after-dinner brandy and the wine she drank earlier is fuelling her annoyance.

"Did you fuck him?"

"That's none of your business."

"So, you did?"

"I didn't say that. You're my partner, not my confessor. Do I ever ask you about the intimate details of your life with Amelia?"

"You're right. I shouldn't pry." He drains his brandy and gestures at Elena to finish her drink. "Time to go. Yvonne will be wondering what's keeping us."

His change of mood from belligerent questioning to agreeing with her is a surprise. Alarm bells ring in her head but alcohol has muted their chimes. They pass the restaurant window on their way to the car park. Steve's profile is visible as he talks animatedly to his companion.

Nicholas is silent on the drive to Woodbine. She tries to gauge his mood and fails. When they enter the living room Henry awakens from a snooze and Yvonne switches off the television. Grace is asleep in her cot. The baby monitor has been silent all night, Yvonne tells them.

"A little angel. She was no trouble at all," she says. "You just need to be more confident with her, Elena. Babies can always tell if a mother is stressed."

Yvonne's inference that she is incapable of looking after Grace annoys Elena but she stays quiet, afraid of breaking the fragile peace between her and Nicholas.

When his parents have driven away, Nicholas sits on the sofa beside her and takes her in his arms.

"Not tonight, Nicholas." She kisses his cheek and tries to rise. "I'm so tired and Grace is due a bottle soon."

"Yes, tonight." He presses her back against the cushions and kneels down in front of her. "I want you to relax. That's all you have to do."

"I don't *want* to relax—" She gasps as he slides her dress over her thighs. Gently but insistently, he eases her legs apart, his breath warm on her thighs. His tongue probes deeply and Elena, surrendering to him, moans softly as the tension eases from her and then falls away.

Unable to find the words to apologise for his earlier behaviour, is he offering sex as an act of atonement? She no longer cares. She begs him to come into her but he refuses, intent only on releasing the ruckus of pleasure he has stirred within her. When her cries die away and he is looking down on her, all askew and spent, she wonders if what he did to her could be defined as rape? This thought, so unexpected and appalling, stuns her. It diminishes the true horror of rape and should not even be considered in the same breath. She is overwrought, reading too much into what was a selfless giving of himself; yet his stance, so contained and controlled, sours the wanton pleasure she has just experienced.

Later that night, aroused and wanting her, he awakens her from a deep sleep. Drowsy and unresponsive, her body bends and shakes, and is ruptured so fast she is unsure if she is still in the realm of dreams.

CHAPTER ELEVEN

Unaware of the tempestuous reaction his meeting with them in the restaurant provoked, Steve will have returned to Paris by now. The passion Elena experienced last night...she should be glowing in its aftermath, not resenting her body for having responded so eagerly to Nicholas's caresses. And later, when he came into her, the force of his desire numbing her, that memory stirs her with an uneasiness she's unable, or unwilling, to name.

Unable to stay indoors, she straps Grace into her buggy and leaves Woodbine.

Her daughter's eyes move to the mesmerising sway of branches overhead as Elena wheels her along the narrow path by the edge of Kilfarran Lane. The width of the road belies its title as a lane but the houses along either side of it are sparse, as are the cars that use it.

Fifteen minutes later Elena reaches Kilfarran Village. She hopes to meet other young mothers in the café or the library, but the streets are quiet, sunk in an afternoon hush. Mornings are the best time to make new friends, the librarian tells her. She hands Elena fliers with information about a mother and baby yoga class that is held in the community centre, a parents' coffee morning organised by the Ginger Nut Café, group buggy walks through the woods and the local cinema, which features films one morning a week for parents and babies. Obviously, the village is not as sleepy as it looks and Elena feels her spirits lifting as she walks back to Woodbine.

She needs an outlet and Nicholas is not yet ready to put the house on the market. His workload has increased since Peter Harris was diagnosed with a heart condition. He is awaiting surgery and Nicholas is now travelling in his stead to the New York office for fortnightly meetings. He had related this information to Elena with relish. He dislikes Peter, whose job he has coveted since he joined the company. To add to Peter's woes, his wife has left him and is demanding a divorce. The indent on Nicholas's forehead deepened when he mentioned this latest piece of office gossip. He called Lilian Harris, "a whinging, mercenary bitch," who was capable of taking her husband to the cleaners in terms of the alimony she would demand. Elena had been surprised by his vehemence. What had Lilian ever done to him? She remembered the group photograph he destroyed. That would explain his reaction. It had obviously been the sight of Lilian, and not Amelia, that had triggered his fury.

Grace is becoming restless. She is due a feed. Elena walks faster. The narrow footpath is edged by a bank of grass that slopes down into a ditch. The stream flowing through it is almost obscured by weeds and bulrushes. She hears its low gurgle as it flows towards the Kilfarran River. Bunches of cut flowers are laid regularly on the grass. Usually they have disappeared by the following day but, inevitably, more flowers appear. It has to be a roadside shrine. A fatality must have happened there and a bereaved loved one has turned the site of the accident into a memorial.

Today, an elderly man stands on the grassy ridge. The carnations he has spread out in a fan shape are just about to open. Elena recognises him as one of her nearest neighbours; he lives in a secluded dormer bungalow and she has seen him working in his front garden as she passes his gate.

He lifts his cap in a salute when he sees her and steps down onto the path. "Well, Elena, we meet at last," he says. "I'm Billy Tobin. Congratulations on the new arrival." He leans over the pram. "A little girl, I see. What a beauty. Does she have a name?"

"Grace."

"A sweet name. I hope she has many graces throughout her life." He peers at Elena from under the brim of his hat. "How are you settling into Woodbine?"

"Very well. It's a beautiful house." She points towards the carnations. "Why don't you put them into a vase? They won't last long without water."

"They won't last long, period." His genial expression hardens. "Vases break easily, as I've discovered. This is the best way."

"Did someone die here?"

"You haven't heard about the accident?" He stands a little straighter. "Surely Nicholas told you about it?"

"Told me what?"

"Amelia's father died here. A hit-and-run."

"How terrible." She blushes, embarrassed before his frank gaze. "I didn't know. Did the gardai ever find out who caused the accident?"

"No. His case is probably closed by now. It was a long time ago."

"You must have known Amelia very well?"

"She was a lovely young woman in the prime of life." He nods, vigorously. "Such a tragedy. Her father was my best friend. But it's a nice summer's day and not the time to dwell on the past. Would you like to walk back to my house with me and have tea?"

"Thank you for inviting me but I can't today. I need to feed Grace." Her daughter is awake, little fists raised and a frown that suggests she is about to give vent to her hunger. "I'd love to have tea with you another time."

"I'll look forward to it. Don't be a stranger when you pass by."

As she walks back to Woodbine, she wonders why Nicholas has never mentioned Amelia's father. Is she supposed to peel away his past life layer by painful layer?

At dinner that evening, she mentions her encounter with Billy Tobin. "He seems like a nice man," she says. "He invited me in for tea but Grace was hungry—"

"Billy Tobin is no friend of mine." Abruptly, he interrupts her. "You are to have nothing to do with him."

"Why ever not? What's the matter with him?"

"He wanted to pick your brains about me. That's the only reason he invited you into his house."

"I don't believe that."

"You spoke to this man for five minutes today and you're prepared to discount what I'm telling you."

"That's not what I mean," she protests. "He never asked about you, apart from being surprised that you hadn't told me about Amelia's father's accident."

"There you go again." He smashes his fist off the table and rises, his meal untouched. "You keep talking about her, even though you know how much it upsets me."

She crosses her hands on her chest, shielding herself against his anger. "I'm not trying to upset you. All I said was—"

He will never find out what she intended to say. On the floor, trying to crawl away from him, she loses a little bit more of herself and wonders if she will ever be whole again.

✦

The carnations are missing from the roadside shrine the following day. Someone, she has to assume it was Billy, has left a spray of purple dahlias in their place. The low growl of his lawn mower reaches her when she passes his house and the heady smell of cut grass sweetens the air. She walks swiftly past before he sees her. Once past his house, she turns the buggy around the corner and into a narrow side lane. Devoid of traffic and pedestrians, it stretches before her, as empty as the days she must endure until her bruises fade.

CHAPTER TWELVE

It's two o'clock in the morning and Nicholas remains sleeping as Elena slips from his side. He is a heavy sleeper but she, aware of the risk she is taking, holds her breath as she rifles through the pockets of his jacket. She has searched every drawer in the house for a key to Amelia's bedroom and now, acting decisively, she grasps the keyring and moves soundlessly across the landing.

Only two of the keys on the ring look as if they could fit into the lock. Both fail to work. Struck by a sudden thought, she stands back and studies the casing that surrounds the door. It curves outwards in an ornate sweep and allows just enough space for her to run her fingers along the gap between the edges and the wall. She finds the key hanging from a hook near the top of the casing. Finally, she will be able to open the door to this mesmerising room. She touches the key for reassurance, then, terrified in case Grace cries and awakens Nicholas, she returns to the bedroom and replaces the keyring in his pocket. He stirs but does not awaken as she eases back into bed beside him.

The following day, her first reaction when she enters the bedroom is one of disappointment. The room she shares with Nicholas is modern and bright; by contrast, this one looks as if it has been used by many generations. The old-fashioned furnishings have a highly polished sheen that suggests care and attention. The bed is covered by an eiderdown that, she suspects, was once a treasured possession of Nicholas's. He would have caressed Amelia on that bed and loved her as he will never love Elena. Now, adrift without her, he has turned into a monster and she stands in the centre of his tortured path.

He has not yet made an appointment with a psychologist to discuss his stress disorder, which is becoming more pronounced. He accuses her of nagging at him when she reminds him of the promise he made to her. If she continues to undermine him, he will be forced to take action. He speaks softly, as if they are sharing an intimate exchange; a promise of pleasures to come, and she, hearing his implicit warning, is silenced.

Amelia's make-up is still on the dressing table. Nicholas has made no attempt to tidy it away. Lipsticks are lined up in rows according to their shade. Tubes of foundation, jars of moisturising creams and bottles of perfume are aligned with the same symmetry. The only item to disturb this evenness is a crumpled sheet of tissue paper. Elena picks it up, then lets it fall when she sees the imprint of Amelia's lips, a vibrant, fuchsia pink. Why has he not thrown it away? Does he hold it to his own lips when he is here, remembering... remembering?

She opens drawers filled with underwear, rainbow colours in satin and lace. Stockings and tights, two suspender belts, fun pyjamas with cartoon prints, some sexy, flouncy nightdresses. Her stomach turns as the intimacy of the life he shared with Amelia is spread before her.

She reaches the en suite just in time. Holding her hair back from her face, she kneels in front of the toilet bowl and retches, convulsively. Afterwards, sitting back on her heels, she wipes her mouth. The last time she was this sick—no, it isn't possible... but that night when they met Steve...she was dazed with sleep and can't remember if Nicholas used a condom. She rises and returns to the bedroom, slams the drawers closed. The nausea has passed. A stomach bug, that has to be the reason. Anything else is unthinkable.

She opens the wardrobe. The coat hangers all face the same way and the clothes—colour-coded and coordinated, look as though they are on display in a boutique. After seeing Amelia's lingerie, Elena finds it hard to imagine her wearing these structured suits, tailored trousers and formal dresses. She had always imagined Amelia floating from room to room in layers of silk. The only dress to attract her attention is the silver lamé one she saw in the photograph Nicholas has burned. Sleek and slim-fitting with a long slit at the side, it must have hugged every curve of her slender body.

The zip is easy to slide down. Elena lays it on the bed and takes off her top, wriggles out of the trousers with the elasticated waist. She used to laugh with Tara when they went shopping and saw these shapeless, chain-store trousers that offered comfort instead of style. Never, in her wildest nightmares, did she believe she would ever wear them but Nicholas had bought two pairs for her—one navy, one indigo—as a stopgap, he said, until she recovered her figure.

She stands before the long cheval mirror and steps into the dress. Amelia was smaller than Elena, and the hem hangs a few inches above her ankles. The zip sticks at her waist and won't go any higher. She tugs hard but it's caught in the fabric. Her tears fall without warning. She can't believe she is making this sound, her body racked with sobs, her face livid and blotchy. The dress, glittering in the mirror, is a mocking tribute to Amelia's beauty and svelte figure.

Downstairs, Grace is also crying. Elena glances at her watch and is shocked at how much time has passed since she entered the bedroom. Her hands shake as she shoves the dress into the back of the wardrobe. The clothes have the musty smell of unopened spaces and Nicholas, she hopes, will never notice that they have been disturbed.

✦

That tingle on her skin, the feathery brush against her cheeks fuels her fear when he comes downstairs from the bedroom that evening. She has become accustomed to his waxen complexion when he is angry, his eyes glazing over as he studies her.

"What were you doing in her bedroom?" he asks.

"I don't know what you mean." It is futile to lie but confessing the truth is not an option either.

He wrenches her from the armchair to her feet and twists her arm behind her. "You are a deceitful bitch." He breathes hotly into her ear. "I gave you the run of my house. Her bedroom was my only refuge from your prying obsessions. All I asked in return was that you should respect my privacy. Was that too much to expect? Was it? Answer me. Why did you have to defy me and enter it?"

She is sprawled on the floor, blows raining on her shoulders, her legs. He is being careful, she notes in the midst of her terror, to avoid her face. When he lifts his foot, she cradles her stomach and finds the strength to breathe a warning.

"I'm pregnant." The words are almost inaudible but they penetrate his fury. His foot freezes. His stillness suggests he is trying to decide whether or not she is lying. Then he bends and helps her to stand.

"How long have you known?" he asks.

"Not long." She has no idea if she is telling the truth but the possibility that she is carrying his child has stayed his fists, his feet. She sobs and pushes him away. Denial is no longer possible. She has fallen in love with a man racked by memories, whose violence stems from the fact that Elena will never replace his lost love.

CHAPTER THIRTEEN

The pressure on Nicholas to work late increases as Elena enters the final months of her pregnancy. Is there another woman in his life, besides the one who haunts him? Is that the reason he is avoiding her? Does he find her repulsive, her wan face and bulging stomach, the constant retching that leaves her without the energy or desire for anything except sleep? The only consolation she has is that his rages have ended. When they are together he is solicitous, soothing Grace and feeding her when she awakens at night, apologetic when he rings Elena to tell her not to wait up for him. His concern, though, only feeds her suspicions.

She phones Rosemary one night when the solitude has become intolerable and asks why it is necessary for Nicholas to work so much overtime.

Rosemary pauses, as if considering her words carefully, and when she does speak, her surprise is palpable. "I don't work with KHM anymore. It's three weeks since I left. Didn't Nicholas tell you?"

Elena, unable to believe she hasn't heard this news, is shocked. "No! But *why*? What on earth happened?"

Rosemary is vague on the detail yet there is an edginess in her tone that alerts Elena's suspicions.

"You should ask Nicholas those questions," she says when Elena probes her for more details. "He's in a better position than I am to explain the reasons."

Nicholas, when he arrives home, is dismissive of her concerns. Rosemary's attitude had become problematic, he says. Clients had complained about her work and an amicable agreement was reached to allow her to take early retirement. His eyebrows rise when Elena continues to question him and, recognising the danger signals, she changes the subject.

She plans to visit Rosemary to find out exactly what happened but Grace is cutting a tooth and has developed a rash on her face. The thought of leaving Woodbine and driving to Rathgar, where Rosemary lives, is too much of a chore at the moment. She will do it next week… or the week after… and Rosemary remains a guilty intention at the back of her mind as the months pass and the date for her delivery draws nearer.

Christopher Keogh organises his annual KHM charity auction for cancer research. At the end of the night, he thanks Elena for being so understanding about the overtime Nicholas does. The market is volatile at the moment and this has increased Nicholas's already demanding work schedule. She knows Christopher would not lie to her. When she was younger he used to invite her and Isabelle to staff barbecues in his long back garden. Elena had never tasted anything as delicious as the home-made lemonade and ice cream that Rita, his wife, gave the children. Was it her imagination or did the sun always shine on those summer afternoons? Christopher smiles and agrees that that is also his recollection. He is considering retirement. His voice flattens. The thought of retirement holds no pleasure for him since Rita died, but—he leans towards Elena and whispers in her ear—it will advance Nicholas's career.

"I'm delighted he's getting a second chance at happiness," he says. "He tells me that being with you is the best thing that's happened to him since Amelia. You've been good for him, Elena.

Soon, he'll be able to add another photograph to the ones he has of you and Grace on his desk."

✦

Joel slides into the world as easily as his sister did. Elena folds her love effortlessly around him and Nicholas is equally enchanted with his son.

"You're not to worry about anything except getting your strength back," says Yvonne when she visits. She has moved into Woodbine to take care of Grace while Elena is in hospital. "I can stay for as long as it takes to get back on your feet again."

"It's not necessary," Elena argues weakly. "I'll be discharged tomorrow."

Yvonne, her expression rapt as she gazes on her grandson, doesn't appear to have heard her. "Isn't he *absolutely* adorable?"

"He's also hungry." Elena stretches out her arms. "I need to feed him."

"Goodness me, have you decided on breastfeeding again? Are you sure you're able—"

"We're not repeating this conversation, Yvonne. I won't stand for it this time."

Elena's response is sharper than she intended and Yvonne tosses her head back, arches a shoulder.

"I'm sorry if you think I'm interfering, my dear. I'm only thinking of your welfare. The sooner you put him on the bottle, the sooner you'll get your life back again."

I don't want my life back again. Elena longs to scream the words aloud. The need to end this polite charade and tell Yvonne what she has endured comes and goes. All that is in the past, Nicholas insists. "A second chance at happiness," Christopher Keogh had said and Elena wonders if this is really possible. That awful first year, when Nicholas was unhinged by grief, is over. He has repeated this so many times to Elena, as if the force of repetition will fade the nightmare. She has to believe that change is possible.

When she is alone, she takes her son in her arms and stands at the window. Post-partum depression: the term terrifies her. Joel whimpers, then changes his mind and continues sleeping. The city winks back at her as she wills the black dog snapping at her heels again to slink away.

CHAPTER FOURTEEN

Nicholas arrives home from work late one night when Joel is two months old. Grave-faced and solicitous, he comes into the bedroom and sits on the side of the bed.

"Hard day?" she asks quietly.

He nods. "One of the toughest. How are you?"

"Tired. Otherwise I'm fine. Have you checked Grace?"

"I peeked. Her cheeks are flushed. Is she teething again?"

"Looks like it. She's been fretful all day but Joel has been an angel. What was so tough about your day?"

"That's what I need to talk to you about. I don't want you to be upset but I'm—"

"What is it?" Her alarm is instant. She knows that he is about to reveal something that will shatter the uneasy truce they have shared. He has met someone else? Her suspicions were right all along. Stolen hours in hotel rooms. She imagines them together, the woman faceless but dishevelled on a bed, and he, leaning over her, uncaring that Elena is trapped with two babies in a house she hates, her days blurred with meaningless chores. Seeing her agitation, Nicholas smiles reassuringly and takes her hands in his.

"Nothing that won't be rectified in time. There's been a glitch on the market. Chinese-related. It affects our plans for the immediate future. It's only temporary though and you must trust me to sort it out." Quietly, he explains how her stocks and shares in KHM have collapsed. The investment he was positive would wield such profits has been affected by the collapse of a Chinese bank. Ripple effects throughout the global market has made the stocks worthless.

He holds her hands more firmly when she struggles against him. He has been trying for months to recoup her losses, and those of the other investors, who have also been affected. It seemed, for a while, as if the company would go under but Nicholas has managed to avoid this catastrophe. His partnership is still intact and Elena's investment will return in time to its full value, when the market settles. He makes it sound like a wild beast that has escaped its leash, temporarily. She hurls furious questions at him but is unable to listen to his answers. How could she have been so trusting? Isabelle had often spoken about the reliability of KHM and had always received a healthy return on her investments. But that was when it was called Keogh & Harris Investments, before Nicholas became a junior partner. Her stomach cramps with panic. She pulls free from him and pushes him aside. Sobbing, she stands, her legs shaking so much she is afraid they will not hold her upright. She leaves the bedroom and crosses the landing, unsure where she is going, what she will do, how she will cope with this revelation. The only certainty she has is that her future has turned to dust.

"Come back to bed." He is close behind her. "Everything will be back to normal, eventually. You have to trust me, Elena. It's just a blip. It happens all the time but the market always recovers."

Unsure and uncaring whether he is anxious or contrite, she turns at the top of the stairs and flails back at him.

"Listen to me." He fends off her blows and reaches towards her. Unable to keep her balance, she claws the air for support and, for an instant, it seems as if she is suspended, motionless, in mid-air. Then she falls. As her face smacks off the wooden staircase, she thinks of Amelia falling from a ladder with the same graceless abandon.

When she recovers consciousness, Nicholas is bending over her. Pale and gaunt from shock, he presses tissues to her forehead. Her head hums and the red mist before her eyes breaks into jagged stars. He helps her to her feet and talks about calling an ambulance.

"No...no, I don't need an ambulance." She is insistent at first, fighting back panic as she imagines Yvonne moving in and looking after the children, but the blood seeping from her head tells her that an ambulance is vital. Has she fractured her skull? Her body will be one dark bruise tomorrow. How ironic that this one will have been self-inflicted.

The paramedics are attending to Elena when Yvonne arrives to look after the children. Her face floats into view and away again, yet not before her shocked expression is replaced by a wary glance from her son to Elena, who is being lifted onto the stretcher. She suspects, Elena thinks, but her thoughts are dulled, her mind unresponsive.

Nicholas holds her hand as the ambulance driver hurtles towards the hospital. The siren is a screech inside her head but even louder is an insidious, taunting question. Did she fall or was she pushed?

CHAPTER FIFTEEN

Susie is unable to hide her shock when she enters the small, private ward where Elena is recovering. "I fell down the stairs." She sounds, she thinks, more defensive each time she repeats this information. "I was wearing socks at the time. Not a good idea on a wooden staircase. Thankfully, awful as I look, I'm going to be okay."

"Your poor face. Oh, my God, Elena."

"I thought I'd fractured my skull but it's okay. I'm just badly bruised, that's all. I'll be fine in a week or so." She is familiar with the palette to recovery; the mottled purple turning to a murky brown before fading to amber, then a sickly yellow. She is briefly tempted to confide in Susie before Nicholas arrives, but shame holds her back. Her inheritance is worthless, frittered away by a man who claims to love her but has brought her to the depths of despair with his recklessness and violence. His chastened expression has done nothing to relieve her fury. It doesn't matter how often he apologises for the vagaries of the market and reassures her he will recoup his losses; he has taken her means of independence from her. Now, with their children binding them ever closer, she is unable to see a way forward without him.

"I'll be discharged tomorrow. I can't wait to see the children again. The nurses have been wonderful. They've helped me to pump milk so that I can continue to feed Joel when I go home."

"They're *so* sweet." Susie is enchanted by the photographs on Elena's phone. "Guess what? They'll have a new little friend in six months."

"Oh, Susie! That's wonderful news."

"You're the first to know, apart from Killian, of course." Susie giggles and presses her hands against her flat stomach. "He's over the moon about it. I'm going to need all the advice you can give me."

Elena's bottom lip bleeds when she tries to smile. Susie dabs at it gently with a tissue. "That looks sore. You must have been terrified when you fell."

"It all happened so quickly." She stops as the door opens and Nicholas enters. She takes the tissue from Susie and holds it against her mouth, unable to bear the thought of being kissed by him.

"My love, is your lip bleeding again?" He ignores Susie and bends towards Elena. "I'll call the nurse—"

"Don't do that, Nicholas. It's okay now." She gives her lip a final dab and introduces him to Susie.

"I've heard so much about you and Killian." He smiles warmly at her. "It's a pleasure to meet you at last."

His teeth look long and sharp, a wolf's teeth ready to tear her apart. How come she has only ever noticed their whiteness until now, and not their lupine appearance? The band around Elena's chest tightens. She has to stop—*stop*. Otherwise, she will have a heart attack and who will love her children as much as she does? She must find a way to strengthen this relationship and build on the shame she has sensed in Nicholas since the night he confessed to beggaring her.

"And you too, Nicholas," says Susie. "Congratulations. I've just been looking at photographs of your children. You must be thrilled with them. They're gorgeous."

"They take after their mother." He strokes an index finger along Elena's swollen face. "I'm a very lucky man."

"Elena has been telling me about her accident. From the sound of it, she's lucky to be alive."

The atmosphere in the small ward changes instantly.

"Wooden stairs. Woolly socks." Elena speaks quickly. "A dangerous combination, as I told you."

"Unfortunately for Elena, that's true. For one dreadful moment when she fell I thought I'd lost her." He looks pointedly at his watch. "As you can see, Susie, she's still in recovery and supposed to be resting."

Susie, taking the hint, stands. "It's been wonderful seeing you again, Elena. Why don't you all come and stay with us for the weekend when you're fully recovered. We'd love to show you what we're doing on the farm. It's quite amazing."

"I'm sure it is," says Nicholas. "But with two babies, a visit is out of the question for the foreseeable future."

"Of course." Susie squeezes Elena's hand. "But don't leave it too long. Our door is always open."

"Why were you so rude to her?" Elena asks after she leaves.

"Rude? Since when has caring for the person you love been considered rudeness?" He kisses the top of her head. "How did she know you were in hospital?"

"I told her when she rang me yesterday." She sits perfectly still. That gentle pressure on her cheeks, as if she has been brushed by cobwebs, is becoming familiar now. "She drove all the way from Galway and you made her feel so unwelcome."

"That's nonsense, Elena. She left because she could see you were exhausted and overwrought from her visit."

"I'm not overwrought—"

"Calm down, *please*. I can't cope with another scene."

"Then watch my lips, Nicholas. I'm *not* overwrought."

"If you say so. But you can't blame me for being worried about you. Remember how you were after Isabelle died? And those months after Joel was born? You were worse than with Grace. All I ever want to do is protect you."

Protect her from what? From herself, is that what he means? From the fear coiling inside her? The throbbing of her head? The jabbing pain in her chest when his face hardens and she realises she has said the wrong thing again?

CHAPTER SIXTEEN

Elena treads lightly, like those women in niqabs who wear soft-soled slippers that whisper their approach. She uses words warily, afraid of the "triggers" that will unleash his temper. The mirror reflects her inner turmoil: her thin face and eyes shadowed from sleeplessness, her stiffened shoulders.

She lifts a pair of scissors and brings them towards her. Clumps of chestnut hair fall soundlessly to the floor, where they coil like a nest of mice. She gags at the harsh chemical smell as she mixes dye and applies it to her bobbed hair. When the time is up she rinses it out until the water runs clear.

Sleek wings brush her cheeks when she swings her head, but the matt black colour drains her complexion. In straightening her springy curls, she has achieved a slightly lopsided effect, as if the scissors had been slanted in the wrong direction.

She should look chic, having copied the short, asymmetrical hairstyle she has seen so often in the photographs of Amelia. But she is not, by nature, chic. She was made for the outdoors, for boisterous waves and challenging heights.

✦

Tara is home to attend her father's sixtieth birthday, a family celebration to which Elena and Nicholas were invited. Elena had sent their apologies and is surprised, the day after the party, to see her friend standing at the front door. Thankful that she had put on a pair of sunglasses before answering it, she takes Tara into the conservatory.

"I took the train to Wicklow, then a taxi out here," Tara says. "I didn't realise Woodbine was so far out in the sticks." She stands back to survey Elena. "I like the shades. Classy. Not sure about the hairstyle. Bit Joan of Arc, if you don't mind me saying so."

"It's easier to manage this way." Elena flicks it self-consciously with her fingers. "Joel was pulling it out by the roots. Excuse the shambles." She clears toys from the floor and dumps them into a toybox. "Why didn't you let me know you were coming?"

"I tried ringing your mobile. You're not answering."

"It's broken. Grace's handiwork. I haven't had time to pick up a new one."

"Oh, my!" Tara hunkers down as Grace walks towards her. "This can't be Grace. I thought she was a baby."

"This little fellow usurped her." Elena gestures towards the carrycot, where Joel lies sleeping.

"Wow!" Tara dutifully admires him. "He's beautiful. How old is he now?"

"Four months."

"And Grace is?"

"A year and six months."

"Irish twins. You *have* been a busy girl since I saw you last."

"Wine," says Elena. "White, I presume?"

"Sounds perfect." Tara collapses into an armchair and coaxes Grace onto her lap.

In the downstairs bathroom, Elena takes off her sunglasses. The bruising is still livid around her eyes and across her forehead. She runs a comb through her hair and splashes cold water over her face. She cannot remember what ignited this last row and anyway it is no longer possible to anticipate the "trigger." Her back aches and a pain at the base of her neck worries her. She walks slowly towards the kitchen and takes a bottle of white wine from the fridge. She uncorks it and returns to the conservatory, where Joel, awake now, is demanding to be fed. Grace immediately abandons Tara and demands her mother's attention.

"How do you do it?" Tara asks as Elena settles him at her breast and perches Grace on the chair beside her.

"It's an innate skill," Elena replies. "You'll discover you have it when your own brood arrive."

"Perish the thought." Tara spins the wine glass between her fingers. "I don't possess a single maternal bone in my entire body." She stops, startled into shocked silence, when Grace, reaching upwards, pulls the sunglasses from Elena's face.

"Oh my God! What's happened to you?" The expression on her face tells Elena that her friend has already guessed the answer.

"I was standing on a stepladder looking for something on top of the kitchen cupboard. I overbalanced."

"Did you go to hospital?"

"No need. No bones were broken. I was lucky it wasn't more serious. I only fell down four steps."

"Four steps too many, Elena."

"It happens." She refills Tara's wine glass and puts the bottle back on the coffee table.

"Won't you join me?" Tara asks. "You look as if you could do with a strong drink."

"My body is an alcohol-free zone when I'm feeding. But I'd love a glass of water. Would you mind bringing me one in from the kitchen?" She needs a moment to compose herself. Tara's expression, that sceptical grimace she was unable to hide, has caused the heat to rush to her cheeks. Grace, still holding the sunglasses, wriggles to the floor and flings them into the playpen. Joel, sated, pokes a matchstick finger into his mouth and drifts asleep.

"Are you happy with Nicholas?" Tara asks when she returns with the water. A slice of lemon floats on top. Elena's face scrunches, as if she has bitten into its tartness. He has destroyed her hopes of independence, shamed her sense of self so severely that she is unable to confide in her friends. She hesitates too long, unable to form the words she needs, and Tara, frowning, kneels before her. "Does he hurt you, Elena?"

The question shocks her into an immediate response. "I've already told you what happened, Tara. Why on earth would you ask me a question like that?"

"I'm sorry. Sorry. It's just... Steve said you seemed different when you met him in that restaurant and Susie told me you were a mess when she saw you in hospital."

"Did you have a conference on my general welfare?" Elena snaps. "Is that why you're here today? To check me out?"

"I'm here because I'm your friend. As are the others. You've cut yourself off from us, Elena. You seldom answer my texts or return my calls. If there's anything—"

They are alone, apart from the children, yet she has a sensation that she can be overheard and it causes her heart to beat faster. "I've told you exactly what happened. As for not being in touch, you try managing two babies and you'll really understand the meaning of busyness."

"I've upset you." Tara sighs. "I certainly didn't come here with that intention."

Her concern is unbearable. What will she tell the others? A black eye, face swollen. Elena imagines a Skype session, opinions hardening, the truth decided. What then? Will they ride off into the sunset with her and her two babies? She doesn't want to think about that night. How she turned on the stairs to hit back at

Nicholas. It happened so fast, her feet sliding from under her. She doesn't remember anything else except his expression as she lost her balance. So detached...she can't forget it, no matter how often she convinces herself it's all in her imagination. Tara is forcing her to confront it. He might have stopped her fall. He might have caused it. He might be completely innocent. He could be a monster.

"If Susie told you I was unhappy, she's wrong. And Steve... meeting an ex-boyfriend when you're with the person you love is never easy." Where does the truth lie in all of this? Her thoughts surge and clash and threaten to undo her. "I want to hear about your new promotion. Senior advertising executive! Sounds pretty impressive. Steve says he wants to poach you but you're incorruptible."

Tara looks as anxious as she does now to change the subject. The talk turns to office politics and an agency full of creative, dysfunctional geniuses, who drive her crazy. It sounds exhilarating. Like the rush of the Big Wave. Nicholas will be home soon. His evening meal needs to be ready, the kitchen spotless.

After a little while, Tara phones for a taxi to take her back to the train station. "You will ring me if you ever need to talk, won't you?" Her fierce embrace suggests she hasn't been deceived in the slightest by her friend's explanation.

Elena closes the front door and leans against it. The setting sun slants through the fan-light. She has squandered precious hours with Tara, whose life is independent, free, well-paid, stimulating. She slaps her hand to her forehead, as if force will dislocate her envy, and winces as pain shoots through her head.

✦

"How was your day?" Nicholas asks, as he does every evening.

"Same as usual." Elena checks her watch. He likes his fillet steak rare, two and half minutes each side.

"*Exactly* the same as usual." He closes the fridge door and stands too close behind her.

"Almost. Apart from Grace emptying the coal scuttle and doing a pretty good imitation of a chimney girl from a Dickens novel."

"Were you too drunk to notice what she was doing?"

"Drunk?"

"On white wine? At a rough guess, you had at least two glasses."

"Oh, that . . ." The oil sizzles hotly as she flips the steak. "Tara called in."

"So, your day wasn't the same as usual?"

"She was only here for a short while." Elena walks to the sink and sieves the potatoes, lowers the heat on the mushrooms, gives the onions a final toss. Golden brown, exactly as he expects. She had been afraid to remove the wine bottle from the fridge, so had just hoped he wouldn't notice the dropped level. His awareness of everything in his house no longer astonishes her. Instead, it terrifies her. He is still shadowing her, demanding to know what they discussed.

"Her father's party. And her promotion to senior advertising executive." She carries his dinner to the table, waits for him to sit down.

"Did you talk about us?"

Elena shrugs. "We're not that important in Tara's scheme of things."

"Answer my question."

What do you think we discussed? That you've beggared me with your reckless Ponzi schemes. That you lift your hand or your foot to me every time I mention your dead wife. That you monitor every aspect of my miserable existence yet I'm afraid to run from this haunted house and become homeless with two babies.

"She asked if I was happy. I said I was. Ecstatic."

"I hope you sounded more convincing than you do now."

"Nicholas, eat your dinner before it gets cold."

"Did you tell her I'm a failure?" He flings the chair out from the table and sits down. "Isn't that what you really believe? You don't trust me to recoup your losses, even though I'm working flat out to make it up to you."

"I know you are. I didn't discuss our personal business with her. Why are you trying to start another argument when there's no reason to do so?"

"This is not an argument. It's purely a discussion as to whether or not I can trust you to be honest with me."

Joel cries. It's time to feed him again. Nicholas grabs her arm as she moves past him. "Don't lie to me again, Elena. I will always find out and that will upset me very much. Do we understand each other?"

"Perfectly." She is free to go. Joel's scrunched face relaxes as she feeds him. Her tiny protector. He is unaware of how often he keeps her safe.

CHAPTER SEVENTEEN

Elena sits on the patio in the back garden and watches Grace
run with growing confidence across the flagstones. Joel, in his
buggy, lies under the shade of the apple tree. He laughs when the
breeze blows through the branches and sets the glass butterflies
tinkling. Their rhythm is disturbed when two pieces, placed too
closely together, collide. This has happened before, but today the
sound clangs through Elena's head. Pain jabs her temples, sudden
flashes that blur her vision.

She settles Joel down for his afternoon nap in the living room.
The French doors are open, so she will hear him if he awakens.
Grace is still playing on the patio when Elena enters the garden
shed. She pauses in the doorway to survey the order with which
Nicholas organises his tools. Each item has a specific hook,
shelf or drawer. This is the same symmetry she saw during her
brief intrusion into Amelia's bedroom and she now applies it to
Woodbine herself. Her old habits of leaving unwashed dishes in
the sink or splaying the pages of newspapers over the table only
displeases him.

He won't miss one butterfly from the cluster, she thinks as she
searches for a wire-cutter and a ladder. Is this the same ladder
Amelia climbed to paint the ceiling in the nursery? It's heavy to
carry but Elena manages to drag it across the lawn towards the
apple tree. The constant colliding has cracked the wing of one

of the butterflies. She cuts it down and shoves it to the bottom of the wheelie bin. What is she doing, hiding evidence like a deranged criminal? Crazy…stultifying craziness. Where is it going to end? He almost drowned her. Almost crashed his car when she was beside him. Pushed her down the stairs—no, he didn't, it was an accident, her own fault, and the car was just a stunt, showing off, and in the water, not knowing his own strength. Frantically, she replaces the ladder and runs a rake over the grass, trying to eradicate the telltale grooves. She opens the organic bin and flings the leaves she has raked into it. She grimaces as the smell of rotting food is released. A bunch of dahlias, crushed and wilting, lie among the potato peelings. They are the distinctive shade of purple that Billy grows in his garden and lays out on the grassy bank. She remembers Billy's expression on the only occasion they met; the certainty in his voice when he told her the flowers wouldn't last long. Was that what he meant? Is Nicholas the person who constantly removes them from the embankment? Why would he dump them in the bin?

They were placed there by Billy to remember Amelia's father. Was Nicholas's relationship with his father-in-law so difficult that he cannot bear to see these floral reminders of him? So many questions—but Elena knows the punishment she will receive for demanding information Nicholas doesn't want to give her.

When she looks up from the bin, alerted by the silence from the patio, she can see no sign of Grace. She hasn't wandered into the living room where Joel is still sleeping, and the side gates are bolted. Elena's knees weaken with relief when she hears a cry from between the trees at the bottom of the garden. A trail, partially obscured by weeds, wends between these trees and Woodbine's boundary wall. She is still unable to see Grace, but her plaintive cry sounds closer.

She calls Grace's name as she runs under the leafy canopy, then spots her sitting under a tree, her legs sprawled out in front of her. Once her daughter is safely in her arms, Elena continues walking, curious to see where the trail leads. It's obvious that no attempt has been made for years to cut back the foliage and it becomes more and more difficult to press ahead. She reaches a wire fence that separates their garden from Billy's land. The fence is broken and allows her access into a meadow where a swathe of bright yellow rapeseed is in bloom. The hedgerow bordering the top of the field is overgrown with elderberry trees and blackberry bushes whose fruits have yet to ripen. She notices a stone arch that she takes to be the brow of a bridge. Dead wood snaps underfoot as she moves closer, expecting to hear the murmur of water but unable to see where it could possibly flow. The red-brick structure, partially hidden in a stranglehold of briar and ivy, turns out to be a small building with a low, arched doorway.

The door is bolted, the padlock rusted. She hurries back the way she came. She has been away from the house longer than she planned and Grace is heavy in her arms. Joel will soon be awake. She runs through the French doors into the living room, where Yvonne is walking up and down with Joel in her arms. He has been crying, his flushed face wet with tears.

"I can't believe you left him alone," she says as Elena lowers Grace to the floor and tries to catch her breath. "How irresponsible is that?"

"I was in the garden for a few minutes." Elena doesn't want to sound defensive, yet there it is again, that high, self-justifying tone she adopts whenever Yvonne calls. How did that happen? How can it be stopped? She takes Joel from the older woman and opens her blouse. Outside in the garden the butterflies, minus one, hang motionless.

✦

"You should have asked my permission before you vandalised my garden," says Nicholas. "I cleared the house of Amelia's possessions but you're still not satisfied. What will be next? The sculptures, the trees and flowers she planted?"

Did he stand beneath the apple tree and count the butterflies or find the broken one hidden at the bottom of the wheelie bin? His obsessive need to be in control is destroying her.

"It's only one butterfly," she says. Explaining is a robotic process, yet she continues to justify her actions. He silences her with his fist. She will wear long sleeves in the days to come.

✦

"Anyone home?" Yvonne sings out as she slams the front door and breezes into the kitchen. Joel cries, as if on cue, while Grace, who had been playing happily in the playpen, knocks her bricks over with a petulant swipe and drums her heels off the floor.

"My poor eardrums." Yvonne dumps a bag of groceries on the table and covers her ears in mock-alarm. "Am I interrupting those temper tantrums again? Nicholas says you've been feeling poorly so I decided you could do with a break. I'll put the kettle on. Nothing like a cup of tea for mending shattered nerves." Still talking, she switches on the kettle, tidies the toys from the floor and sits Grace in her high chair. "Have you had breakfast yet, Elena? I thought not. You sit right here and I'll make scrambled eggs and toast. You know what they say about breakfast being the most important meal of the day. Oh, my dear, you're *not* still feeding Joel. He'll be opening your buttons soon. That's why you look so exhausted." She averts her eyes to the wall behind Elena, a blank space being preferable to the sight of Joel's greedy suck.

"So, tell me what's wrong?" She sets a cup of tea at Elena's elbow and butters toast. "Nicholas sounded quite worried when he rang."

"Nothing's wrong," Elena replies. "I've no idea what he's told you."

"Just that you're down in the dumps again. I reminded him it's no joke having two small babies and any mother is entitled to her off days. Anyway, I decided there's only one thing to do and that's to take this pair off your hands for a few hours. Give you a break from all that feeding and teething. Why not go to the hairdressers? Your roots are growing out again. A new hairstyle will cheer you up and make you look more like your old self again."

Elena holds her temper with an effort. She needs time on her own and if that means enduring Yvonne's implied criticisms, she will smile gratefully as she hands her children over. She pumps milk and fills a bottle. Yvonne's expression, when she takes it from her, suggests that she has in fact been handed a grenade.

As soon as she is alone, Elena removes a slasher and a jemmy from the garden shed. She cuts feverishly through the undergrowth, venting her anger on the snapping branches until she uncovers the wooden door. She forces the bolt with the jemmy and after a few minutes it splinters apart. The mouldering smell of trapped earth rushes at her when she enters. Her suspicions are right. She has uncovered an old ice house that had been built into an embankment of earth. The beam from her torch sweeps over steps leading downwards, an arched ceiling above, a flagged floor and craggy walls. How old is this ice house? How long since it functioned? Eighty, ninety years, maybe more, and since then abandoned and forgotten—no, not forgotten. Candles have burned here; their stalactite remains are still clinging to their glass jars. Mouldering cushions lie scattered on the floor and a pair of old curtains hang from the wall.

Despite the heat from her exertions, Elena shivers. She is not alone here. Someone else is breathing at the same rapid pace. An echo, she realises, as she stills her breath and collects herself. It would be all too easy to allow her overwrought imagination to take flight, yet she knows she came here for a reason. Amelia. Her awareness is instinctive. It explains the reason why she has been unable to stop thinking about her. An obsession, Nicholas called it, but it was her own intuition that led her to this earthy hole.

She shines the torch across stone shelves where beef and fowl and other perishable foodstuffs would once have been stored. Most of the shelves are at a uniform height. All are bare, apart from one, which holds a dusty, hard-backed folder. Cobwebs, glutinous and dense, cling to her hand as she pulls it out. An object on the ground makes a clinking noise when her foot kicks against an ice pick. She lifts it up and runs her hand over the smooth wooden handle. The rusting spike at the end is long and slender, the tip still sharp.

She runs through the trees and back to the house where she sets the folder on the kitchen table, wipes away the dust. Opening the metal clip, she sifts through the documents inside it, taking care to replace each one in the order she found it. She studies photographs of Amelia. Even as a small child, she had that short hairstyle, cut below her ears and framing her cheeks. Her parents are with her in some of the photographs but from her fifth year onwards, she has been photographed only with her father or another couple. She recognises Billy Tobin but not the smiling woman beside him.

Amelia had been a skinny child, the solemnity of her expression emphasised by those almond-shaped eyes that would, in time, become one of her most striking features. She was a typical teenager, pulling faces at the camera, often in the company of a second girl. In contrast to her, this girl was taller and thinner with pale-green eyes. Her long blonde hair, almost as white as her skin, gave her a wraithlike appearance. This image was particularly effective in her mid-teens when she and Amelia cultivated goth images. Dark and light—how arresting they looked, with their heavily pencilled eyes and deadpan expressions. Their appearances changed again, became sleeker, more androgynous as they grew older. Elena recognised the coffee shop in Kilfarran and the high clock tower in the village square, where teenagers still hang out together.

Two boys, in particular, feature in many of the photographs. Hard to tell if they were friends or boyfriends. Certainly, the blonde girl and one of the boys, slightly built and gangly, were just friends; the casual drape of their arms over each other's shoulders and the funny faces they pull at the camera do not suggest romance. His casually tousled hairstyle changes over time: a flamboyant pink Mohican; a sophisticated topknot. She is not so certain about Amelia and the other boy, who was of mixed race, olive-skinned and black-eyed, a wide mouth, always laughing. He disappeared from the photographs after the goth phase. The split between the other three seemed to come in their early twenties. Elena stares at photographs of New York, where Amelia's friend must have been living. They chart the nightclubs she frequented, her sporting activities, her jogs in Central Park. Her cool green gaze suggests she was as much at home in New York as in the small village of Kilfarran.

Elena looks for photographs of Amelia and Nicholas together and is surprised when she can't find any. She opens an envelope and removes a document. Red block lettering states that this is the house deed to Woodbine, dated 1935. The owner's name, Samuel Pierce, is written underneath. She finds birth and baptismal certificates in another envelope; some are yellowed and much-folded and others are more recent. John Pierce, an only child, it would seem, and his daughter, Amelia. She discovers a copy of John's will and testament. His estate, including Woodbine, had been left to Amelia with a stipulation that Nicholas's name could not be added to the deed.

She grapples with this new information. Why has Nicholas kept the ownership of Woodbine a secret from her? The realisation that he will harm her if she confronts him with this information settles like lead in her stomach. Had he told her he had bought this house with Amelia or did she simply make that assumption? It was his attitude, Elena realises, his confident, possessive tone whenever he mentions Woodbine, that has convinced her that it belonged to him. She won't mention her discovery. Why stir dead dust when all that matters is the assuaging of his temper, that tortured fury that overwhelms him so suddenly and swirls her into its vortex?

She will return the folder to its hiding place and forget its existence. But not just yet. Unable to stop rummaging through it, she opens another envelope and spills out the contents. Torn pieces of paper scatter like scraps of confetti across the table. She attempts to join the fragments together and, finally, three frayed edges combine to reveal the word MARRIAGE. She moves with more determination and finds a fragment with the letters IFIC. From then on, the jigsaw visible in her mind takes a physical shape until she is staring at the heading *IRISH MARRIAGE CERTIFICATE*. She pieces together their names. Nicholas Madison and Amelia Pierce. Slivers of information that will disperse if she blows on them. Whose hand tore apart what should have been a cherished document? Amelia's? The drama queen who was always demanding attention? The diva who was never satisfied? Or the hand of Nicholas, who once shattered the glass of a photograph containing his wife's image into the same random pieces?

Elena sits stiffly on the kitchen chair. The only sounds she hears are the clock ticking and the rush of her breath. Her hands, she notices, are trembling. This folder has developed fangs, the charged bite of a dog turned savage. What other unsettling information is contained within it? How will she deal with what she has already discovered?

Walking swiftly through the back garden, she returns the folder to its hiding place and closes the door behind her. The branches she hacked with such ferocity are already wilting on the ground and the ice house, stripped of its unruly cover, is as exposed as a hobbit's lair. If Nicholas comes this way he will know what she has done. Is he aware of its existence? It's on Billy Tobin's land, so, perhaps not. The trail leading to it is barely passable; only someone who had known Woodbine since birth would be able to find their way to it.

But she, Elena, has found her way into his wife's past. Did Amelia guide her there, invisible arms reaching out to entice her to that derelict cranny? Is she watching out for Elena, her spirit rising from the barnacled underworld to warn her? It's no longer possible to know what is chance and what is guidance in this life of uncertainty that she once embraced so willingly. She presses her face to the raddled bark of a tree. It pains her. Gives her proof that she is not yet a husk, nor lost so deeply within herself that nothing else exists except his will. She shivers, as if the chill from the ice house has entered her bones. She waits until her legs are strong enough to carry her back to the house.

✦

"We're home." Yvonne breezes into the kitchen, Joel on one arm, Grace clinging to her hand.

"Oh dear...oh dear!" Her appraising gaze sweeps over Elena. "You didn't go to the hairdressers after all."

"I couldn't get an appointment." Elena takes Joel from her and sits down in the rocking chair she always uses when feeding him. "I spent my time catching up on chores."

"You certainly look as if you've been exerting yourself." Yvonne plucks a twig from Elena's hair. "I'm happy to help out any time but you really should have taken the opportunity to pamper yourself. If we don't do that, who else will look after our appearance?"

"I pampered myself with some thought time, which is just as important."

"I guess it is." Yvonne's tone suggests otherwise. "At least you were out of doors. You need more fresh air to bring some colour back to your cheeks. The children were as good as gold, as they always are when they're with me. I'll take them whenever you need a break. Nicholas says you're exhausted all the time."

An exhausted drudge, neurotic and incapable of managing her own children: is that how Yvonne sees her? Has she formed that opinion independently, or has it been planted in her mind by Nicholas? Still talking, Yvonne, switches on the kettle and opens the tea caddy, stretches up for the teapot. She takes biscuits from the press, sets cups on the table, her knowledge of the kitchen adding to Elena's annoyance.

"You called Amelia a diva once," she says when Joel has fallen asleep in her arms. She lowers him into his carrycot and sits down with Yvonne at the kitchen table. "Why was that?"

"Did I?" Yvonne pauses, teapot in hand. "I don't recall using that word."

"You said she created dramas from nothing."

"I admit she was highly strung," Yvonne concurs. "And she certainly could be a diva when she wanted her own way."

"How?" Elena asks.

"Oh, you know how it is..." Tea poured, Yvonne hands a cup across the table to her. "The number of times I had to listen to her complaining if Nicholas had to work late or entertain clients, especially if they were female. She was very insecure. I guess that must have added to her possessiveness."

"Is that why she haunts this house?"

"What are you talking about?"

"Don't you feel her presence here?"

"I certainly do not."

"Nicholas does."

"Nonsense. I worry about you—"

"She keeps me company when Nicholas is working late. He's still doing it, you know. Coming home after the children are in bed so he doesn't have to entertain them."

"Being a junior partner brings responsibilities, Elena. Surely you can appreciate the effort he's putting into his career to provide for you and the children."

"All the effort he puts into his career didn't stop him beggaring me."

There it is, out in the open at last, and Yvonne draws back, as if from a spray of spittle. Colour mounts her cheeks; but her forehead, which should be furrowed with shock, remains taut and smooth.

"Beggaring you? What exactly do you mean?"

Elena has never noticed the resemblance between Yvonne and her son until now. The chilling impassivity of their expressions when they are angry.

"It's self-explanatory," she replies. "He invested my inheritance and lost it all. I'm penniless because of him. So, you can imagine why I'm not impressed when he tells me he's working late."

"Elena, relax down. Nicholas hasn't lost your money. The market rises and falls and, as a fund manager, he understands its volatility. In time, your money will be returned to you with profits. I should know. The investments Nicholas manages for myself and Henry fluctuate regularly but we always earn our dividend. You need to trust him and stop using inflammatory words like 'beggaring.'"

"What should I use instead? Defrauding? Swindling? Fleecing?" Her anger is reckless, a flare of rage that banishes caution.

"You're being extraordinarily rude, Elena. It's difficult dealing with post-partum depression but that doesn't give you the right to make such appalling accusations—"

"Did Amelia ever complain to you about Nicholas's temper?"

"She certainly did nothing of the sort." Yvonne's tone is hard, flinty, yet Elena senses there is something else behind it, a guardedness, and it gives her the courage to continue.

"Did she accuse him of violence against her when—"

"How *dare* you. He adored the ground Amelia walked on." She stabs her finger at Elena. "You can never hope to compete with his memories of her, no matter how hard you try with that ridiculous haircut. You're the mother of his children and in a position to make new memories for both of you. But you're certainly not going about it the right way. Work on your relationship, Elena. Pull yourself together and seek help for your depression. I can recommend an excellent psychiatrist—"

"It's your son who's in need of a psychiatrist, not me." Elena has gone too far to stop now. "You've both been undermining me since Grace was born and I'm not prepared to tolerate it any longer."

"How dare you interpret my kindness as undermining you? If that's what you think I'm doing, then Nicholas has every reason to be worried about your mental state."

"In future, I want you to phone in advance to let me know you are calling."

"How dare you tell me I need to seek permission to see my grandchildren?" Yvonne pushes the chair back so violently it topples over. Joel jerks at the sound and begins to cry. Grace flings bricks over the side of the playpen and holds up her arms to be lifted out.

"Don't touch her," Elena says when Yvonne bends to pick her up. "I want you to leave my house right now."

"*Your* house."

"Are you implying it belongs to Nicholas?"

"Obviously, it belongs to him!" Yvonne shrieks. "I've heard enough of your craziness for one day. You haven't heard the last of this, young *lady*."

The slam of the front door reverberates through Elena. The fury that possessed her is now spent and she will have to cope with the consequences.

CHAPTER EIGHTEEN

The way he brakes, pebbles spraying like a backwash from the wheels as he parks in front of her car, alerts her that Yvonne has already spoken to him. His stride is fast, briefcase swinging, his shoulders squared. The children are sleeping upstairs, the baby monitor on. Candles are ablaze and cast a soft glow over the throws and cushions on the armchairs. This scene of domestic bliss is a stage, set for action, and the ghost of Amelia trembles in every corner.

"You lying bitch." He closes the door softly behind him and lowers his briefcase to the floor. "My mother takes the kids for the afternoon to help you get yourself together and you reduce her to tears with your deranged accusations. You called me a crook to her face. Accused me of abusing my dead wife." No preamble then. Just a body blow of abuse, which he continues to spew at her.

"I told Yvonne you had a temper," Elena says when he pauses for breath. "It's obvious I was telling the truth. I also accused her of undermining me. Another truth. As is the fact that you've beggared me. I don't have any money, apart from what you condescend to give me—and then you demand a receipt for every penny I spend. I'm sick of living this life, Nicholas—"

"Ghosts." He speaks above her, ignoring the accusations. "What the fuck was all that about?"

"Amelia...she's always here between us." Her cheeks burn, as if his hand has already scorched her skin.

"You are one crazy bitch." He presses his fingertips against his temples. "I feel as if there's a wire being pulled through my head when I try to talk sense to you." He starts slapping his hand against his forehead, his movements becoming more rapid, harder.

"Stop it, Nicholas. You'll hurt yourself." She reaches towards him but teeters back when he lashes out, narrowly missing her face. Before she can recover, she is being walked towards the door. His grip on her arm is light yet firm as they mount the stairs together. The urge to fight back is a fleeting impulse. His strength is contained but capable of being unleashed in an instant.

He unlocks the door of the master bedroom and stands aside for her to enter. The room is exactly the same as she remembers. He locks the door behind them and gestures towards the chair in front of the dressing table. When she is seated, he lifts Amelia's hairbrush and begins to brush her hair. She holds her head stiffly as she endures the slow, deliberate strokes. Strands of hair spring upwards, as if charged with her terror. Is he angry? Or simply playing with her? Unable to assess his mood, she is afraid to stir from her position. He walks to the wardrobe and removes the silver lamé dress. The fabric shimmers under the light, seeming almost to move, and the dress looks as if it is possessed by the rippling elegance of the woman who once wore it.

"Put it on." He lifts it from the hanger and holds it towards her.

"It won't fit me."

"Make it fit," he replies.

Her breasts feel tight. Joel is due a feed. Soon, he'll be awake and crying. "Why are you doing this to me, Nicholas?" A futile question, she knows, yet she asks it in the faint hope that he will see reason.

"You want to be Amelia. I'm giving you the opportunity." He hasn't raised his voice, yet she shrinks back, as if deafened by its force.

"I have to feed Joel—"

"Do as I say, bitch." He lays the dress across the bed and grabs a handful of the hair he had brushed with such deliberation. When she is standing he encircles her neck with his hands, his touch threatening in its gentleness. "You've tormented me for long enough with your inane questions about Amelia. Now's your chance to wear her skin. Put her dress on."

Her throat tightens, as if her air is already restricted. She removes her jeans, then pulls the sweater over her head, noticing as she does so that briars have snagged some of the threads. Her hands are also scratched and there is a line of dirt under the bitten stubs of her nails. He stands behind her as she slides the dress over her hips. The fabric flattens her breasts but he is able to close the zip before steering her towards the cheval mirror. His head tilts slightly as he studies her from all angles. Perspiration trickles under her arms, beads her forehead. Her stomach strains against the fabric.

The weight she has yet to lose is obvious to both of them. She averts her eyes, unable to look at her reflection.

"You disgusting, filthy whore. You've contaminated her dress. Take it off immediately," he breathes into her ear and she, already knowing what she will see, brings her eyes back to the mirror. A damp aureole darkens the fabric and she is shamed by the telltale tingle in her breasts. She covers them with both hands and sways forward, nauseated by his words. Can they hurt more than his fists, she wonders, as he begins to unzip the dress. The zip eases down to her waist before catching on the fabric. Unable to pull it any further, he sits down on the bed and watches her attempts to wriggle the dress down over her hips. In her haste, she breaks the zip and the dress slides to the floor. The energy has gone from the fabric. It looks cheap, gaudy, stained with her secretions. Is it possible to hate herself more than she hates him? Yes, she thinks, as she lifts the dress and flings it at him. It hits his face before he can move and, for an instant, he is contoured in its sheen.

He moves swiftly, a snake uncoiling, and she folds at her stomach before collapsing. When she recovers consciousness, he is kneeling by her side, weeping. All this talk of ghosts had triggered a severe panic attack, he says. What he did was inexcusable. Can she find it in her heart to forgive him? He, too, is haunted by Amelia's ghost. He senses her reproach, her unspoken accusation that when she needed him, he did not accompany her on that last, fatal journey. Yvonne's phone call, Elena's talk of hauntings, triggered his attack of post-traumatic stress. He will seek treatment first thing in the morning.

Joel, in the next room, is awake. His cry is the only sound Elena hears. The only sound that matters. Her head feels light when she sits up. She allows Nicholas to help her to her feet. His touch is repellent but necessary. She sinks onto the side of the bed and pulls on her jeans, hides her face in the sweater. She must concentrate on becoming strong again if she is to escape from a relationship that has become intolerable. She is familiar with the pathways of this thought, which always ends in a cul-de-sac. The impossibility of managing on her own with two babies and no income is exacerbated by the knowledge that their children are his possessions. He will not give them up without a fight to the death.

CHAPTER NINETEEN

She dreams about ice and awakens shivering. Nicholas has turned in his sleep and pulled the duvet from her. Six in the morning. Unable to listen to his steady breathing, she leaves his side and goes downstairs.

Dew soaks the thin soles of her slippers as she walks towards the ice house. Spiders have silvered the bushes with cobwebs, lamé strands suspended on fragile stems. Her torch sweeps across the empty shelves and upwards towards the arched roof. No one else is here, yet the air seems alive with a shivering presence.

"Amelia." The name escapes on an exhalation. "Amelia... Amelia..." She repeats it like a mantra until a gust of wind slams the door closed and shocks her into silence. She reaches into the shelf and pulls out the folder. This time she does not bother replacing the documents in their right order. Nor does she pick up the ones that slip to the floor.

Her disappointment grows as she unearths utility bills, the stubs of chequebooks and Christmas cards from a man named Leo Byrne.

She has examined the entire contents and has learned nothing new about Nicholas. Bending down, she gathers up the fallen pages. Some are stapled together and belong to a file marked "Tax Returns." As she is replacing them, she notices a sealed envelope. The postmark is Irish and shows that the letter came from Kerry. Amelia's name is on the envelope but it is addressed to her interior design studio in Dublin. She draws out a page with the number 3 written on top. The handwriting is flamboyant, exaggerated flourishes that jolt her memory. Where has she seen that handwriting before? She flicks through the stapled tax returns to check if the other pages of the letter have been caught between them. Unable to find them, she begins to read.

> *...a charade. Each time you write my fear grows for your safety. Nicholas's excuses ring increasingly hollow. It's time you stopped pretending you can force him to leave. You can't. Stop trying. I want to help. I'm not crazy, as you suggest. I've never been more clear-headed about anything. All I ask is that you listen to me. Think beyond yourself. Is Woodbine worth it? No! His violence is inexcusable...please...please listen. The chronology of your letters outlines a pattern that is becoming even more destructive and I can only hope that you have the courage to make that final decision. Only then...*

Elena's lips tremble as she rereads the letter. Her ribs hurt. She touches her neck. It feels stiff but the skin where he placed his hands will be unmarked. She is staggered by the force of his deceit. No trigger. No post-traumatic stress. Random violence and carefully constructed cruelty disguised by a veneer of grief.

The door of the ice house opens. Dressed for work, Nicholas stands at the entrance, his tall frame silhouetted darkly against the streaming light. She shrivels into herself, as if she can already feel his fists. She knows, instinctively, that this is the first time he has stood inside the ice house. He strides towards her without speaking and stares at the open folder. His concentration is on the documents but any sudden movement would direct his attention back to her. The contours of his face stand out in stark relief as he plucks the letter from her hand. After reading it, he tears the paper in two, then four, his movements growing faster as he shreds it. A scattering of breadcrumbs, Elena thinks when he walks to the open door and flings the pieces into the air. They swirl briefly before they fall, catching on the briers or lying among the mulching leaves.

"You prying whore." He speaks to her at last. "How dare you sneak around my property without my permission?"

"Billy Tobin's property, you mean," she retorts. "And I know that you never owned a brick of Woodbine. Amelia's father made sure of that. What a convenience her death must have been for you."

"Shut your mouth or I'll shut it for you."

"You never grieved for her. Not for one single minute. Post-traumatic stress. Don't make me laugh." Every word she utters brings her closer to danger. She doesn't care. The caution that has imprisoned her for so long has fallen away. Chains snapping. She is convinced she can hear them. "You inflicted the same brutality on your own wife as you've done on me. Did you kill her? Sabotage the brakes on her car? Drown her so that you could inherit her property? Murderer . . . yes, that's what you are—*murderer*."

One blow to her stomach brings her to the ground. He waits until she stands up again, then moves towards her, his hand raised high. He is upon her when her fingers run along the dusty stone shelf and close around the ice pick. She lifts her arm, unthinking, uncaring, and is filled with a pulsating sureness as she plunges the ice pick into his stomach. As he staggers backwards, she wrenches it out, sickened by the slick feel of flesh separating. His knees buckle like a foal just born, that same trembling need to stand upright before collapsing to the ground.

"Oh, Jesus Christ," he cries. The sound splinters like glass. Is he praying for divine help or cursing her? Blood stains his trousers and spills over his impeccable brogues. His lips stretch around her name as he pleads with her to help him. His pallor reminds her of dead ash. There is an instant when she hesitates. She considers closing the ice house door and leaving him on the floor to bleed to death. Then the mist clears and, chilled to the bone, she comes to her senses. She eases his tie from his neck and ties it round the wound, lays her dressing gown over him. The sky is marbled with red as she runs across the grass. The dew is melting and the footsteps that betrayed her are already disappearing.

Joel is crying, his strident screams ringing in her ears, while she calls an ambulance. She breathes in the scent of her son's hunger as she lifts him to her breast and he suckles from her for the last time.

PART TWO

CHAPTER TWENTY

The Past

The same nightmare. No matter how often it was repeated, Amelia could never succeed in escaping the horror that came with it. Sometimes she was an adult, sometimes a teenager, but, more often, she was five years old again. Dressed in white shorts, a blue T-shirt with an anchor on the front, white sandals and a pink plastic hairband, she was disobeying orders by running along the pier. A forbidden place but her mother was fixing the red beach umbrella that had been blown inside out by the wind and her father was queuing for ice cream cones on the road above. A 99, Amelia had said, with sprinkles of hundreds and thousands. Her mother wanted raspberry ripple, a nice, big, juicy dollop. Amelia's beach ball had blown into the sea and there it was, hurtling like a rocking horse alongside the pier. So easy to stretch out her hand and catch it. But then the wave came pounding over the pier, deafening her, blinding her. She sank and rose—not that she was aware of movement, just the struggle to breathe as her mouth filled with water. All those years later, so real, so utterly real. In sleep, memory had no borderline to stop her roaming through her subconscious.

Her father always knew when the dream came. She used to believe he had heard her screaming, that awful sound she made before the waves silenced her; but the scream, Amelia would discover, had been a whimper, practically inaudible. He too, though, was locked into their tragedy, and intuition, as well as his love for her, brought him into her room on those stricken nights to soothe her as if she was a baby, even when she was ten and eleven and older.

"How do you always know?" she asked him once. Her voice rasped, as if those imaginary screams had leached it dry.

"How could I not know?" His expression was bleak in the filtering dawn light. "I feel it here." He touched his chest, then his head, and said, "This is where I hear her voice telling me to go and comfort you."

"She still talks to you?"

"Of course."

"You loved her so much."

"Yes."

"I feel the same way about Nicholas."

"He's a very lucky man, Amelia." He bent to kiss her cheek, then padded softly from her bedroom.

Love at first sight, she had told him soon after she met Nicholas Madison. "Was that how it was with you and Jennifer?" She never called her dead mother by any other name. Perhaps, once, she had called her "Mama" or just "Mum," but she had no memory of doing so, nor of calling her father anything but John. Compared to her early childhood, Nicholas's upbringing had been uneventful and happy, yet he was still able to appreciate what it was like to walk in darkness. The headiness of being with him and knowing that he shared her feelings still had the power to dazzle her. His hand on hers was strong when she spoke about the guilt she felt over her mother's untimely death. All that talking, a floodgate opening, in those early months.

She told him about Leanne, so far away from her now, yet in touch all the time from New York. Mark, who would later come out as gay to his parents after talking it over with Amelia's father. And then there was Jay, her first love, though they were both only sixteen at the time. The young men she had dated in her early twenties were no different from the boys she had known in her teens. All they had to offer was the added sheen of experience and, apart from Jay, she had never been in love until Nicholas came along.

They met when she was contracted to refurbish the offices of Keogh & Harris Investments. This was Amelia's first major commission. She would never have dared set her sights so high if Leanne had not encouraged—Amelia would say "bullied"—her into applying for it. The staff had been moved to temporary accommodation while work on the redesign was ongoing, but Nicholas had called often to see the progress she was making. As he was a fund manager, she suspected these calls were not in an official capacity. Looking up from a table laid with sample fabrics and tiles, she would find his eyes resting on her and she was increasingly aware of a crackling excitement when he stood too close to her. The real deal, she told her father when the project was complete and Nicholas had asked her out on their first real date. Two months later, John invited him to Woodbine.

❖

The russet Virginia creeper had set the walls ablaze and the old house, bathed in a lilac twilight, had never looked more beautiful, Amelia thought, as she waited on the steps to welcome him. John had prepared coq au vin for dinner. Conversation flowed easily around the table and politics, her father's favourite subject, was discussed at length. After the meal ended, they walked through the garden at the back of the house. Leaves were crinkling into autumn and the first fall crunched under their feet. John was a keen gardener and Nicholas proved to be as knowledgeable on soil types and compost as he was on the machinations of government. Amelia was amused as she listened to him, knowing he was making an effort to impress her father and that the potted plants on the balcony of his apartment on Custom House Quay had long withered through his neglect. She watched the soft bow of his mouth as he listened to her father explaining how roses should be pruned and wondered how long it would take before John excused himself and headed off to his local pub with Billy Tobin. Billy was also a widower and the men, friends since they were boys and both now retired, walked to and from the Kilfarran Inn together three nights a week.

Logs crackled on the hearth as she and Nicholas slowly undressed in front of the fire. His skin on hers, playing his fingers over her body, and she, impatient, wanting him hard inside her, both of them reaching towards the wheeling relief that would leave them spent and sated. He cradled her in his arms afterwards, his long, lithe frame relaxed against her yet, she knew, capable of spilling her into the wildness of his desire once more.

Nicholas had left by the time John returned and Amelia, showered, was waiting in her dressing gown when her father entered the living room.

"What do you think of Nicholas?" she asked.

"He can certainly talk." John's speech was slightly slurred, his face flushed from the cold and the drink.

"That's not an answer. Do you like him?"

"I hardly know him, Amelia."

"You *don't* like him?"

"That's not what I said. He's a handsome lad and entertaining company." He paused and wrinkled his forehead.

"And?" she prompted. "Be honest with me."

He still hesitated, uncertain of his ground, a mild man by nature and incapable of lying. "I'm sorry to say this, Amelia, but I can't help feeling he came here tonight with a script that was well-prepared."

"That's not true." She was stung by his attitude and, also, surprised. Was he suggesting that Nicholas was conniving when he had made such a determined effort to talk about subjects that were of interest to her father?

"I'm not saying there's anything wrong with him trying to create a good impression," John hastened to reassure her. She suspected that the few pints of Guinness he had consumed had loosened his tongue. "But you know me. I don't think there's any man out there who's good enough for my daughter. I'm such a contrary old sod, I had to find some fault with him."

Amelia, knowing he was trying not to hurt her feelings, had to be satisfied with that. She forced her disappointment to the back of her mind as she undressed for bed and fell asleep with Nicholas's name on her lips.

CHAPTER TWENTY-ONE

The nightmares became more frequent. Each time Amelia thrust herself awake, John was sitting on the edge of her bed, his hand cool on her forehead.

"The screams awaken me," she confided to Nicholas. "At least, that's what I think, but my father insists I'm just whimpering. He says it reminds him of kittens. I used to think he had a sixth sense because he's always there when I open my eyes, but he believes it's my mother telling him to go and comfort me."

"And does he comfort you?"

"Always. When I was younger, he'd stay with me until I drifted off again. Sometimes, he'd still be there when I awoke in the morning."

"In bed with you?" He drew back slightly, his eyes opening wide in shock.

"Not *in* bed." She was startled by his assumption. "Sleeping on top of the bed."

He nodded, his expression grave, concerned. "He must have missed your mother very much."

"I used to wish he'd meet someone else who would make him happy again," she admitted. "But he never made any effort to do so."

"He had you to love."

"Loving a child is not the same as loving a wife. His loneliness…" Amelia paused, remembering the effect his aloneness had had on her childhood and teenage years. The impossibility of repairing a fracture that had been caused by her carelessness.

"That loneliness must have been very acute," said Nicholas. "And frustrating for a young man to lose his wife so suddenly."

"I never thought of that when I was a child." She smiled, self-consciously. "To me, being in your thirties was old. Obviously, when I got to being a teenager I'd a better sense of what he'd lost when Jennifer died."

"You're very precious to him, Amelia. You've carried a heavy responsibility all those years."

"He never made me feel like that," she protested.

"Your mother's death obviously created a special bond between the two of you." Nicholas held her protectively in his arms. "And you're still trying to compensate for his loss. You can share anything with me, Amelia. *Anything*."

What had she left to share? At times, she felt as if Nicholas had burrowed down to her bones, his attention never wavering when she described the sense of loss that she had blocked from her memory for so many years.

Amelia's uneasiness after such conversations grew as the animosity between the two men she loved became more obvious. No matter how carefully John tried to disguise his hostility, Nicholas had an uncanny ability to recognise what was hidden in the discretion of silence.

One evening, when she returned from work to Woodbine with him, the tension round the table at dinner became impossible to ignore. John rejected the efforts they both made to include him in conversation, his face set sternly when Nicholas mentioned the banking crisis that had plunged the country into recession after the reckless years of the Celtic Tiger. As a fund manager, he was not in favour of burning the bondholders. He believed the media and politicians would fan the flames of a bigger financial crisis if they kept demanding so-called "retribution." The argument that followed startled Amelia. Her father accused Nicholas of being another "smug, fat-cat banker" along with other insults, which Nicholas took on the chin without once losing his temper.

"He's jealous," he said when John left for the pub. "He sees me as a threat to the control he's always had over you."

Amelia was startled that that was how he viewed her father; yet, when she thought about it, she decided Nicholas was right. John's sense of aloneness had never allowed her a reprieve. Guilt was her caul and Amelia had accepted its tyranny as the natural order of her life. All those dreams, the same theme: guilt…guilt…*guilt*.

"He's never prevented me doing anything I wanted." Rushing to John's defence, she wondered why she needed to justify their father–daughter relationship, and why, in doing so, her voice rose to a higher pitch. "Just give him time to know you. Everything will be all right, I promise."

"Why are you making things so difficult for me and Nicholas?" she asked John that night when he returned from the pub.

"Do you ever look deeply into his eyes?" her father asked.

"Yes, of course I do," she replied.

"What do you see?"

"Enough love to last me for the rest of my life."

"I see only emptiness, Amelia. And that emptiness will break your heart."

"You're so wrong. He's the man I love and you won't make the slightest effort to get to know him. Everyone likes him except you. Why is that so?"

"I'm your father, that's the difference. I'm able to see beyond his superficial charms and it worries—"

"You're jealous," she snapped.

"Jealous? Why on earth should I be jealous? Haven't I welcomed every young man you've brought to this house?"

"Only because you knew they weren't a threat to you. But Nicholas is."

"You loved Jay. You cried in my arms for weeks after he left."

"We were *sixteen*. This is different. Nicholas is the first man I've truly loved and you can't bear it."

"Is he filling your head with this nonsense?"

"I'm perfectly capable of forming my own opinions. You and I have depended too much on one another. It's not healthy..."

The pause that followed felt like a missed heartbeat. "How is our relationship unhealthy, Amelia?" he asked, quietly.

"It just is..." She paused, then blurted out: "I want you to stop coming into my bedroom at night."

"I don't... what are you saying?"

"You know what I mean." Shocked at the direction the conversation had taken, she folded her arms and stepped back from him.

"Are you insinuating—"

"I'm not insinuating anything. I'm just asking you to stop... *stop* making me feel so guilty." Unable to continue, she threw logs into the fire and watched the sparks scatter.

"I've never... how can you even think—you are my life, Amelia." He swallowed, his Adam's apple jerking. "Look at me when I'm talking to you."

Reluctantly, she turned, her cheeks blazing.

"How could such an appalling thought have even entered your mind?" he demanded. His stance, ramrod stiff, reminded her of a wounded animal, shot but not yet feeling any pain. "This is his doing, isn't it? He's brainwashed you. I'll never forgive him for that."

"Why do you keep blaming Nicholas?" she shrieked. "I'm capable of thinking for myself."

"What are you thinking, then? Let me hear it. Spill it out to me so that I fully understand what you mean."

She came to her senses then, drew back from the brink of an accusation that had no foundation. All he had ever offered her was comfort, love, protection. She had always known that and yet...and yet...a worm had entered her brain, creeping in unnoticed and burrowing deep enough to break the bonds that had held them close.

"I didn't mean anything." Stricken with guilt, always guilt, she sobbed into her hands. "I don't know what possessed me to say that. It's just...I want you to like Nicholas and I feel angry when you make him feel so unwelcome."

"I hate him." No mistaking the harshness of his statement. "I hold him entirely responsible for breaking the trust we have always shared." His face, so loved and familiar, looked old all of a sudden, the skin slack under his neck, his mouth clamped.

"Just stop feeling you have to protect me." She was overwhelmed by conflicting feelings. "It has nothing to do with anything Nicholas said. All I wanted to do was bring the two of you together but now, I've only made it worse." She tried to stem her tears and John, seeing her distress, assured her all would be okay. He needed time to adjust to the changes that would come into their lives. Platitudes—she recognised their hollowness and the distance she would have to stretch to receive his forgiveness. In that instant, she realised with a startling clarity that she could never marry Nicholas.

His devastation was obvious when she called to his apartment to end their relationship. He demanded an explanation. She was unable to give him one. How could he make sense of something she could not even understand herself? The words she had spoken to her father, dredged from some dark place within her, would always be associated with Nicholas, even though it was she, not he, who had implied the unthinkable. Love at first sight, she realised, could not always withstand the chilling gaze of second sight.

CHAPTER TWENTY-TWO

Two o'clock in the morning, her screams falling into the fathomless ocean. Amelia struggled awake, the whimper dying. Her nightmares had become more frequent of late but she could no longer see the familiar shape of her father bending over her. Regret tore through her when she realised that something tender and fragile between them had been broken forever. She pushed aside the duvet and put on her dressing gown. He would probably still be awake, attuned to her night terrors as he always was. She tapped on his bedroom door. When he didn't answer, she entered his room and whispered his name. The curtains were still open. His bed was empty, the bedclothes undisturbed.

She ran downstairs. Usually when he returned from the pub, he made tea and toast before going to bed, and left the clearing-up until the following morning. The kitchen was as tidy as he had left it before going out. She searched the other rooms without success. Her panic grew when she rang Billy and he told her they had parted as usual at his gate. The rain had started on their walk home. Billy had wanted him to shelter in his house until it stopped but John pulled up the collar of his coat and said he would keep going. That was two hours ago.

"There's probably a simple explanation." He sounded unruffled but Amelia knew he must be equally alarmed when he told her to phone Kilfarran Garda Station.

The guard on duty knew John and did not waste time asking questions. He promised to alert a squad car immediately. Frantically, Amelia changed into outdoor clothes and rang Nicholas. A month had passed since their break-up but she needed him now, needed his reassuring presence to ease her fear. An automated voice told her to leave a message on his answering machine. She tried to slow her voice, unsure whether he would be able to make out her garbled explanation. She pulled a hood over her head as the rain, driven by a harsh wind, slanted against her face.

At the end of the driveway, she turned left onto Kilfarran Lane and shone her torch over the empty road with its zigzagging bends. Clouds hid the moon and the water reeds banking the ditch below the embankment swayed like the manes of ghostly horses. Her dread increased when she heard the sluggish flow of water wending its way over stones towards the Kilfarran River.

Billy's house was about six hundred metres away and he was already on the road, his torch splaying over the darkness. "We should check the side roads in case he wandered off-track," he said. His expression was hidden beyond the beam of his torch but Amelia heard his trepidation. The network of narrow roads and lanes around Kilfarran all looked the same with their dense hedgerows and overhanging trees, but John knew this labyrinth like the back of his hand.

"No, he didn't." She shook her head. "He could walk home blindfolded from the Inn." Her dread increased when Billy nodded in agreement. She ran to the edge of the grass and shone a light on the stagnant leaves clogging the water. She staggered and cried out, terrified she would topple into the ditch.

"The guards should be here soon." Billy put a steadying arm round her waist. "You check this side of the road and I'll check the other."

A squad car arrived shortly afterwards but it was Billy who found him. Billy who held Amelia back when she, forgetting her fear of water, tried to clamber into the ditch to hold her father in her arms. Billy whose wide, soft shoulders absorbed her cries when the police cordoned off the ditch and erected a white tent around her father's body.

She was still being comforted by him when Nicholas arrived. Unable to drive past the police cordon, he abandoned his car and ran towards her. His arms were strong enough to lower her gently to the ground when she fainted. His face was the first one she saw when she recovered consciousness.

A hit-and-run, she was told by a policewoman. The crime committed by someone who was, probably, drunk or unfamiliar with the bends in the road. The driver, with visibility distorted by the rain, must have noticed John only at the last moment, then swerved and lost control. If there had been skid marks from the tyres they had been washed away, but a full-scale search for clues would begin at first light.

Death, Amelia was told, when the autopsy was performed, would have been instantaneous.

✦

Days and weeks blurred. A searing regret, like pincers around her heart. Sorrow that seemed unassailable. Nicholas carried her through it all. He moved into Woodbine and held her at night when she was unable to sleep. He was patient with her when she turned away from him, incapable of desire, uninterested in food or leaving the house. Even rising from her bed was a struggle. He supported her when she broke down in tears during the reading of her father's will. Apart from a contribution to a horse shelter, Amelia had inherited his whole estate. His solicitor, David Smithson, who had known her since she was born, stood aside when Nicholas took her in his arms to console her.

She allowed him to clear her father's possessions from Woodbine and distribute them to charity outlets. But the house she loved so much still breathed with reproach. She considered putting it up for sale. She could move into Nicholas's bright, brash apartment, where she would not be haunted by the knowledge that she had wounded her father so grievously. Nicholas explained that this was not possible; he had sold his apartment and invested the money he'd received into a junior partnership with the company. Henceforth, it would be known as KHM Investments.

She had always known that Nicholas was ambitious. He had been impatient with the slow progress of his career and now, as a junior partner, he could change the company and drag it into the twenty-first century. He needed her by his side as his wife. She refused at first. She did not deserve happiness.

"These feelings will pass," Nicholas assured her. "No one deserves happiness more than you do. Please, Amelia, make me the happiest man in the world."

Once again, he proposed, down on one knee among the bluebells in Kilfarran Woods, a glittering solitaire in his hand. Clouds spiralled around the sun and the countryside, bathed in its brilliance, took Amelia's breath away.

John seemed very close at that moment. She could see into the dark eyes that had watched over her so carefully, their sadness never allowing her to forget the tragedy she had visited upon him. She willed him away, stemmed the blame that had stunted her growth. Nicholas made her forget. He made her whole again.

Leanne flew in from New York and was her bridesmaid. Jay came from California with his fiancée Hailey, and Mark, who had moved to Dublin, came with Graham, his partner. All of them celebrated with Amelia when, two months after her father's death, she married Nicholas and signed her name on the register as Amelia Madison.

CHAPTER TWENTY-THREE

My father told me once that I'd murdered my mother. I was five years old at the time. Old enough to understand the pressure of responsibility but not to understand the fantasising mind of the alcoholic. He never repeated his accusation. I doubt he even remembered making it. If he did ever have a sudden, hazed recollection of my scared face, the duvet clutched to my shoulders, and wished to apologise for his loaded accusation, it was too late. The damage was done.

When his alcoholism became too pronounced for his superiors in the civil service to ignore, he was then transferred to deal with nondescript responsibilities in the back room of Kilfarran's council office. Moving from a Dublin suburb to Kilfarran with its narrow streets, scattered houses and outlying farms was never going to be easy for either of us as we orbited each other in our separate capsules. I had been so influenced by his illusions that when, in secondary school, the new girl in a one-horse town, I became fodder for the class bully and her sycophants, I believed it was only natural that such punishment should be meted out to a mother-killer.

There was nothing particularly original or inventive about the bullying I endured. It followed a normal process: name-calling, isolation, whispering girls who fell silent as I walked past, their laughter breaking out in my wake. My hair, being long, blonde and tangled, was ideal for pulling and I was constantly being asked if I'd ever heard of an antiperspirant called HBO, which I eventually discovered was an acronym for Hides Body Odour. These were just some of the methods used by Lisa Lynch and her friends to diminish me.

I was pinned against the school corridor wall one afternoon, holding on to my lunch money, which Lisa was determined to take from me, when Amelia Pierce came upon us. I'd admired her from a distance, envied the way she walked that tightrope of being neither the bully nor the bullied. I'd watched her perform incredible flips and forward rolls in gymnastics, her slim, small frame belying her strength.

She dived into the fight when she saw what was happening and I, unable to believe my luck, stopped cowering and fought back. A few minutes later Lisa was running towards the bathroom, her nose streaming blood. One of her friends, sobbing as she followed her, left strands of her hair twined around my fingers.

"Let's go find a table in the canteen," Amelia said. "Nothing like a bare-knuckle fight to whet my appetite."

My lunch money was still in my pocket when I walked away with her, our friendship sealed.

We had much in common, Amelia and I. No mothers, widowed fathers, mine crazed by drink, hers by a protective need to shelter her that, she admitted, could sometimes be stultifying. Try alcoholism, I wanted to shout, but I stayed silent. We shared the same taste in music, clothes, books and dance. She was a natural dancer. I lacked her grace but made up for it in energy. How we talked in those days. Boys, bands, teachers, classmates and that golden bubble where our futures floated.

We were fourteen when we discovered Billy Tobin's ice house. Billy had no objections to us using it and gave us the key to open the rusting padlock. The interior smelled mouldy, dusty, earthy. We imagined spiders and other creepy-crawlies scurrying for cover as the light from our torches flooded the dark cavern. We dared each other to go first, then held hands as we took tentative steps forward, *lighting up the shelves and nooks that had stored perishable foods in the days before electricity made the place defunct. We returned the following day with sweeping brushes, dusters, candles, jar lanterns, rugs, blankets. We hammered a set of old curtains Amelia had found in her attic onto the back wall and called it our Hobbit Den. We filled it with books and magazines, listened to the Spice Girls on our Walkmans. After reading Wuthering Heights, we discovered Kate Bush and became goths. We wrote poems of unrelenting grimness that made us weep at the time and, years later, laugh uproariously when we read them aloud again.*

When Amelia's father introduced us to his album collection, our taste in music changed. We abandoned the net gloves and eyeliner for a slight man in a purple suit and became Prince fans. David Bowie was next. We were developing an interest in older men, especially those with an androgynous allure.

Nothing androgynous about the boys we befriended, except for Mark, who came out as gay when he was fifteen. He was one of our closest friends, as was Jayden Lee-O'Meara, known to us as Jay. Mark and Jay came everywhere with us, except to the ice house. That remained our own private domain and it was where Amelia cried as if her heart was breaking when Jay, her first love, moved to California.

I, too, left Ireland when living with my father became intolerable. I returned to Kilfarran, though, to nurse him through his final year. We made peace with each other before he died but it was too late for the wounds he had inflicted on me to heal.

Amelia had fallen in love with Nicholas by then. Such happiness, the walking-on-cloud-nine kind that was not yet affected by John's dislike of him. When she introduced us, Nicholas held my hand in a firm grip. He looked into my eyes and I shivered. He knew. Without words being exchanged, he was able to see beyond the friendship I shared with Amelia and it spawned his jealousy. This realisation was instinctive. I didn't trust my own judgement and, unwilling as

I was to say or do anything to mar my friend's joy, I decided it must be an overreaction.

Afterwards, when she phoned to tell me John had died, I came back to Kilfarran to comfort her. But Nicholas had stepped into that role and held her with a possessiveness that must have taken her breath away.

I remember their wedding day with gritty clarity. The country church at the foot of the hill. It was a small gathering, compared to the massive attendance at John's funeral. Billy Tobin stepped into the role John would have played and was a sensitive surrogate as he accompanied Amelia up the aisle.

She was dressed in pale gold and I, her only bridesmaid, wore dusty rose. Vows were made, love sealed. We dined afterwards in a nearby hotel where, inevitably, gaiety broke out when the champagne was uncorked. The guests raised their glasses to the blushing bride. To the beautiful bridesmaid. To the handsome groom. And a toast to absent loved ones. Yvonne wore an elaborate fascinator with many feathers and was dressed in purple silk. She was upset that her son's wedding was not the gala affair she had always envisaged and shed many tears during the ceremony.

On that wedding day, as Nicholas Madison walked down the aisle with his bride, it seemed for a short, blissful period, that love would conquer sorrow and triumph in happy-ever-after land.

CHAPTER TWENTY-FOUR

The Past

They talked about starting a family but they had careers to build before committing themselves to nappies and feeding on demand. Amelia's public profile had grown after she successfully completed the interior design of a U.S. multinational tech company with a base in Cork. The project attracted the attention of the editor of an architectural magazine, who was interested in doing an interview with her. Other media features followed. So, also, did commissions. Exciting opportunities that reflected her growing reputation. Nicholas's star was also rising and he appeared regularly on television to discuss investments and the stock market. His down-to-earth approach to the intricacies of choosing the right investment portfolio made him a popular business pundit and he, like Amelia, had acquired a public persona. They were admired for their style and elegance at business functions. Gloss, glitz and colour—they made it look as though it was easy to maintain an idyllic marriage and two demanding careers.

The only problem was Nicholas's insecurity, living as he was on Amelia's charity. He had tied up his capital when he sold his apartment to buy into the junior partnership with KHM and it would take another two years before he would see a return on his investment; only then could they move to a new house that was not steeped in another man's history.

But selling Woodbine was unthinkable to Amelia. Her desire to leave the old house after the death of her father had passed and her love for her childhood home had grown stronger. She wanted their children to play in its spacious rooms and leafy garden, climb the old trees, explore the surrounding fields. After long discussions with Nicholas, who admitted that, despite his reservations, he had also grown fond of Woodbine, they made an appointment to see David Smithson, her father's solicitor, to have Nicholas's name added to the house deed.

"I'm afraid it's not possible to do that, Amelia." David tapped his index nail against his office desk, then, noticing, relaxed his finger. "Your father added a codicil to his will. The ownership of Woodbine must remain in your name only."

"But that can't apply to Nicholas." She was more surprised than shocked. "Why would my father add such a stipulation? I can't understand his decision." But she knew the reason, as did Nicholas, who sat stiffly beside her.

"He didn't confide his reasons to me," David replied. "It wasn't my business to ask why. The codicil was only to be revealed to you if you made the request you've just outlined to me."

"Can it be challenged?" Nicholas asked.

"Anything can be challenged," David replied. "But, as the law stands, it was John's property and he was within his rights to make that decision."

"The ownership of our home doesn't matter," she assured Nicholas when they left David's office. "A piece of paper, that's all it is. Woodbine is our home. It's as much yours as it is mine."

"They're just words, Amelia." Nicholas's hurt was palpable. "They mean nothing. I'd be afraid to put a nail into a wall for fear you'd object."

"That's silly," she protested. "Maintaining Woodbine is a full-time job. Your input will be just as important whenever we decorate it together."

Unknown to him, she contacted David to check the date on the codicil. Her father's signature had been added shortly after that awful night when she had sullied his love for her. How bitter he must have been, how shattered. This guilt, her caul, was she to be bound for ever by its constraints?

She returned from an overnight business trip a month later and discovered that in her absence Nicholas had organised the refurbishment of the old-fashioned bathroom. The antique slipper bathtub with its claw legs had been removed and replaced by a whirlpool bath that bulged outwards from the corner where the spindle-legged cupboard for storing towels used to stand. State of the art, Nicolas said as he bent to demonstrate its swirling effects. The familiar linoleum had been torn up and replaced by shiny marble tiles. A new power shower unit had been installed, along with wall tiles and a panel of blue lights that shone directly on the bath and added a chilling effect to this now unrecognisable bathroom.

Her shock quickly turned to outrage at the decision he had made without consulting her. She would never have agreed to any of this. She shouted him down when he tried to reason with her. Never once losing his patience, he explained how he had hoped to surprise her on her return home. The slipper bath was chipped and fit for nothing but the scrapyard. This new bath with its jacuzzi effects was exactly what they both needed after a stressful day at work. Room for two, he added. If they could bathe together, Amelia would soon overcome her fear of water.

She had climbed mountains, zip lined and bungee jumped, parachuted for charity, hot-air-ballooned for pleasure, but, since her mother's drowning, she had never gone near the sea. When she was younger, hanging out with Leanne and their wider circle of friends, she would accompany them to the beach on condition that they sunbathed on the sand dunes where the long marram grass hid her view of the waves. Standing under a shower, even all these years after the tragedy, she averted her face from the water; and she kept her hair short so that she could shampoo it as quickly as possible. The idea of sitting in a bath with water gushing from whirlpool jets appalled her. How could Nicholas be so insensitive to her feelings?

He was hurt by her reaction, and bewildered, also. Why was she so annoyed? She had told him to make whatever changes he believed were necessary to Woodbine, and he had believed that the bathroom with its cracked tiles and woodwormed furniture was the best place to begin the renovations.

"So much for allowing me to hammer a nail into your precious walls." His disappointment was acute but Amelia was beyond caring.

"Hammer a nail, yes," she shrieked. "But not this—this monstrosity." She pushed him away when he attempted to reason with her. Was it that push that finally ignited his anger and caused him to slap her across her face? She struck him back, then ran from the bathroom to their bedroom and locked him out. Covering her ears, she drowned out the thump of his fist against the door, his pleas to allow him in. She had snatched greedily at happiness, believing it would compensate for the loss of her father. It mocked her now, this illusion that one would cancel out the other.

His face was blotched and wet with tears when she eventually relented and opened the door to him. They clung together, silencing each other's apologies with frantic kisses. He carried her to their bed and promised to organise the removal of the new bath in the morning.

She was still in his arms when she awoke. How trivial their argument seemed in the light of a new day. His sense of insecurity since their marriage had disturbed her yet she had fought with him as soon as he made his first independent decision. Was John controlling her from beyond his grave? Was that why she was so reluctant to change anything in Woodbine?

The bath remained in place and she eventually became used to its bulbous shape. Nicholas used it regularly in the evenings but never again suggested that Amelia share it with him.

✦

Summer came. Jayden Lee-O'Meara returned to Kilfarran for his annual visit to his father. He phoned Amelia, as he always did on these occasions, and arranged to meet her after work for a meal in the Kilfarran Inn. Jay's career as an engineer had turned him into a global traveller. He was much changed from the gauche teenager who had given Amelia her first kiss and left her broken-hearted—or so she had believed then—when he moved to California. Love had now turned to friendship. They kept in touch through email and phone calls, always falling back into a familiar, easy conversation when they were together again.

On this occasion, though, he was subdued. His engagement to Hailey was off.

"Incompatible and irreconcilable differences," Hailey had said when she gave him back his ring. These differences had largely to do with the amount of travelling he had to do but she had also accused him of "mental infidelity." A state of mind, he told Amelia ruefully, that caused both his head and his heart to be elsewhere when he and Hailey were together. By the time he and Amelia had dissected his broken relationship and put it back together again, Jay looked more relaxed. He admitted that Hailey might have had a point about his "mental infidelity."

"I left so much of myself behind in Kilfarran when my mother uprooted me," he said. "It's only in these latter years that I've understood what a wrench that was, especially leaving you. As the song goes, the first cut is the deepest." He smiled to show he was joking but, just for a moment, the memory of the sunshine days when they had kissed in the long grass in Kilfarran Woods, heedless and in love, kept them silent.

She had stayed later than she intended with Jay and, having lowered the sound on her phone, was unaware until she was back in her car that Nicholas had been trying to contact her. Five texts and three missed calls. She rang him but his phone went to message.

He was waiting for her in the living room, seated erectly in the armchair where John used to sit. Was he angry or anxious? Unable to read his mood, she was nonetheless filled with a sense of foreboding as he stood up to greet her. Her good humour plummeted as his questions turned into accusations. He had been expecting her home at eight. He spoke quietly but emphatically. It was now after ten. How could a meal booked for five in the evening have lasted so long? What was so fascinating about Jayden Lee-O'Meara that Amelia had forgotten to text her husband, who had spent the last two hours out of his mind with worry in case she had had an accident?

Was Nicholas her husband or her custodian, Amelia demanded. How dare he accuse her and Jay of being lovers? Did he expect her to fill out a time sheet for him to study and approve every time she met her friends? He silenced her with his fist. A blow to the side of her head that sent her reeling. Stunned, she collapsed to the floor, blood in her mouth, her hands protecting her cheeks. Ashen-faced and contrite, he knelt beside her and begged her forgiveness. She shoved him away from her. That first slap, when she had retaliated, why had she not given it more thought? She had assumed it was an aberration, just as her instinctive response had been, but this was different. Everything had changed in an instant. Like a drowning. A hit-and-run. A world turned upside down by a random act.

Jealousy was his undoing, he begged her to understand why he had reacted so angrily. It consumed him when she was with other men and twisted his feelings into a fist. An apt metaphor, she thought, and one she hoped he would never use again. They made up, of course they did. Love was not yet a choice to give or withhold. He wiped her tears and stroked her forehead until she was calm again and able to forgive him.

When, two months later, she was on the floor again, the shock was all the greater because the lull in between had been idyllic. They had loved more fervently, tenderly, determinedly. Amelia, desperate to rationalise his fury, tried to appreciate his furious response when she accidentally knocked a glass of vodka over the keyboard on his laptop. The corrosive alcohol had burned the components and wiped the contents. Nicholas did not have a proper backup system to recover his files and, he said, her clumsiness had wiped out years of confidential client information.

"You're wrong," she argued. "We can drive to Mark's house straight away. He's an expert at data retrieval—"

"Shut up, you drunken bitch," he roared. "Have you any idea of the damage you've done?"

"How dare you speak to me like that?" She reeled back from his insults. "I had one drink and I didn't knock it over deliberately. It was an accident—"

"I don't give a fuck what it was. I warned you not to touch my laptop." This time he avoided her face but he still brought her to her knees.

Later, she listened to his apologies, his pleas, his promises. The loss of his clients' files meant nothing in the context of what he had done to her.

"I'm sorry, so sorry… I love you so much, Amelia. You must forgive me. You *must*…"

As she had expected, Mark was able to restore the files from the hard drive and he also established a backup system that would prevent a similar accident occurring in the future. Amelia had become wary of Nicholas, though. How could someone who claimed to love her so passionately abuse her on a whim? She searched for reasons to explain his sudden mood swings, his ability to freeze the air around them with a word, a frown, a body movement that could signal anything. Was it fear that trapped her? Or love? She struggled with both and, at such times, he often ended an argument by carrying her to the sofa or the bed, pinning her beneath him until she stopped resisting his kisses. The lovemaking that followed had a charged choreography; edgy with pent-up passion, fear shivering through ecstasy.

Nicholas was particularly resentful of Leanne, who, he claimed, was in love with Amelia. She heard her voice rising defensively whenever she contradicted him but he knew he had picked up on something that Amelia was unwilling to share with him. She kept her silence. What she and Leanne felt for each other could not easily be defined by a jealous husband.

"Our feelings don't matter," Leanne insisted when Amelia discussed the growing tensions she sensed between her husband and her close friend. "Are you happy with him? That's all I care about."

"Very happy." Amelia wondered how Leanne would react if she revealed her bruises. The arrogance that made her believe her love would vanquish Nicholas's insecurity. Insecurity...the word has a soft sound. Not like violence, a word redolent with danger and a growing fear; a fear that she must force herself to confront. Yet, there were spells of tranquility, even happiness, and they trapped her into believing he had succeeded in managing his anger, jealously, resentment, impatience. She was never able to figure out what provoked him most, but she welcomed those interludes when it was possible to dream that all would be well between them.

CHAPTER TWENTY-FIVE

Amelia was aware of the many glances being cast in her direction as they entered the Capella Hotel where the annual KHM Investments Christmas party was being held.

"Dazzling," said Nicholas, stopping to admire the Christmas tree in the foyer. "But it's only a pale imitation of my beautiful wife. Everyone is admiring your dress. I knew it would be perfect on you as soon as I saw it in the window of Brown Thomas." He basked in the fact that he had chosen it, along with the shoes, the gauzy wrap and the make-up that accentuated her cheekbones, glossed her lips and nails. His arm encircled her waist as they entered the ballroom. The dress shimmered when she moved. Silver lamé; she wore it like a sheath. She knew he would have accused her of dressing like a tart if she had bought this dress but, in choosing it for her, he had found another way to dominate her.

The ballroom was ablaze with chandeliers and the tables tastefully decorated with long-stemmed winter roses. Christopher Keogh was seated at the main table. He had arrived on his own, the first time without his wife. Rita Keogh had cancer, Nicholas had told Amelia before they left Woodbine, and Christopher was talking about taking early retirement to look after her. As Nicholas's future would be affected by this decision, Amelia must pay special attention to him. What about your insane suspicions, she had wanted to shout at him, but she kept this thought to herself, unwilling to start another argument before they had even left Woodbine. She had stopped making eye contact with men when they were out together. The change had happened so slowly that it had taken time for her to realise she was taking precautions to avoid provoking his jealousy.

Peter Harris, the other senior partner at KHM, was also seated at the main table. A debonair father of four, he had a mistress in New York who, according to Nicholas, ensured that his business trips were always combined with pleasure. His wife Lilian had the clamped lips of someone used to dealing with lost illusions. As she air-kissed Amelia, she glanced down at her flat stomach and said, softly, yet loud enough for Nicholas to hear, "No news, yet, I guess."

Amelia had no idea if this comment was deliberate or unintentional but, with it, Lilian had touched the latest bone of contention in their marriage. Nicholas had changed his mind about starting a family and was talking persuasively about the joys of parenting together. She had not argued back, knowing that to do so would only harden his determination. Privately, though, she thought, if he was unable to endure her staying away on overnight business trips or dining with male clients how was he to cope with a baby, who would demand so much of her love and attention?

Finally admitting that what he called his "insecurity" was harming their marriage, he had agreed to couples counselling. Amelia had had to cancel their first appointment when he was unavoidably delayed at work. She had made another one for next week and, afraid he would stop using condoms, she had also made an appointment, without his knowledge, at the Well Woman Centre to discuss alternative methods of contraception.

She sat between Christopher and Peter's personal assistant, Isabelle Langdon. Sitting opposite Amelia, and looking regal in midnight-blue organza, was KHM's contract solicitor, Rosemary Williams. Amelia had met both women at a previous function and had discussed Isabelle's plans to downsize to a smaller house as soon as her daughter left home. She had shown Amelia photographs of a bungalow and asked her opinion on whether or not it would be a good buy. Amelia, noting the location and condition of the property, had advised her to go for it.

She was now living in the bungalow and her daughter was in Australia, she said, after greeting Amelia warmly.

"She's become a beach bum." She laughed as she clicked into the gallery on her mobile and showed the photographs to Amelia.

The Pacific Ocean, glistening. Vast waves, as curved as question marks, hurtling towards shore. A young woman soaring above them on a bodyboard, poised and assured as she rode through the froth and the fury. Amelia's heart skipped a beat, as it always did at the sight of an untrammelled ocean.

"Your daughter obviously loves the sea," she said.

Isabelle smiled and nodded. "Elena was a water baby who grew into a mermaid."

"You must miss her."

"It was difficult in the beginning," Isabelle agreed. "But the move to the bungalow has been a good distraction." She paused, apologetically, her mobile still in her hand. "I know this is small fare compared to the work you do but I hope you don't mind if I ask your advice about one of the rooms?"

"Not at all," Amelia replied. "Ask away."

"This one has very little natural light. Any tips on how I can brighten it?" She showed photographs of a small living room and listened intently as Amelia made suggestions about well-positioned mirrors, wallpaper and lighting.

"You make it sound so easy," Isabelle said. "I can see exactly how that will work. You've quite enlivened me. To be honest, I've been finding it difficult since Elena left."

"How long will she be away?"

"Who knows? She loves it over there. I don't see her coming back to settle here, at least not in the immediate future. I don't blame her breaking away from me, not really. Her father died when she was young. He was the love of my life and she always felt she was playing second fiddle to him."

Amelia blinked back a sudden rush of tears. They came at unexpected times and now, in the midst of the annual HKM Christmas party, she was filled with an urge to lay her head on the table and weep.

The band began to play. The crowd looked reluctant to move from their chairs but Nicholas, without hesitation, took her hand and led her onto the floor.

"What was Isabelle bending your ear about?" he asked.

"Her new house. I was giving her some design tips."

"She's worth a fortune yet she's cadging free advice off you."

"She was simply asking my opinion. I like her."

"You're certainly getting on well together...not too well, I hope. You know that she and Rosemary have a thing—"

"That's office gossip," Amelia protested. "They're just good friends. Anyone can see that."

He held her closer, whispered in her ear. "You're an expert on that subject, of course."

"Stop it, Nicholas. I'm enjoying the night. Don't spoil it for me."

As soon as they returned to the table, Peter Harris asked her to dance. Instinctively she glanced at Nicholas, whose nod was imperceptible to anyone but her.

Peter was an excellent dancer, his hands moving smoothly over the back of her dress. "You dance beautifully, Amelia." He brought his mouth close to hers, the smell of brandy on his breath. "Have you ever danced professionally?"

"Only in my dreams, Peter. But I did attend classes with a friend when I was in my teens. We did everything from contemporary to ballet, ballroom—"

"Ah! Ballroom. Wonderful. You're a woman after my own heart." He stopped dancing and held her at arm's length. "I'm going to have a word with the band, get them to play some decent dance music." He strode to the stage and stopped the singer in the middle of singing "All I Want for Christmas is You." After a brief consultation, the band began to play a tango.

"Let's show 'em." Beaming widely, Peter pulled her into his arms, his back erect, head rock steady as he glided her forward. Amelia's legs moved in step with his long, dramatic stride, her body pliant when he bent her backwards. The dancers surrounding them stopped and formed an admiring circle. Peter stood behind her, one hand close to her breast, the other low on her back, their bodies fusing for an instant before he spun her round. Nicholas had joined the circle. He smiled, as if amused, when Amelia flicked her leg high and the slit at the side of her dress opened to reveal her thigh. The younger men watching whistled and stamped their feet. Exaggerating the sensual chorography of the tango, Amelia stepped lightly to the music, giddy with a reckless need to taunt Nicholas. He was still smiling when the dance ended and Peter lifted her into the air. She glimpsed her reflection in the ballroom mirror. Dazzling in silver, her black hair falling back from her cheeks, her arms raised to acknowledge the applause. Her face glowing. What a picture. What a lie.

"Where did you learn to dance like that?" Isabelle asked when Amelia returned to the table.

"Dance class, years ago." Amelia sat down beside her and steadied her breathing. "My friend Leanne and I used to practise every day. Luckily, I was always the woman. Otherwise, Peter would have had some problems on the floor." She laughed and fanned her face with a serviette. "Whew. Your husband is one tough taskmaster, Lilian."

Amelia's efforts to draw the other woman into the conversation failed. Lilian Harris, who had been drinking steadily throughout the night, simply nodded and signalled to Peter that she needed another vodka.

Nicholas sat beside Lilian and enquired about her family. Two sons, two daughters, adults now; he knew their names and the details of their education and careers. Amelia listened to his easy flow of conversation. His memory was a tool he used to charm and control. Why was she only seeing this now?

He continued talking to Lilian, who reached into her evening bag for her lipstick and drew a red slash on her lips. "We've had this fascinating conversation about my family every year since you joined the firm, Nicholas." She snapped the bag closed. "I've always admired your ability to entertain me for my allotted time span."

"Lilian, you make it sound like a chore," Nicholas protested. "I always look forward to talking to you and catching up on your family's achievements."

"But you never ask about me. My achievements."

"Your achievements are obvious. Four wonderful children—"

"Indeed. When are you going to provide me with an opportunity to ask about *your* children? I sincerely hope you're not firing blanks into your lovely wife."

A nerve twitched in his cheek but, otherwise, Nicholas seemed unaffected by her comments.

Peter coughed and slammed his glass on the table. "Time to go, darling." He lifted a black velvet pashmina from the back of Lilian's chair, his discomfort obvious as he draped it over her shoulders. "I've an early flight to catch in the morning."

"Of course you do, *darling*." Lilian stood and gripped the edge of the table. "He's off to New York for his Christmas shopping."

She nodded vaguely at the group around the table. "Peter always knows where the best tat is cheapest and available."

"You take care of yourself, Lilian." Christopher Keogh's expression was sombre as he kissed her cheek.

"You too, Christopher." Her brittle shoulders lifted and fell. "Give Rita my love. I hope she'll be back to full health soon."

"That reminds me." Christopher reached for his camera. "I want a group photograph before you go. Strict orders from Rita." He set the timer and joined the group in time for the flash.

"Lilian's rudeness was unfortunate." He pulled his chair closer to Amelia after the Keoghs left. "I've never seen her behave like that before."

"Do you think she was upset because I danced with Peter?"

"She's an unhappy woman, Amelia. I suspect you're the least of her worries."

"How is Rita?" Amelia asked. "I'm sorry she wasn't able to be here tonight."

"The chemo's tough," he replied. "But we're both hopeful of a good outcome."

The band had finished playing and a DJ was erecting his turntables on the stage. This was a general signal for those remaining at the main table to leave. More smiles, more handshakes and hugs.

Apart from giving their address to the taxi driver, Nicholas remained silent as they were driven through the glittering city. His fingers drummed against his knee and his profile, reflected in the taxi window, could have been carved from granite.

CHAPTER TWENTY-SIX

Back at Woodbine, he opened a bottle of cognac and poured two measures into tulip-shaped glasses.

"A toast to my beautiful wife." He handed one to Amelia and lifted his own glass in salute. "You were quite sensational on the dance floor."

"Thank you," she said and clinked his glass with hers. His mood was benign. When had she started using that word? Benign, as opposed to malignant. She swirled the cognac and sniffed its nutty aroma, the hint of honey, vanilla. This was an aged cognac. Billy Tobin had bought it for her father on his fifty-fifth birthday and John had only used it to celebrate special occasions. She sipped it slowly, aware that Nicholas, seated in John's favourite chair, had already finished his. Did he think he was drinking a shot? Some cheap concoction that would give him a quick buzz? How dare he take over her father's chair, open his precious cognac, plant such ugly suspicions in Amelia's mind? She lowered her eyes, afraid that Nicholas would realise what she was thinking.

When she had finished her drink, he followed her up the stairs and steered her towards the bathroom, his hands planted firmly on her hips.

"What are you doing?" Amelia paused in the doorway, her body, so pliable on the dance floor, tensing.

"Something you'll like." He gently but firmly propelled her forward and closed the bathroom door. Standing behind her, he turned her towards the full-length mirror set into the tiled wall and unzipped her dress. Slithery as a snake shedding skin, it fell to the floor. Amelia released her breath. The fabric had encased her like a suit of armour, yet she had been unaware of its restraints until she was out of it.

"Let's go into the bedroom, Nicholas," she said.

"Not tonight." He breathed the words against the nape of her neck. "I want this to be extra special."

He moved away from her and turned on the taps. Water cascaded into the bath. Steam rose and obscured her reflection.

"I've been looking forward to being alone with you all night," he said. Slowly, deliberately, he eased down the thong she had worn and unhooked her bra. He removed his own clothes and left them in a tidy bundle beside hers. She used to enjoy watching him undress, his unselfconscious suppleness as he kicked off his shoes or unbuttoned his shirt. Now, as the muscles on his arms rippled, she thought of a panther, its graceful stealth as it drew closer to its prey.

"Not here, Nicholas." Amelia stepped back from the bath and tried to ignore the gushing water. To show nervousness would only make the situation worse. "I want to be with you, too. But this is not going to work."

"Yes, it is," he replied. Aroused and eager, he took her hand. "We can make it happen. I love you. I know you doubt that sometimes. I'm sorry I give you reason to do so. But nothing will ever change my feelings for you." He cupped her face, kissed her lips. "I want you to be happy with me."

"I am, Nicholas."

He shook his head. "You've lived with fear since you were a child. It's distorted your ability to know true happiness. Your father—"

"Please don't talk about him. I can't bear it."

"You're shaking. Are you frightened of me?"

"No...no. I'm cold. And tired. Let's go to bed."

"Don't be afraid, Amelia. I've been waiting all night for this moment."

His grip was firm and confident as he led her towards the bath, where bubbles frothed and the blue lights shining on the wall cast an unearthly hue over their bodies.

"Take my hand," he said. "I won't let anything happen to you."

She searched his face for anger, the hardening of his features that always signalled a mood change. The violence that would start soon afterwards. Could she trust the emotions she saw there, his tenderness and desire, the love that he claimed to be an enduring one? She lowered herself into the fragrant water. Jasmine, she thought. The sweet scent clung to the steamy air.

Nicholas sat beside her and slid his arm round her shoulder, drew her closer to him. "Do you know what I was thinking when you were dancing with Peter?" Without waiting for a reply, he continued. "It takes two to tango and I'm the only one who knows the right moves." He slowly stroked a sponge across her breasts. "How does that feel, Amelia?"

She unclenched her teeth. "Good," she whispered. "So good."

He leaned forward and turned off the taps. "That's not so frightening, is it?"

"Not with you beside me." She was no longer able to distinguish between a lie and the truth. The heat from the water was draining her energy and making it difficult to focus.

"Every man at that party desired you tonight," he said.

"You've a vivid imagination, Nicholas."

"Don't call me a liar."

She tried to concentrate on what he was saying but his voice seemed to be coming at her from a great distance.

He did not sound jealous, nor angry, but she had ceased trying to judge his moods by these outward signs. "I'm not," she replied. "Let's just say you're *slightly* biased." Her body jerked when he pressed a button on the side of the bath and a jet of water surged against her back. A second jet erupted between her thighs, the pressure sending rippling waves across the surface. A racing tide; she needed to escape but her body refused to obey her.

"You breathe sex when you move, Amelia." He continued stroking her with the sponge. "You're a flirt. Such a tease . . . those poor slavering goons watching you. If they could see us now."

"I love you, Nicholas," she said. "I'm not remotely interested in flirting with anyone but you. That's not what's bothering you. It's Lilian Harris. What she said. Her behaviour was appalling."

"But you were responsible for it."

"If anyone was responsible for upsetting her, it was her husband."

"Whom you encouraged. It's not the first time Peter Harris has made a fool of someone at the Christmas party. It's a standing joke in the company. Who will it be this year? I never thought it would be my wife. You made quite an exhibition of yourself."

"That's so unfair." Her voice should be trembling uncontrollably. Instead it was flat, expressionless. "We danced the tango. I followed Peter's steps. It's a dramatic dance."

"From where I was standing it looked more like a lap dance. All you were short of doing was screwing him on the floor."

"Don't you dare speak to me like that. Have you any sense of the damage you're doing to our marriage by treating me this way?" She should sound angry but her words had slurred into a drawl that sounded unfamiliar to her. She tried to grip the edge of the bath and stand but her fingers slid helplessly away. She was unable to struggle when he grabbed her legs and pulled her down, shoved her head under the water. It roared in her ears, filled her mouth, blinded her. This was her nightmare, her memory, ready to claim her once again. She surfaced, gasping. She had to escape but her body was flaccid and she was unable to find the strength to push him away. He was smiling when he forced her down again. Blackness filled her eyes and it was no longer possible to fight him.

✦

Nicholas was spooned against her when she awoke. Amelia wrinkled her nose against the rancid smell of stale alcohol permeating the bedroom. Her mouth was dry and had the sour taste of too much drink. The cognac she had had when they returned from the HKM party was strong and Nicholas had poured a large measure. Before that she had had wine with her meal and vodka afterwards. This was going to be a severe hangover. She touched her lips, convinced they were cracked, bleeding, but they felt smooth under her fingers. She shivered, cold despite the heat from his body, and swung her feet to the floor.

Anxious not to awaken him, she moved quietly to the window and pulled back the edge of the curtain. The sun was a blurred disc behind an early morning mist. Her dress lay across the back of a chair, her underwear folded beside it, her shoes underneath. The muzziness in her head increased as she tried to remember undressing. The bathroom. Her mind steadied. She had been in the bathroom with Nicholas, her dress slithering from her body. Beyond that, nothing.

She crossed the landing to the bathroom and stood beside the ostentatious bath with its jets and lighting effects. The shower gel and deodorants Nicholas used were arranged on the shelf above the bath and the surface was spotless. She was overcome by a sudden wave of nausea. Her knees weakened. Afraid she would collapse, she pressed her hands to the wall and gasped for air. She exhaled loudly but was still unable to ease the constriction in her chest. For a dizzying instant, the bathroom swayed. A memory returned. Shoulder to shoulder—they had sat together in this bath as bubbles frothed and jets of water pummelled her.

"Amelia!" The bathroom door opened and Nicholas, wearing a T-shirt and boxers, entered. His hair was ruffled, his eyes slightly bloodshot. Otherwise, he looked the same as always, yet when he took her hand she had to stop herself from instinctively recoiling.

"The morning after the night before is never easy," he said. "Come back to bed. This has to be your duvet day. I'll make breakfast for you."

"No, I'm okay. I'm up now."

"You drank a lot last night. You need to sleep it off."

"I've work to do—"

"Work can wait. It's Saturday. Come on, do as I tell you." He had switched on the electric blanket and when she was back in bed he tucked the duvet tightly around her. "Cocooned from everything." He smiled down at her. "I'll be up to you with breakfast shortly."

Alone in the room, she lay motionless. A blackout, that had to be the answer. It had happened once before, in her teens. A party at Mark's house when his parents were away on holiday.

They had raided the drinks cabinet, making cocktails from a recipe book Mark produced, and she had ended up being collected by her father, who carried her to his car. The following morning, chastened and still suffering, Amelia had promised him she would never take another drink until she was eighteen. Her friends remembered everything that had happened that night but Amelia's memory had stopped functioning shortly before she collapsed on the floor.

Nicholas returned with a tray. Freshly squeezed orange juice, toast lightly buttered, scrambled eggs sprinkled with slivers of smoked salmon, a pot of tea. She didn't think she would be able to keep the food down but it was easier just to smile and thank him. He sat on the edge of the bed and waited for her to eat.

Her hand shook as she raised the fork to her mouth.

"It's the alcohol," he said. "Don't worry. It'll pass." He cut her toast and fed her, coaxed her to swallow. Somehow, she managed to finish her breakfast without throwing up.

"What happened last night?" she asked when he had cleared the tray away. "I remember being in the bath with you but I can't remember getting out of it."

"You were pretty far gone," he admitted. "I'm not surprised it's all a blur." He tilted his head, quizzingly. "Can you remember what we talked about?"

"Were you angry with me?"

"Why should I be angry?"

"Peter. That silly dance."

"That's all it was. A silly dance." He traced his finger across her lips. "We talked about love."

"I'm sorry, Nicholas." She shook her head, helplessly. "All I remember is being frightened of the water."

"Initially, yes. But you overcame your fear, as I knew you would. Even when you slipped in the bath, you didn't panic."

"I slipped?"

"You were trying to stand. That's how you bruised yourself." He pulled back the duvet and exposed her legs. Shocked, she stared at the swelling below her knee and the bruises on both thighs. "I helped you out of the water and dried you off. I put you to bed. I'm amazed you can't remember."

"I didn't realise I was so drunk."

"Then rest and recover. Everything will come back to you in time."

"You said we talked about love?"

"We did. You told me you would love me until the day you die. I need to believe you meant it."

The silence stretched as he waited for her reply. Her mind remained blank, unmapped, without direction, and he was waiting—no, he was demanding an answer.

"I meant it," she replied, dully.

"I made the same commitment to you," he said. "Only death can ever separate us."

Alone again in the bedroom, her mind raced. He had helped her to face her fears. Why would he lie? And why did the terror she had spent her life trying to curb now feel even more overwhelming? It was so bad that, later, when she entered the en suite and switched on the shower, she was too frightened to stand underneath it. Nicholas found her hunkered on the floor, naked, weeping. He switched off the shower and filled the handbasin with warm water. He drew her to her feet and began to wash her. She quivered, her skin shrivelling, or so it seemed, as he gently ran the sponge over her and wrapped her in a towel before carrying her back to bed.

CHAPTER TWENTY-SEVEN

The nightmares returned, only this time it was her father's face staring back at her from the waves. Nicholas always woke her. Talking it through with him would banish these night terrors, he believed. Drowning, she said. My dreams are always about drowning. She didn't tell him the same images haunted her during the day. Water pummelling...bubbles...his face disappearing, appearing, disappearing...cocooned in a towel, on the bed...what then—what then...? At night, in his arms, she was unable to respond to him. Afraid of upsetting him, she faked a pleasure she was far from feeling, her limbs heavy, her mind dull and unresponsive.

'Til death do us part. This then was her marriage. Her wardrobe was filled with his choices. Structured suits, high-collared blouses, sensible shoes, shapeless jogging pants. A blueprint for conformity.

Couples counselling had been cancelled too many times for her to bother making another appointment. Nor had she attended the Well Woman Centre. Nicholas had found the appointment on her phone when, mistaking it for his own—or so he claimed—he picked it up accidentally.

A phone call from Terry Wall, part-owner of Knob Needs, snapped her from her lethargy. The family business in the centre of Dublin had specialised in doorknobs for a hundred years and Terry believed this anniversary was the perfect time for a makeover.

Eric, his father, disagreed. Why fix something that wasn't broken? Amelia, having arranged a meeting, was convinced she could persuade Eric to change his mind once he saw her presentation. She checked the wardrobe and chose a navy suit from among the clothes Nicholas had bought for her. She buttoned a pink blouse with a bow and tucked it into the skirt. Matching navy shoes with block heels and light-coloured tights, densely woven. She chose a lipstick from the row of pink shades on her dressing table. Clutter, Nicholas believed, was the sign of a disorganised mind. Her hand shook as she applied the lipstick and smudged her top lip. Simple acts that were once second nature to her were becoming laboured and clumsy.

Knob Needs had the grey slump of a building long neglected. The interior, though clean, felt oppressive, as if old dust clogged the crevices. Eric greeted her with a grudging handshake but Terry, whose certificate was framed on the wall behind him, had the confident smile of an entrepreneur with a master's degree in retail marketing.

Amelia switched on her laptop and began her PowerPoint presentation. Eric jutted his bottom lip and crossed his arms, barricading himself against this intrusion into tradition. She ignored his body language and explained how she could lift the old building out of its grimy past. The construction industry was moving out of recession and this was the perfect time for Knob Needs to introduce its doorknobs to a new generation of house buyers.

Suddenly, her mind went blank, like a light switching off, and she floundered in darkness; the words she had rehearsed were forgotten and she was unable to move her hand towards the laptop—... *the sea roaring—no—in the bath... water cascading, bubbles... her legs going from under her... floppy body—eyes open... watching—unable to fight back...*

Terry was staring at her in alarm and even Eric had abandoned his truculent pose and was sitting straighter in his chair.

"Is everything okay, Amelia?" Terry reached her before her legs collapsed and helped her into a chair. She pressed her face into her knees and waited for the dizziness to pass.

"I'm so sorry." She held the back of the chair as she stood up. "I've no idea what all that was about."

"We can call it a day if you like." Eric was clearly eager to get back to his doorknobs; but Terry handed her a glass of water and nodded at her to continue. She managed to finish her presentation without any further mishaps but was still feeling shaky when she switched off her laptop.

"You take care." Eric winked at her as she was leaving. "And make sure you get plenty of rest. The early months are the toughest."

CHAPTER TWENTY-EIGHT

Nicholas was thrilled. Blame it on a faulty condom, he said. Water churning. Steam rising. A bedroom door opening. Her body spread-eagled—Amelia forced the bewildering images from her. Yvonne and Henry arrived at Woodbine with champagne. They toasted the future. The first of many babies, Yvonne said. Amelia smiled as she sipped iced water. There was still a hope, faint enough but worth holding onto, that once their child was born, everything would be different. New beginnings were always imprinted with optimism, no matter how dark the circumstances.

In the early bloom of her pregnancy, Amelia felt wonderful. No morning sickness, just some tiredness in the evenings, which passed by the third month. But her hope that her pregnancy would make a difference to Nicholas's jealousy was short-lived. One night, having returned late from meeting Leanne, who was visiting from New York, Amelia lay doubled up on the floor. Afraid to battle back, as she had done in the past, she was nonetheless no longer thinking only of her own safety as she struggled to catch her breath and pacify Nicholas.

"Our baby," she gasped. "What are you trying to do?"

"My baby?" He knelt before her and grabbed her shoulders. "Swear to me it's my baby you're carrying."

"You tell me you love me yet you have the nerve to ask such a question." Still on her knees, she cradled her stomach protectively.

"As your husband, I've every right to ask it." He spoke fast and furiously. Her lies and deceit. How could she blame him for being suspicious? Like moths to a flame, she attracted other men with her tight skirts and low-cut tops. In an effort to appease him, she allowed him to help her to her feet. She knew the pattern by now. She had married a man who uttered meaningless apologies, found meaningless excuses for actions that stemmed from only one source. Violent anger. She was no different from the battered wives who she had always imagined as being meek, bedraggled women, worn down by constant abuse. She had refused to equate herself with them. Allowed love to blindfold her. It was easier to be in denial than to admit she had made a catastrophic mistake. Her father had been right all along. Emptiness. Her husband's eyes were devoid of emotion if one cared to look deep enough into them, as he was now forcing her to do.

✦

He arrived home the following evening with flowers, a twine-tied bouquet of pale pink lilies and roses. His ability to act as if everything could continue as it did before his outbursts had baffled her in the beginning. Was it a deliberate ploy to normalise their lives in the aftermath or did he genuinely believe his behaviour could be forgiven and forgotten so easily? When he was relaxed—and she was still able to recognise the man she loved—he always dismissed her efforts to reason with him as overreactions, exaggerations, histrionics. Somehow, in the flow of words between them, she had lost the power to argue. In doing so, she minimised his brutality. Boxed it off until the next confrontation.

Unable to tolerate another token of his repentance, Amelia took the bouquet with her when she left Woodbine the following morning. She braked at the spot where her father's body had been found and hunkered down before the small white cross she had erected soon after his funeral.

Cremation was what he had wanted when he died, he had told Amelia once. Her mother had also been cremated. Both of them had had their ashes scattered from the summit of the Sugar Loaf. She was five when her mother's ash-scattering took place. The ashes whirling in the wind had reminded her of the starlings that speckled the sky above Woodbine in the evenings.

She had felt unable to let go of John's ashes until the first anniversary of his death. Billy Tobin had accompanied her and Nicholas to the Sugar Loaf. She had been standing a short distance from Nicholas when she emptied the urn and the wind, turning freakishly, had blown the ashes back into his face. Shocked and repulsed, his hands over his eyes, he had stumbled down the mountain. She had been unable to keep up with him. When she reached the spot where he had parked his car, she discovered he had left without her. Billy drove her back to Woodbine, where she found Nicholas in the bath, scrubbing furiously at his skin.

The white cross on the crest of the grassy embankment had become Amelia's place of repose. Once a week, she left fresh flowers in front of it, and she stopped there every day for a few moments to remember her father. Not that John was ever far from her thoughts. She removed a bunch of wilting daffodils from a terracotta vase and replaced them with the pink bouquet.

That evening, as she drove past the white cross, she noticed that the vase had toppled over. She stopped her car and crossed the path to the grass. The flowers had been removed.

Below her, she heard the low gurgle of water running, wending its way past clusters of bluebells and cowslips. It sounded louder than usual, rising as it always did at this time of year. The roaring filled her ears . . . and the choking sensation returned, of not being able to breathe, her face in water...in the bath...Jagged images, their velocity shocking her to a standstill. That was how those images came, like rags fluttering on a prayer tree, too scattered to form a coherent shape.

When she got back to Woodbine, the cloying scent of lilies filled the hall. The bouquet had been returned to the glass vase on the console table. The roses had yet to open but the orange stamens on the lilies arched towards her like vulgar tongues. She entered the kitchen, where Nicholas, wearing a striped butcher's apron, was preparing their evening meal.

"How was your day?" He smiled across at her, knife in hand as he sliced peppers and tomatoes. Minced beef and onions, flavoured, she could tell by the smell, with cumin, paprika and chilli, sizzled in a saucepan on the hob.

"Busy, as usual." She unbuttoned her jacket and laid it over the back of the chair. This game could be played by two. "When did you arrive home?"

"About thirty minutes ago. The traffic was okay for a change. I made good time." He added the peppers and tomatoes to the saucepan. "I hope you're hungry. I'm making chilli con carne."

"Sounds good." Her eyes stung from the spicy aromas as she set the table. She strained the rice, dressed the salad. They worked well together, a coordinated team. When they sat down to eat, he opened a bottle of Merlot. She drank Ballygowan water with a slice of lemon. The flowers were never mentioned.

They wilted over the following fortnight, their leaves browning, the blowsy rose petals falling. Dust from the stamens peppered the console table and their overpowering scent nauseated her whenever she walked through the hall.

Finally, one evening, they were missing when she returned from work. The table had been polished, the rancid water emptied from the vase. A small victory? She felt no elation, no sense of having scored a point. This was a waiting game and she had no idea how the next round would go.

✦

He lay beside her in bed, his hand on her stomach making a gentle, circular movement that was meant to soothe her. His touch was repugnant to her but she stayed still, afraid to jeopardise the tiny life they had created.

The following day as she was discussing a project with a client, her mobile rang. She was about to cancel the call when she realised it was Billy Tobin. Startled, she apologised to the client and walked out of earshot. Billy would never ring her at work unless it was an emergency.

"Is something wrong, Billy?" she asked.

"I'm not sure," he replied. "I thought I'd better check with you, just in case. There are a couple of boyos here from the council. They're taking John's cross down. They say they've permission to do so. You didn't mention anything about it when I was talking to you a few days ago, so I'm just letting you know."

"I never gave anyone permission to touch that cross. Where are you now?"

"I'm standing right beside them."

"Let me speak to whoever's in charge."

"Jim Jackson here, Missus." The tone was brusque, impatient. "What's your problem?"

"My problem is that you've no right to touch that cross. I had permission from the council to erect it."

"There's been complaints. It's a traffic hazard."

"That's nonsense. It's such a small cross. It's hardly visible from the road."

"Orders are orders, Missus. I'm afraid it has to go."

"We'll see about that. Don't dare touch it until I speak to someone in authority."

"That'll be Maura Gowan."

"I want her number." Amelia jotted it down, conscious that her client was glancing at his watch.

"I'm so sorry for that interruption." She returned to her drawing board, where she had sketched some preliminary ideas.

"You look upset," he said. "Is everything all right?"

"It's a mix-up. I'll sort it out later." She tapped a pencil on the sketch. "As I was saying, vertical blinds would be the best option on those windows." She hurried through the remaining details and rang Maura Gowan as soon as he left. An automated voice asked her to press a number, then another. Finally, she reached the woman's voicemail. Clipped and authoritative, Maura Gowan ordered her to leave a message.

She rang Billy. "What's the situation?" she asked.

"They're still here but they haven't removed the cross yet," he replied.

"I'm on my way." The waiting game with Nicholas was over.

CHAPTER TWENTY-NINE

The traffic had yet to reach its evening peak when she drove onto the N11, heading for Wicklow. The council workers were gone by the time she reached Kilfarran Lane where poppies, crushed by the boots of the workmen, splashed a blood-red stain on the embankment. The last flowers she had left there had also been trampled underfoot and the terracotta vase was broken in half and partially covered by a mound of mud. It marked the spot where the cross used to stand. She knelt down and touched the earth. When she closed her eyes, the same well-known image assaulted her. She gasped aloud, as she did so often in her nightmares. Only now she was awake and conscious of the hard earth under her knees. The chilling east wind rising.

Her mobile rang. "Mrs. Madison, Maura Gowan here. Regarding your query about the roadside shrine—"

"Why was my father's cross removed?"

"We wrote to you twice outlining the complaints we'd received from motorists. As you ignored our correspondence we had no option but to take action."

"I never received any letters."

"They were sent from this office. The second one was registered. I have the details of its delivery in front of me. And when your husband spoke to us—"

"My husband?"

"We rang your landline, Mrs. Madison, and left a message with him. I'm sorry for any distress the removal of the cross has caused you. But we *did* give you ample opportunity to address this issue with us."

✦

No sign of Nicholas downstairs, no cooking smells emanating from the kitchen. A sound from an upstairs room alerted her. She opened the door of the room they had chosen as the nursery. A two-sided, folding ladder stood in the centre of the floor and Nicholas, in paint-splattered dungarees, was painting the ceiling.

"You're home early." He replaced the roller in the paint tray and climbed down.

"So are you."

"I'd a business meeting in the Shelbourne. It was cancelled when I was on my way there so I decided to call it a day. What's your excuse?"

"I came home to prevent my father's cross being removed. Unfortunately, I was too late."

"Ah, yes. I meant to tell you about that. A woman phoned from the council. Seems you ignored their letters. Motorists were complaining—"

"Stop lying to me," she snapped. "There were no complaints, apart from the ones you manufactured. You must be very satisfied with your day's work."

"You can't believe I had anything to do with this."

"No one else is responsible."

"You're calling me a liar?"

"A *vindictive* liar. I was a fool not to heed my father's warnings."

"Your father had only one reason for hating me."

"Don't you dare sully his memory with your disgusting insinuations."

"He broke you, Amelia. He left you incapable of love or trust. That's why we have problems in our marriage. You can deny it all you like but you need to name it. The two of you alone here. Those night terrors. You were too scared to understand what was happening to you. The sooner you accept what was going on, the sooner you can seek help and start to rebuild our relationship."

The mesmerising tenor of his voice. She had listened to him once but that was before she discovered that violence took many forms, apart from bruises and cracked ribs.

"He said you'd break my heart. How right he was." She could feel it sundering, the fissure widening. "He saw through you from the beginning but I was too besotted to heed him. I had to wait until you attacked me before I realised he was trying to protect me from a nightmare, like he always did." Her hand moved protectively over her stomach. "I'll never forgive myself—or you. *Never.*"

"I wasn't the one who accused him." Nicholas took a step towards her, then stopped when he saw her expression. "No one twisted your arm, Amelia, or forced you to confront him. You did that all by yourself. Putting up a cross in his memory may be a salve to your guilt but to me it's the height of hypocrisy. He told me he'd do everything he could to break us up, which is not surprising considering—"

"When did he say that?"

"He didn't tell you, did he?"

"Tell me what?"

"He hired a private detective to check on me. He found nothing, of course. What would I have found if the tables were reversed? Hmm?"

"Stop it. *Stop.* I won't allow you to poison my love for him into something hideous. You've wrecked our marriage. I'm not prepared to put up with your behaviour any longer. You've freeloaded off me for long enough. I want you out of my life."

"*Freeloaded?*" She forced herself to stand still as he walked towards her. "That's not what we agreed. What's mine is yours. Isn't that what you told me? I've no intention of going *anywhere*. My child—"

"Your child? You thought otherwise when you knocked me to the floor."

"You provoked me, Amelia, just as you're doing now." He grasped her shoulders, twisted her head so that she was forced to look at him. "*Our* child belongs to both of us. Remember our vows? 'Til death do us part. I've no intention of breaking mine or allowing you to do something as foolish as breaking yours."

"Leave me alone. You've raised your hand to me for the last time."

"We'll see about that." The blow, so swift and sudden, sent her spinning away from him. She fell, her body crashing against the ladder. It tilted, the legs on one side lifting. For an instant it seemed to defy gravity, and Amelia, also frozen in that same suspended pause, was assailed by images. The memory rushed away from her as the metal frame struck her head and she was knocked senseless.

✦

An ambulance, siren screaming. The pain low down in her back, her stomach cramping.

"My baby…" Her breath rasping, Nicholas holding her hand. "Don't talk. We're nearly at the hospital. Everything's going to be all right."

Amelia could see the truth in the eyes of the paramedic, who leaned over her and asked her to score her pain on a ratio of one to ten.

"I can't give you a number." She wasn't sure if the paramedic could hear her or if she had even spoken her thoughts aloud. "How am I supposed to calculate such pain?"

Nicholas clung to her hand. She did not want to listen to him sobbing or look at his tears falling. Crocodile tears, shameless, and she was unable to tell if she was clinging to him for support or if it was the other way around.

✦

The edge was tempting. A bottomless hole waiting for her to fall forward. No space to burrow, no way to escape. Here, there was just darkness. Her baby, gone now, gone like thistledown on a spring breeze, leaving behind a weight too heavy to carry. Nicholas stayed by her side, pulling her back when she strained against him.

"We are one," he said. "Now, more than ever, we must work to make our marriage stronger. I love you, Amelia…love you… until death do us part."

His promises sloughed off her. Dead tissue falling from a marriage that no longer had meaning. She would talk to David Smithson as soon as she was strong enough to face the inevitable confrontation when she demanded a divorce from Nicholas. Living with him was no longer an option, yet she knew how hard she would have to fight to reclaim her freedom. She would move slowly, warily. Wait for the right time to lock him and his possessions out of Woodbine for ever.

CHAPTER THIRTY

Nicholas was in London on a three-day business trip when I came back to Woodbine to see Amelia one sunny afternoon in June. Love had not served either of us well. I was pale and drained from the ending of a passionate but destructive relationship with a graphic novelist, but I was shocked by the change in Amelia. Make-up could no longer disguise her pallor and her face was gaunt from the weight she had lost. She moved slowly, as if the ground beneath her was unstable and she had to feel her way to steadiness. She was still recovering from her miscarriage but I knew that her loss had simply intensified a grief she could no longer hide.

I'd left New York by then and was living back in Ireland. My father had died and left me his house in Kilfarran, along with two ramshackle cottages situated beside each other on an isolated headland overlooking the Atlantic. The sale of his house had paid for the renovations of the cottages and the establishment of my studio on Mag's Head.

I'd suspected, for some time, that she was very unhappy. For the first year of her marriage, I thought she was grieving over John but I'd soon realised it went deeper than that. Nicholas's behaviour early on in their relationship had made me suspicious of his possessiveness. I'd chosen to ignore the signs then, and, though I was horrified by what she confided in me that afternoon, I was not surprised. The hairs on the back of my neck lifted as she recounted the accident that had preceded her miscarriage. Had he deliberately pushed the ladder on top of her or had it fallen accidently? She claimed it was the latter but I was unsure if that was what had happened or just what she needed to believe. Otherwise, how could she keep going?

I told her to leave him before he returned from London. Woodbine was bricks and mortar, I argued. Life was flesh and blood. She could fight him through the courts and have him evicted from her home, but once life was taken that was the end of the story. Then, I offered her an alternative solution. It swept over me in waves of certainty and an acceptance of my own future. I loved Amelia. I would do anything to protect her. But all my pleas were tearfully rejected. She put her hands over her ears, insisted that I must stop making preposterous suggestions. I could tell she regretted her decision to confide in me. By then, it was too late to put the genie back in the bottle, so to speak. We had both bared our souls to each other and were unable to return to a safer space where we could convince ourselves that we were exaggerating the awfulness of our realities.

Amelia agreed to make an appointment the following day to see a divorce solicitor. She promised to keep me informed in detailed letters about any further violence Nicholas inflicted on her. That way, she would create a record of his brutality, along with photographic evidence that we would use to discredit him when the time was right.

Later, we went outside to the garden to hang the glass butterflies from the apple tree. She held the ladder steady as I attached them to the branches. I'd crafted each one with love and their glittering hues rippled a rainbow across her upturned face. They swayed in the breeze as we made our way along the overgrown path at the end of the garden. We pushed through the overgrowth in search of the ice house. There it was, its red arch almost obscured by briar and ivy. That same mouldy atmosphere when we opened the door. The cobwebs and the cushions, the burned-out candles, the old curtains still hanging from the wall.

✦

This scene, so instantly familiar, brought me back to an evening when I told Amelia about my father's accusation. I was fifteen then and had carried it like an echo in my head for all those years. He'd seldom mentioned my mother's name or divulged any information about the catastrophic event—my birth—that had caused her death. He'd snap at me if I questioned him about her or asked to see photographs of myself as a baby. The reason for the latter, I would later discover, was that he had never taken any. I spat out the words he'd shouted at me in his drunken fury. It was the first time I'd spoken them aloud and Amelia listened until I could speak no more.

She put her arms around me. We would search for my mother's medical records and lay his lie to rest, she said. In the flickering intimacy of the ice house, I kissed her. A kiss of gratitude that turned into something else. Something neither of us were prepared to name at that stage. Her lips moved when she felt the brush of mine, but they did not open or surrender to my hunger. I pulled away and stared into her eyes. They glistened in the candlelight, tears at the corners ready to fall. Regret. Her eyes, not her lips told me I had to let the hope die, if I was to save our friendship.

That was the first time I acknowledged my yearning and accepted that this was not an erratic hormonal urge; it was something more profound. Something that would shape my future. I no longer had to pretend to enjoy the pulsating fumbling of teenage boys that I'd found to be amusing or irritating but which had never awakened me as Amelia did during that first hesitant kiss.

A week later, we found my mother's medical records among the clutter of old documents in my father's attic. Some secrets are best left beneath the eaves; some need to be dragged into the light. My anger grew as I read through the notes and discovered that I had just been delivered by emergency Caesarean when she, Anna Rossiter, the mother I would never know, suffered a fatal post-partum haemorrhage. How could I, a baby still gasping for breath, have caused her death? Why not blame the act of love between my parents nine months earlier? Or their mutual friend who'd introduced them to each other two years previously? How far back could I go on this interlocking chain reaction—back to the Garden of Eden, perhaps? That alluring apple? I felt light-headed, as if my father's words had finally escaped from a poisonous crevice in my mind.

We stopped using the ice house soon afterwards. So many projects to be undertaken and the dreaded Leaving exam hanging over us like the sword of Damocles. Excuses that made sense and prevented us from confronting what we were still unable to understand. In time, I confided in Amelia. Not the full truth—that I loved her and believed my feelings would never change—but a truth that would fork our lives in different directions.

As I grew more confident in my own skin, I told my father what I'd understood that evening in the ice house. He refused to believe me. There'd never been anything like that in his family, he said, as if lesbianism could be laid at the door of genetics. He waited for my "confusion," as he called it, to pass. When I showed no signs of bending to his will, he told me I'd degraded my mother's memory. She had sacrificed her life for an "aberration."

After that, it was impossible to live with him. I was twenty when I moved to New York and changed my name by deed poll to Annie Ross. I continued my training under an eccentric Italian who had learned his craft in Venice. In time, I became confident enough to establish the Clearwater Stained Glass Design Studio.

I was happy in New York, free in a way I would never be in Kilfarran. Heartache doesn't warm the other side of the bed and my expectations were not as demanding when I lowered the bar. Then, it was easier to settle for second best, third and fourth. They left me, those wonderful women, some tearful, some angry, all claiming I lacked commitment to our relationships. They were right. I remained unlucky in love, a woman in constant search of happiness. Was that where I went wrong? Should I have remained faithful to an ideal? Yearned for the moon? For her? No, that was not my nature but when my future changed in a way I'd never envisaged, the Big Apple proved too frenzied and challenging for me to continue living there. I needed the peace and isolation of a cottage on a rugged headland where, on a clear day, I could look across the ocean and imagine I could see America.

✦

That afternoon, when we closed the door of the ice house on our memories, neither of us mentioned the kiss. Had Amelia forgotten it, crushed it under kisses from the lips of others? Men like Nicholas, who had brutalised their love, or Jay, who had loved her so briefly before they were separated by his warring parents?

He'd returned to Kilfarran to visit his father and came with Mark that evening to Woodbine. They arrived with wine and pizzas and it seemed, for a short while, as if time stood still and it was like old times again... almost.

Amelia drank too much and danced with me, laughing as we reminisced about the dance school we had attended in our teens. As we moved together, tuned in to the same internal rhythm, I felt the slow burn of an old desire but I'd learned to hide my longing in the strength of her friendship.

When she danced with Jay I watched the spark between them reignite. Theirs had been such a short-lived passion, yet there was something so familiar about the sight of them together that the years in between seemed inconsequential.

We'd never understood how Jay's father had persuaded his mother —whom he had met when he was a student working in Californian *vineyards for the summer—to marry him and move to Kilfarran. California was sunshine and surfboards. Ireland was dulled by mist and history—but perhaps it was this colonised history that kept her here. Dolores Lee-O'Meara was African-American, a genealogist specialising in tracing the roots of those, like her, who were descended from African slaves. For seventeen years she'd tried to fit into this small village on the slopes of the Wicklow hills but she missed the sun and dreaded the drawn-out Irish winters. When Trevor O'Meara stubbornly refused to leave his sheep-breeding farm to move to California, she left him, taking her son and daughter with her. After their departure I'd comforted Amelia and reassured her that broken hearts mend. Watching them together that night at Woodbine, I wondered if either of them had really recovered from that summer when they exchanged hot-blooded kisses in the shade of Kilfarren Woods.*

In the taxi on the way back to the village, I told Jay the truth about Amelia's marriage. Was I right or wrong? Did my revelation change the direction of their lives or had destiny preordained what was to come? All I can say in my defence is that sometimes right and wrong don't matter. It is fate that determines the outcome of our decisions.

Jay loved Amelia. Perhaps he could achieve what I'd been unable to do and rescue her from a precarious and ugly future.

CHAPTER THIRTY-ONE

Amelia had already cleared away the wine bottles and the pizza cartons when Nicholas Skyped from London.

"Are you alone?" he asked.

"Yes, of course I'm alone." How easy it had become to lie to him —though, strictly speaking, she was being truthful. Mark was on his way back to Dublin and Leanne had left for Kilfarran Village in a taxi with Jay, who was flying back to California in the morning.

"How are you feeling?" Nicholas looked concerned, or was it suspicion that crossed his face? She could no longer tell the difference.

"I'm okay."

"You don't look okay, Amelia. Have you been drinking?"

Yes, suspicion—as always. "A glass of wine," she replied. "No need to stay off alcohol now, is there?" Her words, instantly regretted, hardened his expression.

"Are you blaming me again for the accident—?"

"No. I don't want to talk about it."

"Sooner or later, we have to talk. But for now, you need to rest. Yvonne will come over tomorrow with food."

"There's no need for her to call."

"There's every need." His eyes narrowed as he brought his face closer to the screen. "Have you seen yourself in the mirror? You're drunk."

"I had a glass of wine, Nicholas. I'm far from being drunk."

Could he detect her panic? Suspect that Jay's arrival had lifted her from the dulled apathy she had been unable to shake off since the loss of her baby?

"If you say so, Amelia. You can't blame me for worrying about you when I'm away from home. It's lonely here without you. Have you any idea of how desperately I miss you? I love you so much." His mood changes could occur in the middle of the mildest conversation and she could never gauge when his tone would soften or harden.

"Do you miss me?" he asked. His question was pointless. No matter how often she answered it, the constant reassurances he demanded from her would never be enough to satisfy him.

"Yes, I miss you."

"Then say it as if you mean it."

"I'm tired, Nicholas."

"Too tired to talk to your husband?"

"Yes."

"Obviously the wine has loosened your tongue."

"Probably." She knew this was true. Alcohol begot recklessness and blunted her fear.

Unable to endure the sight of his face any longer, she ended the call. She entered the small room she used as a home office and rummaged through a folder of documents. She removed some, including the house deed and the copy of her father's will that she had secretly requested from David Smithson. She stored these in a separate folder and replaced the original one in its filing cabinet. She shredded her marriage certificate, shoved the pieces into an envelope and added it to the new folder. Tomorrow, she would remove it to the ice house. No danger of Nicholas ever finding it there; the hostility between him and Billy Tobin had become irreconcilable since the removal of John's cross. He and

Jodie, Billy's late wife, had been like second parents to Amelia when she was a child. Now, her life had reached such a pass that she only visited Billy in secret.

She collected albums of photographs and spread their contents over the desk. How carefree she and Leanne looked; all those different teenage phases: brash Spice Girls, theatrical goths, the edgy post-punk rebellion of their late teens and the androgynous stage when they were in art college. Jay was in the photographs until he was sixteen. All those tears after he left. Amelia had believed she would never stop crying. She laid her hand over the dark eyes that stared back at her from a photograph taken at a school disco. Tonight, he had been wearing jeans and a T-shirt with a print of a music festival he had attended in Australia. His world seemed so expansive compared to her own narrow confines. Heat flowed through her as she recalled how they had danced together, laughing over his clumsiness when he stepped on her feet. The music had slowed and silenced them, late-night blues stirring old longings. Like a dream that had lain dormant for years until the touch of their hands brought it back to life. Could the past be resurrected so easily? she wondered. Or had she simply snatched a brief respite from the heartache of her marriage? Afraid to answer the question, Amelia switched off the light and climbed the stairs to her bedroom.

The doorbell rang as she was undressing. She dressed again quickly and ran downstairs in her bare feet, alarmed in case something had happened to Billy. No one else would call at this hour of the night.

Jay was standing outside and the lights of a taxi were disappearing round the bend in the driveway.

"What is it?" She was instantly alert. "Is everything all right with Leanne?"

"She talked to me—" He stopped, swallowed, steadied his voice. "Why didn't you tell me?"

She opened the door wider and walked ahead of him into the living room. "What exactly did she say?"

"Enough to know you have to leave him."

She sank down onto the sofa. That was the worst thing about confiding in others. Pretence was no longer possible. A truth she had tried to contain was loose and already beginning to change its form.

"This is my home. I can't just walk away from it. I've already discussed this with Leanne."

"Yes, I know. Like me, she can't understand why this house is more important than your own safety."

"It belongs to me. My father refused to allow Nicholas to have any share in Woodbine. I didn't understand his reasons for doing so but now, even though it's too late to make up for anything, I'm going to honour his wishes. I accused him, you see, and hurt him deeply. I deserve everything that's happened to me."

"Accused him of what, Amelia?" Jay sat beside her on the sofa and pulled her into his arms.

Overwhelmed by this memory, she began to cry. How easily she had allowed Nicholas to warp her mind, seeding it with innuendo and resentment, while the truth, the undeniable spark of his violence, had been hidden from her behind a gloss of charm. All this she told Jay, who gave her space to cry when she found it difficult to continue.

She was acutely aware of his nearness, and that his body, having shed the gangling awkwardness of those teen years, had the strength and fullness of a man in his prime. Finally, when she fell silent, it seemed so natural to lift her face to his, and to kiss his lips, as she had longed to do when they had been dancing together.

When did comfort change to passion? A spontaneous surge of desire that was at once familiar, yet thrillingly new. They undressed and lay together, skin on skin, electricity running through their fingers, everything forgotten; all swamped in the tumult of desire. He stayed with her until dawn had lightened the sky. He begged her to come with him to California. She had spent holidays in New York with Leanne and had the necessary documentation. But she remained firm in her decision to stay. Unlike Woodbine, love and passion were transient and she had learned to mistrust the storms of the body. Nicholas would never force her to abandon her home.

✦

Yvonne arrived at noon with home-made soup and a bowl of mixed salad. She heated the soup and set the table in the conservatory for two. The soup, thick and creamy, smelled delicious. Amelia barely tasted it.

"You have to start eating properly again." Yvonne gazed reproachfully at the bowl. "Nicholas is worried about you. That's why I'm here."

"Is he really?"

"What kind of question is that, Amelia? Obviously, he's worried. This depression—"

"I'm not depressed." She brought her attention back to her mother-in-law. "I'm recovering from a miscarriage and a blow to my head that could have killed me."

"If only you'd had the good sense to let Nicholas take care of painting the nursery." Yvonne sighed heavily, resignedly.

"You've made that point already, Yvonne. Please, don't let's go over it again."

"I'm sorry." Yvonne patted her knee. "I don't mean to keep reminding you of what you've lost."

"You're not reminding me. I remember what I've lost every moment of the day."

"Well, that's not good either." Joining her fingertips together, Yvonne pointed them towards Amelia like a gun. "Sad things happen. We have to put them behind us and move on with our lives."

Tearful and reproachful when Amelia was discharged from hospital, Yvonne had chided her for being so reckless. What on earth had possessed her daughter-in-law to climb a ladder in her condition? Why take such a risk when it was her responsibility to protect not only herself but her unborn son? "Sad experiences teach us hard lessons," Yvonne had said. "But you're young and strong. You and Nicholas will move on from this unfortunate event and have a brood of children."

Tell her . . . tell her the truth now. End this charade once and for all. The thought had surged through Amelia's mind but Nicholas's hand in hers, the warning pressure hurting her fingers, had kept her silent.

Amelia stared out at the garden, where the glass butterflies glinted, their incandescent wings poised in suspended animation. "Yvonne, I know you're anxious to help and I appreciate the food. But now, I just want to be left alone."

"I drove over here to oblige Nicholas. But I certainly don't want to intrude where I'm not wanted." Yvonne pursed her lips. Engorged from a recent injection of collagen, they dominated her small face and reminded Amelia of plump garden snails. Hurriedly banishing the image, she attempted to pacify her mother-in-law. "I'm tired, that's all. I told Nicholas not to bother you."

"He was anxious about leaving you alone. I promised him I'd have a chat with you, woman to woman." Yvonne pulled her chair closer to the table. "I've had my share of ups and downs in my marriage so I feel qualified to give you some advice. Nicholas loves you, Amelia. He wants to help you to get back on your feet again. Antidepressants are not the way forward and it's—"

"I don't take—"

"Have you considered counselling? It doesn't do any harm at certain times to let someone else help us to recover. I know an excellent woman—"

"I *don't* need counselling."

"How do you know until you've tried it? Unresolved issues can arise during pregnancy and, sadly, also after a miscarriage."

"What unresolved issues?"

"Your father's death, for instance. Nicholas said you accused him of having that cross you erected on the embankment removed."

"Does he always run to his mama when he's upset?"

"You're being rude, Amelia. He's my son and I can always tell when he's upset, no matter how hard he tries to hide it. He had nothing to do with the cross's removal but it suggests to me that you should talk to someone about…well, you know…" She paused. As always, her carefully bland expression was hard to read but Amelia, her senses painfully attuned to her mother-in-law's reaction, noticed the speculation in her gaze.

"Know what?"

"I'm not trying to upset you, dear. But I need to ask you a very sensitive question. Was your father always kind to you?"

The question oozed across the table towards Amelia. "What exactly do you mean?"

"John drank a lot." Yvonne stared at a spot above Amelia's head, the lift of her eyebrow suggesting she had noticed a cobweb dangling from the wall. "He was killed coming home from a pub. The coroner said the alcohol in his system—"

"My father was walking along a dark road and was knocked down by a hit-and-run driver. How dare you talk about him in that way?"

"In what way?" Yvonne dismissed the imaginary cobweb and stared at her daughter-in-law. "I simply asked if he gave you the respect and privacy a father should allow his daughter? Nicholas told me you and John had a painful conversation before he died."

"Nicholas had no right to discuss that with you. No right whatsoever." Amelia locked her fingers together, nails digging into the skin. "But I'll answer your question. My father's love for me was unconditional and pure. I made a dreadful mistake and will never forgive myself for doing so. Unlike your son, he had no dark side to his nature."

"Dark side?" Yvonne's shoulders shot back, her arms rising and opening out in a puzzled V. "What's that supposed to mean?"

"Nicholas beats me, Yvonne." Saying it aloud at last. Naming it, the accusation flat, ugly, free. "I'm your son's punchbag when he's upset. Does he discuss that with you?"

"Heavens above! What absolute nonsense."

"It's not nonsense. I've stayed quiet for far too long. You must know that Nicholas has a vile temper. When he doesn't get his own way, he can lash out without thinking about the consequences."

"I know nothing of the sort." Yvonne was on her feet, her cheeks enflamed. "How dare you turn this conversation round and imply that my son is violent towards you? Your father—"

"My father saw right through his charms. He never wanted us to marry. I should have listened to him."

Yvonne pulled on her jacket, her fingers trembling as she buttoned it. "It's just as well I have an understanding nature and can appreciate the stress you're going through. Otherwise, I'd find it impossible to forgive you." Her lips puckered in a bow of disbelief. "You need help, young woman. And soon, if you want to have any hope of saving your marriage."

Come away with me, Jay had begged until he ran out of words.

Bricks and mortar, Leanne had said. Not important enough to risk her life. With each entreaty, Amelia had felt her resolution harden, her determination growing. But, now, with Jay on a flight back to California and Leanne leaving soon for Kerry, her fear came crawling back. Nicholas would be home tomorrow. Would he, with his knack of burrowing into her thoughts, somehow realise that she had been unfaithful to him? A bloodhound feeding off suspicion, he was bound to notice something—a stray hair, a non-aligned cushion, her lips bruised with pleasure, her heart breaking.

After Yvonne drove away, the wheels of her car stirring dust into a fury, Amelia entered the ice house and hid the folder that held the tattered remnants of her marriage certificate.

CHAPTER THIRTY-TWO

She waited for Nicholas to bring up her conversation with Yvonne but, instead, he talked about New York. The limitless energy and opportunities in a city that never slept. They would sell Woodbine and with his severance package from KHM, they would begin again over there. A fresh start for both of them. He had bought her gifts, a cashmere pashmina, perfume, gold earrings that she had seen in a magazine and admired. He poured champagne into slender glasses and toasted their future. She answered him in monosyllables and sipped the champagne slowly, reluctantly, yet afraid to offend him, or upset his affable mood. Did he really believe she would sell Woodbine and leave her beloved home for a future with him? He filled her glass again, ignoring her protests that she had drunk enough, seemingly unaware, or uncaring, that she showed no interest in his plans.

The following morning, Amelia awoke to the sound of music. Gentle and soothing, it floated in and out of her consciousness. Her mind drifted, then gained force as she gathered her thoughts. The curtains were still drawn, the light in the bedroom dim. The ceiling began to spin as soon as she sat up. She fell back against the pillows, closed her eyes and lay perfectly still. Vertigo—she had had it once when she was a teenager. Her doctor had diagnosed a middle ear infection. She remembered the nausea, her staggering footsteps and her belief that the floor would pitch her forward if she wasn't holding on to the wall.

The door opened and Nicholas entered. "Breakfast is ready," he said.

She heard him set the tray down on the bedside table, felt the mattress sag as he sat on the side of the bed. His hand on her forehead was cool, his touch light as his fingers massaged her temples where two pincers of pain jabbed deep.

"Wake up, darling," he said. "It's almost noon. I'm going to open the curtains and let some light into the room."

She felt the sunshine press against her closed eyelids when he whisked the curtains across. Cautiously, she opened her eyes. He was back on the bed beside her, smiling. The warmth of his gaze, his tender touch. Terror cramped her stomach and she was afraid she would throw up over the duvet.

"Let me help you." He moved behind her and lifted her upright, plumped the pillows behind her. Why was he treating her like an invalid?

He suggested she start breakfast, but she shook her head. The tray was set with freshly squeezed orange juice, scrambled eggs, slivers of smoked salmon. The same breakfast as that previous occasion when she had tried to struggle her way out of the blackness. The morning after the KHM Christmas party, those images ingrained. He had fed her like a timid fledging then. Not this time.

"I don't want anything." Thankfully, the dizziness had passed and she was able to speak clearly. "Take the tray back downstairs."

"You're obviously still in shock but you must try to eat something. If you can't manage the scrambled eggs, at least have some tea and toast." He buttered toast, spread it with lime marmalade, poured tea.

"I'm not in shock," she snapped. "And I'm not hungry. I'll make something to eat later." Her headache was so intense that she was only vaguely aware of a stinging pain in her arms. Now, as that pain pulsed more strongly, she noticed the bandages for the first time. She stared at the white strip wound round her right upper arm. On her left arm a bandage had been wound below her elbow. Was she dreaming? No—the pain was too real to belong to a nightmare, throbbing, sharp as a blade. What had happened? She was unaware she had asked the question aloud until Nicholas clasped her face too tightly between his hands and said, "Thank God I found you before it was too late."

"What did I do?" Her skin felt dry and abrasive when she pressed her palms together. "Why are my arms bandaged?"

"Don't you remember?" he asked. "You did it in the bath. Both arms cut." His voice broke. "How could you do this to yourself? To us?"

"I wouldn't go near that bath." She pulled back from him and began to scrabble at the bandage on her right arm until she found the opening.

"I stopped the bleeding and cleaned you up. You kept talking about your father. I'd suspected as much but to hear you admit it was horrendous. All that hurt and resentment finally pouring out of you. My poor love, what you were forced to endure."

Insinuations. How many tentacles did they grow? Each one clinging to the same lie. Blood had seeped into the inner wrapping, rust-coloured and sickening to see. She unwound the last stretch of bandage. It had stuck to the wound, which began to bleed as she eased it off. She took the tissues he handed to her and stemmed the flow. The swipe of a blade. Pain, so sharp, the warm spill of blood, cries that no one but Nicholas could hear. This chilling certainty stayed with her.

"You can't make me believe I did this to myself," she whispered.

"Who else would do it?" He flung the challenge like a gauntlet before her. "You were zonked on those tablets you take at night and not responsible for your actions."

The bleeding on her arm was slight, the wound clean, superficial. The cuts on her other arm would be the same, she thought; but they came with a warning.

"You found release in pain," he said. "But cutting yourself is not the answer, my love. It's destructive, dangerous. Do you remember anything about last night?"

She shook her head, numbed by the horror of her suspicions. Her breakfast was cooling on the bedside table. Why had he chosen the same menu? That night had also been a shadow, dark and threatening. Then, as now, she was unable to emerge from its shade.

"Do you remember?" he repeated.

Numbly, she shook her head.

"Could you have double-dosed on those tablets?"

"Why would I do that?" She had taken a sleeping tablet shortly before she went to bed, welcomed the relief it would bring for the next six hours. Nicholas had remained downstairs, working on his laptop.

"Only you can answer that question, Amelia." He walked to the laundry basket and removed a bloodstained towel and her nightdress, similarly stained. "We need to talk about what you're going through. Self-mutilation is dangerous. Repressed memories equally so. I'm going to arrange an appointment with a therapist for you."

"I'm not the one who needs to see a therapist."

"This self-harming must never happen again." He ignored her comment and bundled her nightdress, along with the towel, back into the laundry basket. He removed a silver bowl in the shape of a curved leaf from the dressing table. Amelia used it to hold her rings and earrings. The only thing resting in its hollowed centre when he carried it back to the bed was a razor blade. He sat back down and balanced it lightly between his fingers.

"Why did you feel it necessary to lie to my mother?" he asked.

"What lies did I tell her?" A reason at last. Amelia fixed her gaze on the razor blade. Such a slender weapon, so slick and fast.

"You accused me of being a violent husband."

"How else would you describe yourself, Nicholas?"

"A husband who adores you. I don't have a 'dark side' to my personality, as you so dramatically put it. All I've ever wanted to do, and will continue to do, is to love you until death do us part. Think about what that means, darling. You could have slashed your wrists last night and drowned in the bath, especially as you had taken an overdose of tablets. I might not have found you in time. The preciousness of life. How easily it can be taken from us."

✦

She stayed in bed all day. She was unable to eat and refused food each time he carried a tray into the bedroom. What had happened to her last night? Another blackout? That was impossible. Apart from the two glasses of champagne he had pressed upon her, she had not touched alcohol since that evening with her friends. Two days since they were here. Two nights since Jay. The freedom in the air then. So palpable she could have hugged it. Now, it was sucked dry, acrid, and even the memory of Jay, his tenderness, the joy she had experienced in his arms, all gone, dispersed by this new terror. She pulled her nightdress from the laundry basket and examined the splatters of blood on the front of it. How could she have cut herself and been unaware that she was committing such a violent act? The only answer was the obvious one. Nicholas had cut her. This accusation almost choked her when he returned to the bedroom and laid a cup of coffee on the bedside table, but she forced herself to remain silent.

She stood in front of the full-length mirror after he left and examined the bruise on her left breast. Reddened skin, as if teeth had sunk deeply into the tender skin around her nipple. The same kind of mark on her thigh. Did it explain the dull, throbbing ache between her legs? The bloodstains on the nightdress blurred as she felt her mind exploding. The night of the Christmas party; she was back there again, hearing the roar of the sea. No… no… She clamped her hands to her head as she tried to force the images into a shape she could understand. She had been in the bath, water cascading, bubbles. Her legs going from under her. Eyes open, her body floppy, unresponsive, jolting. Tendrils of wet hair in her eyes, unable to fight back. Last night had been the same. Whatever had occurred during those forgotten hours was somewhere in her consciousness, waiting to be freed. He had found another way to violate her. Another memory stirred. Paper, she had signed something. She recalled the pen in her hand and Nicholas picking it up when it fell from her fingers. What document would demand her signature? Her will? It was the only answer. She had willed Woodbine to him in the event of her death?

The bandages had been tight on her arms, wrapped with clinical precision. No need for them. The wounds would heal easily. It was what they symbolised. A binding. Her throat tightened, as if his thumbs were already pressing hard against the carotid arteries.

Rohypnol. When he left for work the following morning, she keyed the word into her laptop. Impaired memory, partial amnesia, especially when mixed with alcohol, confusion, panic attacks, breathlessness. It was as she suspected. The drug of choice for men who need to prove they are not firing blanks. She wiped the history from her laptop, knowing that Nicholas would find a way to probe through the sites she had opened, the information she had absorbed, the memories that had been returned to her.

She walked to the empty space where her father's cross had stood. Leaves were beginning to turn, their green vitality seeping into the rustic hues of autumn, but Amelia could only see his body falling into the ditch below her. Water flooding his mouth, blinding him. Echoes rustled between the reeds and, in their sway, Nicholas's voice rushed upon her once again. It gurgled in the rising stream and it seemed as if her disjointed memories had become the spate of a river in full flow... *blue lights shining—jets of water... his hand on her mouth—whore, bitch, cunt—'til death do us part... I'll find you if you dare to leave me—I'll find you even if it takes forever...*

✦

The madness of those first letters. What a purging. Each violent act held up to the light and judged for what it was. Leanne wrote back by return of post, addressing the letters to Amelia's interior design studio. Nicholas opened every envelope that came to Woodbine. Nothing was safe from his curiosity; emails, texts, phone calls—all could be the breeding ground for her infidelity.

She shredded the letters as soon as she had read them, afraid to leave anything to chance. When he arrived unexpectedly at her studio one evening just as she was destroying Leanne's most recent letter, she shoved the page and envelope she was about to shred into her pocket.

It was, Nicholas said, the anniversary of their first date and he had booked a meal for her in their favourite restaurant, the Peach Tree. How could he remember a date that she had wiped from her memory? When she returned home, she added the envelope to the store of mementoes in the ice house, rushing back to the living room before he could notice her absence.

Her fear grew as the gap between sanity and madness began to close. Her fear of his willpower became deeper than her fear of water. Her longing to escape deeper than her love for Woodbine. Her affection for the old house had turned it into her prison and, two months later, knowing there was only one way to escape from his violence, she made her decision.

PART THREE

CHAPTER THIRTY-THREE

The Present

The policewoman is gentle but firm as she pries Elena's children from her arms. She hands them over to the social worker who has arrived to take them to a place of safety. Elena is escorted to the squad car and driven to Kilfarran Garda Station. In the interrogation room, she huddles in a chair, her mind spinning from one fragmented impression to another. Joel crying, Grace shrieking, black uniforms, hi-vis jackets, cold steel handcuffs on her wrists, the smell of coffee brewing on a hotplate, faces pressed too close, asking questions she can't answer, a glass wall with ears and eyes, a table in the interrogation room with scars scored into its surface . . . her children gone—*gone*—and Nicholas, his blood spilling from him.

She narrowly missed the aorta in his abdomen. Dully, she absorbs this information. Yvonne and Henry are keeping vigil by his bedside. He will recover, providing he does not develop sepsis from being stabbed with a rusting ice pick. She rocks back and forth as she lists the assaults she has suffered at his hands. Some are too hazy to remember clearly and she shakes her head each time she is asked for evidence. The only bruise she can show is on her neck. She knows what her interrogators are thinking. A bruise administered in self-defence when Nicholas tried to ward off her grievous attack. Why didn't she go to hospital when she was beaten up? they ask. Why didn't she call the gardai? Why didn't she leave Nicholas, take out a barring order against him, confide in her friends?

She is adrift, unable to think straight until Rosemary Williams arrives. She had heard about the attack on Nicholas from Christopher Keogh. KHM is in turmoil but Christopher, remembering the friendship between Isabelle Langdon and Rosemary, had decided to inform her that Elena had been arrested.

Rosemary had practised as a defence lawyer early in her career before retraining as a specialist in contract law. Her arrival at the police station proves that she has lost none of her assertiveness in the intervening years.

Elena is released on bail, the conditions clearly outlined to her. She must reside at Rosemary's address and not leave that jurisdiction until her next appearance in court. Nor is she allowed to trespass near Woodbine or Nicholas's parents' house, where her children will live for the foreseeable future. Elena knows she is lucky to be freed on bail. It is Rosemary's tenacity that has made it possible and this fact penetrates the numbness that has possessed her since she confronted Nicholas in the ice house. In the office of the small law firm that Rosemary opened after she was forced to resign from KHM, she silences Elena's tearful gratitude. She has appointed a barrister, a close friend from her student days, to represent Elena in court at her arraignment. The judge has demanded reports on her psychiatric and psychological state of mind before then.

Appointments are made. The experts nod sagely as they burrow into Elena's mind to try to understand why she would attempt to kill the father of her children. Was she suffering from post-partum depression? An inability to manage two babies? Depression after her mother's death? Labouring under the belief that Nicholas stole her inheritance? Scribble, scribble—they remain impassive as Elena struggles to prove she is not a vindictive and neurotic would-be killer. The evidence proves otherwise. After all, she did attack the man she had loved in happier times with an ice pick. They focus on her obsessive jealousy of his dead wife when Nicholas was struggling to move on from that tragic history. What are they to make of that?

Once again, Amelia Madison has become a headline. *Husband of Tragic Drowning Victim Stabbed*. Pictures of Mason's Pier have been plucked from the archives and shown on the news. So, too, are the replays of Nicholas leaving the church after the memorial service. Yvonne, supporting him, is dabbing her watery eyes with a handkerchief. Then, as now, she is offering him her unconditional love.

Maurice Turnbury, Elena's barrister, is a soft-spoken, colourless man with rimless glasses and sparse grey hair. His desk appears to be too large for him, but when he stands to greet her he projects an air of authority that reassures her.

"He looks harmless but don't be fooled by his appearance," Rosemary warned her on the way to their meeting with him. "He uses it to disarm the opposition. In court he's a viper and that's what you need in your corner."

Physical and mental abuse is difficult to prove without evidence. Maurice comes straight to the point. Is there anything Elena can say to convince him that Nicholas Madison is capable of violence?

"I found a letter in the ice house," she says. "I think it was written—"

"You *think*?" Maurice's question is sharp. His reptile gaze demands more than conjecture on her part.

"I *believe* it was written to Amelia. The sender warned her that her life was in danger."

"The name of her friend?"

"It was just one page. There was no name on it."

"Where is this letter now?"

"Nicholas tore it up. That's when I..." Elena hesitates, then decides she has to name it. "When I stabbed him."

"Did you mention this letter to the gardai?"

"Yes."

"What was their reaction?"

"The same as yours."

"Are you surprised?"

Dully, she shakes her head.

"You failed to convince the gardai that you were a victim of domestic abuse and now you want to add another layer to your defence by bringing his dead wife into the equation."

"Nicholas doesn't leave signs behind him." Rosemary interrupts the barrister's questioning. "I know that to my cost."

"I believe you're telling me the truth." Maurice ignores her comment but smiles at Elena for the first time since she entered his office. "But that's only because Rosemary wouldn't waste my time with a dud. However, a jury won't know that. Nor will the judge. Post-partum depression, that's our best line of defence."

"I wasn't depressed."

"How can you say that when you've told me you were being physically and mentally abused by your partner? It's the view of your psychiatric team that you display the classic symptoms. Low self-esteem and lack of confidence, an inability to cope, irritability, exhaustion."

"My baby is not responsible for that."

"I'm quoting from your medical notes. If we can prove that you were of unsound mind—"

"Unsound mind?"

"Temporarily."

"I was distraught, frightened for my life. That's not insanity."

"I never said you were insane, Elena. I'm just explaining what I consider to be the best course of action. You haven't been able to produce any evidence that you were acting in self-defence. If you plead not guilty, you'll be charged with grievous bodily harm. A guilty plea will do away with a trial and post-partum depression can be offered as a viable legal defence. You'll receive the necessary psychiatric treatment while you await your court appearance—"

"An asylum, that's what you're suggesting? Where's the justice in that?"

Maurice is patient but determined that Elena must listen to him. "The alternative is a prison cell. I'm not suggesting you'll be committed to an asylum, anyway. You're in Rosemary's care and you'll receive outpatient treatment. Nicholas's legal team will strongly oppose this measure, so the slightest infringement of your bail conditions will be disastrous for you."

A current of air passes through the small office and plays over Elena's face. She is convinced there are cold fingers pressing on the back of her neck. Amelia. This tingling awareness gives her the strength to listen carefully to Maurice. She thinks about the fatal decision Amelia made to escape the misery of her marriage. So many parallels. Elena could be her pale reflection. But there is one difference. Amelia chose death. Elena is determined to choose life. She is alert now, listening to Maurice as he elaborates.

Post-partum depression is the only explanation that makes sense. It's understandable, fixable, unlike the unseen fist and boot. Maurice will enter a plea of guilty by reason of insanity and a judge will sentence her to a rock or to a hard place.

Which will be more endurable?

CHAPTER THIRTY-FOUR

The word *Kingsdale* has been carved into a granite rock that stands at the entrance to the housing development where Yvonne and Henry live. The houses are detached and spread out around a large communal green space. Elena doesn't stop as she walks past their house, but nor does she quicken her pace. A slow saunter and a sideways glance over the gate. Only one car in the driveway. Henry must be at work. The house is screened by a high privet hedge and the gate has been tied with rope to prevent small children escaping.

She once lived in a similar development called Leeway Valley, where children played on the green and the residents organised annual sports days. In her teens, she would congregate there with her friends, drinking cans and smoking, until the council, tired of complaints from neighbours about noise at night, cut down the shrubbery and deprived them of their shelter. "The graveyard," that's what they used to call Leeway Valley. Elena had despised its suburban symmetry and unchanging routine. Now, she longs to wrap those safe structures around her once again. Instead, she must deal with a new normality. But this—this deliberate taking of her children—what is normal about that?

Yvonne and Henry's hatred towards her remains implacable. She almost killed their son and they are not prepared to listen to excuses about self-defence. They believe her unhinged from her inability to manage two babies and they have taken them into their care. Elena's court hearing to grant her visiting right to Grace and Joel has been postponed three times. Rosemary warned her that Nicholas's barrister would find every available legal loophole to delay the case. No matter how anguished the wait becomes, Elena must not do anything reckless or foolhardy to jeopardise her chance of a fair hearing. She has tried to be patient. All she wants is a glimpse of Grace and Joel. That will be enough—just a glimpse—and she is prepared to wait all day, if necessary. Her face is shaded by a hood and her zip-up hoodie and jogging pants are a nondescript grey.

Four days a week, she works at Rosemary's law firm. Business is beginning to pick up and being busy keeps Elena sane. Since that terrible morning Rosemary has been like a surrogate mother to her, a kind friend and a wise advisor. She is an early morning jogger who encourages Elena to rise early too and pull on a tracksuit. Elena hated it in the beginning, her body protesting as the road rose and fell under her. But only her body cried. She had no energy left for tears. She is swimming again, old rhythms returning. Sometimes, as she battles with the waves and the cold rush of the Irish Sea, she feels the return of that familiar exhilaration and welcomes it, despite its briefness. To forget everything except the buoyant waves and sting of salt is amnesia at its most powerful. But as she drags herself from the water, it is no longer possible to pretend that her life—and her children *are* her life—has not been taken from her.

A man emerges from a neighbouring house and jogs past her. Further up the road, a silver-haired woman is walking two dogs on leads. Elena crosses the road to the green, where a horse chestnut tree has shed its leaves. The tree and a semicircle of dense foliage form a natural boundary to the road. It will shelter her from the houses on the opposite side but she will be visible if anyone walks across the green. A stranger in a hoodie will be enough to alert suspicions in this quiet development.

Children have forged paths between the shrubbery's burgeoning roots. So, too, have teenagers, if the empty beer bottles and cans are any indication. Some things never change. She moves into this leafy space and crouches down. Drivers leave for work and children amble towards the nearby school. This spurt of activity is soon over and Kingsdale settles back into a mid-morning quietness.

Her patience is rewarded when a car draws up outside Stonyedge. Nicholas has changed his Porsche for an ice-blue BMW. Adrenalin pumps through Elena as she watches him untie the rope from the gate. His jeans and bomber jacket suggest he has taken a day off work. She searches for signs that her attack on him has had an impact but he appears to have fully recovered, if his brisk walk is any indication. Yvonne opens the door before he reaches it. Unlike her son, she is dressed formally, in a red, pencil-slim skirt and matching jacket, a scarf draped over her shoulders. Nicholas hunkers down and holds out his arms to the children. Grace... How fast she runs, fleet on her feet, while Joel clings to Yvonne's neck. Their shrieks reach Elena, as does Nicholas's laughter. Once so familiar and dear to her, now it grates against her ears. She longs to drown it out and listen only to her children. She parts the branches for a better view. Nicholas takes Joel under his arm and holds Grace's hand. Her daughter's excited voice reaches Elena, who strains forward in an effort to hear what she is saying. Yvonne accompanies them to the car, nodding, talking, making hand gestures, as Nicholas straps them into the back seat.

Elena reads his impatience in the lift of his shoulders as his mother continues talking. Unlike Elena, Yvonne has never been forced to analyse his body language, listen for his change of tone, the lift of an eyelid that signals a mood swing. Is it possible that she has no idea that her son is capable of both instinctive and calculated violence? Could his childhood have been as exemplary as Yvonne insists? Surely, there must have been signs of his cruelty: flies with wings torn off, schoolboys who had been bullied and battered, tearful girls who were charmed, then belittled and sullied by his scorn, his indifference? All Elena knows about his past is what she has seen in that album of smiling family photographs. She clenches her fists, beats them silently against her knees as he eases his long body into the car and turns on the ignition. Yvonne waves him off. Have Grace and Joel waved back? It's impossible to see through the tinted windows. She has pins and needles in her legs. They will give way if she tries to stand.

When the car has disappeared from sight and Yvonne has returned to the house, Elena rises, grimacing as she stamps her feet. She is about to emerge from the makeshift shelter when Yvonne reappears. Her bridge morning. Always on a Friday, Elena remembers as she hunkers down again. Yvonne reverses from the driveway and, in the hush that settles after her departure, Elena is taunted by the sight of that empty house.

She resists the pull until her head begins to throb and another form of reasoning takes over. This graveyard place will be devoid of life until the afternoon. All she needs is a few minutes to check out whether her children are receiving the love they deserve.

If Rosemary knew what she was doing on her day off... Elena refuses to think about her reaction. She crosses the road before she can change her mind. The privet hedge shelters her when she enters the driveway. She rings the doorbell, ready to run if she hears movement from within. The chimes have an echo, a harsh pitch that suggests too much empty space. Moving quickly, she enters the side passage, where she is hemmed between the gable wall of Stonyedge and the dividing wall that separates the two houses. A wooden gate at the end of the passageway blocks her entry.

The distance between the detached houses is slight, about the width of a wheelie bin, she reckons. The wall is low enough to climb and allows her the momentum to heave her body over the gate. A jump to the ground; she lands catlike, a cat burglar, and smiles grimly. She opens the door to a garden shed. Nicholas once mentioned that a spare key was always kept under a tin of paint. She examines the tins lined up along a high shelf, hoping that this is still true. All have been opened and used, dried stains on their outsides. She checks underneath three tins before she uncovers the key.

The house to the rear of Stonyedge has been built on a rise and the occupants have an unobstructed view into the Madison's back garden. Exposed, Elena imagines eyes fixed on her as she unlocks the patio door. She has gone too far to stop now and steps quickly inside when the door slides open. The kitchen is spotless. She touches the sterilising unit containing Joel's bottles. She opens the fridge where Yvonne has stored the children's dinners in food storage containers, each one labelled with its contents and the child's name. Yvonne, methodical and practical as always. What a disorganised muddle Elena must have seemed to her.

Upstairs, her footsteps sink silently into soft carpets as she moves from room to room. Grace's bed has a duvet with a picture of Peppa Pig. Her clothes are folded in drawers, rows of underwear, jumpers as neat as a display in a department store, tights, leggings, dresses. Elena cannot see anything her daughter had worn before they were separated on that fateful morning. The pictures on the walls are also unfamiliar. She searches for a photograph of herself, unable to believe Yvonne or Henry have made no effort to provide one. The photograph on the bedside table is of Grace and Joel at a picnic with their father and grandparents. She resists the temptation to raise the frame above her head and smash it off the wall. Fury will not serve her purpose. She needs to remain in control but her hands tremble when she replaces the frame in its original position. She lifts a jumper from a drawer and holds it to her face. She longs to breathe in the scent of her daughter but all she can smell is fabric freshener. She could be standing in the room of a child stranger. The jumper looks lumpy when she attempts to fold it back into the drawer with the same precision as she found it. She shakes it out, tries again. She must focus—*focus*. This time, her attempt is passable and she slides the drawer closed.

She glimpses her reflection in a pink-framed mirror. The natural colour is returning to her hair. She has had it cut short to hasten the process and the cropped style highlights her haggard features. Her eyes seem enlarged, their colour dulled from medication. She is afraid to stop taking the correct dose of prescribed tablets in case it jeopardises her hard-gained bail, yet here she is, risking everything for what? She must leave now, this minute, slip away as quietly as she entered. Head down, she moves across the landing—and stops at the open door to Joel's room.

Thomas the Tank Engine is obviously his passion—or Yvonne has decided that for him. Duvet, curtains, wallpaper, all the same. His drawers are as organised as Grace's and the photograph beside his bed shows the same configuration, only this time the five of them are sitting on a bench in a playground. Nicholas is preparing his ground for a custodial hearing, each photograph projecting the smiling features of a caring father and adoring, trustworthy grandparents. Elena remembers the nights she waited in vain for him to come home from work to say goodnight to his children. Whenever he did manage to see them before they fell asleep, his interaction with them was brief, the earlier enthusiasm he had shown when they were newly-born fading as they grew more demanding.

"They're not interesting at these ages," he told her once. "It'll be different when they're older."

The front door slams. Rigid, her hands gripping the edge of Joel's cot, she hears footsteps mounting the stairs. The bedroom door is still ajar but the footsteps stop before they reach her. Another door is opened, closed. She sags with relief and moves to the window to check the driveway. As she suspected from the heavy tread, it's Henry who has arrived home.

Relieved that he hadn't entered the kitchen and noticed the unlocked door, she leaves Joel's room. Rosemary's warnings ring loudly in her ears as she descends the stairs. The step that creaks sounds like a scream. Afraid to stop, she runs through the kitchen and locks the patio door from the outside. In the shed, she crouches down and tries to remember which paint tin was used to hide the key. Had she found it under the green or the yellow? Unable to decide, she shoves it beneath a tin in the middle of the row.

"Stay where you are, punk." Henry is standing behind her, no longer soft-voiced or affable. "If you move I'll crack your head in two with this axe."

Elena stands and pulls both ends of the hood tightly over her forehead and cheeks. He is correct about the axe. It swings loosely from one hand, deceptively so. She recognises the charged-up energy Nicholas always projected before he struck her. But Henry is not violent like his son...or is he? What does she know about anyone anymore? Elena thinks over her options. She can charge into him and try to knock him over, but he will catch up with her before she has climbed the gate.

"Don't even think about it." Henry, reading her mind, blocks the shed doorway. Does he have that same canny awareness as Nicholas? The ability to know how she will react to a given situation? Maybe he is more like his son than she thinks. "There's a squad car on the way," he continues. "You can explain to the guards why you broke into my house."

"Put the axe down, Henry." She pulls back the hood and lifts her chin defiantly. The last time she saw him he was stony-faced, avoiding her eyes across the courtroom while the judge decided whether or not bail should be granted.

"Good grief!" He steps backwards, his craggy face wrinkling with shock. "What the hell are you doing here?"

"I had to come." The explanation is simple but useless. "I've tried so often to see my children. Nicholas keeps delaying my appeal for visiting rights and no one answers my letters or takes my calls—"

"That's because we're under no obligation to do so." His tone is harsh but the pumped-up aggression has left him. Keeping his eyes on her, he reaches behind him and props the axe against the wall. "You lost your right to the care of those children when you attacked their father."

"He was violent towards me. You must believe me. How long are you and Yvonne going to close your eyes to his behaviour?"

"My son is not a violent man. He loved you—"

"He pretended to love me, just as he pretended to love Amelia. He destroyed us both."

"You're lying." He sounds sad but certain. "I was so pleased when Nicholas met you. A new beginning for him, I thought. But you could never cope with playing second fiddle to his feelings for Amelia."

"Is that what he's told you?"

"It's what I saw with my own eyes. You imitated her. The hairstyle, the make-up, the same clothes. You lost yourself, Elena. And then you turned on Nicholas—"

"You're right." She nods, dully. "He mesmerised me and I allowed it to happen. When he beat me, he made sure the marks didn't show. He'd had time to practise on Amelia. That's why she went into the water. Death was preferable to being married to your son."

She thinks he will bring her to the ground. The tension in his body—she knows the signs. The closing down of emotion until all that remains is the blood urge. She shrinks back, as if she can already feel the impact of his fists.

"I won't allow you to make those wild accusations about my son." His shoulders slump, his hands uncurl. "You've broken your barring order. I'll make sure you take full responsibility for breaking into my house."

"I *won't* be silenced, Henry—"

"We both know what will happen when the police arrive." He cuts her short and checks his watch. "They should be here in two minutes or less. Whatever chance you had of getting your children back again has been wiped out by your recklessness. Nicholas could have died by your hand—"

"Amelia told you, didn't she? That's why Yvonne called her a diva. She said there was always some drama going on around her. But, being beaten up is not a drama—"

"*Stop.*" He licks his lips, as if aware that spittle has dried on the corner of his mouth. "You retracted the statement you made to the police. My son has a clean slate but you, on the other hand, are mentally deranged. What credibility does that give you?"

"Did Amelia confide in—"

"No, she did *not*," he shouted. "I refuse to listen to any more of your babbling nonsense." He steps to one side and stares above her head. "If you have another truth, then go and find it."

The doorway is clear, a channel to freedom. Is he toying with her? Will he pin her to the wall as she runs past, drag her down from the gate when she tries to climb it? Henry is not like his son . . . not like his son . . . Elena lowers her head and sprints past him. He makes no effort to detain her as she clambers over the gate. She is free and running towards the shrubbery on the green.

A squad car is coming. Blue lights flash and the silver-haired woman, returning with her dogs, stops and then hurries onwards, afraid, no doubt, that burglars have been at work while she was out walking. Elena watches through the leaves as the squad car pulls up outside Stonyedge. Two policemen in hi-vis jackets walk up the driveway to where Henry is waiting for them. At the end of the road, there is a shortcut into a shopping centre. He points towards it and when the squad car disappears in that direction, Elena moves from her hiding place and walks away.

Is Henry watching her? *If you have another truth, then go and find it.* Did he really utter those words? Is it possible that he believes her? Does he know the truth about Amelia's marriage? Unlike Elena, she had not been too proud to confide in a friend. A few sentences from a torn letter. Elena tries to remember the order in which she read them. *It's time you stopped pretending you can force him to leave... His violence is inexcusable... please... please listen...*

CHAPTER THIRTY-FIVE

Henry is a tormented man. I met him only once, and that was shortly after my conversation with Amelia. I'd returned to Kilfarran for Mark's thirtieth birthday, which he was celebrating at his parent's home with his partner, Graham, who would soon become his husband. Amelia and Nicholas had also been invited on that Saturday night but Nicholas had phoned late that afternoon to explain why they would be unable to attend. Amelia, it seemed, had a migraine.

The following day I called to Woodbine in the afternoon. When no one answered the doorbell, it was obvious from the cars in the driveway, three, to be exact, that they were at home. I heard voices and followed the sound round the side of the house to the back garden, where a barbecue was underway. His parents were present and Nicholas, masking his displeasure, made me welcome. Amelia flung her arms around me and held me too tight. "Stay," she whispered. "Please stay."

The sun shone for the afternoon and Nicholas, in a butcher's apron and chef's hat, made a great show of cooking steaks, burgers, sausages, kebabs. His charm was effortless, an embracing web of strands that Amelia seemed unable to break. I'd no appetite but he piled my plate, even though all I managed to eat was a kebab. He remarked on the weight I had lost and claimed I was just a few pounds off being scraggy. He was right about my weight. Climbing a headland and bending into the wind blowing off the Atlantic burned energy.

I saw the look Amelia gave him. The anger that flared in her eyes but died away just as quickly.

Yvonne's manner towards her that Sunday afternoon was chillingly polite. They had argued over Nicholas. Amelia didn't go into the details but it was obvious that bitter words had been exchanged between them.

Later, when I was sitting alone in a bower on a bench for two, Henry joined me. I still don't know what possessed me to tell him about Nicholas. It needed to be said but there was no easy way to explain what was going on between him and Amelia. What did I hope would happen? That a father would turn against his beloved only son? Henry's face became ever more austere as he listened to my stammered suggestions that he speak to Nicholas about his violence. He accused me of being jealous.

"I know you have feelings for my daughter-in-law," he said. "But that's no reason to tell such slanderous and hateful lies about my son." He said much more than that, and I to him, our voices pitched low, as if our argument would strike a tinderbox if overheard. That is why I think he believed me. We parted on bad terms. A weak man like my father, living with his own illusions. Most of us do, one way or another. We mould the world to our own reality and then wonder why it leaves us on the outside looking on in bewilderment.

CHAPTER THIRTY-SIX

Elena wheels the mountain bike that once belonged to Rosemary's husband from the garage. Unused since his death four years previously, it needs dusting off but it's still in working order. The journey to Woodbine takes over an hour. She is flushed and sweating by the time she reaches Kilfarran Lane. A canopy of bare branches twine overhead and the sun spangles the country road. The jittery feeling in her stomach is almost unbearable as she nears the old house. As usual, a bunch of fresh flowers lies on the grassy embankment. Nicholas mustn't have had a chance to dump them in the bin yet; and even when he does so, Billy will just ensure that new fresh flowers will be on the same spot tomorrow.

"He's remembering his friend," she said to Nicholas once. "Why should you object to that?"

"For reasons I'm not prepared to discuss with you," he'd replied in the flat, expressionless voice he used when she irritated him. "Don't ask me again." His warning was implicit. As well as silencing her, it prevented her accepting Billy's invitation to have tea at his house. This fear had caused her to walk straight past him whenever they saw each other on the road or in the village. She had always kept her head down on these occasions, fearful that, if she talked to him, Nicholas would discover she'd disobeyed him. Even when he was abroad on business, his eerie ability to know when she was lying or hiding something from him had had a paralysing effect on her.

Christmas had passed without Elena's custodial case being heard, cancelled again on a technicality his barrister unearthed. The new year slid into spring and Grace's second birthday in March came and went without Elena being able to see her daughter. She had resisted the urge to lurk outside Stonyedge on the day, knowing she would be unable to restrain herself if she saw balloons attached to the gate. Joel's first birthday came shortly afterwards. As it had been with Grace, the card and present Elena sent were returned to Rosemary's address, unopened. Once again, she had resisted the temptation to see them. Henry would have been watching out for her. No more second chances with him. She still finds it hard to believe he did not report her break-in to the police. He can't have told Nicholas or Yvonne; if he had done so, Elena would be incarcerated by now and not free to break her bail conditions once again.

Billy is on his knees weeding the borders of his lawn. The helmet and dark glasses gives Elena a degree of anonymity but she still increases her speed in case he recognises her.

She stops a short distance beyond the boundary wall surrounding Woodbine. A small gate leading into a field is almost hidden by an overhanging hedgerow. Cautiously, checking her surroundings, she opens the gate and wheels the bike along a narrow trail by the side of the field. It curves around the back of Woodbine and the broken boundary wire has been trampled underfoot by those who investigated the scene of her crime.

The ice house is still standing. A police cordon, broken in places, sags from supporting poles. Elena pushes the door open and shines her torch into the interior. Nicholas's blood forms a black, grotesque map on the floor. Even when it is cleaned away, that residue of violence will have permeated the old stone. She reaches into the shelf where the folder had been hidden and feels only dust, grit, cobwebs. Henry probably took the folder away on Nicholas's instructions. It must now be in his possession. She checks the shelves and hollowed spaces. There must be something here that will help her to fight for custody of her children. Otherwise, why the compulsion to come here?

Eventually, she is forced to accept that she has had a wasted journey. A gust of wind whips the door open. She recoils from the dust that it stirs and coughs at a dry tickle in her throat. A flicker of white catches her eye. A mouse scurrying to safety, she thinks, but quickly realises it is a piece of paper. An envelope. She picks it up and brings her torch closer to it. The handwriting is instantly recognisable; she remembers dropping this envelope when Nicholas entered the ice house. It must have lodged in one of the crevices before the wind could blow it free. Her hand trembles as she studies the address. This is the reason she is here. She can feel Amelia's presence around her. Amelia's breath on her face, her hand gently pushing her from the ice house, where it could be dangerous to linger any longer.

She blinks as she emerges into daylight and makes her way through the trees. Woodbine is visible from this vantage point. Nicholas is at work, and the old house is empty. She had always felt like a stranger there, but now, forbidden to go near it, she wants to touch its walls, walk its floors, as she did so often with Grace or Joel in her arms. Nicholas had broken her so easily and she had blamed Woodbine for her own self-loathing and the obliteration of her identity. Finding herself again, shattered in heart but whole in person, is restoring her confidence but fear can still force her to a sudden standstill. She continues on without stopping until she reaches the end of the field, then wheels the bike onto Kilfarran Lane.

As she cycles past Billy's house she glances across to see if he is still in his garden. Startled, she pulls on the brakes, unsure whether she has imagined his crumpled figure on the ground. She abandons the bike outside the gate and runs towards him. As she approaches, he tries to rise, then collapses again. His pallor reminds her of putty. Beads of sweat stand out on his forehead.

"What's wrong?" She is unsure whether he can hear her. "Do you need an ambulance? Where's your phone, I'll call emergency." Despite this crisis, Elena's self-survival reflex has kicked in. Even if Billy won't recognise her in the helmet and dark glasses, she can't risk a phone call being traced back to her. The ambulance driver might ask her name and how she came upon the scene. If she is caught breaking her barring order, she will have lost all hope of visiting her children.

"No need," Billy gasps. "Too much exertion."

"I don't think so." She helps him to sit up. "Whatever is wrong with you, it needs to be checked out."

His legs wobble when he tries to stand. He leans heavily on her as she leads him to the stump of a nearby tree. He removes his mobile from his pocket and hands it to her. She dials emergency and explains his symptoms: dizziness, shortness of breath, excessive sweating.

"I need another stent," Billy says when she finishes the call. She has to bend close to hear him. He sounds resigned, unsurprised.

"Don't worry," she reassures him. "An ambulance will be here shortly and the paramedics will have everything they need to look after you."

He sways and closes his eyes. If he collapses she will have to resuscitate him. She learned how to do the procedure in Australia. She and Zac took classes together with a view to training as lifeguards. How long ago that seems. Another world entirely. To her relief, she hears the ambulance siren in the distance.

"They'll be with you in a moment." She needs to leave now. "Everything is going to be all right."

"Thank you, Elena," he says.

His eyes are open, his dulled gaze focused on her. She pulls off her dark glasses, hunkers before him. "Are you going to tell Nicholas I was here?"

"I wouldn't tell that weasel the time of day. You go on, now. I'm a tough nut to crack." He forces a smile and gestures towards the gate.

Head down, feet pumping, she cycles in the opposite direction to the ambulance.

✦

Later, alone in her room, she tries to decipher the postmark on the envelope. It is smudged and dusty but with the help of a magnifying glass, she eventually makes out the name *Rannavale*. Google Maps shows its location. A small town in West Kerry. She holidayed in Dingle once with her mother. A dolphin jumping, mountain peaks hidden in cloud, magnificent scenery, vast, wild and expansive. Picturesque villages, cattle meandering along rutted lanes, scattered farms; finding the sender in that huge area would be like searching for a needle in a haystack. Her earlier elation fades. That is how she is these days, either feverish or apathetic. She holds the envelope up to the light as if there was a name in invisible ink that will be revealed to her. She is no wiser when she slips it into a drawer and goes downstairs to prepare an evening meal for Rosemary.

Later, as she is about to fall asleep, she remembers where she has seen the handwriting. A scrawl on the back of a photograph, that was it. The woman with the shaggy white-blonde hair and the cool, appraising, green stare. Her life in New York chronicled. Somehow those flourishes suit her.

CHAPTER THIRTY-SEVEN

Four days later, Billy is out of bed and sitting in an armchair when Elena visits him in hospital.

"Two new stents," he says. "That makes four altogether. Piece of cake." He sounds proud enough to brandish a "heart recovery" trophy at her. "I'm to be discharged tomorrow."

"I was very worried about you." Elena perches on the edge of his bed. "You look a lot better than the last time I saw you."

"You saved my life."

"I doubt it. Like you said, you're a tough nut to crack."

"Enough about me. How are *you*?" He lowers his voice, as if asking such a question might upset her.

"I've been better, as you can imagine."

He nods, his expression grim. "I don't know you well, Elena. But this much I do know. There was a reason for whatever happened in that ice house. You're a kind young woman and Nicholas is a hard man. I never liked him, and that's a fact."

"You must be the exception to the rule, Billy. Most people find him utterly charming, including the police."

"John didn't."

"John?"

"Amelia's father."

"Ah . . . the flowers."

He nods. "Amelia used to leave them there all the time. After she died, it seemed right to carry on the custom."

"Why did Nicholas always remove them?"

"He could never forgive John for trying to break up his relationship with Amelia." Billy scratches the nape of his neck. "Nicholas doesn't forgive easily, even if the person who crossed him is dead. I always hoped you'd drop in for tea with the young ones."

"I'm sorry, Billy."

"No need to apologise. It wasn't difficult to see that he was changing you."

"How could you tell?"

"You reminded me of Amelia before she died. Your demeanour, the way you dressed. And the way you walked, like there was lead in your shoes, yet I'll hazard a guess you were a vibrant lassie before you met him."

"Was Amelia?"

"She was a terrified little girl after the accident that took her poor mother. Wouldn't go near water for love nor money. Jodie, my wife, used to look after her. For months afterwards, she'd just sponge Amelia down and the poor child would be trembling like a leaf. Terrible it was, for a while, but between the two of us we brought her through it—and John too."

Elena imagines Amelia as a child. A skinny little girl, trembling at the sound of running water. She blinks, her eyes glistening, but tears are only a distraction.

"She grew out of it, eventually," says Billy. "She was a lively kid growing up. Me and Jodie never had children so we used to call her our 'almost daughter.'"

"You must have known her friends."

"She used to hang out with Jayden and Mark. Can't remember their surnames now. The old memory, you know. Then, of course, there was Leanne. A right pair, they were, always up to some devilment. They used to put on concerts. They were great dancers but not so good at the singing. Not that that stopped them. I remember they loved the spicy girls."

"You mean the *Spice* Girls?"

"Whatever." Billy shrugs. "Then there was that time when, I swear to God, the pair of them looked like Dracula's brides. White faces and net stockings, that kind of thing. Then Leanne dropped out of art college and left for New York."

"Is that where she still lives?" Elena's spirits sink, but Billy is shaking his head.

"Last I heard she'd come back and was living somewhere out West Kerry way."

"Rannavale?"

"Could be, though that name doesn't ring a bell. It was some headland or other. Named after a horse, far as I remember. Amelia was married to that weasel by then and I don't think they were much in touch with each other. Nicholas made sure of that. How Amelia stood for it, I'll never know."

"But she didn't, Billy."

"True enough." His brow furrows. "Strange to think that mother and daughter went the same way, God rest their souls."

"Would you recognise this handwriting?" Elena shows him the envelope. "Could it belong to Leanne?"

"Could be," he says after studying the writing. "But I wouldn't swear an oath on it."

"Do you have a surname for her?"

"What is it now?" He taps his forehead. "Like I said, my memory's shot to hell these days. As soon as I try to remember names, they run away from me... ah, yeah, Ross—Rossiter, that's it. Leanne Rossiter. Her father was a martyr to the drink. Took him in the end, it did." He pauses, wary of intruding. "Any word on when your case will go to trial?"

"The arraignment will take place in three months."

"How are you pleading?"

"I did it, Billy. There's only one way to plead."

"Did you tell the police he was violent?"

"They didn't believe—"

She stops abruptly when the patient next to Billy curses loudly as he tries to leave his bed. His right leg is in plaster and his struggle with his crutches adds to his colourful vocabulary. For an instant, he looks as if he will topple over. On regaining his balance, he swings round on his crutches and says, "I'm going to the shop for a paper. Can I bring you back anything, Billy Boy?"

"Nothing, thanks, Red. I can hardly close the door of the locker for the amount of biscuits and chocolates in there."

Billy introduces her. Red is a biker, bearded and heavyset, his ponytail as grey as his fuzzy beard. He broke his leg when he took a tumble off his Harley.

"Did Amelia confide in you?" Elena asks when Red has left the ward.

Billy frowns, shakes his head. "I wish she had. I'd have taken him apart if I'd known for sure. Did you ever tell anyone how he treated you?"

"I was so ashamed and frightened, also, of what he would do. I still am."

"Will you come and see me when I'm discharged?"

"I'm not allowed near Kilfarran Lane. I took a chance the last time. I might not be so lucky the next time."

"Then we'll meet somewhere neutral. I want to talk to you about something but this is not the place for it."

He stops as a nurse wheeling a blood pressure monitor walks towards him.

"I'll have to ask you to leave," she says to Elena. "Visiting time is over." She briskly pulls the screens around the bed, her stern expression warning Elena not to linger.

CHAPTER THIRTY-EIGHT

Rannavale is exactly as Elena imagined. Flower baskets above shop doorways, a pub with white wrought-iron furniture out front. A busy petrol forecourt with a convenience store attached. The post office is located in the centre of the main street, a nondescript, grey building, quiet at this time of day.

"What can I do for you?" The woman behind the grid has a protruding lower lip and a pale-blue stare that tries to place Elena in some recognisable context. Unable to do so, she waits for her to speak.

"I'm searching for the sender of this." Elena slides the envelope under the grid. "It was posted from here by someone called Leanne Rossiter."

The woman's lower lip drops fractionally as she studies the postmark. "That was posted years ago."

"This is all I have to go on. It's important that I contact her. Does anyone by that name come in here regularly?"

"Are you from the gardai?" Her eyes narrow to a squint.

"Absolutely not. But I need an address and I'm hoping you can help me."

"I'm afraid I can't give out confidential information about our customers."

"Please, it's *vital*—"

"Let me stop you there." She shakes her head, apologetically. "Even if I knew anyone called Leanne, I wouldn't be able to help you.

But I can't recall anyone by that name using this post office. We're a small community and I know everyone. Perhaps the person who sent the letter was passing through. We get a lot of tourists here."

Elena is not surprised. Rannavale has a postcard quality that seamlessly unifies the past with the present. Unable to tease any further information from the postmistress, she continues along the main street, stopping now and then to ask the same question of people passing by. No one is able to help her.

At the end of the main street, the sound of rushing water draws her towards a bridge. Down below, a river freewheels over stones. On the riverbank a heron, head erect, appears to be staring directly at her. A dog runs towards the bridge, yellow-coated and sturdy. A male dog, who plonks his front paws against the bridge wall and barks at the heron. Elena tries to guess the breed but there's too much of a mix in him to decipher. His owner has shrunk into old age and walks slowly with the help of a stick.

"Good day to you, Miss." He touches a cap pulled low over his brow and stops beside the dog. "I see you've met Custard."

"He's a fine dog."

"He's like his name, soft and yellow-bellied."

"He looks fierce." Elena stretches tentatively towards the dog and fondles his ears.

"Just shows, doesn't it?" The man nods. "Appearances can be deceptive."

"I agree." Her mouth twists her smile away.

"You're a stranger to these parts." He states this as a fact, not a question, and makes no attempt to hide his curiosity. "A Dublin lass, from the sound of the accent. Are you visiting or staying?"

"Visiting. I'm trying to find someone called Leanne Rossiter but I don't have an address for her."

"Let me see now." He lights a pipe, his movements slow and certain, his fingers still nimble. The dog, clearly knowing he won't be moving for a while, lies down on the bridge and closes his eyes. "Did you check with Kitty at the post office?"

"Yes. She wasn't able to help me."

"She'd know, right enough. I can't recall a Leanne Rossiter myself. What makes you think she lives in Rannavale?"

"It's on the postmark." She shows him the envelope. "A friend told me she's living on a peninsula called after a horse. Is there anywhere like that around here?"

"The nearest peninsula is Magdalen's Head. Nothing horsy about that." He puffs vigorously on his pipe and observes her through a pall of smoke.

"Is there a riding stable nearby?" She can't give up on Leanne Rossiter yet. "Could there be a farm or a pub with a horsy name?"

"Not to my mind, there isn't. But, wait a minute, now." He removes the pipe from his mouth and studies the bowl. "We call it Mag's Head for short. Your friend wouldn't have got it wrong and called it Nag's Head, by any chance?"

"I've no idea. How far away is it?"

"About twenty miles out the road. It's a lovely spot but lonely, I always think. Now that I remember, there's a woman living there called Annie Ross, if that's any help to you. The only reason I know her name is because she came to me once looking for a soldering iron. I used to run the hardware store here. Retired since then. It's been turned into a Chinese, so it has. I didn't have what she wanted and that was the only time I'd any contact with her."

Leanne Rossiter...Anne...Annie Ross. It's too vague to be taken seriously, yet Elena is filled with a tingling elation. That sense, again, that she is being guided by Amelia. "I'll check her out. How can I get there?"

He checks his watch. "There's a bus leaving here in about an hour. It runs by the foot of the headland. Most of the houses on Mag's Head are deserted. Too much wind and too little to do for the young ones. You should have no bother finding her place. That's if she's still there." He lifts his cap to her and prepares to move on. "Good luck with your search."

Below them, the heron opens its wings with a languid flap and flies away. The dog, rising, scratches his belly with a back foot before ambling on.

✦

Elena's stomach lurches when the bus driver turns another corner. She is the only person left on the bus. The surging rim of the Atlantic weaves in and out of view along the corkscrew road before finally disappearing behind a soaring headland.

A few shabby buildings crouch at the foot of Mag's Head. A small pub with boarded-up windows and a padlock on the front door suggests that the locals once gathered there. Two rusting petrol pumps stand in the shell of a one-time forecourt. This is the village that time forgot. Elena almost expects to see a bale of tumbleweed wheeling towards her. The only shop, Lily Howe's Grocery Provisions, although open and lit by a fluorescent tube, is empty of both customers and staff. She coughs loudly to attract attention. The shop is too small to be called a supermarket, yet its cramped interior contains everything from waders, hardware and groceries, to sacks of turf and coal stacked outside.

An elderly woman in dungarees and a grey topknot puts her head round a wooden partition. "Looking for directions, are you?" she asks in the resigned tone of someone who has had to give out the same information too many times.

"Yes." Elena moves closer to the counter. "I'm looking for a woman called Annie Ross. I believe she lives around here."

"She does and she doesn't." The woman has a high, rolling timbre to her voice, as if she is only a note away from breaking into song. "I haven't seen her for a while so she could be abroad. She does that, sometimes."

"Is her house easy to find?"

"It is, if you're an eagle." She juts her thumb towards the headland, which is visible from the window. "For us mere mortals, it's a different matter. Are you on foot?"

"Yes."

"Then I hope you've got your walking clogs on." She nods approvingly when she sees Elena's mountain boots. "She lives near the summit. You'll see a windbreak of trees and her gate is just beyond." She waves her hand around the counter, where a display of sweets and buns are on display. "Can I get anything for you?"

The buns look surprisingly fresh considering the fusty atmosphere in the shop, and the smell of baking wafting from behind the partition suggests that home baking is another service the place provides.

Elena's mouth waters. She had not eaten since breakfast and it is now after one o'clock. She buys two buns and orders coffee. The coffee maker with its shining pipes looks incongruous among the shelves of fly spray and rat poison. "Are there many people living around here?" she asks.

"You'd be surprised," the woman replies. "There's a few locals close to the village and the headland will always attract them hippie types. They come here to paint the scenery or write a poem about the bright, blue ocean but hightail it out of here after one winter. Not her, though. She's sat out a few winters up there with her kid. If you see her, tell her I have the coffee she likes. Ordered it in especially for her."

The climb up Mag's Head is easy at first. Slight inclines give way to plateaus where the gable walls of abandoned cottages rise like pyramids through the overgrowth of decades. She imagines families living here once. Sons and daughters marrying and building a new home beside their parents. They would have toiled in the shade of the massive boulders that protrude from the landscape and remind Elena of standing stones. They look as though they could be toppled over by a finger push but they are welded to this rugged headland, as are the sheep clinging to its hazardous clefts. As she climbs higher, the wind, sweeping in from the Atlantic, forces her to stop to catch her breath. Down below, the ocean lurches towards the steep side of Mag's Head. The rising spray reminds her of Australia. The thrill of riding those waves. The tumbling freedom she took for granted and, now, seems as ephemeral as a dream.

She notices a black, serrated line in the distance. Drawing nearer, the colour changes to the green sheen of conifers. The density of the trees shelters a grey-stone cottage with high, double gates. The name *Clearwater* is etched on the gatepost. Spiky red hot pokers add a blaze of colour to the garden, as does the red-belled fuchsia bushes.

Elena enters. No car in the driveway. It would be impossible to survive here without one. Elena swallows and bends forward to ease a stitch in her side. The garden is carefully maintained. No weeds grow among the plants and the soil under one of the conifers has been turned recently.

She studies the home of Annie Ross and realises it was originally two cottages that have been joined together. That explains its breadth; it is much wider than the ruins she passed on her way up. She sits down on a bench by the front window and steadies her breathing. Her phone rings. Rosemary—she recognises her number and, unwilling to lie to her, cancels the call. The ocean has a perpetual rhythm as it beats off the cliff and prevents her hearing a Land Rover until it has almost reached the cottage. The engine stops and a little girl with black braids runs to unlatch the gate. She stops, surprised to see it open, and notices Elena. The child—Elena reckons she must be about five years old—walks slowly towards her.

"Are you a visitor?" she asks.

Elena stands, suddenly uncertain as the words she had rehearsed so carefully desert her. "I guess I am," she replies. "I came to talk to your mother."

"She's in the jeep." The child turns as the woman at the wheel enters and brakes a short distance away. When she steps down from the jeep, the wind instantly flails her long hair around her face. She, as well as the child, is wearing jodhpurs. They have obviously come from a riding stable.

She walks slowly towards Elena. Sunglasses cover her eyes and reflect Elena's terse face back at her. Is that how she appears to this woman? Wild and flushed, her features starkly outlined. Impossible to tell by her expression—but Elena has recognised her from the photograph she found in the ice house. There's no mistaking that cascade of unruly white-blonde tresses.

"Can I help you?" she asks. Unlike Lily Howe with her rich Kerry accent, she speaks with a slight drawl that suggests she has lived for some time in the States.

"Are you Annie Ross?"

The woman nods and waits for Elena to continue.

"Are you also called Leanne Rossiter? I'm searching for someone by that name and am hoping I've come to the right house."

"I'm afraid you've made a mistake. I don't know anyone by that name." Her tone is definite, a hard snap of denial that causes Elena to step backwards.

"I'm *so* hungry, Mammy." The little girl, anxious to go inside, pulls at her mother's hand. "You said we could have toasties."

"So we shall, Kayla. Now, go and change into your jeans and trainers. I'll be in to you in a moment." She unlocks the front door and her daughter runs inside, the coloured beads on her braids clattering. Annie Ross returns her attention to Elena. "If you'll excuse me, I need to feed my daughter."

She is lying. Behind her glasses her eyes must be glittering with deceit.

"Please, I desperately need your help." If Elena has to plead on her knees, she will do so. "Did you know Amelia Madison?"

The woman raises her hand to settle her unruly hair, then lets it fall to her side. "Amelia who?"

"Madison. She was from Wicklow."

"I've never heard of her. What makes you think I should know either of those women?"

"It was a hunch. I thought your name might be short for Leanne."

"And Ross short for Rossiter, I suppose?" She sounds amused but remains unsmiling. "Don't you think that's a massive assumption to make?"

"I came a long way to find Leanne. It was worth taking a chance."

"Well, I'm sorry your chance didn't work out. You've had a wasted journey, I'm afraid."

Elena wants to rip the sunglasses from her eyes and scream, "Liar—*liar*!," into her face. "Amelia Madison received a letter in this envelope and I desperately need to find her. Please look at the handwriting."

"I told you already, I'm—"

"*Please.*" She holds the envelope towards the woman, who barely glances at it before shaking her head.

"Why are you lying to me?" Elena cries. "I know you were friends with her. I found photographs of the two of you in the ice house."

"I've no idea why you think you know me or what you are talking about." She whips off her sunglasses and stares unflinchingly at Elena. Her eyes glitter, anger intensifying their dark-green hue. "You've made a mistake and I won't stand for being harassed on my own property. If you don't leave immediately, I'm calling the police."

"Mammy, can I have my toastie? I'm *starving*." The child's plaintive wail comes from inside the cottage.

"Coming, sweetheart." She pulls a mobile phone from her jacket pocket and swipes the screen. "Just because I live in isolation doesn't mean I'm beyond help. A squad car will be here shortly, so I'd advise you to start walking now." Her mouth has stretched into a hard, defiant line.

She waits, her arms folded, as Elena turns towards the gates, then slams the front door closed.

The journey down the headland is more difficult than the ascent. She had hope then, a sliver, admittedly, but it had kept her going. Halfway down and flagging, she sits on the crumbling brick wall of a derelict cottage to catch her breath. Why has Leanne Rossiter chosen to rear her child is such an isolated setting? Elena longs to go back and shake her by her shoulders, shake and shake her until she forces the truth from her lying lips.

The sun disappears behind a grey bank of cloud. The air is misty and damp. The sheep on the gradients bleat mournfully and fluttering tufts of wool, caught on barbed wire, warn Elena that she has stepped too close to the edge of the road. In this bleak terrain, there are no smooth pavements to mark her passage, no trees with leafy crowns to guide her to safety. All that grows here are straggly, windswept bushes that rear from the deepening mist like hunched famine victims. Her feet sink in swampy grass and she slips, her ankle twisting under her.

She is limping now, unable to put weight on her injured foot. Is she still on the main road or has she branched off onto a side trail that could lead her over the edge? Confused, she stops and tries to get her bearings. A stretch of barbed wire is her only protection against the ocean crashing below her.

She sees a shape in the mist. Chilled fingers brush against her cheek. There is someone beside her, a willowy sylph in palest gossamer. Amelia...She understands, logically, that the mist is shifting. A will 'o the wisp is playing mind games with her but the feeling that Amelia's ethereal presence is nearby causes her to cry out.

"Amelia, help me to find my way. Don't let him destroy me as he destroyed you."

CHAPTER THIRTY-NINE

Yellow fog lights penetrate the mist. Elena makes out the shape of the Land Rover.

"Get in." Annie Ross brakes beside her and leans across to open the passenger door.

In the back, round-eyed, the child watches as Elena clambers into the warm interior.

"Thank you." Her ankle throbs and swells in her tight mountain boot. "The mist fell so suddenly. I'd no idea where I was."

"It comes down fast here," Annie says as she turns the car smoothly on the narrow pass. She is obviously used to this terrain, but the back wheels are so close to the edge of the cliff that Elena grits her teeth.

"I figured you'd find it difficult to make your way back down." Annie has changed into sandals, jeans and a blue jumper with a crew neck. Her hair, still tangled, shields her face as she drives upwards towards her cottage.

"You can shelter here until the mist lifts," she says curtly when she brakes in the driveway. "I wouldn't like to have it on my conscience if something happened to you on the headland."

A picture window in the kitchen looks out over the Atlantic. The view, obscured by the mist, must be stunning when the sun is shining.

"Sit down." Annie gestures towards a chair. "I'll make some tea. Or would you prefer coffee?"

"Tea is perfect. I'm sorry about earlier. I thought...Never mind." Elena sits down and unties her lace. Her ankle is ballooning and she is unable to pull off her boot.

The child hovers by the chair, inquisitive yet too shy to speak. She has also changed, from jodhpurs into a pair of leggings and a Charlie and Lola T-shirt.

"That's nasty." Annie kneels and gently eases the boot from Elena's foot. "You need ice to take down that swelling. Lots of ice."

She wraps a tea towel round Elena's ankle, adds two ice packs from the freezer and secures them with a scarf.

"I'm sorry if I was rude earlier." She hands Elena a mug of tea. "We're not used to visitors and I'm very protective of Kayla."

Elena's hand is shaking. The hot liquid slops over her fingers and onto her jeans.

"Missy *messy* moo." Kayla covers her mouth and giggles.

"Come on, Kayla, let's see if Charlie and Lola are on the telly." Annie lifts the child and carries her into the room next door.

A television is turned on and the sound of animated voices comes faintly through the wall.

"I shouldn't have intruded," Elena says when Annie returns to the kitchen. "But I was anxious to find someone who knew Amelia Madison."

"As I already told you, I don't know anyone by that name."

"She's dead."

"I'm sorry to hear that." The comment is meaningless and Elena doesn't bother acknowledging it.

"You look like her friend. At least, that's what I thought when I came here." Up close, Elena can no longer see the compelling resemblance to the woman in the photograph; and even her memory of that is suspect.

"What led you here?" Annie asks.

"The Rannavale postmark on that envelope I showed you."

The evening is darkening and the mist is still dense. There is someone outside. A face at the window, staring through. White-blonde hair, green eyes glowing. They remind Elena of a cat's eyes caught in light. The figure lifts her hand as if to wave goodbye. Elena is about to cry out when she realises it's Annie, tossing an unruly hank of hair from her forehead and reflecting back at Elena in the glass. This is crazy. Hallucinating and chasing illusions. She drags her gaze away from the window.

"Do you believe in coincidence?" she asks.

"That depends." Annie sounds cautious.

"Ghosts?"

"No." An emphatic shake of her head.

"Neither did I until recently," says Elena.

"What changed your mind?"

"Amelia Madison is haunting me. I saw her in the mist earlier." The words coming from her mouth defy logic. She is unable to meet the surprised stare of the woman sitting opposite her.

"You were lost on the headland. Anything seems possible when the mist falls so suddenly. You could have died. People have, you know. Walkers who didn't pay attention to the weather forecast. Some locals, too." The tea Annie had poured for herself is cooling on the table. "You were in shock when I found you. I'm not surprised your imagination was playing tricks on you."

Elena winces. The ice is burning her ankle. "I know it sounds crazy but I've had this feeling for so long. As if she's trying to reach me. It's muddled...so confusing. You're right to think I'm crazy."

"Troubled, not crazy." For the first time since they came face to face, she notices Annie's expression softening.

"Do you know who I am?" Elena asks.

"Should I?"

"If you read the tabloids, you must."

"I don't."

"The tabloids call me the Ice Pick Stabber but my name is Elena Langdon. I stabbed my partner with an ice pick." It shouldn't sound like a boast but that's how it comes out. In the room next door, Kayla laughs and shouts, "Mammy, Lola is *so* funny today."

Annie's eyelids flicker but, otherwise, she remains composed. What an effort that must take. She walks towards the counter of an upright, old-fashioned kitchen dresser where a set of knives jut from a wooden block.

"Was it an accident?" She removes one knife and lays it on the table.

"No."

"Did you have a reason?"

"Oh, yes," Elena replies. "I certainly did. I thought you could help me to bring him down. I was wrong. But don't worry. I'm not going to harm you or your daughter."

"Whatever reason led you here, it was a wrong call." Annie speaks slowly, each word emphasised. "I'm not the person you're looking for."

The mist is beginning to lift. Elena stands and tentatively puts her weight on her damaged ankle. The pain is sharp, intense. "I have to get back to Dublin tonight." She forces her boot on and hobbles across the kitchen. "I've to attend a group therapy session tomorrow or I'll be in serious trouble. If you can just give me a lift back to the grocery shop, I'll catch the bus from there."

"There's no bus at this time of the evening. This isn't Dublin—"

"I know that. But I'm causing you trouble and it's obvious you don't want me here. I can hitch a lift—"

"Mag's Head is the end of the road. There won't be many cars passing. I'll drive you to the medical centre in Rannavale. They have X-ray facilities there and you'll be able to catch the last bus back to Dublin."

She returns to the next room to persuade Kayla away from the television. The little girl can be heard protesting loudly as the animated characters are silenced, then she emerges from the cottage with a rag doll in her arms. Elena limps beside her and climbs into the Land Rover. Kayla, strapped into the back seat, starts to sing to the doll, her annoyance forgotten as soon as her mother starts the jeep.

Elena tries to think of something to say but polite conversation seems like an impossible ask after the confession she has just made.

"Do you get lonely here?" She is curious about this woman who lives this hermitic existence with only her daughter for company.

Annie shakes her head. "I don't have time for loneliness." She offers no further information. They reach the foot of the headland and drive past Lily Howe's Grocery Provisions. The shop is closed, the light off.

"Lily has the coffee you ordered," Elena says.

"Thanks. I'll call tomorrow and pick it up."

"Does anyone else shop there except you?"

"Enough to keep her open. Appearances can be deceptive."

"You're the second person to say that to me today."

"Then it must be true." Annie smiles and drives onwards.

When they reach Rannavale, Annie supports her into the clinic's waiting room. Kayla tags behind, the doll in her arms. Elena will be seen shortly by the triage nurse.

"Goodbye." Annie shakes her hand, then bends to scoop Kayla into her arms. "They're very efficient here. You'll be discharged in time to catch the bus back to Dublin."

"Bye bye, Elena." Kayla holds on to her doll as she reaches out to kiss Elena. In doing so, she pulls the top of her mother's jumper out of alignment. A medallion at Annie's neck is briefly visible before she pulls her jumper back into position. A stained-glass butterfly, wings raised in flight. Then she's gone, her child in her arms, leaving unanswered questions trailing in her wake.

Her demeanour had given nothing away when Elena blurted out her confession. No curiosity, no flicker of sympathy or understanding, no fear, even when she laid a knife on the table as a warning. Annie Ross. Leanne Rossiter. On the bus travelling back to Dublin, Elena visualises the medallion. Branded on her retinas, it has the glistening vibrancy of an oil painting that has yet to dry.

Such butterfly jewellery is common, she thinks as she travels through the night. Forged in silver and gold, gilded and burnished —or, sometimes, those iridescent hues are stained in glass. Her mind darts at that same fluttering speed back to Woodbine. Nicholas's foot on her neck, pressing hard as he demanded to know why she'd dared to remove one of the butterflies from the apple tree.

✦

"Why didn't you take my call or return it?" Rosemary is waiting for her when she finally arrives back. Her stern expression warns Elena not to lie. Blurting out the reasons that had drawn her to the headland, she tries to make Rosemary understand why a few sentences on a crumpled piece of paper had convinced her that a stranger called Leanne Rossiter would have known about Nicholas's violence.

"So, did you find out anything?" Rosemary demands. "Apart from the fact that you met someone called Annie Ross, who insisted you'd made a mistake?"

Elena shakes her head, knowing it would be useless to tell her about the medallion.

"What if you'd been unable to get back in time for your group therapy tomorrow?" Rosemary asks. "You are my responsibility until you go to trial. Break any of your bail conditions and you'll put my professional reputation at risk. It's suffered enough already. I don't need Nicholas to spread any more rumours about my incompetence."

"I'm sorry, Rosemary."

She is unmoved by Elena's contrition. "Without evidence, you'll simply come across to the judge as petty and vindictive if word of this gets out."

"Is that how you see me?"

"No. But my opinion isn't important. The judge is the one you need to impress."

CHAPTER FORTY

Two cyclists and a lone trekker are sitting on beer barrels outside Lily Howe's Grocery Provisions, enjoying coffee and Lily's home-made scones.

"Well, Annie, did your visitor find you?" Lily asks when she enters the small shop.

"She did. But I wasn't able to help her."

"Poor girl. She came a long way to find that out," Lily says. "I was afraid she'd get lost when the mist came down."

"Then you won't be surprised to hear she fell and sprained her ankle."

"She's not the first and she won't be the last." Lily sighs, unsurprised. "Was she okay?"

"She stayed with me until the mist lifted. Then I dropped her into the medical centre."

"That's your good deed for the week done. How's the work going?"

"Good. I finished the Charmeuse order. Manged to get it off on time, too."

"Beats me how you do it." Lily reaches under the counter and hands her a packet of coffee beans. "That online stuff is far too complicated for my old head. How you manage to run a business and you stuck up on that headland with only sheep for company is beyond me."

"The power of the internet, Lily. I keep telling you to get a computer."

"Ah, sure, why would I be bothered at this stage of my life? I'm done with newfangled notions. Are these the beans you want?"

"They are indeed. Thanks for ordering them."

"Any time. Have a coffee on the house. What would you like? A cappuccino, americano, latte?"

"You say you're done with new newfangled notions yet you handle that machine like a qualified barista."

"A barrister? What are you on about now, Annie?"

"Never mind." She laughs and sits on the high stool in front of the counter. "An americano would be lovely."

One of the cyclists enters the shop with two empty coffee mugs.

"Magnificent scenery," he says to her. "Do you live around here?"

"Nearby." She nods, non-committally.

"Are you an artist?"

"No."

"Annie is more the techie type," says Lily. "But I paint." She points to a picture of Mag's Head, which, for reasons known only to herself, she painted in lurid purple. "It's for sale, if you're interested."

The cyclist rolls his eyes away from the painting. "A most interesting landscape," he says, smoothly. "However, my taste in art veers more towards the abstract. Can I buy a soda bread and four of those delicious scones?"

Lily stares out the window as he cycles off with his friend. "I could see his nuts in that Lycra. Disgraceful." She sounds appreciative rather than disgusted. "Did you notice how he was giving you the eye?"

"No, he *wasn't*." She sips her coffee. It's too hot to drink quickly, really, but she is anxious to return to the cottage.

"He certainly was," Lily insists. "And why wouldn't he? He's a red-blooded male and you're an attractive woman, even though you live like a hermit up there."

"This hermit has work to do." She leaves the coffee unfinished and swings her handbag over her shoulder. "See you tomorrow."

The trekker bids her goodbye in Italian.

"*Slán leat*," she replies in Irish and beeps the horn as she drives off. She drives past the two cyclists straining up the slopes of Mag's Head. Lily the matchmaker; she never stops seeking a suitable husband for her. Heads down, helmets thrust forward, they remind her of determined wasps. Their ride back down will be exhilarating, if they have any energy left to enjoy it.

The silence of the cottage bears down on her when she unlocks the hall door. Kayla's doll lies on the floor, dropped and forgotten when she put on her schoolbag. It's too early in the morning to hear back from Greg Ahearn, Charmeuse's marketing executive in New York. She's confident he'll be pleased with the information she sent to him. She checks her emails. A potential new client in Canada is interested in hearing from her. She reads a report from a satisfied manufacturer in Portugal and a plea for help from a regular client.

Her mind feels dull, apathetic, occupied with thoughts of Elena Langdon. Did she make that last bus? Is she, right at this moment, participating in another group therapy session where she will try, once again, to analyse why she tried to kill her partner? The Ice Pick Stabber. Her photograph had been on the front pages and on television. Not as thin then as she is now, she was laughing, with her children in her arms, Nicholas Madison, proud father, standing beside her.

Even with her hair cut close to her scalp, and her weight loss, Elena had been instantly recognisable. Those woebegone eyes, smoky-blue; they would once have been her most arresting feature, until brutality dimmed their luminance. The knuckled cheekbones, her mouth clenched in disappointment when she finally accepted that she had come to Mag's Head on a wild goose chase.

Her mobile rings. "Ross Creative Designs," she says. "Annie Ross speaking."

"Hi Annie, Oscar Sayer here." The caller is male, his accent clipped, English, probably London posh. "I'm interested in your suggestion. I just need to clarify the numbers."

"Let me bring up the details and I'll go through them with you." She turns her attention to her laptop. When the call ends she begins to work again on the Canadian proposal but, unable to focus, she stands up and goes to her living room in the centre of the cottage. The fire is set with logs that will not be lit until Kayla comes home from school. She stops at the side of an open hearth. It's raised on bricks above the floor and built within a granite fireplace. Logs and kindling are stacked beside it. She removes the logs one by one and lays them on the hearth until only a few remain in the stack. The switch on the wall that she reveals is barely visible; a slight protrusion that allows a panel to slide silently across when she presses it. A light turns on automatically when she steps inside a dark recess. This small room fills the space that once existed between the two cottages. It is rarely used and the cardboard box she opens is covered in dust. The letters inside it are arranged according to their dates, the most recent one on top. A chronology of violence at her fingertips. *Help me, Leanne. What am I to do? He'll kill me if I leave him.* Each beating, arm-twist, kick, broken ribs and bloodletting listed. She trembles as she reads them. Time has not diminished their ferocity. The desperation she had seen on Elena Langdon's face was a reflection of that terror. She sees it also in the photographs that accompanied these letters. She finishes reading the last one and closes the box. It's time to collect Kayla from school but, first, she must shower the residue of dust and memory from her skin. She works late into the night to make up for lost time. The wind blows hard around the cottage. If there is an electrical outage it will affect her schedule. She has been lucky so far, with only short outages, but Lily has told her she once had to cope for four days before her electricity was restored. No wonder families fled this wild terrain with its orchestral gales and drumming waves. Kayla, born to these sounds, sleeps soundly in the next room and the light in the cottage window is the only glimmer in the enveloping darkness of Mag's Head.

CHAPTER FORTY-ONE

Finally, there has been a court ruling. Elena can see her children for an hour twice a week in the Kingsdale Community Centre, but always under the supervision of a social worker.

They meet in a room with bright yellow walls and toys to distract Grace and Joel should the reunion with their mother become difficult. The social worker's name is Sophie. She looks far too young to be writing a report on this reunion and summing up emotions she will only experience if she is unlucky in love. But she sits at a discreet distance and Elena is grateful for that.

Grace runs into her arms but Joel cries when she takes him on her knees. He is sturdy and long-legged, almost unrecognisable as the baby she held to her breast while his father lay bleeding on the floor of the ice house. He wriggles too quickly from her arms, intent on playing with the toys.

Grace wants to know when she is going home with Elena. She pushes out her bottom lip in a once-familiar pout when she hears she must stay with her grandparents for a little while longer. Elena is conscious of Sophie's eyes on her as she plays with her children. Her voice is pitched too high, the tone fake with forced jollity. Then they are gone, Grace in tears and Joel, who has finally relaxed into her embrace, clinging to her neck when she hands him over to Sophie.

She watches from the window as Yvonne and the social worker speak together in the car park. Yvonne, who appears to be arguing with Sophie, is probably insisting that this first visit is having a traumatic effect on her grandchildren. Elena is consumed by a savage desire to run out and silence her. Is this how Nicholas feels before he attacks? The uncontrollable anger that can only be appeased by brutality?

When Yvonne has driven off, Sophie pauses on her way back into the community centre to stare at the car Elena came in. Difficult to miss Rosemary's flamboyant, orange-coloured Citroën. Last week, she replaced it with an Audi SQ5 and handed Elena the keys to this one.

"You'll need it for your visits," Rosemary had said, waving her thanks away.

Each time Elena sits inside it she thinks of a pumpkin, but she is grateful to have wheels under her again.

"Ms. Langdon, are you okay?" Sophie has returned to the room.

Elena blows her nose and crumples the tissue in her fist. "Is Yvonne trying to stop me from seeing my children again?"

"You have been granted visiting rights in a court of law." The social worker assumes the evasive mask of a professional. "Only a judge can reverse that decision. Would you like a cup of tea before you leave?"

"No, but thank you. I've to go to work."

"Then I'll see you at the same time on Friday. You did well today, Ms. Langdon. The first visit is always the hardest."

Elena drives into the city and circles Mountjoy Square searching for a parking spot. Usually, if she is unable to take a lift with Rosemary, she cycles to work and locks her bike to the railings of the building. Her basement office is accessible via an exterior set of wrought-iron steps. She is convinced her office must have been a broom cupboard in an era when these houses were grand residences. Moving around in such a cramped space will be good training for a prison or a psychiatric cell, she thinks in moments of black, bleak humour.

✦

Billy rings that evening and asks her to visit him at his house. His invitation surprises her; he knows she must not go too close to Woodbine. Having finally gained access to her children, Elena is determined not to take any further risks.

"I could be recognised going into your house," she says. "Can't we meet somewhere else?"

"I wish I could, Elena." His breathing is laboured and fast. "The news from the hospital is not good so I'm confined to barracks. There's something I have to tell you. I won't keep you long. Come on Friday—"

"I'm seeing my children on Friday."

"Then Saturday."

"What if Nicholas…" She pauses. Billy would not ask her to break bail without a good reason. Nicholas always goes to the gym on Saturday afternoons, as well as two evenings a week. Pumping his fury into iron. Why was that never enough to assuage it? An attempt on his life has hardly changed his self-discipline. Elena agrees to have lunch with Billy at one o'clock on Saturday.

She arrives on time. Billy has prepared a salad with cold chicken and ham. Their conversation flows easily throughout the meal. No sign that there is anything on his mind, yet she can tell he is troubled.

They take coffee beside an open fire in his living room. "The old ticker is not behaving as well as it should," he admits. "It's progressive. Six months if I'm lucky, according to my cardiac specialist."

She is shocked by his blunt statement, yet not surprised; Billy has deteriorated since she saw him in hospital. But he shows no sign of distress as he outlines the specialist's verdict.

"I've had a good innings and things haven't been the same since Jodie died. And John, too. He's the reason I asked you here."

"Amelia's father?"

"Yes. John was a gentle person but he was dead set against Amelia marrying Nicholas. I'd met Nicholas and liked him well enough at the beginning, so I found it hard to understand why John was so opposed to him. He used to work for a credit control company and he had friends in far-flung places. He found out information on Nicholas that you or I would never uncover in a month of Sundays. I never heard the full details but I remember it had to do with an embezzlement scandal that was hushed up when Nicholas was working in Hong Kong—"

"Nicholas was never in Hong Kong."

"He was, Elena. Two years there and a year in China before he joined Keogh & Harris, as it was known then. John was going to tell Amelia what he'd uncovered but when she decided to end things with Nicholas, he kept the information to himself. There was some trouble between him and Amelia at the time and that could have made things worse. But he confronted Nicholas and warned him he'd release the information if he attempted to persuade Amelia to change the decision she'd made not to marry him."

"I never knew Amelia broke it off with him. But, then, I never knew anything about him, anything truthful that is. It's my own fault. I was so stupid—so *stupid*... I let him embezzle every penny I owned." Elena beats her fist against her knee. "I took everything he told me at face value and look where I am now."

"Everything passes, Elena. Karma has a way of balancing us out."

"That's a nice thought, Billy. But I'm afraid it's for the birds."

"Hear me out, girl. Knowing when you're going to make your final exit has a way of concentrating the mind and there's something I need to tell you. Remember that hairy lad in the next bed to mine when you were visiting me?"

"Red? With the beard?" She remembers his expressive language as he struggled to master his crutches.

"That's him. Red Boland." Billy laughs. "He was red before he went grey. Nicknames can be hard to shake. I told you he took a tumble off his Harley, out Glendalough way. Luckily, he wasn't killed. I used to be a biker back in the day. Jodie, too. The bike kept me going after she died. I only gave it up when the old knees started giving me trouble."

What is he talking about? Karma and bikers and his dead wife—where is this conversation going? Elena wants to hear about Nicholas and how she can get her children and her inheritance back; but there is something about Billy's posture that stops her restless movements.

"Me and Red, well, we got to talking about bikes," he continues. "He showed me photos of his Harley. A fine-looking bike, if ever I saw one. He told me the man who sold it to him was one of those slick financial sorts. Gave him some investment tips. Red made a packet as a result. I don't know what made me ask when he bought it but I did." Billy pauses, frowns, as if unsure whether or not he should continue.

"Go on," Elena prompts him. She has no idea what is coming next. It will be bad, though, of this she is certain. Anxiety has become her bowstring, finely tuned to premonitions.

"It was two days after John's death," Billy continues. "Red remembered the date because it was his birthday. But he couldn't bring the name of the seller to mind."

"What are you trying to tell me, Billy?"

"It rained hard on the night of John's accident." He sucks in his breath, as if he too can't believe what he is going to say next. "The road was very slippery. The police always assumed that a car driver skidded on the wet surface and then drove off after the accident. By the time we found John, there were no tracks to prove otherwise. But I saw a bike on Kilfarran Lane that night. I'd walked to the gate to call the dog in. John wouldn't have reached Woodbine by that stage. I knew it was a Harley going by. It's got a distinctive sound because there're two pistons and only one pin in the crankshaft." He stops, shakes his head. "Never mind the technicalities. What I'm trying to say is that I heard that sound and also recognised the bike by the headlights. I reported what I'd seen to the gardai but the following morning they found one of those metal Mondeo logos near the scene. They were convinced it had fallen off the car that hit John."

She stares into the fire. Nicholas is the father of her children. The heat stings her eyes, flames her cheeks. How can her heart continue beating so fast, so violently, without collapsing into stillness?

"You're not suggesting it was Nicholas who sold his bike to Red?"

"I'm not suggesting it. I'm *telling* you he did. Red rang me a few days ago. He'd found the chequebook he used when he bought the Harley. Nicholas's name is on the stub. So is the date."

"That can't be true." Billy has no reason to lie to her, but what she has heard is too horrifying to accept. "All that proves is that Nicholas sold his bike around the time Amelia's father died. It has to be a coincidence. Nicholas is violent but to call him a murderer...it's ridiculous. I won't listen to this. I won't—"

"Sit down, Elena. Please." The colour has drained from Billy's face. Aware that his heart is also in turmoil, she does as he asks.

He opens his wallet and shows her the cheque stub. "I got that in the post from Red. Like you say, it could be a coincidence."

"It *has* to be a coincidence." She doesn't want to think about the photograph in Yvonne's album but it flashes before her like a danger signal. Nicholas, relaxed in leather, leaning against his Harley, and Yvonne's admission that he'd kept it in her garage long after he had stopped using it.

Billy hands the cheque stub to her. "Take this. I've photocopied it. I've no idea what you can do with it but someday maybe…" His body sags in the armchair. Elena is conscious of his fragility. She finds his tablets and he slips one under his tongue.

"Stress busters." His smile is strained; his concave chest rises and falls fast. "No matter how you do it, I hope you can bring him to justice, Elena."

When they part, she is still in a state of disbelief. She will visit him again, she promises.

His house is close to a bend on Kilfarran Lane and she is edging the car cautiously out of the entrance when she notices Nicholas's BMW. Two wheels are up on the narrow pavement and the car slants, half on and half off the road. Nicholas must have returned early from the gym and parked opposite Billy's house. The driver's seat is empty and her children are not in the back. Elena is wearing sunglasses, her hair covered by a hood, yet she feels as exposed as she always did in that instant before he struck her. From the corner of her eye, she sees him emerge from the trees that shadow the pavement. She only catches a fleeting glimpse of him as she bends her head over the steering wheel. Her foot shakes when she presses it against the accelerator. The rage that seized her when she attacked him had been an impulse, scalding and visceral, passing through her and fading as quickly as it had come. But the deliberate taking of a life, the methodical planning and ruthless execution… how could she have been so deceived in love?

Billy must be zonked on medication. Dementia setting in. The fear of death disturbing his mind. But the cheque stub lies on the seat beside her. It flutters, as if disturbed by the jerking speed of the car as she turns and drives from Kilfarran Lane. She glances sideways at the wing mirror. Nicholas is standing in the middle of the road and, as if aware that she is looking back, he lifts his hand and waves.

✦

Billy Tobin's death makes the morning headlines.

> *The elderly man was pronounced dead at the scene and his body removed from his home on Kilfarran Lane. Time of death has yet to be ascertained but it is believed he had been dead in his living room for four days before his presence was missed and the gardai were called. Foul play is suspected and gardai are appealing to anyone who was in the vicinity of Kilfarran Lane on Saturday and noticed anything unusual to contact them at Kilfarran Garda Station.*

Hands over her mouth to stifle a scream, Elena leaves the breakfast table and climbs the stairs to her room. Four days—since Billy died. She imagines his body stretched in front of the fire that had crackled and sparkled as he revealed a terrible truth to her. She would understand what had happened if his heart had given way after the stress of their conversation? That would make sense but what she had just heard on the radio ruled that out. *Foul play is suspected . . .* what does that mean? How soon after she left had the attack taken place? Did Nicholas recognise her as she drove away? No, that would not have been possible, not with the sunglasses and the hoodie. But he had waved, a deliberate gesture of acknowledgement, a mocking salute of recognition.

She needs to compose herself before leaving for another day at the office. Rosemary, who shouts from the hall that she is ready to leave, must not suspect anything is wrong. Elena splashes cold water on her face and runs downstairs.

More details emerge in the evening papers. The alarm had been raised by the owner of the Kilfarran Inn, who noticed the absence of his regular customer. When the guards broke in, they found Billy in a pool of blood, his skull cracked. A burglary that went wrong, they believe. Thugs targeting the elderly, especially those who live in quiet places. Jewellery that once belonged to Jodie has been stolen, also Billy's wallet.

CHAPTER FORTY-TWO

In St. Malachy's Church, Elena recognises faces from Kilfarran Village. Sideways glances, unbridled interest; she senses the unease caused by her arrival. On the way to Billy's funeral she almost changed her mind on two occasions and, now, as she finds a seat among the mourners, she imagines the whispered comments. *That's her? The Ice Pick Stabber. A real nut job, she is. Better not get on the wrong side of her.*

The tension rises a notch when, towards the end of the funeral mass, Nicholas stands at the altar and pays tribute to his neighbour. Unaware previously that he was in the church, Elena is stunned to see him, without notes, eulogising Billy's life. If she leaves now, everyone will know why she is fleeing. She listens to the familiar cadences that once seduced her and is assailed by images that have haunted her since the news of Billy's death broke. Nicholas returns to his seat on an appreciative round of applause.

In the cemetery, the crowd are sombre, still shocked that a local man could die in such circumstances. No one speaks to Elena or shows that they recognise her. Once again, she is facing Nicholas across the width of an open grave. As always, he stands out from those surrounding him. His flawless skin is lightly tanned from a recent holiday with the children in Spain. His forehead is smooth, a high plane without furrows, guiltless. His eyes compel attention, engender trust, beget love.

She notices a stranger standing behind him. He is losing his hair and has shaved off what remains. Square-rimmed glasses and a neatly trimmed goatee beard add to his air of gravity. She has no memory of having seen him before, yet there is something about his face that tugs at her memory. He lifts his head and, as if aware that he is under scrutiny, he looks across at Elena and smiles. She looks down quickly. Smiling at strangers in cemeteries has consequences.

When the burial is over, a portly man pumps Nicholas's hand and slaps his shoulder. Congratulating him on his speech, no doubt. Elena walks away. She has watched the reports on television, listened to a grave-faced detective inspector plead with the public for information from anyone who saw Billy in the lead-up to the time of his death. How long can she hide the truth? How long before the fragile house of cards she had built around herself collapses?

The man who had smiled at her is walking ahead. He slows until she is abreast of him.

"I'm Mark Patterson," he says. "Amelia was one of my closest friends."

Elena remembers him now. A photograph of teenagers, Amelia, Leanne and two boys lounging on grass with them. Mark's features are unchanged but he had hair then, a pink Mohican.

"Billy was always kind to us when we were kids," he continues. "His death was an obscenity."

"He was kind to me, too," she replies. "I hope they find whoever is responsible. They should throw away the key when they lock him up."

"I agree." When they reach the car park he reaches for her hand and squeezes it. "Have courage," he says.

Before she can respond, he walks swiftly ahead of her towards his own car. Such a fleeting encounter, almost imagined, yet she is aware of a quickening in her step, a lifting of her heart.

Nicholas is standing beside the orange Citroën. When he holds out his hand to shake hers, there is a perceptible pause from those who have still to drive away.

"Get out of my way." Elena ignores his gesture and pulls the car keys from her handbag.

"Why?" He leans back against the door on the driver's side, his tall frame relaxed, one foot crossed over the other. "Will you stick me with an ice pick if I don't?" Once, his laughter was contagious. Now, when he laughs, it sounds in her ears like breaking glass.

"You can do better than that with the insults, Nicholas. You've done so in the past, usually before you knocked me to the ground."

No longer laughing, he ignores her comment and smacks his hand off the side of the car. "When did Rosemary give you this heap of junk?"

"If you don't leave me alone, I'm calling the police and reporting you for harassing me," she snaps.

"By all means, call them." He speaks softly so that only she can hear him. "Then you can tell them what you were doing at Billy Tobin's house on the day he died. Or have you informed them already that you were the last person to see him alive?" He shakes his head and answers his own question. "No? How very remiss of you. I can accompany you to Kilfarran Garda Station, if you like. It must feel like a second home to you by now."

"I wasn't—"

"You weren't there?" His forehead furrows in mock-surprise. "I apologise if I've made a mistake. I could have sworn I saw you driving away from the scene of a murder. Practice makes perfect, don't you agree? And this time you succeeded. The only reason I'm alive is that you failed to find my heart."

"That's because you don't have one."

"Answering back now, I see. Found you had a backbone after all. Congratulations."

"Don't you dare threaten me." Some of the drivers are clearly delaying their departure to witness this encounter and she, like Nicholas, speaks softly. "I wasn't with Billy and you can't prove otherwise."

"I certainly can. I photographed this car outside Billy's house, so don't waste my time denying you were there. I also have a video of you driving away—very erratically, I should add." He removes his phone from his pocket and holds it towards her. "Would you like a preview?"

"If you have the proof, why haven't you already reported me?" She averts her eyes from the phone. He will not see her tremble, though she feels as if she is gripped by a fever. "You've done your utmost to separate me from my children. This gives you the perfect excuse."

"I'm a protective father. Do you blame me for worrying about their safety?"

Before she can step aside, he takes her in his arms. She gasps as she is crushed against him, his grip iron-like, his fists digging into her back.

"You've been talking to a lot of people lately," he murmurs into her ear. "First Billy and now that poofter at the cemetery."

It takes an instant before she realises he is referring to Mark.

"Let me go." She struggles to break free, aware that they are still being watched by the onlookers. A teenager standing nearby raises his phone. A video for Facebook or Instagram; it will be uploaded within minutes.

"All in good time, Elena." He is speaking faster now. "Billy Tobin was a demented old fool. I want to know why you were at his house."

"I wasn't anywhere near his house."

"You've a big mouth on you, bitch," he whispers as he releases her. "Tell me the truth or I'm going straight to the police. You *do* know what that means? You'll be placed on remand straight away but don't think you'll be cossetted in an asylum."

"This is the only truth you'll get." To draw her hand back and slap his face is the wrong thing to do. Uncaring, Elena glories in the warm sting of satisfaction against her palm. She is aware of the effort it takes Nicolas not to retaliate. And something else, almost imagined, yet she sees it in the flicker of his eyelids. Why is he fearful when he has the upper hand, has always had it?

"Showing your true colours, Elena." He holds his fingers to his cheek, then turns and walks away.

She gets into the car, her hands sweating as she holds on to the steering wheel. A video of an orange Citroën leaving the scene of a crime. This time, she will stand trial for murder. Why should anyone believe her innocence?

She returns to Rosemary's house and showers that feel of him from her skin. Cycling to work, she takes deep breaths, inhaling, exhaling, determined to be composed when she sees Rosemary, whose questions about Elena's free time have become more probing.

✦

She has gone viral. The Ice Pick Stabber strikes again. Her face twisted with hatred as she smacks his face. Nicholas looks stricken, wounded, forgiving. Elena reads the comments on social media and is sickened by the vitriol. No sense searching for comfort in the world of virtual reality where there is only room for opinion.

CHAPTER FORTY-THREE

She works late to make up for the time she lost at Billy's funeral. No interruptions from couriers, no coffee breaks, no phones ringing. Climbing the stairs to Rosemary's office, she leaves a stack of documents on the solicitor's desk to be signed next morning. This house was once a grand Georgian residence and then a slum. Children sleeping four or five to a bed, a communal toilet that left the stench of poverty on their skin. Now, it is a business premises and, in the quietness of the hour, she hears a sound drawn from the old stone and wonders if the ghosts of those who once walked those stairs are stirring.

Back at her own desk, she finishes an email to Tara and sends it off. Her friend has flown from London twice to see her and emails her every day, as does Steve. Killian and Susie have invited her to stay on their farm until the date of the trial but going away is impossible; still, it helps to know they are concerned for her. She checks the time on her phone and is surprised to discover it's after ten o'clock. She will turn off the computer and return to Rosemary's house. Searching Facebook again is a destructive act but she is tormented by a voyeuristic curiosity about herself. The Ice Pick Stabber. The name will haunt her always. Decisively, she shuts down the computer and switches off the gas fire.

Her coat hangs from a hook on the door. As she puts it on she is startled by a movement outside the window. Her fingers freeze on the buttons until she realises it's her reflection. She closes the blinds and turns off the lights.

The exterior light that automatically turns on when the basement door opens has broken. First thing in the morning she'll call an electrician to fix it. The glow from a streetlamp filters through the wrought-iron railings above her and illuminates the passageway leading to the steps. Cracks on the surface have made it uneven in places and she must be careful of her ankle, which is still painful. She locks the door and pulls down the security shutter.

"Elena." He speaks her name softly. Before she can move, he is behind her, his arms encircling her. He pushes her against the wall and forces her face into the rough stone.

"One word from you and I'll smash your head in." His breath is warm on the back of her neck, his tone an obscene caress. "Are you listening to me? Repeat every word that demented fool told you." His knee crashes into the back of her legs and her body jack-knifes in a spasm. "Speak to me, Elena. I'm waiting."

"I told you already," she gasps. "I wasn't there."

"Don't lie to me." He pulls her head back from the wall by her hair.

"Why would I risk breaking bail—?"

"I'm asking the questions, bitch."

Once again, her forehead is smashed against the wall. Her mouth fills with the metallic taste of blood. It rolls slickly down her cheek.

"He hated me because I knew his friend was a fucking paedophile. He'd do anything to slander me so you'd better start talking. What did he say?"

Tears run from her eyes but she is afraid to cry out in case he attacks her again. A trembling suspicion has turned into conviction. Billy alone in his house, answering a knock on the door late at night. Questions asked and a blow to the head when he refused to answer them.

Her arm has been twisted so violently behind her back she fears it has been dislocated from its socket. How long can she withstand the pain before she breaks? And if she breaks and reveals what Billy told her, what then? Death? She knows now that he has killed twice. Why not a third time? She will never hold her children again, hear their voices, wipe their tears, share their laughter. She whispers their names: *Grace... Joel... Grace... Joel...* if these are the last words she utters, she will repeat them until she has no breath left to do so. He releases her arm and encircles her neck. Gloves, soft leather, flexible, untraceable. *Grace... Joel... Grace... Joel...*

"Do you want me to strangle you, Elena?" He has still not raised his voice. Anyone passing above them would think they were a couple embracing in the shadows. "You always liked a bit of rough and this will be as rough as it gets unless you tell me everything. The police didn't believe a word from your lying mouth when you tried to kill me. I'll make sure you—"

Suddenly, the locked security shutter springs upwards with a loud clatter. The office window cracks outwards, as if blown apart by an internal explosion. Startled, Nicholas reels back and releases his grip on her. Elena collapses to the ground as shards of glass shatter around them. She hears a sigh, as if a beast imprisoned for too long has been released. Unable to tell if Nicholas is injured but knowing she only has seconds to escape, she staggers to her feet and runs, sobbing hysterically as she mounts the steps. Nicholas, too, has risen. He grabs her ankle but his grip is weak and he overbalances when she kicks back hard with her other foot. He curses as he slides back down the wrought-iron steps. She reaches the footpath. The bike is locked to the railings. She leaves it there and runs onto the road, searching for a taxi. Her right arm hangs limply by her side. Blood is still streaming from her forehead.

Nicholas has reached the pavement, his tall frame forming an elongated silhouette under the streetlamp. "That was only a taster tonight, Elena." His voice, now rough with fury, reaches her. "Just remember that you were the last person to see Billy Tobin alive. One mention of tonight and the police will be knocking on your door so fast you won't have time to blink before you're in handcuffs." She hears him walking away, his footsteps fading.

A taxi draws up beside her. "Good God, lady! What happened to you?" the driver asks when she collapses into the back seat. He rummages in the glove compartment and hands her a wad of tissues. "You need an ambulance, not a taxi. I'll call one for you."

"It's superficial. I'll be okay." She scans the road but Nicholas has merged into the night. "I was cut by flying glass." Perhaps that's true. There could be splinters of glass embedded in her skin, along with grit from the wall. "There was a gas explosion in my office," she continues. "I need to ring Bord Gáis and report it."

"I'll do that for you, lady. Then we go to the hospital." The driver is Nigerian, broad-cheeked, his dark eyes filled with concern. A medal of St. Christopher hangs from his rear-view mirror. His deep voice with its rhythmic intonations helps to calm her down. She speaks to an official from the gas board and gives him the address of the office, as well as Rosemary's phone number.

The driver, having escorted her to the emergency department of the Mater Hospital, refuses her offer of payment. "You are alive to tell the tale," he says. "It is a miracle to survive a gas explosion. Someone in heaven was watching over you."

CHAPTER FORTY-FOUR

Elena arrives at the community centre early. Sophie makes coffee and polite conversation. It's Yvonne's bridge morning, so Henry will bring the children today. Usually, their grandmother takes them as far as the entrance and hands them over to Sophie but today, Henry comes straight into the room where Elena is waiting. He is carrying Joel but Grace has already let his hand go and is running towards Elena's open arms. When she sees her mother's face she falters and begins to cry. The bruises are livid, a palette of violence, and scabs have formed on her skin where it was torn by the brickwork.

"Sweet Jesus, what happened to you?" Henry stops, shocked by her appearance and obviously unable to hide his apprehension in case she screams *Your son did this to me*.

"I fell on the steps coming out of work." If she repeats this lie often enough she might begin to believe it herself. Billy Tobin is the spectre that keeps her silent. So far, she has heard nothing from the police. That can mean only one thing: Nicholas has not reported her visit to Billy. Instead of relief, she feels a growing agitation that eases only when it is announced on the evening news that a young man has been taken in for questioning. Perhaps she was wrong about Nicholas and he is simply trying to torment her. But her relief is short-lived: the suspect is released without charge the following day. A garda statement claims the police are following a definite line of enquiry. Every time the phone rings or someone knocks on Rosemary's door, she trembles. As always, Nicholas has her where he wants her, helpless and at his mercy.

"I'll collect the children in an hour." Henry averts his eyes from her face. "Joel may be difficult." He speaks directly to the social worker. "He's cutting another tooth."

Joel crawls to the box of toys and flings them to the floor. She has applied to the courts for longer hours and is waiting on a date for a new hearing. She longs for those visits, yet when they are over she feels no sense of fulfilment and is conscious only of relief. A relief that used to overcome her when she had undergone a difficult test and passed it. The hour she spends with them twice a week is too short. Grace and Joel have only just begun to relax when their visit is over. She is running out of things to say to them. This frightens her. Is it so easy to break the maternal bond or are words hard to find in such an unnatural environment? She must depend on touch to break down the barriers that keep her and her children apart. She holds Grace to her, strokes her hair, kisses her face. She hunkers beside Joel, who has pulled himself upright and is clinging to the side of the toybox. As she reaches towards him, he lets go and takes a step, then another. A beatific smile spreads across his face as he manages another one before falling into her arms.

"Those were his first steps." Henry's delight is evident when he comes back at the end of visiting time and hears the news from Sophie.

"I'm so pleased he took them when he was with you," he says to Elena and walks away before she can reply.

✦

The pain in Elena's arm awakens her at two o'clock in the morning. When she switches on the light she is confronted as usual by the life-sized poster of a rugby player. This bedroom belongs to Rosemary's son, who used to be play for his local football club before he moved to Brussels. The bedroom is crammed with medals and trophies, triumphant photographs, and framed jerseys scrawled with signatures. She feels as if she is sleeping in a stadium but is reluctant to change anything. Staying with Rosemary is a stopgap until she gains custody of her children and life can begin again. Illusion and hopelessness dominate the small hours when reality lies down and plays dead.

The venom in Nicholas's voice when he called John Pierce a paedophile was unmistakable. What secrets had Amelia carried with her into the depths? Would Elena ever be able to decipher them when all she had was a grubby envelope with a faded postmark?

She goes downstairs in search of ice and painkillers. Sally, Rosemary's cat, winds around her legs and laps gratefully at the milk Elena pours into her bowl, an unexpected treat. She mews to go outside. Elena stands in the open doorway. A full moon hangs heavy in the black sky. She imagines craters and soundless depths, an abiding calm. If only she could instil some of that quietude in her mind and stop it racing from one catastrophic scenario to another. Had Billy confronted Nicholas without realising the fury he would unleash? Or had he decided it was preferable to name the truth rather than carry it to his grave?

A rustle in the bushes startles her. It's probably a hedgehog or some other nocturnal creature foraging, yet she feels the darting fear that she so often experiences these days and nights. She calls the cat in and locks the back door behind them.

The ice pack hurts her skin but the painkillers are taking effect. She is sleepy yet returning to bed is a useless exercise.

"I thought I heard you moving about." Rosemary enters the kitchen in her dressing gown and sits down beside her. "Is the pain keeping you awake?"

"It woke me up and I couldn't settle again." Elena adjusts the ice pack.

"Is the poltergeist on your mind?" Rosemary's smile is grim. The inspector from the gas board was unable to find any trace of a gas leak and the explosion in the office remains a mystery. Unaware that her sarcasm could carry a grain of truth, Rosemary suggested that the damage must have been caused by a ghost.

"What do you mean?" Elena asks.

"Don't take me for a fool." Rosemary wraps a fresh ice pack in a towel and applies it to Elena's arm. "I don't believe you fell on those steps. If you are in danger, I need to know."

"I told you—"

"Nicholas attacked you, that's what I believe. What I don't understand is why you feel the need to protect him. You must tell me what's going on."

The strain of setting up her own law firm and combatting insistent rumours about her sudden departure from KHM is etched deeply on Rosemary's face. The whispering campaign she endured took place shortly after she'd held a meeting with Nicholas and questioned him about his dealings with an Asian bank. The same bank that left Elena penniless and dependent on Rosemary's generosity.

"You know what happened." The lie lodges in her throat. The longing to confide in her friend is a constant struggle but blurting out the truth will bring no relief. Rosemary, her reputation as a law-abiding solicitor at stake, will insist on going directly to the police. Elena is under no illusions as to how they will react, especially if she accuses Nicholas of murder.

Rosemary, clearly unconvinced, rises stiffly from the chair and returns to her bedroom. Elena follows her up the stairs and lies sleepless until morning.

CHAPTER FORTY-FIVE

On Mag's Head, the knock on the cottage door startles her. As always when an unexpected caller arrives, she tenses and, in doing so, her features tauten into a chilling rigidity. She checks the front window. Beyond the gate, an orange Citroën is parked close by the side of the road. She doesn't know anyone with such a distinctive car but tourists sometimes call looking for directions. When the caller knocks a second time, a prolonged rat-a-tat that sets her teeth on edge, she checks through the peephole. Elena Langdon. How long will it take before she gives up and drives away? After the fourth knock, she pulls the door open, furious yet frightened by the woman's determination.

"I had to come back." Elena stands square in front of her, her face bruised, stitches in her forehead. "You must tell me the truth about Amelia Madison."

"I told you I don't—"

"You lied." Elena's eyes are fixed on the butterfly pendant at her neck. "Amelia made that for you. I recognise her design. I've seen them often enough in her back garden."

"No, she did not." Such a tiny clue. The one mistake that could change everything. "How many times do you need to be convinced I'm not the person you're searching for?"

"Annie, please listen to me. You must have been close to Amelia. She would have confided in you. You knew something about

Nicholas's cruelty to her but it went further than that. Much further. Please let me in. You have to hear me out."

She pulls the front door closed behind her and confronts Elena. "Before you say anything further, I want to show you something that will end your suspicion once and for all." She leads Elena along a flagstone path at the side of the cottage. The windbreak trees provide shelter, yet the wind is still strong enough to stream her hair like a pennant behind her.

The studio fronts onto the ocean and has two wide picture windows on either side of the door. *Annie Ross Glass Design Studio* is written on a sign that clearly once hung from a pole but now lies on the ground. Below the studio, a cliff stretches down to the ocean. The flaking paint on the windowsills, and the residue of spume on the glass, give the small studio an air of neglect. She unlocks the door and stands aside for Elena to enter.

Some half-finished stained-glass pieces rest on a table, glass-cutting and soldering tools beside them. A stack of business cards with *Annie Ross Stained Glass Artist* embossed on them sit on a table by the door. A kaleidoscope of colours glitter in a showcase filled with butterflies, owls, birds in flight, roosters and peacocks, fish and dolphins.

"This is my studio," she says. "I made that medallion for myself. It's part of a collection I designed and sold some years ago. Now, please, leave me in peace. I hope you find this person you're searching for. But I can't help you. I never knew anyone called Amelia Madison."

Elena picks up a piece of glass, uncompleted but clearly intended to take the form of a dolphin. Her mouth stretches in a rictus of disappointment. A crack on her lip opens and begins to bleed. The sight of it is unsettling, as are the bruises and scabs on her face.

"Why did you close down your studio?" she asks.

"Logistics." Each time she is asked this question, she gives the same excuse. "My location made it too difficult to receive materials and deliver the finished product." She taps her index finger against a carousel of horses and sets them dancing.

"I see." Elena raises her right arm to rub dust from the dolphin, and winces. "I've evidence that Nicholas Madison killed Amelia's father." She makes this announcement flatly, without emotion. "The only person to know the truth was Billy Tobin. Now, he's also dead. Battered to death by a thug, as yet unnamed."

Elena Langdon has the tortured expression of a fanatic. *The Ice Pick Stabber*. It's not surprising the tabloids had a field day with that one. Obsessed with his dead wife, they said. Jealous and vindictive—and here she is, trying to pull apart the serenity that pervades this studio. What is she talking about? Nothing she says makes sense. A biker called Red, who owns a Harley and has a ponytail. What biker doesn't? Why on earth did she allow this crazy woman into the studio to spout gibberish that has nothing to do with her, nothing at all? Elena hands her a cheque stub. The name and date blur into a meaningless blob. Her head begins to spin. She holds onto the table for support, aware that Elena's expression has changed to one of concern.

"Annie…Annie, I'm sorry, I've upset you," she says. "Can I get you a glass of water?"

She is afraid to nod in case the dizziness returns but Elena is already walking towards the studio sink. So long since that tap was turned on. The water should taste of rust or decay, but it is as pure as she remembers.

"Who gave you this?" she asks after drinking the glass of water.

"Billy Tobin," Elena replies. "He died that night. And I'll be dead too if Nicholas finds out I came to you for help."

The silence that fills the studio is thick with grief. She walks to the window and stares at the Atlantic, as she has done so often when the sky is clear. A walking trail runs from here to the summit of the cliff where a high, slanted rock leans like a watchful guardian over the turbulent waves below. Tourists write their names on that rock, draw love hearts and doodles. She believes it is likely that worshippers must once have gathered before it to honour the sun as it rose above its mighty incline. Witches too, she thinks, when it was silvered by the moon. Lightning struck it once. She saw it happen, a flash that dazzled her eyes and seemed to split it in two. But when she checked the following morning, it was still rooted to the earth. A fishing boat rounds the headland and heads for the harbour at Rannavale. The beat of the ocean is familiar to her. Like the shriek of seagulls, it is a backdrop to her days, a lullaby at night.

"How dare you come into my house with your ludicrous accusations." Suddenly, she is screaming, her shrill wail of denial bouncing off the glass. "Amelia's father was knocked down by a car. A drunk driver, most likely, who drove off and left him to die in a ditch. Get out of my house this instant and leave me alone—leave me *alone!*" Dead memories clutch at her throat. They snatch her breath away. Tears run from her eyes. A dark road. Rain falling. A voice calling. *John . . . John . . .* The cracking is inaudible, yet she feels the sundering of two identities separating.

Elena's arms are around her. They look too brittle to support her, yet they are surprisingly strong as they hold her upright. Together, they leave the studio and enter the living room. She removes the logs and opens the hidden door. Elena kneels inside this small chamber and removes the letter at the top of the bundle. The bare light bulb hollows her face and illuminates her eyes as she skims over the written words. She stares at the photographs and sighs heavily, as if a long-held suspicion is finally being exposed to brightness.

✦

Out on the headland there is room to breathe. The jeep windows are open and the smell of seaweed drifts on the spume. Lily waves from the doorway of her shop as she drives past. In the rooms above the padlocked pub, an artist, a potter and a writer reside in relative harmony. A commune of new age travellers took over the defunct community centre that closed down when the recession hit and the young people fled to London, New York, Sydney. Like the ebb and flow of the tide, others will come and more will leave this rugged enclave. Constant motion, destabilising secure foundations and piledriving new ones.

Elena Langdon, alone in the cottage, searched for the truth and has now unveiled it. The façade of a marriage laid bare. Children stream from the small school towards the bus that will carry them to outlying farms and bungalows.

"Mammy, look. I made this card for you." Kayla proudly shows off her handiwork. The youngest pupil in her small class, she is surprisingly talented at drawing for her age. Two figures, one small, one tall, one pale, one olive-skinned. Always alone, mother and daughter. She turns the car round and begins the steep drive upwards.

CHAPTER FORTY-SIX

"Uncle Mark is here. He's *here*." Kayla dances on her toes and spins away from the window, where she has been waiting for the first sight of his car. Down the front path she runs and straight into his arms.

Mark swings her into the air. "Who are you?" he asks. "I came here specially to see Kayla, not a big, beautiful, grown-up girl like you. What's your name, big, beautiful girl?"

"You're a silly billy." She giggles. "I'm Kayla."

"That's not possible," he gasps. "Kayla is just a titch. At least she was the last time I saw her."

"I'm Kayla," she repeats and smacks his head. "Where's all your hair gone, Uncle Mark?"

"I sold it to the fairies to weave into a coat of gold."

"That's a big fib. Your hair was black."

"Haven't you heard of black magic? It turns to gold when a fairy is the weaver." He throws her over his shoulders and marches towards the front door.

"Is it gold like Mammy's hair?"

"Even more golden. Where is she?"

"She's baking cupcakes for you. I had two. They're yummy."

"Yummy yum yum," he chants as he marches towards the front door, where she stands waiting for them. "Annie! Why didn't you tell me Kayla had changed from a titch into a giant toadstool?"

"It happened overnight," she replies. "I was as surprised as you were when I saw her the next morning."

Kayla giggles and wriggles her legs as Mark lowers her to the ground. "I'm going to find Bluey," she shouts and runs out the gate. "I want him to meet Uncle Mark."

"Bluey?" Inside the cottage, he hangs his jacket on a hook. "Who or what is that?"

"A lamb," she replies. "He's an orphan. His mother died giving birth. Kayla has adopted him. She's supposed to feed him from a bottle five times a day but you don't have to be a genius to guess who does the six-in-the-morning feed."

"Ouch!" He takes her hands and holds them tight. "It's good to see you again."

"You too, Mark." She tilts her head, quizzingly. "Have you been burning the midnight oil?"

"Do I look that bad?"

"Just tired. Otherwise you look wonderful. How's Graham?"

"Good. He shaved off my hair. Said he refuses to live with a combover." He runs his hands self-consciously over his scalp. "I'm still getting used to it."

"It suits you. Adds character to your face." The chicken casserole she has prepared is ready to serve, the table set.

"I told you to keep Bluey outside," she says as Kayla enters the kitchen, a small lamb with a blue patch on its back at her heels.

"I want to show him to Uncle Mark."

"After dinner." She carries the casserole dish to the table and shoos the lamb away. "Now, do as I say and wash your hands."

Kayla chats throughout the meal and the lamb, staring through the glass patio door, bleats piteously.

"She's obviously devoted to the little fellow," Mark says when Kayla has filled a baby's bottle with warm milk and headed out to feed Bluey.

"He's a substitute for friends," she replies. "We live a quiet life here. So far, she hasn't realised what's she's missing. It'll become more difficult when she grows older and wants her friends to visit." She bites the edge of her nail, unaware that she is doing so.

"Jay was in touch last month. Back on his annual visit to his father. We had lunch together."

"How is he?" she asks. Outside, Kayla sits on the edge of a wooden picnic bench, the lamb feeding greedily from the bottle.

"He's in good form. Travelling a lot. High-pressure but he's coping. He spoke about her."

"You didn't—"

"Of course not," he says quietly, reassuringly, and opens his laptop.

"What have you managed to do so far?" she asks.

"It took a lot of figuring out but the fact that I restored his database once makes it slightly easier to gain access to his computer." He hits the keyboard and numbers flash onto the screen. "His assets are well protected and that money is buried so deep it's going to be one hell of a job to trace it. I have to be careful."

"If it puts your job in jeopardy..."

"Don't worry. I'm being cautious."

This virtual world was once unknown to her. A language she believed she would never understand or be interested in acquiring. Now, watching his fingers fly across the keyboard, she can see what he has achieved as he hacks into firewalls and breaches dark secrets in Panama, the Cayman Islands, Jersey, Puerto Rico.

"Will it work?" she asks when she has seen everything.

"Yes." He sounds grimly satisfied. "But I need to move slowly and not alert his suspicions. I'm worried about you."

"I can look after myself."

"Don't be foolhardy. You should consider moving somewhere less isolated. If Nicholas discovers—"

"He won't. Have you spoken to Elena?"

"Briefly by phone," he replies. "I'm meeting her on Friday evening."

"I showed her the studio."

"Can I see it before I go?"

Each time she opens the studio door, she imagines suspended animation; a fairy story where all the characters are caught in a spellbound sleep.

"Do you believe she's at peace?" she asks.

"I hope so."

"I dream about her sometimes. Really vivid dreams. We're children again, or teenagers, always the four of us."

"They were good days," he says. "Or am I sinking into the mire of nostalgia?"

She laughs, shrugs. "Probably. I'm told it's a disease that gets worse with aging. But one dream was different. She was on her own in a garden. The flowers and bushes, the waterfalls and trees shimmered, as if they were made from glass. She was standing at a bridge with steps leading up to it. In my dream she was at peace but when I woke up, I knew she was not at rest."

"That's because you can't let her go," he says. "Your feelings keep getting in the way. Maybe that dream is her actual reality."

"Mammy? Uncle Mark...where are you?" Kayla's cries draw them to the window. She runs towards the studio, her black braid clattering, the lamb, round-bellied, padding behind her.

✦

Darkness is beginning to settle over Mag's Head when Mark says goodbye. Before leaving, he takes her hair in his hands and lifts it from her shoulders, pushes her fringe back from her forehead. She resists the urge to pull away from his gentle touch. Apart from Kayla, she has become unaccustomed to human contact and is uneasy under his scrutiny.

"It's good to see you," he says and kisses her forehead. "To know you haven't changed and never will."

When he releases her hair, she gathers it around her like a cloak.

"Goodbye big, beautiful, grown-up Kayla," he shouts from the car. "Goodbye Annie."

She stands with her daughter at the gate and waves until he is lost from sight.

CHAPTER FORTY-SEVEN

Mark Patterson is waiting for Elena in Neary's Bar. He has found a quiet corner where they won't be overheard but she remains uneasy. Nicholas could be nearby, watching, waiting for her to drop her guard. The pub is busy, noisy, people milling around the bar and spilling outside onto the pavement. She is unable to pinpoint anything to confirm her suspicions and, gradually, she relaxes. She liked Mark from the moment he spoke to her in the cemetery and felt his light, reassuring grip.

He talks about Woodbine. How the door was always open to Amelia's friends. John Pierce was like a second father to him. To the four of us, he adds. He remembers the horror of his death, Amelia supported from the church by Nicholas, who formed such a protective barrier around her that her friends were excluded from her grief. That was the beginning of the change but they, like Amelia, were hardly aware of it until it was too late.

He remembers her checking her watch constantly when he met her for a drink or a meal, evasive when he questioned her about Nicholas, interrupting conversations to read texts from him, always the first to leave because he was outside in his car, waiting to drive her home. Elena could be listening to her own story. She thinks of her friends, how she allowed them to slide from her life and how invaluable their support is now, when she needs them. He tells her why Leanne changed her name by deed poll to Annie Ross as soon as she moved to New York. An act of defiance against her father. And Jay—Elena remembers him from the photographs, striking dark eyes and skin, dreadlocks, a rangy teenager who fell in love with Amelia.

Dropping his voice ever lower, as if the walls can eavesdrop on them, Mark outlines what he has been doing. As he reveals the information he has uncovered about Nicholas's financial transactions, Elena begins to fidget.

"Mark, I need some air." She finds it impossible to sit still and listen to how she has been defrauded. "I'll be back in a few minutes."

He nods, appreciating her distress. The glasses wobble when she stands up and her knees knock against the table.

Outside the pub, she leans against the wall and breathes deeply. Couples stroll arm in arm along Chatham Street. Flower sellers entice passers-by to purchase tiger lilies and brown-eyed sunflowers from their stalls. Elena is unaware of all this sound and movement. Nicholas ruined her. Coldly, calculatingly, he destroyed her only means of independence. Financial control led to mind and body control; and she allowed it to happen. She isn't interested in hindsight or excuses. She remained silent when she should have spoken out. Named it for what it was and named him for being the perpetrator of that violence.

She pleaded guilty at her court arraignment. In two months her trial will begin. Post-partum depression. But she is not depressed. Instead, she is possessed by a raw, red fury that causes her body to tremble uncontrollably.

"Are you all right, dear?" An older woman, her expression concerned, taps her arm.

Unable to reply, Elena gazes blankly at her.

"Are you feeling all right? the woman repeats. "Is there anything I can do to help you?"

I'm beyond help, she wants to shout but the woman gestures towards an empty seat outside the pub. Elena slumps down on the chair. The woman removes an unopened bottle of water from a small backpack and twists off the cap. The cold water revives Elena. She attempts to hand the bottle back but the woman declines it with a shake of her head.

"You keep it, dear. The colour is coming back to your cheeks again. This humid weather, it's affecting us all and Neary's is always so crowded."

"You're very kind."

"Not at all. Happy to help." She is a wiry woman with tightly permed hair and an inoffensive expression. "You remind me of my daughter."

"How so?" Elena asks.

"You're both very pretty and, like Danielle, I suspect you're finding life difficult at the moment."

Elena looks away, uneasy under the woman's scrutiny. The strains of a guitar being played by a street busker reach her. The woman is waiting for a reply but she feels no inclination to answer her.

"Thank you." She stands, her legs steady again. "I'd better go back and join my friend. He'll be wondering what's happened to me."

CHAPTER FORTY-EIGHT

Standing outside Clearwater, the woman looks undecided as to whether or not she should open the gate. Having made up her mind to enter, she stops for a moment to admire the garden. Her knock on the door is gentle, as if she is reluctant to disturb the owner. Kayla runs around from the side of the cottage to see who is calling. She is dressed in a bikini and droplets of water drip from her hair, shimmer on her arms.

"Can I speak to your mother or father?" The woman smiles apologetically. "I've lost my way and need directions."

"Where are you going?"

"To the summit. I've been told the view from there is magnificent."

"It's okay." Kayla doesn't share her enthusiasm. "Sometimes, there's mist."

"Not today."

Kayla nods. "I'm playing in my paddling pool."

"You're a lucky girl to have your own swimming pool."

"It's not a *real* swimming—"

"Is your mother at home, dear? Or your father."

"Mammy's working."

"Are you all alone then?"

"No, she's inside. I'll get her."

"Mammy...Mammy!" she shrieks. "A woman at the door wants you."

"I'm in here, Kayla." Another lost tourist. Reluctantly, holding tightly to her daughter's hand, she walks to the front door.

"I'm sorry to take you away from your work but the road seems to be impassable from here on." The woman, who had bent to admire a cluster of purple heather, straightens. Her face is flushed and beads of perspiration have gathered above her upper lip. She dabs at her mouth with a tissue, then smiles apologetically. "The journey up Mag's Head is more arduous than I thought. Can you tell me where I went wrong?"

"About a half a mile back you'll find a fork on the road. That leads directly to the summit, where there's a viewing platform."

"I saw that fork." She smacks the side of her head. "As usual, I made the wrong decision. Story of my life." Her walking boots have a lived-in shape and her trekking poles suggest she is a seasoned hillwalker.

"It's an easy mistake to make."

"You have a beautiful garden," she says. "I love how you've cultivated those wildflowers yet allowed them to flourish in their natural surroundings."

"Thank you."

"I'm sorry to intrude further on your time but could I ask you for a drink of water?" This time, she mops her forehead with the tissue and sways forward. Her grey roots are growing out and her curly hair is limp from the heat.

Work has been difficult this morning, a constant flow of emails demanding attention. She hesitates, reluctant to waste any more time, but this woman with her faded blue eyes looks as if she's about to collapse on the doorstep.

"You'd better come in and sit down for a few minutes." She opens the door wider. "I'll make you a cup of tea."

In the kitchen, the woman introduces herself as Moira Ward and offers a moist handshake.

"Annie Ross." She extricates her hand and resists the urge to wipe it on her dress.

"Annie? What a sweet name. Have you always lived here?"

"Not always." Already, she is regretting the decision to invite Moira Ward into her home. She switches on the kettle and wonders what they will talk about as she waits for it to boil.

"Do you mind if I use your bathroom, Annie?" Moira's flushed features have faded to a pallid grey that is probably her natural complexion.

"It's the last door at the end of the hall."

"Thank you." Taking her handbag with her, she leaves the kitchen.

Outside, Kayla, back in the paddling pool, is trying to persuade Bluey to join her. The lamb ignores her pleas and nibbles contentedly at the bark of a fallen branch. The cottage feels contaminated by the stranger's presence. She knows this is an overreaction, yet she is unable to dispel it. Moira is taking too long to return to the kitchen. Could she have fainted, or is she doubled over with cramps, unable to continue her journey? Alarmed by this possibility, she checks the hall. Moira is standing opposite a table of photographs. She turns quickly, her phone in her hand.

"I was just admiring your photographs." She points to a framed selfie, taken on Mark's recent visit. "Is this gorgeous man your husband?"

"No," she replies shortly. "He's a close friend. Your tea is ready."

"You're so kind. Thank you."

Back in the kitchen, she slowly sips the tea, her bird-like eyes darting around the room and then to the window. Outside Kayla is teaching her doll to swim.

"What a charming child," she says. "What age is she? Five? Six?"

"She's almost five."

"She has amazing eyes. Just like yours. Does she go to school locally?"

"Yes."

"You wouldn't imagine there'd be enough children living around here to keep a school open."

"You'd be surprised."

"I spoke to a man in the grocery store. He said you work with stained glass."

"I'm sure he told you I've closed down my studio."

"No, he didn't mention that. How very disappointing. I collect stained-glass pieces from everywhere I go." She butters a scone, smears it with jam. "Is this home-baked?"

"Yes. By Lily, the woman who owns the grocery store."

"Delicious. I'd like to buy one of your designs."

"As I said, I no longer work with stained glass." Kayla's shoulders are reddening. Another layer of sunscreen is needed. "I'm sorry. I have to attend to my daughter. She burns easily."

"Of course, I'm delaying you. You've been so kind. I'll say goodbye to Kayla and be on my way." She opens the back door and steps down into the garden. "I'm off, Kayla. It was a pleasure to meet you."

Kayla stands, water streaming from her. "Are you going to the summit now?"

"As soon as I take a photograph of your lamb. What's his name?"

"Bluey."

"You stand beside Bluey and I'll snap the two of you." She swipes her mobile and hits the camera. "Lovely." She checks the photograph and shows it to Kayla. "Now, let me take one of you and your mummy together."

"I want my lamb in the photograph as well." Unselfconscious in front of the camera, Kayla calls Bluey back to her side and crouches beside him.

"Annie, will you stand over here?" Moira gestures to her. "I'd like to get the ocean in the background."

"I'd rather you didn't take photographs." She can no longer ignore the uneasiness that besets her when unexpected people call to the cottage.

Moira lowers her mobile immediately and clasps it between her hands. "I'm invading your privacy. How rude of me. I don't think before I act, that's always been my problem. I'll leave you in peace. Thank you so much for your hospitality." Her eyes alight on the studio. "Oh, my goodness, Annie. Is that your studio?"

"I told you, it's no longer in use."

"But have you anything I can buy?"

"You have dolphins, don't you, Mammy, and lots and lots of butterflies like the ones in my room."

"Stained-glass butterflies? Oh, please, Annie. Let me buy one from you."

Reluctantly, she opens the door to the studio. Moira gasps with delight when she sees the display case. "You're so talented. Why on earth would you give up such a wonderful skill?"

"I lost interest." She removes a small frame containing a butterfly, its wings in flight, from the display cabinet and puts it into a carrier bag. "Please accept this as a gift, Moira. Now, I'm afraid I really must get back to work. It'll take no time at all to reach the fork in the road and you'll be at the summit shortly afterwards." She holds the studio door open until Moira, gushing her thanks, moves away from the display case.

"This view of the ocean is amazing." Once again, Moira is taking photographs. She swings around, her camera still raised. "It must be inspirational to live here." She slips the phone into her backpack, along with the carrier bag. "This beautiful butterfly will always remind me of your kindness."

CHAPTER FORTY-NINE

The Past

On the morning of her departure, Amelia walked through every room in Woodbine. She breathed in the smell of the old house and breathed it out again. She called to see Billy, who insisted, as he always did, that she have tea and Kimberley biscuits with him.

"Goodbye, Billy." She hugged him so hard he gave a small gasp of surprise.

"Are you sure you're okay?" he asked. "I hope that man of yours is treating you right?"

Coming to say goodbye to him was a mistake. Better a clean break—but he was her last link with her father. John always seemed a little closer when she was drinking tea in Billy's kitchen.

"No, I'm fine," she said. "Just running a bit late, so I'd better be off. Take care of yourself." A few kisses flung from her fingers and she was gone.

Nicholas had wanted to come to Galway with her and extend her overnight business trip into a short holiday. They would eat oysters in Clarinbridge and trek through Connemara, as they had done on their first weekend away together. Did she remember how *happy* they were then? Amelia remembered that happiness, the lightness of their footsteps, the music of their laughter. Nothing, she had believed, could ever come between them.

She should have spotted the cracks. There must have been signs she'd overlooked, swept up, as she was, in a delirium. A few days of relaxation would put the bloom back on her cheeks, he said. As he planned what they would do, where they would stay, she hid her panic, knowing that this would only increase his determination to come with her. She needed to unwind and become again the woman with whom he had fallen in love, he said. Not this nervous shadow who flinched at sudden movements and lay like a statue with her back to him at night. Being in love meant being patient. *Very* patient. He had taken to emphasising certain words and turning them into threats. He was willing to work through this difficult stage in their marriage as long as she showed signs of *appreciating* his efforts.

She showed him her work schedule for the coming week. Meetings with architects, tilers and painters, an office outfitter, the managing director of a company considering a revamp. Bored by her busyness, he eventually lost interest.

"Another time," he said.

"I'll look forward to it," she replied. "I'm only going to be away for a night. I'll be back before you know I've left."

✦

She reached Galway in the early afternoon and presented her proposal to the management of a pharmaceutical company. They were moving to new premises and at this, her third interview, she was awarded the commission. It would be one of her most prestigious projects. After lunching with Betsy Poole, the human resources manager, they drove to the industrial estate where the new premises were nearing completion.

By the time they parted, the peak hour traffic was moving sluggishly through Galway City. Stalled at the entrance to a roundabout, she chewed her knuckles and allowed the fear that she had controlled throughout the day to take over. Madness… she had to turn back… there had to be another way. She would take the next exit on the Dublin route and drive home. It was the only sane decision she could make.

Nicholas rang. She saw his name on the screen and allowed his call to go to message. His words slid like oil over her and away again. She exited the roundabout after the Dublin turn and headed for Mason's Pier.

✦

Twenty-five years since she had been there, yet her surroundings were heartbreakingly recognisable. She drove to the holiday home her parents had rented for that fateful week. The cottage was still thatched and the jutting window in the loft bedroom where she used to sleep was exactly as she remembered. One night she had woken to a roar of thunder. She had stood on a chair to watch as flashes of lightning skimmed across the waves. Five years old, her fearlessness taken for granted until it was destroyed. She drove on into the seaside village. Like the cottage, Mason's Hook was unchanged, the wending main street with its colourful shops, the cars parked any which way outside them. Past the village, a quietness fell. No houses broke up the stark descent along the cliff road to the pier.

Memories churning, she fought back nausea as she approached the slipway. In those moments before her car reached the water, she entered a dreamlike trance. A child running along the pier. Her mother struggling with a beach umbrella. A ball bobbing on the white-fingered waves.

Amelia shuddered and gripped the steering wheel, her palms slick with sweat. The fury of his fists. The kicks that left her gasping for air as she lay doubled over on the floor. The mark on her left breast where he, a non-smoker, had branded her with a cigarette. The nights he had held her and wept, promised to change; and, for a time, how possible that had seemed.

The tyres still had traction on the slimy slipway. It was not too late to change her mind. The life she was leaving behind and the future she faced clashed in an instant of doubt. Then she was composed again—or was it numbness that steadied her resolve? She was unable any longer to understand the signals her brain was sending to her. She felt a change in tempo, an almost imperceptible movement as the wheels began to lose their grip on the downward slope. The ocean had turned red. Tongues of fire, kindled by the setting sun.

She was aware that she was sinking, but not fast as she had expected; or maybe time had slowed so that she could enjoy a few seconds more of this rapturous sunset. She wondered if her car could straddle the ocean like a flat-bottomed boat. Could it carry her beyond the horizon where she had always imagined her mother lived in a dazzling, parallel universe? This fantasy was fleeting and water began to lap against the windows. Soon, she would be unable to see anything except cascading bubbles evaporating into the fathomless depths.

✦

For months, she had prepared herself for these final moments. Alone on Kilfarran Strand, furrows of wet sand squiggling under her toes. Gannets and guillemots beating their wings against the sky. Terror slicing through her as the sand shifted in its rush to meet the incoming tide. A scampering wave sliding away before it reached her bare feet. Bracing herself as the next wave splashed over her toes. Telling herself, three steps... three steps will be enough for today. Enduring the shock each time she was buffeted by a fresh wave even though the sea, running dizzily past her, was still no higher than her ankles.

Back at Woodbine, showering. A residue of sand left on the floor of the cubicle. Frantically spraying it away. Down on her knees to check if she had missed a grain. He was at a business meeting but he might have been looking over her shoulder, demanding to know why she had been standing up to her ankles in the petrifying sea. Sitting back on her hunkers, thinking it would be easier to fling her body against the walls of a padded cell than to continue living this existence.

She changed beaches regularly. Each one threw up a new challenge. Each one buoyed her confidence. She had never been able to imagine herself swimming yet her father had told her many times that she had been like an eel in the water before the accident.

Leanne had kept in touch, letters flying back and forth, insistent that Amelia did not change her mind. The die was cast, she wrote, if you'll excuse the pun. Her sense of humour was dark and, sometimes, all Amelia could do was laugh at the absurdity of it all. It was never going to happen, yet she had kept swimming, knowing that if she could conquer this fear, anything else was possible.

Thinking about Leanne always brought tears. They had fused with the waves and were washed away by the sea.

✦

A beach ball hurtling. A woman's screams. Her mother's arms reaching for her. To be enfolded in her embrace again. This time she would reach Amelia and they would be together at last. A joyous reunion, a glorious new beginning in a sphere where the sun never set and happiness was their eternal reward. This vision was dangerously close and enticing, as her car lurched and continued its downward plunge.

Amelia grabbed the red boot she had left on the passenger seat and smashed the window. Water surged around her, assaulted her eyes and nostrils, lifted her from the driver's seat. Her body flailed, free-falling, an astronaut in space. She clung to the steering wheel and willed herself to remain focused as the return of a familiar panic stabbed her.

The car door was jerked open. A figure was beside her, round-helmeted and sleek as a seal. Was he a figment of her imagination or a knight in shining armour? She released her death grip on the wheel and was lifted upwards, her lungs straining against the pressure to breathe. Then, with what seemed like an explosion of splintering glass, Amelia surfaced into the light.

She was swept forward by the incoming tide towards a curvature of rocks. A sliver of sand was visible under the overhanging cliff. The diver, swimming stroke by stroke with her, encouraged her when she slowed or showed signs of panic. The waves were rushing to claim full possession of the cove when they staggered ashore. He supported her up steps cut into the cliff face. Down below them, the waves rolled over the sand and obliterated their footsteps.

The interior of the van was warm, the heating full on, yet Amelia shook convulsively as Leanne helped her to change from her sodden clothes into thermal underwear and a fleece. Wrapped in a thermal blanket, she lay down on an airbed in the back of the van. Jay unzipped his wetsuit and pulled on the clothes Leanne handed him. Mark started the engine. Gradually, her trembling stopped and Amelia, drifting in and out of sleep, was barely aware of time passing. Whenever she awoke, Leanne was beside her to whisper reassurances that all was going as planned.

✦

Her first impression of this wild place that was to become her home was an audible one. Leanne assured her she would become so used to the wailing wind that she would sleep soundly through the mightiest gales. In the bathroom, Amelia showered. Her skin felt abrasive, brine in her pores. A plan that had seemed beyond crazy had worked—but for how long?

Nicholas was bound to become suspicious sooner rather than later. She had promised to ring him as soon as she arrived in Galway. He would be angry that she had not obeyed his instructions and even angrier when he was unable to contact her later in the evening. Not enough to alert his suspicions, though; he would see this as just a small gesture of defiance. One that he would quash easily once she returned. Her legs weakened. She gripped the edge of the handbasin to steady herself. He would ring the hotel where he believed she was staying overnight and discover she had cancelled her booking? He would ring the pharmaceutical company and discover that she had told Betsy Poole she was unable to accept their commission?

At first, he would believe she had run away. He would check her laptop, looking for clues. Failing to find any, he would search her possessions, hurling her clothes from the wardrobe, upending the drawers in the dressing table that he had filled with the lingerie of his choice, searching, searching for the tiniest clue that could explain her disappearance. Then, tomorrow, the knock on the door. Two grave-faced gardai who would enquire whether her car had been stolen. When he shook his head, they would ask if his wife had been wearing red boots? They would tell him that a car had been discovered at the foot of Mason's Pier at low tide, and that a red boot had been recovered from the silt, a second boot wedged between the driver and passenger seat. She envisaged the search that would follow, the divers, the boats and helicopters. How long would it last? Was she now a criminal? Wasting valuable resources? Her survival instincts were stronger than the shame this caused her. She touched her stomach. Another few weeks and Nicholas would have noticed the swelling, slight as it was.

CHAPTER FIFTY

How mightily the strong fall when illness strikes. I was a healthy child, who became a healthy adult. My constitution could go fifteen rounds with an infection and win. Contagion looked me in the eye and fled. If I could claim unrequited love as an illness, it would be the only one that made my eyes water and my breathing short.

When I was afflicted by a strange tiredness and sensations of pins and needles in my legs began to trouble me, I refused to recognise this as an illness. It was easy to find reasons for my symptoms. I was working too hard, taking on too many commissions, sitting for too long at the cutting table in my New York studio and ignoring my posture. Denial became harder when I was cutting glass one day and my right arm began to shake uncontrollably. The attack passed but I knew I must consult a doctor. I found myself undergoing tests in the unfamiliar environs of a hospital. It took time for the medics to reach a diagnosis. When the disease was named, a rare and fatal syndrome with a name I wanted to instantly forget, I discharged myself back to my apartment. Ignoring something, I believed, could force my mind to conquer matter. For a while that seemed possible. But when I was no longer able to ignore the gradual weakening of my limbs, I returned to Ireland and moved to Mag's Head.

My creative vision had always embraced large spaces but there, beside that restless ocean, I set up my studio and worked small. In those early months I wondered if the medics had been wrong. My energy was good, my productivity boundless. Looking back, I see this brief remission as a final handout from the puppet-master of fate.

I persuaded myself to endure the pain, the increasing sense of weakness, of losing possession of my own body. I thought I could tough it out, as others have done, using their guts and grit, but I was never born to endure the unendurable.

My mind was made up, my plan set when I came to Woodbine and hung the butterflies from the apple tree. When the time was right, I would go quietly into the darkness, or, if there was a bonus to be gained, I would pass into the brightness.

Amelia had been devastated when she heard what I intended to do. We'd argued fiercely. She said it was a crazy solution to both our problems; outrageous, bizarre, and without any possibility of succeeding. Fate, however, had decreed otherwise.

My hair had always been my flag of identity, so striking that people seldom noticed much else about me. I used to cry in the mornings when my father combed it, dragging the comb through the tangles until my scalp ached. He'd become impatient and, eventually, give up and fling the comb at the wall. A bad hangover kills parenting skills flat-out. I managed it myself from the age of eight. At one stage I could sit on it. After I became friends with Amelia, she brushed it every day until she'd removed the tangles of years. I was just as patient when I searched online for the wig she would use when she came here.

I became a tactician, slotting all the pieces together and plotting carefully, knowing that one slip of the cutting knife would shatter the glass. Our friendship, forged in love, would give my death meaning. What had seemed unmanageable when the thought first came to me took on a semblance of possibility, then normality. Nicholas believed I had returned to New York. Amelia had told him so, and, as he did not know about my illness, he'd believed her. I had no children who would mourn me, no partner who would care if I slipped away for ever. Jay and Mark would grieve, this I knew, and Amelia, this woman I was born to lose, would be freed from the burden of my love.

CHAPTER FIFTY-ONE

When she realised she was pregnant, and that she had no idea if this new life had been conceived in love or violence, Amelia was conscious of only one emotion. To protect her child was all that mattered to her. To do so, she must create a secure space where both of them could be safe from Nicholas. If she ran away from him, she knew with absolute certainty that he would not rest until he found her again. She must disappear, leave no trail of breadcrumbs for him to follow, but, if she had to vanish without trace, she must first overcome her fear of the ocean. Only then could she lay claim to the new future that Leanne had offered her.

Jay did not know the true reason why Amelia had chosen to embark on such a dangerous subterfuge. The scars on her arms had healed but the internal ones would never fade. She had struggled to overcome the blur of amnesia that followed that lost night when Nicholas cut into her flesh and branded her as his own. That other night—those passionate hours she had spent in Jay's arms—she could remember every blissful moment of their time together. Dawn had been rising over Woodbine when he parted reluctantly from her and returned to his life in California. He had been unaware of the legacy he could have left behind him and this still remained the case. If he suspected the truth, and the possibility that he could become a father—or even if he had not fathered her child—he would try to persuade her to leave with him. Her husband had the instincts of a tracker, the cruelty of a hunter. If she chose the life Jay would offer her, she would always imagine his shadow following her. If she refused to leave Mag's Head, Jay would insist on staying here with her. What future could she offer him on this barren headland? No, he must leave as soon as he and Mark completed work on the chamber that Leanne had insisted was necessary for Amelia's protection. How was she to face her uncertain future without him? With courage—it was the only way. She had claimed possession of this gift that Leanne had offered her and must find the strength to step into her best friend's skin.

Four days, that was the length of time it took Jay and Mark to create the chamber and install a phone alarm system within it. It would be effective should help be needed from the police in Rannavale Garda Station, but Amelia was aware of the length of time it would take for a squad car to arrive. Living on Mag's Head would be a see-saw of survival and she must struggle to find a perfect balance.

When the chamber was complete, she stood with Jay on the summit of Mag's Head and told him he must leave. She had never loved him, she said, even when they ran hand in hand through the trees in Kilfarran Woods, stopping under their shade to kiss until their lips were bruised. Nor had she loved him on that tumultuous night when he lay above her, and under her, beside her and inside her, so deep she wondered if they could ever be separated. She ordered him to go to back to California and forget her. She was assuming a new identity and cutting off all links to her past life. He had gone down on his knees and begged her to move with him to California or let him stay with her in the misty climes of Mag's Head. How hard it had been to turn away from him, but true love, she had discovered, was conjoined with sacrifice. Leanne would lay down her life so that Amelia could create a new existence. Amelia was willing to lay down her own happiness so that Jay, unhindered, could move on with his life. She lied to him and her deception broke him. He believed her and his acceptance broke her.

In those early weeks, she found it impossible to visualise Leanne in her reflection and was startled every time she glimpsed herself in the mirror. In art college, they had studied stained-glass design during their first year. Leanne had continued her studies until she dropped out and left for New York but Amelia had preferred a softer, more tactile material. In Leanne's studio, she was a fish out of water. Her hands shook too much to handle a soldering iron or a glass-cutter. Seeing how distressed it made her, Mark persuaded her to stop trying to take over the business. He helped her to set up an online company and provide a specialist finder service. Her database was exhaustive and she was soon sourcing the elusive furnishings and textiles her clients sought.

Her hair's natural wave returned after years of being straightened into the helmet style she loved. She dyed it and let it grow long. Did anyone notice her features, the shape of her nose, her eyes, so like Leanne's but a deeper green? The difference in their height—slight, admittedly, but Leanne had always been the taller. No. People saw what they expected to see. It was easy not to look beyond the obvious, unless, like Nicholas, total possession was the endgame.

Mark was with her when Kayla was born. The midwife masked her surprise as she glanced from him to Kayla and realised he could not be the baby's biological father. He behaved like one, though. Holding Kayla with wonder, besotted by her perfect fingers and Cupid mouth, her mother's green eyes, her father's dark, velvety skin.

Amelia, weeping with relief that she had given birth to a love-child, was consumed by a new dread. Kayla must always remain her secret. Fear for Jay's safety if Nicholas discovered the truth overrode all other considerations. Kayla Ross would be written on the birth certificate. Father Unknown. Her daughter must be her only love and yet... and yet... sometimes the isolation of her surroundings was almost too much to bear. As time passed, she merged into the quiet life of Mag's Head and, eventually, found it possible not to jerk with grief when she answered to the name of Annie.

✦

Loneliness is her companion now. To break loose and risk everything to be with the man she loves is an intolerable burden. She was able to carry it until Elena Langdon came knocking on her door with her bruises and harrowing facts but now this loneliness is combined with uneasiness, a nervous tension that has heightened since Moira Ward stood inside her cottage and radiated hypocrisy.

CHAPTER FIFTY-TWO

The Present

Amelia watches the car from the back of the cottage, where she has a view of the twisting road. The BMW is out of place on Mag's Head, where four-by-fours, jeeps and quad bikes are a more normal means of transport.

The driver brakes outside the cottage. She has imagined this moment so often. Imagined her heart thudding to a shuddering halt or her brain imploding. Now that he is here, though, she is alert and resolute. Kayla is at school. The front and back doors are securely locked but her jeep will indicate that she is at home. Moving quickly, she enters the chamber and huddles down. When it had been completed, she had left two packed suitcases of clothes and toiletries inside it, along with passports for Kayla and Annie Ross.

He knocks four times. The sound reverberates through the cottage. Each bang on the door feels like an electric charge on her skin. She draws her knees towards her and breathes silently into them. She doesn't move from this position, even when the silence suggests he has given up and left. An hour later, she emerges from hiding. His car is missing, but she is not deceived by this obvious sign of his departure. She rings Lily to ask if she has noticed a BMW coming and going from the headland. This is a rhetorical question. Nothing escapes Lily's eagle eye.

"I saw him heading up the head and coming down again," Lily says.

"Has he left the village?"

"I reckon he has. He called in here to ask about you on his way out. Said he'd been knocking on your door for ages but got no answer. I told him you were in New York and wouldn't be back for a few months. I hope I did the right thing."

"Yes, you did, Lily. Did you talk to him about Kayla?"

"Don't worry. I never said a word about the child."

"Is there any chance Bart could pick her up from school today?" Despite Lily's assurances that Nicholas has gone from the village, she is still too frightened to leave the cottage. "I'm busy tracing some textiles that I need for a client, who is expecting an answer from me in the next hour."

"Bart!" Lily shrieks at her husband, who makes deliveries of coal and turf to the small community at the foot of Mag's Head when he is not helping out behind the counter. "Will you collect Annie's kid from school and drop her home?" She pauses, then reverts to her normal voice. "He says he'll pick her up in the van."

"Tell him not to talk to anyone."

"You mean your man in the BMW?"

"I do. Make sure to tell him."

"Don't worry about Bart. I'll be sure to tell him to keep his big trap shut."

"Thanks, Lily. I don't know what I'd do without you."

"Ah sure, isn't that what neighbours are for? When he first came into the shop and asked about you, I thought all your dreams had come true. Such a handsome hunk and a charmer, to boot. He even admired my painting. There's not many around here do that so I figured then and there that he was a right chancer."

◆

Kayla is sleeping. Her mother is staring at the stars. The sky is clear tonight and the constellations dazzling. She talks to Leanne, as she always does last thing before she goes to bed. Do you believe in ghosts, Elena had asked the first time she came to Clearwater.

Amelia's reply had been emphatic. No ghosts haunted this craggy peninsula but sometimes a play of light, a darting bird, the swirl of a butterfly brought Leanne to mind with such vividness that she was forced to a standstill, her heart filled to bursting.

CHAPTER FIFTY-THREE

In the dead of night, shadows tell no secrets. I'm insubstantial but I'm not a shadow, of that I'm certain. Billy Tobin is dead. One blow from a weapon that has yet to be found. Nicholas recognised Rosemary Williams's orange Citroën that afternoon. Guessing it was being driven by Elena, he knocked on Billy's door that night, demanding to know what she had been doing there. When the fear of death has been conquered, we become unconquerable. And, so, Billy didn't bend. He had solved a mystery that had tormented him for years and he made the accusation to Nicholas, loudly, defiantly. How easy it was to crack his skull. The gardai were convinced it was a cricket bat or, perhaps, a mallet. It wasn't either. The knob on Billy's walking stick was the weapon of choice. He died from the third blow. It lay beside him, washed clean of blood and unfamiliar fingerprints. A less deadly weapon to the one that killed John Pierce, but just as effective.

Initially, Nicholas had no reason to query the financial transactions that were taking place in his offshore accounts. The dark web had too many layers to infiltrate, he believed, and, with the confidence of a true narcissist, he was convinced he would never be found out.

Nicholas is unaware of the extent of the discovery, yet his instincts tell him something is wrong. His habitual charm has disappeared. He no longer flashes his white teeth at the female staff at KHM and tells them how stunning they look. He is wary, verging on panicky, working late at his computer to try to combat information that threatens his future. It has taken time to trace the changes to his online account. The payouts that he never authorised yet which have his imprimatur. His accounts were being hacked but he was unable to figure out how it was happening or who was responsible—until he saw the photographs he had obtained from a private detective.

Moira Ward is a chameleon who blends into her surroundings. An inconspicuous woman of uncertain age and grey hair dyed a mousy beige. Nicholas recognised Neary's, where old-fashioned lamps and wooden panels add an authentic charm to the old pub. How intense Elena looked as Mark explained how he would destroy the man who had destroyed her.

Other photographs puzzled him. An untamed landscape overlooking the ocean. Rocks slanting towards the sun. Stained-glass designs that were familiar to him. A child, dark skin glistening with water, green eyes staring trustfully into the camera and, by her side, a slim figure, white-blonde tangles hiding her features as she raised a hand to block off the invasive lens.

✦

Mark does not hear the footsteps gaining on him, nor feel the air stir with menace. Ducks are sleeping in a row, the ones at the end keeping one wary eye out for perilous encounters. He crosses a humpback bridge and stops on the crest to admire a lone swan, gliding on the water like a ghostly ballerina. He phones Graham and apologises for his lateness. He'll be home in thirty minutes.

"Hurry," Graham says and the longing in that one word sums up the tenderness of their marriage. It is the last word Mark will hear before he is struck down by a one-punch blow to his head.

That night when Elena was helpless in a basement and fighting for her life, my fury struck a spark in this nameless heartland. It shattered glass, wrenched steel. Tonight, I feel it again. The swan rises on the crest of my rage. Wings outstretched, a clumsy take-off that turns to grace when she is airborne. She flies so low that Nicholas is startled by her appearance and the blow he delivers is weakened.

Why am I forced to witness these visions? I am helpless, invisible chains and walls separating me from those I love. Pinned like a butterfly in a shadowbox, my wings stilled as Mark collapses, his face smacking against the pavement, his brain stunned. A couple, attracted by the swan, appear from behind the Pepper Canister church and approach, cautiously. The swan flies in a circle above the spot where Mark lies. Nicholas slips away, his footsteps making no sound on the pavement as he blends into the darkness, and the swan returns to her nest among the reeds.

CHAPTER FIFTY-FOUR

"No change," Graham tells Elena when she arrives at the hospital. He holds on tightly to her hands, his cheeks knuckled with shock, and asks her how anyone could do this to Mark.

Photographs of the couple who found him unconscious on the pavement and called an ambulance have appeared on the front pages of the newspapers. They have been interviewed on the morning news bulletins. Last night, walking in the opposite direction to Mark, they noticed a swan rising from the canal and doing what they described as "acrobatics" in the air. They returned to watch her glide back to the water and discovered Mark. No one else was on the scene.

Mark remains in intensive care and on life support to help his breathing. She sits with Graham in the hospital corridor and tries to console him. They strain forward each time they glimpse a nurse or doctor in scrubs hurrying past but the medics keep their eyes averted. They are used to the desperation of loved ones waiting to hear the latest update.

Graham has seen the tabloid headlines. Gay-bashing. Where did they get that information? The term has an ugly resonance that belongs to the past. He refuses to believe it was the reason for the attack. Mark has no enemies, he knows; and there are no secrets between them . . . He screws up his forehead at the latter thought. And yet, and yet . . .

"He was working late so often lately," he tells Elena. 'We both have to do that occasionally. It's never been an issue before now but this time there was more to it than late hours.

"He brought it home with him, not the work itself but the energy of it. He wasn't sleeping well. I'd awaken some nights and he'd be downstairs on his laptop. He wouldn't tell me what he was doing and that's unusual. We talk about everything, including our work." He continues searching for reasons. Maybe the tabloids have it right. Maybe his attacker mistook him for someone else. Maybe some crazy coke-head turned vicious and Mark was in the wrong place at the wrong time. The conversation goes round in circles. Elena lets him talk. There is only one possibility. Nicholas knows. Somehow, he has gained knowledge of the fact that his computer was being hacked and identified Mark as the hacker.

✦

She arrives at the community centre early. As usual, Sophie meets Yvonne at the entrance and brings the children into the room to meet their mother. For the next hour they will play on the slides and bricks, and Elena will read to them, *Are You My Mother?* by P. D. Eastman, as she does on every visit.

Ghosts don't exist. She knows this now. She never experienced Amelia's cool breath on her skin or moved to the bidding of her unseen presence. There was a logical reason for the shattered office window, the rattling shutter. Sooner or later she would understand it. Imagination, overstretched and stressed, had played tricks on her. What did exist, she discovered on her second visit to Mag's Head, was enduring friendship and selfless love.

In the hidden chamber, she read the letters Amelia had written. She saw her bruises in the photographs scattered before her and, in the muddled and sometimes indecipherable writing, her words had revealed an awful truth. Desperate to protect her unborn child, she had jettisoned her own identity to emerge from the chrysalis of violence. How must that feel? To live in a dead woman's shoes? Elena understands this overwhelming protectiveness. If she could snatch Grace and Joel and bring them to a place of safety, she would do so without hesitation.

Today, Yvonne has a hair appointment and Henry will collect his grandchildren. Sophie's professional mask is dropping; Elena has noticed a softening in her voice when they speak together.

As the hour draws to a close, Elena asks her to watch the children while she uses the bathroom.

"No problem." Sophie kneels down beside Joel, who pushes a toy helicopter across the floor.

As soon as she is outside the room, Elena hurries towards the entrance. Henry, punctual as always, stops abruptly when he sees her.

"I have to talk to you." Elena steps in front of him. "It's important."

"Then speak to me in front of Sophie. You're well aware that any contact between us is strictly forbidden if she's not present."

"I just want a moment of your time."

"You could be in serious trouble for accosting me." His tone has become hard, inflexible. "Stand aside and allow me to collect my grandchildren."

"Henry, please listen to me. I'm worried about Nicholas."

"Worried? You have a strange way of showing it."

"His violence is—"

"Oh, for God's sake, Elena. No more pathetic lies about my son."

"I didn't fall on the steps outside Rosemary's office. Something interrupted him while he was attacking me. Otherwise, he could have killed me."

"I presume you can name this 'something' that prevented my son from killing you?" His mockery is overdone, his eyes darting past her, seeking an escape. Unlike Nicholas, he's incapable of hiding his feelings and she can see how nervous he is.

"It doesn't matter what interrupted him," she says. "A man is on life support in hospital. I'm convinced Nicholas attacked him—"

"For Christ's sake, Elena. Is there no end to your vindictiveness? Yvonne is right when she says you're unhinged."

"Do you believe her?"

"Absolutely."

" 'If you have another truth, then go and find it.' " Wasn't that what you said to me, Henry?"

He steps closer and grabs her shoulders. "I was a fool not to report you for breaking into my house. You need to be locked up and I'm going to make sure that happens. Starting right now."

"The only way Nicholas can keep me from revealing the truth is to kill me," she says. "If that happens, I want you to remember this conversation."

Without replying, he storms ahead of her into the other room, where Joel is lying on the floor, red-faced and drumming his heels. Grace, her hands clasped over her ears to drown his shrieks, is weeping quietly in Sophie's arms.

"They were afraid you'd left them without saying goodbye." She glances apologetically at Elena, who has lifted Joel and pressed him to her shoulder. Gradually, his shrieks quieten into hiccupping gulps. Her neck is wet with his tears. She waits for Henry to report her for accosting him. He bends and begins to pick up the toys. His face is hidden from her, his shoulders stooped.

"Say goodbye to your mammy." He speaks softly to Grace and takes Joel, relaxed now, from Elena's arms. He does not look at her or speak again.

He will ring the police as soon as he returns home. What else can he do? Elena is a stalker, intent on destroying his son with her insane accusations. This time there will be no mitigating circumstances. The post-partum depression argument is a spent force and will not soften a judge's heart.

CHAPTER FIFTY-FIVE

Henry is in an agony of indecision. He remembers that afternoon at the barbecue. How he shut me down when I appealed to him for help. He has blocked the words we exchanged, believing I had been driven by malice or, even, jealousy. Excuses can be found easily if you search for them as desperately as Henry does. He had seen the flint in his son's eyes, witnessed his sudden outbursts if he was challenged or questioned. Not that it happens much these days. Unlike his childhood tantrums. They left Henry whey-faced and desperate for a professional opinion as to why their son could shatter his parents with his mood swings and then charm them back with a smile.

Yvonne refused to acknowledge his fears. Small boys were aggressive by nature, she said, and Nicholas was just going through a phase. One he would soon outgrow. Henry must stop being jealous of the attention she gave to their son. Stung by her attitude, afraid that, if they continued to argue, she would leave him and take Nicholas with her, he buried his misgivings. Today, Elena forced him to confront them again, as did Joel's ear-piercing shrieks, the pitch of his distress sweeping Henry back in time. The only difference was that Elena had pacified her son. Nicholas could never be silenced by soothing arms, yet it seemed that Yvonne always knew best.

Henry had relaxed as his son grew in assurance and self-control. It was easy to dismiss the odd incident. Like the boy in hospital with the fractured arm and the Year Head's belief that he had been bullied by Nicholas. A lie, as it turned out. What else could it be when the boy had insisted he fell off his bike on his way home from school? Yvonne threatened to bring the Year Head to court for slander and only stopped the proceedings when he resigned. Then there was the incident with the girl, doe-eyed and hungry for Nicholas. Her father had the nerve to accuse Nicholas of rape, which his daughter denied as soon as she realised that she would have to admit in court how she had stalked Nicholas and constantly demanded his attention. Nicholas was right to go abroad afterwards. He needed time to recover from her slanderous accusation. The wealth of experience he gained in China and Hong Kong was invaluable. Henry never admitted, even to himself, that the happiest time of his married life was when his son lived abroad. The knot in his chest—so familiar that he was hardly aware of it—only tightened again when Nicholas returned.

I am witness to his tormented thoughts. I don't want to be there but hither and thither like a feather I float and land. It would be easy to blame Yvonne. An easy target, indulgent and obsessed with her only son, unable to see the mote in her own eye and in his. But Yvonne is not to blame for his murderous intent. Nor are his antecedents, though there was a great-grand-uncle who terrified both of his wives into early graves. When it comes to the final roll-call, we are all responsible for our own actions and Nicholas knew from the beginning that he was set apart from others. He was gifted with an intuition that recognised vulnerability and could prey upon it. He chose well when he captivated Elena. An only child, no siblings or parents to give her support, her friends scattered. As isolated as the wife he had lost. Unable to see beyond his tragic past, no one makes that connection... except, perhaps, Henry, half-blinded by paternal love but beset by doubts he is now forced to acknowledge.

At Woodbine, where he takes Grace and Joel after their visit with their mother, he feeds his grandchildren and settles them down for an afternoon nap. He passes the bedroom Nicholas once shared with Amelia. The key, no longer hidden, falls at his feet and clatters on the wooden floor. He picks it up and replaces it in the keyhole. Why is the door locked? Why does he feel the urge to unlock it? Why is his skin crawling, as if beset by small, scurrying spiders?

Henry does not know what he expects to find there, yet he keeps looking in drawers, under the bed, in the wardrobe. He is shocked to see Amelia's clothes still hanging neatly on hangers. Clothes so different from the ones she used to wear in those early years. The only eye-catching dress is the silver lamé one and even that, he knows, though he has no sense of fashion, is one Amelia would never have chosen for herself.

His movements become more frantic and finally he finds what he has dreaded, on the top shelf. Photographs of Elena going to and coming from work, at the supermarket, emerging from the sea, a swim hat in hand, walking with Rosemary in a park, entering the community centre to visit her children, and one that shows her outside a pub. He examines other photographs. A mother and child, an unruly lamb, the ocean thrashing below them.

"Leanne." He breathes my name. The child is a stranger to him but the last photograph Henry comes upon will torment him forever. He recognises Neary's distinctive décor. He had sat in that pub with Nicholas, comforting him, when tragedy came out of the blue and the woman he loved disappeared without trace. Now, he wishes he had the wisdom of Solomon. If he could cut the truth in half, he could endure it. But there is no middle ground. Either Elena Langdon is an insane liar or his son is a monster. The face of

the person in the photograph is familiar to him. He has seen Mark Patterson on television. He has heard the request from the gardai for information from anyone who noticed him in the vicinity of the Grand Canal on the night he was attacked with a one-punch blow to his head.

CHAPTER FIFTY-SIX

Rosemary is visiting her sister for the weekend and will not be back until Sunday night. On Monday, she has an appointment to meet with Christopher Keogh. "He has some very interesting information to share with me," she said to Elena before she left. "He wants to discuss why I became suspicious of Nicholas. I wonder who could have alerted him that something was wrong? It appears that his golden boy is made from gilt."

Alone in the house, Elena waits for the knock on the door. Henry will have reported her by now. She imagines the authoritative voices, the clink of handcuffs. Outside, there will be media, cameras flashing, questions shouted.

The night passes. She tries to distract herself by watching television. A crime drama is playing on every channel she zaps. Finally, she discovers a nature documentary that looks gentle enough to soothe her—until the animals obey their primal instincts and kill for their dinner. Giving up, she decides to go to bed. An envelope lies on the hall floor. She picks it up, thinking it will be addressed to Rosemary, and is surprised to see her name printed on it in block capitals. Opening it, she removes a sheet of paper that has been wrapped round a USB key. The message is stark and brief. *Be careful, Elena. You are being followed.*

The USB key opens up as soon as she inserts it into her laptop. She stares at photographs that can only have been sent by one person. Henry's phone is switched off when she rings him. His answering machine tells her he is unavailable.

✦

The eyes that follow her must sleep at some stage and Elena has chosen the quiet of the small hours to drive through the slumbering streets. No car headlights beam in her rear-view mirror. The only traffic she encounters is trucks heading towards the ferry.

It is after five in the morning when she reaches Lily Howe's Grocery Provisions. A light is shining from the window and Lily, muffled in a quilted dressing gown, waits in the doorway. She opens a gate at the side of the shop and gestures at Elena to park the car in the back yard where sacks of coal and turf are stored.

Mag's Head, rising to meet the dawn, stands like a brooding sentinel over the small hamlet. The jeep arrives shortly afterwards. Elena and Amelia do not embrace. Their kinship, conjoined by secrets, is still too tentative for touch. They have accepted that their lives are in danger. Not to act now is to look over their shoulders every time they hear footsteps behind them.

Inside the cottage, breakfast is ready. Fresh fruit and poached eggs, a pot of strong tea, home-baked scones that Lily pressed into Elena's hand as they were leaving. The radio playing early morning music and the heat in the kitchen from the wood-burning stove add to the cosy normality of their surroundings. The décor in each room has a flawless simplicity that combines comfort with style and reminds Elena of Woodbine.

Kayla is excited when she runs into the kitchen. She is on her school holidays and her mammy is taking her to a special farm where there is a new baby for her to mind. Elena waves goodbye as they hurry towards the jeep. She yawns, tired and stiff from her journey. She will rest for a few hours in the spare bedroom. The sounds of the morning are muffled. The jeep leaving, the shriek of seagulls and kittiwakes, the radio still playing as she drifts towards sleep.

In a few hours, she is due to present herself at the garda station. Her disappearance will be reported to Nicholas. The eyes that he has hired to watch her will have no idea of her whereabouts. He is the only one who will figure out where she has gone.

CHAPTER FIFTY-SEVEN

Amelia enters her daughter's bedroom. It is empty of clothes, toys, books and the many possessions Kayla loves. Today, Amelia drove her to Lemon Grass Hill, the farm run by Elena's friends. Kayla had been enraptured by baby Lucy but had wept loudly when the time came to say goodbye, unable to understand why, for the first time in her life, her mother was leaving her. She had cheered up a little when Killian brought her to the stable yard to meet their horse, Cassandra, and her newborn foal Jolly. Since then, Susie had sent photographs of Kayla holding Lucy, and feeding the hens, her face alight with excitement, yet Amelia still feels as though she has lost a limb.

When she returned from the farm, she had packed everything belonging to Kayla in boxes and left them in Lily's storeroom. All photographs have been removed and there is nothing in the cottage to remind her that she has a child who was conceived in love.

Thinking of Jay causes pain. She has deprived him of the right to know of his daughter's existence. A harsh decision that she has never regretted. This realisation steadies her resolve when the isolation of Mag's Head fills her with longings to ring him and utter the words he yearns to hear. Feelings pass, no matter how agonising they are to endure. On such occasions she sits beside Kayla, her secret safe within the thick, strong walls of Clearwater.

Mark sees Jay when he returns to Kilfarran to visit his father and talks him out of driving to Mag's Head to persuade Amelia to change her mind. Thinking about Mark, Amelia pauses in her preparations. Yesterday, she had missed the morning news bulletin and was unaware of the attack on Mark until Elena rang late in the night to inform her that she was on the road, heading for Mag's Head. The connection on their phones broke occasionally and their conversation was disjointed. But one thing was clear. Mark was in a coma and Nicholas was responsible. Fury had followed Amelia's shock and action had replaced the anxiety that she had managed to control ever since she came here.

She kneels on the stony floor. Her prayers have never matured beyond those she learned by rote in her childhood. Here, on this isolated headland, she knows that praying takes many forms. She stills her mind and brings her consciousness to Mark's bedside. Her love for him flows from her through his unconsciousness and penetrates the darkness that still possesses him.

Gradually, Amelia returns to her surroundings and rises. She has much to do and time is running out. The search for Elena will have begun by now. How long before it lands on the doorstep of this haven that Leanne created for Amelia and her daughter?

On her last visit, Elena had been battered and bruised. Amelia, fighting against the swarming memories of her own beatings, had wanted to slam the door in the face of this dangerous interloper. Elena's bruises have healed since then. The emptiness in her eyes has been replaced by a steely determination. Her shoulders are no longer slumped with defeat.

CHAPTER FIFTY-EIGHT

I always suspected I would die young. Not tragically young, as in my teens, but a little later, after life had tossed me around a bit. Turns out I was right. How much time has passed since I reached this uncertain shore that rests between the rapture and the inferno? Years? A nanosecond? Does it really matter anymore?

Jay left Mag's Head with me, his heart breaking as he waited in vain for Amelia to call him back. So long since I travelled under my own name and, as we passed through airports, those who checked my old passport gave it just a cursory glance. It's all about the hair, you see. My crowning glory, windswept as the tresses of a banshee.

On our last night together, we ate in a restaurant where a musician played on a piano. I called it my last supper and was the only one who laughed at my joke. I considered telling Jay the truth about Amelia, as I had once before, but, this time, too much was at stake for compassion.

We slept side by side in an anonymous hotel room, chaste yet linked in love. I love them all. Mark with his quiet determination. Amelia . . . what more can I say? And Jay, who came with me to that strangely peaceful house of death. The calm before the storm of passing.

I was curious but not frightened by the thought of what was to come. I'd jettisoned the dogmas of faith when I was sixteen. My church had turned its back on me, refused to recognise that I had a unique identity that desired to be fulfilled. Outside the mould, I *became an atheist who believed that death was the void. Was I right or wrong? Would I wilt like a flower into the mulch when I drank the cup of hemlock—or travel towards a rapture that stretched far beyond my imagination?*

Jay held me as my heart slowed and my eyes were filled with visions. Soon, very soon, as I was unwoven from life's canvas, I would know the answer to that eternal question.

I was wrong. There was nothing here to reflect my surroundings back at me, apart from those brief laser blasts. That's how they came, such visions, always catching me unprepared. All I had to sustain me was her name. Amelia. And then another name that echoed like the chimes of a bell when it stops tolling. Elena... Elena...

Could I have interceded when she stared at him across the width of her mother's grave and fell into his eyes? To do so would have made sense. Why else was I forced to witness such an encounter and others over which I had no control?

I never believed in psychics. Never had my palm read, tea leaves studied, tarot cards analysed. Never wondered if those who claimed to have visions were the chosen ones or simply charlatans, experts only at reading the runes of the body, hearing the unspoken words, tracking the unshed tears. I had to die to discover that to be so gifted is to accept a wound that will never stop bleeding.

CHAPTER FIFTY-NINE

Night settles over Mag's Head. The cottage blends into the rocky bluffs and windswept trees, the blue shutters on the windows securely closed, the door of the studio locked. The only noise to penetrate the restless swish of the ocean is the growl of a BMW as it negotiates the steep bends in the road. Sheep stir, eyes glazed with sleep as they are caught in the headlights.

Amelia lifts her head, suddenly alert. Accustomed to the reverberations of the headland, she recognises this alien sound for what it is. Her scalp bristles. The moment she has always feared is upon her. Elena, who has been talking about Grace and Joel, tenses when she sees her expression change. It's audible now, the gears straining against the upward slant, then easing down when he reaches the plateau where Clearwater sits. They have planned each detail of this confrontation yet, suddenly, there is a void where moments before there was a strategy.

They hold hands, squeeze hard. This is their first physical contact, though they have poured their hearts out to each other, drinking black coffee to keep them awake, knowing he will come at a time when he believes they'll be unprepared.

In the living room, Amelia slides the hidden door across and enters her refuge. The BMW is silent. The gate bangs. He strides across the gravel, making no effort to disguise his arrival. He knocks on the door, an assertive sound that he quickly repeats.

"Hello, Nicholas." Elena swings the door open. "What took you so long?" Her life depends on remaining composed, yet the urge to cower away from him is as strong as ever. She holds her head erect, conscious that Amelia, who found the courage to face her greatest fear and escape from his brutality is close by.

"I'm relieved to know you're safe." His forehead furrows with concern and he speaks quietly, as he often did before he struck her. "What on earth brought you to this godforsaken hole?"

Elena stands aside and gestures for him to enter. "Come in and I'll explain everything."

"Thank you." He does not hesitate as he walks past her and enters the living room. His confidence is threatening, as he intends it to be. "Nice décor." He stares around him, slowly turning to take in every detail. "It reminds me of somewhere. Can you enlighten me as to where that could be, Elena?"

"I'm afraid not." She will play his cat and mouse game, if that's what he wants. "This cottage belongs to Annie Ross. I'm afraid you've missed her. She's in New York."

Ignoring her, he rests his hand on the mantlepiece. "No photographs? I would have thought this was the ideal place to display them."

"There's no accounting for taste, Nicholas."

"I agree. I must say you're looking well for someone who has just jumped bail."

"I'm still in one piece, as you can see. Not a single bruise. How amazing is that?"

"Don't get too used to it. Your luck won't last long when you're sent down. Are you looking forward to your first night on remand? Women prisoners are more vicious than men, I'm told, and they enjoy the taste of fresh meat."

"After living with you, jail will be a walk in the park."

"You do realise there's a warrant out for your arrest?" he says. "Unfortunately, the gardai are searching in the wrong direction. Not for long, though. They were afraid you might have taken your own life rather than serve a long jail sentence. They'll be relieved to know it's the latter."

"If anyone is going to jail, it's you."

"A sense of humour was never your strong point, Elena. Where is this so-called Annie Ross?"

"I told you."

He lifts an eyebrow, smiles his disbelief. "You could never lie, Elena. Another one of your weak points."

"You were good at pointing them out," she retorts. "How come you never looked at your own failings?"

"What would they be?" He spreads his fingers and taps on them. "Helping you through your depressions? Loving you, even though you did your utmost to make that impossible? Dealing with your obsessive jealousy? Your pathetic whining? Your constant demands? Would you like me to continue?"

"Why not? You're on a roll."

"I came here to talk about her, not you. Where is Leanne Rossiter?"

"I don't know anyone—"

"Don't play games with me. Annie Ross, Leanne Rossiter... it did take some figuring out but then Leanne always had a problem with her identity."

"You won't find her here, Nicholas. I told you, she's in—"

"Yeah... yeah. I know. The Big Apple. Is her charming daughter with her?"

"She doesn't have a daughter."

"To be honest, I did find it difficult to envisage Leanne as a mother, considering her predilection."

She meets his challenging gaze and holds it. His stance is relaxed, a half-smile playing across his lips. The silence stretches, taut enough to snap.

"Nothing to say." He laughs, shrugs. "That makes a change."

"I have the evidence I need to put you behind bars, Nicholas. Letters Amelia wrote to her friend. She told Leanne everything about your so-called love. That page you shredded? Imagine the information it contained, multiplied many times. I've left her letters with a solicitor. If anything happens to Leanne or to me, they'll be handed over to the gardai immediately."

"Really? You should know by now that I don't scare easily."

"Did you ever love Amelia?" she asks. "Or was that just another way to dominate me?"

"I loved her," he said. "You, however, were a pathetic substitute."

"Yet you used your fists on both of us."

"Sarcasm? You *have* grown up. There's not one scintilla of evidence to prove I ever laid a finger on Amelia, except in love."

"Love?"

"We've talked enough, Elena. For the last time, where is she?"

"In New York."

He points his index finger at her mouth. "Frankly, I couldn't care less whether Leanne Rossiter is hanging out in New York or is six feet under. So, let me put my question another way. Where is my wife?"

There it is. The words she has been waiting to hear since his arrival are out in the open at last.

"Your wife is dead," Elena replies. "I know you find it difficult to accept that Amelia preferred death to living with you. Only I can understand why she would make that choice."

"My wife didn't drown. She's here, hiding out with her bastard child." He grabs Elena's shoulders and shakes her. "That's the truth, isn't it... *isn't* it?"

"If you lay one finger on me, those letters will be read," she warns him. "I strongly suspect the evidence of your brutality will persuade the gardai to investigate her drowning. If they search hard enough, they'll know you had everything to do with it."

He ignores her threat, his tone robotic and certain. "This sub-terfuge has gone on long enough." He releases her so abruptly she staggers and almost overbalances. He pulls a photograph from his inside pocket and shoves it under her nose. "Does Amelia really believe I wouldn't recognise her? Or that I'll leave here without finding her?"

"I don't care what you do or don't believe." Elena pushes the image away. "I've stared at enough photographs of Amelia to know that the woman you're looking at bears no resemblance to her." She encircles the room with her arm. "If you're so convinced she's here, why don't you search for her?"

"That's exactly what I intend to do."

He rampages through the cottage, banging doors, opening wardrobes, climbing into the attic, exploring the studio and the outhouses, checking any space where he thinks it would be possible to hide. Eventually, he returns to the living room. He appears unperturbed but his thin veneer of calm is belied by the stretching of the tendons in his neck.

"I want the truth now," he says. "I'm tired of playing games with you."

She is conscious of the hairs rising on her arms, on the nape of her neck, a cool breath on her face. Not so long ago she would have believed it was Amelia linking with her from some transcendental sphere. Now, she knows that what she is experiencing has nothing to do with benign spirits and everything to do with terror.

"You killed her father." The accusation flies from her like an arrow, fired too fast. She watches him falter as it strikes him. Their conversation has gone beyond dangerous. Not that she has felt safe for an instant, but she has stepped over a line now and it's too late to pull back.

"I never understood why you were allowed bail, Elena. Your psychiatrist will be disappointed when he discovers you're still as crazy as ever."

"I have proof, Nicholas."

"How can you have proof of something that never happened? John Pierce's case was closed years ago. He died in a hit-and-run—"

"Which was never solved. Billy Tobin gave me enough information to put you behind bars for life." Coldly, using all her reserves of courage, she continues. "As you also killed Billy, I have to be his voice. You are a murderer, a wifebeater and a rapist. I think that should qualify you as a psychopath."

"If that was true, you should be very, *very* afraid."

"Why should I be afraid? I will do everything I can to bring you to justice. Think carefully before you lift your fists, Nicholas. If anything happens to me, those letters will be opened by the gardai in Rannavale."

"Bitch! You're bluffing." He shouts the accusation so suddenly that Elena jerks back, convinced he is going to slam his forehead against her face. "I'm not prepared to waste my time on this bullshit. Where are—"

"You killed John with your Harley. Billy knew—"

"Bill knew fuck all and you know even less." His fist moves so fast she is unable to evade the blow. She reels backwards but manages to keep her balance. The sensation of teetering on the edge of a cliff is sickeningly familiar but she avoids shrinking into the familiar posture of self-survival.

"You can silence me but that won't stop the truth coming out. You killed those men and you would have killed Mark, only your luck ran—"

This time he brings her to the floor. Struggling for breath, she coils away from him in a vain effort to avoid being kicked.

"That fucking paedophile had it coming to him, and so have you. I'm going to shut your mouth once—" He stops in mid-movement, the admission he has made freezing him into a shocked silence.

She is dragged upright and shoved against the wall. He runs his hands roughly over her. The coldness of his touch against her skin is petrifying as he searches for the wire he believes she is wearing.

"You lying, vicious bitch," he whispers. "Where is it?"

She has trained for this moment, dreamed of it, visualised it in her imagination. When she drives her knee into his groin and his body doubles over, his lips puckering with pain, she feels a brutal rush of satisfaction. Is that what compels him to behave so monstrously? The intoxicating sensation of being able to reduce someone to a whimper or to absolute silence?

When he straightens, his hands pressed against his testes, she drives her fist into his chin with such force that his head snaps back. She only has an instant to push her advantage before he retaliates, and he is too fast for her. She staggers back, her ears still ringing from his earlier blows, and falls clumsily against the stacked logs. They clatter as they roll over the floor and he, startled by the noise, bends to pick up a log. He remains in that crouched position, his eyes fixed on the wall, his head moving closer to study it, his breath whistling through his teeth as realisation dawns on him. Triumph blazes through his pain as he grips the log and stands. She lifts her arms to protect herself and manages to blunt the force of the blow to her cheek. Her eyes roll as red stars spin. She knows what he is going to do. Helpless to intervene, she watches as he presses the switch and the panel begins to slide across.

He calls out to Amelia. Her name on his lips becomes a moan, fury and longing dragging the harsh sound from him. He will recognise her instantly. The fall of her hair and its unusual blonde sheen diminishes her features but he will identify the oval sweep of her face, her almond-shaped eyes, her nose with its slight tilt, the full lips he kissed so often. Elena pitches into unconsciousness, or so she believes, as the room darkens and he is lost from sight. But how can this be oblivion when the pain in her face is too severe and her fear too overpowering?

She tries to concentrate. This must be an electrical outage. Amelia had spoken about them, how their unpredictability often hampered her work. She hears Nicholas curse as a log rolls under his foot. The thud of his body when he falls. He is close to her. She smells his sweat, shot through with his aftershave, a sharp citrus scent that he orders from abroad. He scrabbles across the floor, trying, like her, to find his bearings in this impenetrable blackness. Blood streams from her nose and bubbles in her mouth. Silently, afraid to make a sound in case she draws him to her, she tries to prevent her stomach from retching. Her cheek is swelling rapidly and tightening her skin. She suspects that he has broken her cheekbone. Does terror have its own unique smell? If so, he will be upon her soon. Nicholas does not need light to kill.

CHAPTER SIXTY

The gardai are on their way from Rannavale. Amelia phoned them as soon as Nicholas admitted he had murdered her father. But they will arrive too late. She tests the tip of the knife against her finger. It is the same knife she placed on the table when Elena first came to Mag's Head. It's impossible to see in front of her but she heard the soft whirr as the panel slid across. Her hiding place has been discovered. She expects the light to return at any moment and expose her. When that happens, she will plunge the knife through his heart.

Elena is in danger. Amelia heard her cries but she has been silent since then. Which way to turn? She keeps a store of candles and a storm lantern for such emergencies. Usually when there is an outage she can find her way to the sideboard where she keeps her supplies, but she is lost in this darkness, unable to make out anything familiar that will guide her towards Elena and away from Nicholas.

Her task had been to record him, Elena's to goad him into an admission. The eerily familiarity of his taunts, as fresh as yesterday, had stirred up emotions she believed she had overcome. *That fucking paedophile had it coming to him*…those words pound inside her head. She had hoped desperately that, somehow, Elena had got it wrong when she came to Mag's Head the second time with her horrifying revelations. To believe that her father was

struck down by the man she had married seemed too heavy a
burden to carry. Now, she has recorded the truth. Enough proof to
put him behind bars and give her the freedom to reclaim her life.

She takes one step forward but stops short when she hears
Elena moan.

"Damn you, where is she?" Nicholas shouts. "If you don't tell
me where she is I'll...I'll..."

She hears his panic, his fear that his threat will be recorded.
He is disorientated also but he has found Elena. His hands are
clasped round her neck—Amelia recognises that strangled wheeze
and is horrified by the thought of knowing he can take Elena's
breath away if he decides to apply more pressure.

"I'm here, Nicholas," she says. She grips the knife tighter and
raises it. "Leave her alone and I'll come to you."

"Amelia." He doesn't sound surprised. "I *knew* I'd find you,
even if it took a lifetime to do so."

"Elena, are you okay?" she calls into the darkness. She imagines
Nicholas straining blindly towards her voice.

Elena doesn't reply but her abrasive breathing is still audible.

"Switch on the light, Amelia." He has moved closer to her.

"I didn't create the darkness," she says. "You did, as soon as
you came into our lives."

"Don't lie to me."

"The electricity has gone. I can't fix a power failure."

"But it wasn't beyond your power to come back to life. Or to
carry another man's bastard to full term. *Whore.*"

A citrus scent cloys the air. On a weekend trip to Paris, she
had bought the aftershave for him in an exclusive men's boutique.
He had liked it enough to continue ordering it. Now, she recoils
from the scent and the memory it stirs.

The shutters rattle as the wind sweeps in from the ocean. They
are normally secure enough to withstand the weather and the

sudden noise startles her. It also offers her a sense of direction. If she moves to the left, she will reach the window and from there she can feel her way to the door. If only she can find Elena and bring her to safety.

She has always believed that the thick, stone walls of Clearwater would protect her, that if danger threatened her it would come from outside. At night, lying in bed and listening to the pitch of the wind, she would compare it to the exultant strains of an overture but, now, it is a gale of unconstrained fury. The walls shudder from its force. She feels the vibration in her feet and wonders if the floor has been charged with electricity. The glass panels of the front door shatter. This is not a gale, Amelia thinks. It's a tornado roaring through the hall and twisting its way towards them. The living room door bursts open. She braces herself against the onslaught. Objects fall around her, crashing, clanging, thudding. She hears Nicholas grunt and the dull thump of his body as he hits the floor. She drops to her knees and crawls forward. Her hand touches something soft. Flesh, stubble. Nicholas is flat on his back and silent. She touches his closed eyelids, feels the rise and fall of his chest. Her arm is steady when she lifts the knife.

The wind dies away as suddenly as it whipped up. Someone or something has entered the room. A new energy is breaking through this rage that has consumed them all. Elena moans. The anguished sound stops Amelia, forces her to concentrate. She lowers the knife and the urge to kill her husband passes from her like an exhausted sigh.

The outage is over. Light floods the room. Books have been blown from their shelves, cushions and throws scattered, pictures tilted. A hand sculpted in glass, palm curled in supplication, lies beside Nicholas's shoulder. The wind must have hurled it from its position on the windowsill and smashed it against his forehead.

She is amazed it did not break when it fell. His eyes are closed, his mouth a rictus of shock and pain. The swelling on his left temple shows where he took the blow. Up close to him, she sees that he has changed little over the years since she left him, yet she notices, as she never did before, the dominant thrust of his eyebrows, the aggressive slant of his chin. Now he is unconscious and unable to project his charm, the finely chiselled lines of his face map his true personality.

Her only concern is escaping from him before he recovers consciousness, and bringing Elena with her. She kneels beside her and feels her pulse.

"Elena. Elena...can you hear me?"

"Yes." Elena's voice rasps as she slowly uncurls from her foetal position. Her face is streaked with blood. She struggles to open her eyes but the swelling on her cheek has already closed the left one.

"Can you stand?" Amelia whispers to her.

Elena nods, but cries out when Amelia helps her to her feet. "Have you got the evidence?" She is still dazed and disoriented, yet aware that this is all that matters.

"It's on a memory key," Amelia reassures her. "I've contacted the gardai in Rannavale. They're on their way but it'll take time to reach us. Lean on me. We have to get out of here before he comes to."

The feel of the knife in her hand repulses her. She stretches up to the top shelf of the bookcase and shoves it out of sight. The hall door is still open. Shards from the shattered glass panels crunch under their feet. One glance at the gate tells them that escaping in her jeep is impossible. Nicholas has blocked their exit with his BMW.

"I'll have to go back and get his keys." Amelia tries to disguise her fear, yet it ripples from her to Elena.

"You can't," she whispers. "He'll kill you. Leave me here and find somewhere to hide. I'll only slow you down—" She presses her hands to her head and staggers, almost falling before Amelia steadies her.

She opens the door on the passenger side of the jeep and helps Elena up into the seat. "I'll only be a minute," she promises as she shoves the keys into the ignition and closes the door quietly.

His black bomber jacket is open, the quilted lining visible. He used to keep his keys in an inside pocket and that is where she must search. She kneels beside him and folds back one side of the jacket. The pocket is zipped but she sees the bulky shape of his keys inside it. The thought of touching him is petrifying but his stillness might not last much longer. Her hands shake so much she has to pause and breathe deeply. Carefully, she pulls at the zipper. It refuses to budge at first and she is forced to apply more pressure before the zip slides across.

She grasps the keys to prevent them jingling and pulls them out. The glass hand that struck him lies at an angle to his neck. The palm with its beckoning curve is finely lined, head and heart lines, a life line that has changed much since Leanne traced Amelia's fate in glass.

The light flickers. Her senses are alert to the danger of another outage but the flickering stops and the room remains bright. She is about to rise when she registers the position of the hand. It had fallen close to his left shoulder but it is now positioned to his right. Too late, she tries to stand but Nicholas has grabbed her wrist. He jerks her so violently that the keys drop to the floor and she, overbalancing, is brought to her knees. His free hand closes over one of the fallen logs, chosen, Amelia knows, because he can clasp it with ease and swing it unerringly at her head.

Easily, as if she is feather-light, he carries her in his arms from the cottage. Glass breaks under his feet as he walks across the shards. Stunned but still conscious, she is unable to see if Elena is still in the jeep. He lowers her into the back seat of the

BMW and lifts a length of rope from the floor. He deals easily with her struggles, faint as they are, and when he has bound her hands behind her and tied her ankles, he walks back to her jeep. He opens all the doors then slams them closed. Unable to move yet desperate to see what he is doing, she lolls helplessly and falls forward, banging her face off the back of the passenger seat. He returns to the car alone and pushes her roughly into a sitting position.

"Did you really believe I'd never find you?" He holds her face in his hand and forces her to look at him. "Answer me, you whoring bitch."

Her lips are puckered from his pressure and when she refuses to answer him he leans forward and kisses her. "That's the last time you'll ever be kissed by anyone," he says. "I hope it brings you comfort when you're drowning."

He slams the back door and gets into the driver's seat.

"Where are you going?" she asks as he drives over the rutted trail towards the junction where a smoother road leads to the summit.

"To the edge of the world." He stares at her in the rear-view mirror, his eyes marbled with hate. "Isn't that where you went to escape from me?"

CHAPTER SIXTY-ONE

Something is wrong. Elena is too familiar with the signs to ignore them. The prickling feeling on her skin, the cold air that comes with a warning. From where she is sitting, she watches the flickering light above the porch. It steadies again and shines over Nicholas as he emerges from the cottage with Amelia in his arms.

Elena slides painfully to the floor and hunkers down to avoid being seen by him. As soon as he has passed the jeep, and she is sure he has reached his car, she peers over the passenger seat. The interior bulb in his car flashes on when he opens the back door. Unable to see what he is doing, she reaches upwards and switches off the jeep's interior light and opens the door. Her ears seem to be ringing, as they often did when Nicholas struck her, but when she is outside, hunched at the side of the jeep, she realises that the tinkling sounds are coming from the direction of the studio. The door must have been torn open by the gale and the butterflies are dancing.

She avoids the broken glass in the hall and enters the living room. Crossing to the window, she watches Nicholas search the jeep for her. The knife that Amelia failed to use is now in her hand. She will not hesitate if he enters Clearwater. But he returns to his car. The headlights sweep over the hulking bluffs and the lopsided rocks that gleam like the scales of prehistoric reptiles, rising on their hind legs.

Elena waits until he is out of sight before she turns on the engine and reverses the jeep onto the road. She can only see from one eye and the jolting road intensifies the pain in her head. The BMW is out of sight but she drives with dipped headlights in case he sees her. Unable to steer a straight course, she veers off the road. The wheels sink into spongy grass. She straightens the jeep, her hands clenched on the wheel. At the junction she hesitates, unsure of the direction he has taken. Unable to see his rear-view lights winking on the downward slope, she negotiates the narrow turn and drives upwards towards the summit. The road twists continuously. She catches an occasional glimpse of his headlights before his car disappears round another bend. Sections of the hedgerows have been cut away to provide an area for cars to pull in and allow approaching traffic to pass. Before the final ascent to the summit, Elena parks the jeep in one of these, gets out and moves forward on foot. She carries a torch in one hand and grips the knife in the other.

✦

Amelia wriggles her hands, but they are too tightly bound to allow any leeway. The moon shines on the white rim of the ocean below them. Nicholas is driving erratically, veering from one side of the road to the other. She doesn't know if he is doing it deliberately to add to her panic or if he is unaware of how close they are to the edge of the headland.

A stone hits the windscreen. The glass cracks but doesn't shatter. Nicholas curses as the cracks widen and multiply into a web of many strands. Unable to see in front of him, he struggles to bring the car under control. Amelia opens her mouth to scream but only a whimper emerges. The same anguished whimper that always brought her father to her side. Nicholas's knuckles whiten as he brakes on the viewing platform on the summit of Mag's Head.

The cracks in the windscreen have formed a shape. A face appears. Amelia recognises her reflection in this distorted mirror. She blinks but it's still there, clearer now. The pale cameo made visible convinces her that she is staring not at herself but at Leanne. Windswept hair and feline eyes, that strong, concentrated gaze that looked with love upon her so often.

Nicholas wraps a chamois round his fist and breaks the glass. The reflection disappears. This is an untamed landscape where imagination is honed on terror... it has to be. Leanne is dead, her body cremated. Her ashes scattered by Jay from the summit of a faraway hilltop.

Nicholas opens the back door and leans in to lift her out.

"Nicholas—" she begins but he clamps his hand over her mouth.

"Shut up," he hisses. "It's too late for apologies. This time when you hit the water I won't be left wondering whether you're alive or dead."

He unties the rope from round her ankles and drags her from the car. Her numbed legs give way. When she falls to her knees, he takes her under her arms and drags her towards the edge of the viewing platform. It's guarded by a steel safety barrier and, beyond it, rocks and rough tussocks of grass look hunched and distorted under the moonlight. Her view of the ocean is blocked by the smooth slant of the highest boulder but she can hear the waves pounding against the craggy face of the cliff.

His fist in her face, her head jerking back from the force of the blow, the pain he inflicts on her has a terrifying familiarity. He hits her again and lets her fall to the ground when her eyes close. She feigns unconsciousness but has enough awareness to realise that he is loosening the rope that binds her wrists. He

stops, startled, as she is, when his car headlights start flashing
and the alarm goes off. His BMW is sitting like a beacon on the
summit of Mag's Head, the ricocheting shriek amplifying its
presence. Forced to loosen his grip on Amelia, he reaches one
hand into his jacket in search of the keys. When he realises they
are still in the ignition, he curses loudly and hesitates, seemingly
unable to decide whether to ignore the clamour or drag her back
to the car. He bends over her and tries to slide his hands back
under her shoulders. The pressure from the rope has eased and
she has enough strength to link her fingers together and swing
her fists upwards towards his chin. Pain shoots along her arms
when she makes contact but, as he jerks backwards, his grip on
her loosens. When he tries to grab hold of her again she rolls to
one side and kicks out at him. He crashes against the steel barrier
and falls heavily to his knees. He is still stunned when she rises
to her feet, limping at first and then running towards his car.
She flings the rope aside, knowing that if she reaches it before
he gains on her, she will drive it in only one direction. A knife
or a car—it matters little how she destroys him.

Nicholas commands her to stop. Even now, he believes he has
the power to dominate her. Hate lends her strength, fear gives
her wings, or so it seems; but he is gaining on her, his threats
ringing in her ears. It's too late. She will never reach the car in
time. She veers away from it, heading towards the trees and the
scraggy overgrowth in a desperate attempt to outrun him.

CHAPTER SIXTY-TWO

The shriek of a car alarm stops Elena in her tracks. She sees headlights flashing, figures running across the viewing platform. She is too far away to distinguish them but it has to be Amelia and Nicholas. Exposed in this open space, she switches off the torch and moves forward, cautiously approaching the car. The alarm is silenced and the night is black again, apart from the interior light, which shines like a lone star brought to earth. The wash of the ocean is the only sound she can hear. No running footsteps to alert her to danger as she examines the BMW. A back door is open and a length of rope hangs half in and half out of the car. The windscreen is broken and the serrated shards still set in the window frame are whetted to an ice-pick sharpness.

She is about to move on when she hears footsteps. They're too heavy to be Amelia's. She hunkers down at the front of the car, shoves the torch underneath a wheel and waits for him to come closer. He slams the back door and the interior light goes off. Nothing to guide her but the moon. She waits until he has opened the door on the driver's side before rising. As she moves forward, her boots splinter a shard of glass. He spins round as she is about to lunge at him. The element of surprise has gone and when her arm is twisted behind her back, the new pain on top of the injury he inflicted on her outside Rosemary's office saps the last of her strength. As the knife falls harmlessly to the ground, she knows she has lost.

He picks it up and holds it to her throat. How many times has she faced him like this, helpless while he decides what punishment to mete out? This time will be different. She senses it in the steadiness of his hand as he prepares to take her life from her.

The ringing in her ears is back again and is even louder than the waves roiling below them. Can he not hear it? The chime of butterflies making music as they flit against each other in a deserted studio? How has the sound reached them? Has the wind carried it this great distance? The same wind that sighs his name. "Nicholas...Nicholas..." A voice floating on the air, familiar yet unrecognisable, its cadences enticing him to listen as she sings out his name, louder this time. When he turns from Elena, his attention distracted, he is unable to see who is calling him but he knows, as Elena does, that Amelia is offering herself as a decoy.

Elena wants to shout at her to run—run without stopping towards a new haven where she and Kayla would be safe. But her tongue is fused to her palate, her throat too dry. He shoves Elena aside and switches on the headlights. Amelia is visible on the other side of the barrier. She lifts her hand, as if to shield her eyes from the glare, then walks slowly away from him. The grass sways and leaves a trail for him to follow. She disappears behind one of the largest standing stones before coming back into view.

Nicholas climbs the barrier and drops easily to the other side. Amelia looks back over her shoulder and continues walking. What is she doing? Elena, finding her voice, screams at her to run but the wind, rising again, flings the warnings from her. Nicholas is gaining ground and Amelia, finally realising the danger she is in, begins to run. Moonlight infuses the silvery blonde strands of her hair and the folds of her dress are sculpted to her slim form. They are close to the edge of the cliff when she veers right in a zigzagging movement. Nicholas is gaining on her with every second that passes. Amelia will never outrun him. Elena grabs the torch and climbs over the barrier. She screams again but it is too late. Nicholas has caught up with Amelia. They look as if they are dancing together, their bodies entwined in a deadly waltz beneath the standing stone. It reminds Elena of a sacrificial altar; a stark, bleak slab where blood is shed so that others might live.

When it moves Elena is convinced she is caught in the madness of a fantasy. The torch beam wavers wildly over the stone as it falls soundlessly over Amelia and Nicholas. Horror drives her across the grassy plateau. Where it stood, magnificent in its looming solitude, there is now a view of the ocean. The ground that cradled it is as hollow as an empty grave. The stone lies flat upon the space where they had performed their deadly dance. Elena kneels beside it. She is aware that the butterflies have stopped chiming and the waves have a softer wash.

She had envied Amelia, been fascinated by her, yearned for Nicholas to love her with the same passion she used to believe he had felt for his wife. Lies, all of it. What he had wanted was to dominate her, possess her, and, now, unable to succeed in doing so in her life, he had achieved it with her death. Together again forever, and Elena, who had barely begun to know this stranger, is weeping by their grave for the friendship they could have shared. She sees Nicholas's hand by the edge of the stone. It is visible in the moonlight, his strong, brutal fingers that could clench into a fist or sensuously shiver over her skin. Now, the palm is curled inwards. Was he begging Amelia's forgiveness, or clasping her slender neck, when his life was wrenched from him? She will never know. Horrified by the sight, she averts her eyes and fights back the nausea that rises hotly in her throat. She hears a siren in the distance. The gardai have arrived, but too late. Two squad cars are visible, blue lights whirring as they are driven onto the viewing platform. As she staggers across the grass, she pitches forward, tearing her knee on the rough shingle. The urge to lie there overwhelms her but she rises and hobbles towards the group of uniformed guards, who are making their way to the barricade.

She tries to explain what has happened but she is sobbing too loudly to be coherent. A policewoman wraps a blanket round her and leads her towards the first car. She is gentle with Elena as she opens the door and assists her into the back seat. Tears blur Elena's vision. Tears that cause her to hallucinate—for how else can she explain the pale vision who stirs, as if awakening from a deep trance, and whispers her name?

Amelia Madison is also swaddled in a blanket. Twigs are tangled in her hair. Her wrists are grazed and ringleted in red. Her voice shakes as she explains what had occurred after she escaped from Nicholas. How she hid in a wilderness of fuchsia, burrowing deep within the red bells, scrabbling for cover as Nicholas's footsteps drew nearer then faded. How she was afraid to emerge until she heard the sirens of the squad cars and knew she was safe.

In the months to follow, they will try to find reasons that can logically explain the sighting of a woman on a clifftop, whose power unearthed a boulder that had been rooted in the earth for millennia. And how, when the boulder was finally lifted, there was only one body to be found. Such questions can wait. And does it really matter if they are never answered? As Elena Langdon and Amelia Madison embrace, they are aware that on this terror-stricken night they were not alone. Somewhere in those dark reaches, beyond moonlight and shadows, beyond illusion and comprehension, they had caught a glimpse of the mystery that lies beyond the veil.

EPILOGUE

Rewind, play, fast forward, rewind… how was I to define these flashes? What were they? Three-dimensional holograms? Light waves, delusions, illusions? I received no guidance when I came here. No divine voice directed me; yet there were moments when I was ether, brimstone, energy. I was the wind and the dark, a face in the mist, the air that brushed against a cheek and brought comfort. I was a siren waiting by the edge of a cliff; a hurtling force that toppled a rock from its slanting stance. I was a web, each strand connecting me to the past, the present and the future.

Before I went to that house of death, I deposited a letter in a bank vault with instructions for it to be handed over to Amelia's solicitor, if she decides to reclaim her identity. Thanks to Elena, the feverish letters Amelia wrote to me, and which I kept safely until I could give them back to her, are now with him. They will give her the freedom to find herself again. The recording she made in that hidden chamber will be used by Elena's barrister to exonerate her.

All this I've seen, and more. Mark's struggle back to consciousness; Elena's joy when she opens her arms to her children, knowing they are back where they belong. Yvonne will mourn the son she never really knew. Henry will mourn the son he knew too well. And Jay, such wonder, such bliss, when he meets his daughter for the first time; this, too, has been shown to me. He will walk with Kayla and Amelia through the garden at Woodbine, where my glass butterflies *will glitter between the branches and the low cooing of doves will be the only melody to break the stillness.*

As these chains of attachment fell away from me, Nicholas's voice was the last one I heard. His threats and promises: "Amelia... Amelia... Bitch. Whore. Liar. I love you... hate you... love you...'til death do us part we are together as one."

As he chased me along a cliff path that was once familiar to me, his intent was clear. Hate had conquered love, flattened it and smote it into an ugly weal. He stretched out his arms to crush what was immaterial, and I, released from all earthly ties, yet filled with a rapturous certainty, took him with me.

A LETTER TO MY READERS

The Wife Before Me was inspired by many stories. I listened to them on radio and television. Occasionally, they were breathed secretly into my ear and, once, when I was active in journalism, I interviewed women on the subject of domestic abuse for a series of features I was writing.

I also volunteered for a number of years in a support group that offered legal advice to women caught in such harrowing situations. A world that existed behind closed doors opened up to me and I became familiar with cover ups, underfunded refuge centres and the reluctance of some women, even in the midst of their struggles, to free themselves from the bonds that imprisoned them. The reasons for not leaving such relationships were complex and diverse. But bonds that are forged from love are the hardest ones to break.

I'd like to believe that such abuse, both physical and mental, belongs to a darker era when awareness and communication were not as honed as they are today. But I would be foolish to think so. The urge to explore the smouldering secrecy, the shame, the lies, the damage inflicted on a partner who begins to see herself through the prism of her abuser, lay dormant within me for a long time. Then, last year, I watched a documentary on television that showed footage of a man savagely beating his partner. Words can be a powerful tool but such raw brutality, caught on camera, has the impact of a fist to the face. Shortly afterwards, I started to write.

Needless to say, once I began, my idea moved quickly from a simple reporting of facts into fiction. It assumed its own shape, its distinctive voices, and its own unique territory. Despite the fictitious narrative, I hope I've managed to convey the truth of the subject I've explored while allowing the writing to develop its own momentum, especially when my character, Leanne, put her hand on my shoulder and demanded, "Let me in…let me in."

Thank you for reading my latest novel. If you've enjoyed *The Wife Before Me* I would be thrilled if you could review it on Amazon or Goodreads. Such reviews are vital to the life of a book and it is always a pleasure to hear the views of my readers. You can also contact me through my website: lauraelliotauthor.com.

ACKNOWLEDGMENTS

My family mean everything to me and each one, in their own unique way, have made my writing journey so much easier.

Thank you, Sean, my beloved husband, for keeping our home fires burning when I'm chasing deadlines, and for your unwavering support down through the years.

To my son, Tony, I appreciate your patience and your advice in times of tech stress. You've saved my sanity, and my manuscripts, on more than one occasion. To my daughter, Ciara, your editorial advice and support always renews my energy and clears away the fug of over-writing. Thank you, Michelle, my youngest daughter, for reading *The Wife Before Me* at its draft stage. Your sensitive comments added greatly to its development. To Roddy, my son-in-law, thank you for the conversations we've shared about writing and for always being such a thoughtful listener. Thanks, also, to Louise, for the unfailing care you have given to my family in times of need. To Harry, the quiet efficiency you always show when helping out in emergencies, especially when business cards are needed *yesterday*, is greatly valued. A special thanks to you and Michelle for presenting Sean and me with our precious grandchild—Nina, who was born in 2017, and is a joy to hold and behold.

To my other beautiful grandchildren, Romy and Ava, who, despite my strict instructions to allow time to stand still, insist on growing up so fast—thank you for the love and the many occasions you've tempted me to abandon my computer and enjoy the great outdoors in company with you.

My extended family are exactly that—extending rapidly—and too numerous to name individually. Thanks to one and all for the friendships we share, the fun occasions we enjoy together, and the support we have always offered each other.

A special word of gratitude to friends, Betty Reddy, Geraldine Byrne, Colette O'Hora and Patricia O'Reilly. Over coffee, brunch, lunch and early birds—you are the conduits through which my ideas flow. To all my other friends, those here and abroad —time, events and distance cannot diminish the friendships we share—and I am grateful for them.

Bookouture has become the power house of digital publishing in recent years, expanding in many new directions and establishing a cohort of wonderful writers. I'd like to compliment them on achieving this success without losing the personal qualities that drew me to them in the first place. So, thank you to my editor, Claire Bord for your insightful editorial comments and perceptive interpretation of *The Wife Before Me*. I'm grateful to designer, Stephen Mulcahey, for such an eye-catching book cover, which I love. To my line editor, Jacqui Lewis, and my proof reader Claire Rushbrook, thank you for your thoughtful editing and eagle-eyed concentration. To Kim Nash and Noelle Holten for looking after my publicity so effectively.

I write for pleasure but, ultimately, that joy would be meaningless if readers showed no interest in my books. Thankfully, that is not the case, so, last but by no means least, I wish to express my gratitude to the readers, reviewers and bloggers who have been so instrumental in building my career. Your blogs and reviews have added so much pleasure to my days and are rays of sunshine when the cloud of seclusion needs lifting.

ABOUT THE AUTHOR

Laura Elliot was born in Dublin, Ireland. She lives in Malahide, a picturesque, coastal town on the north side of Dublin.

The Wife Before Me is her seventh novel and, writing as June Considine, she has twelve books for children and young adults. Her short stories have appeared in a number of teenage anthologies and have also been broadcast on the radio. She has also worked as a journalist and magazine editor.

Learn more at:

https://www.lauraelliotauthor.com/

@Elliot_Laura

http://facebook.com/lauraelliotauthor/